CHANCE ENCOUNTER

AN LCR ELITE NOVEL

BY CHRISTY REECE

Chance Encounter
An LCR Elite Novel
Published by Christy Reece
Cover Art by Patricia Schmitt/Pickyme
Copyright 2015 by Christy Reece
ISBN: 978-0-9916584-7-3

To obtain permission to excerpt portions of the text, please contact the author at *Christy@christyreece.com*.

PROLOGUE

Her arms wrapped around herself, she rocked back and forth as she sat on the edge of the sofa. Only vaguely aware of her sharp nails gouging her skin, she watched, and she suffered. The recording was pornography…disgusting, vile. There might be worse—more graphic, much more disgusting—films. Having seen only a few porno movies in the past, she really wasn't a good judge. But for very personal reasons, this film was the pinnacle of revolting.

The man on the screen was overweight and middle-aged, definitely not porn star material. Wearing clothes, he had looked distinguished, sophisticated. Nude, he had the kind of body that revealed what overindulgence and lack of discipline could do to a person. That, along with gravity and the natural process of aging, had taken a toll on his already less-than-superior physique. The recording was over five years old, but the camera had been the best money could buy at the time. Every sag and bulge showed with humiliating clarity. Even the freckles on his dimpled, cellulite-covered ass showed up.

The unattractiveness of the man was made all the more evident by the contrast of the woman with him. She, too, was nude. But she was young, beautiful, with the kind of looks that came from good genes and an overly generous creator.

The man moved on top of the young woman, blocking the camera's view of her body and exposing his pudgy ass in an even more revolting way.

The temptation to fast-forward was strong—just the press of a button—but to understand everything, to refuel the fury and accept what had to be done, she knew she must endure the entire footage one last time.

As the old man moved his body, the young woman's face was once again revealed. She lay there, partially compliant, partially participating. The vacant, glazed expression in her eyes left no doubt about why she wasn't protesting. Five years ago, William Harrington III had arranged for the woman to be taken for his own pleasure. She had been drugged and every perverse act he had performed with her had been recorded.

Harrington was killed when a rescue organization found his secret hideaway. Several women had been rescued that day, including this one. This one had been his favorite, the one he had called his *precious jewel*.

When Harrington's home had been raided, his private stash of homemade porn had been discovered. All recordings had been confiscated, all destroyed. With the exception of one. One recording, one copy.

After the young woman's rescue, she had disappeared. Even the most tenacious investigator had not been able to find her. When she had finally reemerged, she had been a whole new person with a new name. Only her closest friends and allies knew the truth. Until now.

The woman thought she had disguised herself enough to hide her real identity, and to most of the world, she had. Her hair, face, body looked different—more mature, less childish. Yes, she had fooled the world, but there was one person she hadn't been able to deceive. The only person who mattered.

The beautiful, oh-so-innocent-looking Kacie Dane was on the peak of becoming one of the most recognized faces and names in the world. She was adored. She was worshipped.

And very soon she would be dead.

CHAPTER ONE

New York City

Dear Kacie, I feel like I've known you forever. We are kindred spirits, navigating the travails of life, connected but not yet bound.

"Oh brother," Kacie muttered and put that message in her *no answer* stack.

Dear Kacie, You are my absolute most favoritest person in the whole wide world. I want to be just like you when I grow up.

Smiling at the innocent words, Kacie put the message aside to answer later.

Dear Ms. Dane, Your concern for the refugees in Manitoba Province prompted me to contact you regarding a matter of grave concern.

She put the letter in another stack for research and then rubbed the middle of her forehead, hoping to head off the looming tension headache. Normally, reading her correspondence was either entertaining or uplifting. Occasionally, it was boring. Today, because of one particular message, it was a pain in the ass and the head.

"Stop rubbing your forehead like that. It causes wrinkles."

Tara Greenfield, personal assistant and self-appointed nag, often threw out homilies and advice as if she were fifty years older than Kacie, when in actuality she was a year younger.

Resisting the childish urge to stick her tongue out at her like the smart-ass kid she'd once been, Kacie scrunched her nose instead. "Just trying to prevent a headache."

Tara's golden-brown eyes went soft with concern. "Want me to set up an appointment with Alberta?"

"No. Unfortunately, a massage won't fix this problem."

"What problem?"

Pulling a letter from one of the stacks in front of her, she read aloud: "*Kacie, it's been much too long since I've heard from you. Your lack of concern for my welfare is both unattractive and selfish. If you don't contact me soon, I will come to you.*"

"Whoa. Somebody's got some nerve. Who's it from?"

"From my…" She mentally shook herself. Good heavens, she must be tired. "From a distant relative."

"You don't talk about your family very often."

She didn't talk about them at all and for a lot of different reasons. Besides, the woman who had given birth to her had no interest in Kacie except for what her daughter could provide. "I stopped sending her money last month. She's not pleased."

"Uh oh."

"She recently remarried, and her husband is wealthy. She doesn't need my money."

"So she wants her husband's money and yours, too?"

"To some people, you can never have too much."

Kacie rubbed her forehead again. There had been several reasons to send the money, but most of them had nothing to do with her mother needing the extra funds. Kacie had realized the futility of her efforts long ago. However, she had continued. When her mother remarried, Kacie had looked upon it as an opportunity for a clean break. No surprise that her mother disagreed.

"I'm tired of thinking about that." She handed Tara a small stack of printed emails. "Would you mind answering these for me? Just use your best judgment on the replies."

"Sure. But what about the other ones? Want me to do those, too?"

Kacie glanced back at her desk. She'd taken a swift glance at them all, including the ones that Molly, her secretary, referred to as the *you really need to see this for yourself* stack. None of them was urgent.

"I'll handle those later. There're not that many."

Paper rattled as Tara pointed her handful of pages at Kacie. "Why don't you take a few hours off? Go do something fun for a change."

Fun? That word hadn't been in her vocabulary lately. She worked, she came home, ate, and slept. Such was the glamorous life of a successful model.

"The fundraiser starts at eight."

"So? You've got a gazillion people working on that to make it run smooth as glass."

"But I'll need to get ready."

Tara snorted softly. "It only takes you about forty-five minutes to get made up and dressed. Then half an hour or so to get to the Plaza. You've got plenty of time to relax. Go have some fun. Do some window shopping. Go to the park and breathe in the not so fresh air of spring. Hell, grab a hot dog." Her eyes twinkled with mischief. "I won't tell Gustav. Promise."

Kacie laughed. Her personal trainer would make her pay dearly if he found out she'd indulged. But the idea sounded so enticing. Dare she? It had been months since she'd taken a few hours off for junk food and some mindless fun.

Before she knew it, Tara was gone and seconds later returned with a Tennessee Volunteers cap that Skylar Maddox, Kacie's best friend, had sent her. Tara handed it to Kacie, along with a pair of obnoxiously big sunglasses.

Laughing, she took the cap and sunglasses. "Okay, Tara the Tyrant. I'm gone."

Grabbing her purse and cellphone, Kacie scooted out the door, feeling more lighthearted and carefree than she had in months. It wouldn't hurt to take just a few minutes for herself, would it?

She was glad she'd let Tara bully her into this break. It had been the perfect remedy, and she was feeling tons better. She loved living in New York City. Every season brought a different kind of flavor and excitement, but spring, with its abundance of blooming trees and flowers, was her favorite.

She inhaled a deep breath and then grimaced at the noxious fumes from a passing bus. Okay, not everything had the fragrance of flowers. Turning a corner, she spotted a street vendor, and her day got even brighter.

Without the least tinge of guilt, Kacie ordered the works. And like a kid who knew she was doing something she shouldn't, she glanced around just to make sure no one had noticed that a fairly famous model was about to down a ginormous hot dog.

One more thing to love about New York City. No one paid her the slightest attention. She paid the vendor and, preparing to thoroughly enjoy herself in style, headed to the park just two blocks away. The tantalizing aroma of her early dinner enticed her to walk even faster.

Within minutes she'd settled onto a bench and unwrapped her delicacy. Then, without a thought that she could easily be on the front cover of a tabloid tomorrow with a glaring headline about a hidden eating disorder or some other nonsense, she took a giant bite, almost groaning as the flavors hit her tongue. She chewed contentedly and then washed it down with a long swallow from an icy, sweet soda.

If Gustav, her trainer and literal pain in her ass, could see her, he'd go all Gestapo on her. Probably put her through a week of detox cleansing plus an extra hour a day in the gym. Kacie couldn't bring herself to worry too much about that, though. It had been months since she'd taken a day off to just be nobody at all. A nameless, faceless person dwelling in this vast, beautiful, and fascinating city.

For over a year after her rescue, she hadn't wanted to be anyone, least of all herself. It had taken her a long time to be comfortable in her skin again. She'd hated every single particle of her being, body, heart, and soul. Every day she'd woken with her inner demons reminding her of her sheer stupidity and naïveté. She'd been the one to go blindly into the situation. It had been her fault and hers alone.

Having no one to blame but your own blind ambition gave a person nowhere to go. She'd been forced to look deep inside herself for answers and had hated what she discovered. She could blame poor judgment and an unhealthy desire for fame and money as the culprits, but after digging even further, she'd accepted the real cause. She had wanted validation. Somehow, she had believed that being a famous model would give her what she craved.

Changing her name had been harder than she'd thought it would be. Not the actual process, but accepting that she was someone else. In the end, she realized she'd had no other choice if she wanted another life for herself.

She was now living the dream she'd originally wanted with every breath of her being—the modeling career that she'd once believed would make her the happiest person on earth. Thankfully, she had developed a healthy dose of common sense to go along with her ambition. Fame and fortune did not and should never define a person. It was what they did with it that mattered. And she'd learned the hard way what really mattered.

Refusing to dwell on those dark days any longer, Kacie took one last bite of her super-bad-for-her-but-oh-so-delicious meal and then stood. The break had done her a world of good. So much so that she even had the energy to deal with the issue of her mother before getting ready for tonight's event.

Breathing in the fragrance of a coming rain, along with the delicate scent from the cherry trees a few yards away, Kacie dropped the remains of her meal into a nearby garbage can and strolled leisurely back toward her apartment.

Refreshed and renewed, she was ready to take on the world once more.

She never saw them coming.

One moment she was on the sidewalk, the next she was doing a clumsy midair tumble like an inebriated gymnast. She came to an abrupt and painful landing on the soft, forgiving earth.

Stunned and breathless, Kacie lay still for a few seconds, trying to figure out what had happened. Had she gotten dizzy and fallen? Had she run into something?

A multitude of whispers floated toward her. Twisting her head slightly, she blinked her confusion as she realized several people were standing over her. Were they here to help her?

One of them, a young man, moved closer and whispered something.

Kacie blinked up in confusion. "What?"

The whispers started up again. What were they saying? It sounded almost like a chant.

The one who'd come closer leaned over her. His breath coated her face with the smell of something strong and spicy as he whispered in an eerie, monotone, "He's. Coming. For. You."

Any breath she'd gathered left her again. Kacie managed to croak, "Are you crazy? What are you talking about?"

"He's coming for you. He's coming for you." The voices around her increased in volume in a creepy, mantra-like symphony.

The man who leaned over her straightened, and then almost as one, the entire group disappeared from sight.

What the hell?

"Miss. Are you all right?"

Kacie looked up into the concerned eyes of an elderly man who stood over her.

Gathering her wits, she drew in a shaky breath and assessed the damage. Other than getting the crap scared out of her and a couple of bruises, she was unharmed. "I think so."

"My wife called 911. They should be here soon."

"Oh...I..." *Don't be stupid, Kacie. Not calling the police because you want to avoid publicity is insane.* "Thank you." Feeling both vulnerable and foolish for just lying on the ground, Kacie attempted to sit up.

"Maybe you should stay put until the paramedics can check you out."

"I'm okay...really." She sat up, pleased that she spoke the truth. Other than an accelerated pulse that was beginning to slow down and a couple of aches on her shoulder and hip, she felt fine.

Pushing herself up, she flashed a grateful smile at the elderly man as he put out a shaky hand to help. Though she took his hand, she did her best to get up under her own strength. The kindly gentleman was bone thin and so frail looking she feared she'd pull him down on the ground if she tugged too hard.

Her legs wobbled only slightly when she was finally standing. She looked around, pleased to see that, other than the man and his wife, who was still on the phone, no one else was around.

"Did you see what happened?" Kacie asked.

"Just a glimpse when they were leaving. There were six of them, all on skates. I told my wife the other day that those kids are going to kill somebody someday." He looked around. "Did they steal anything?"

"No. I didn't have a purse or anything. They just startled me."

The man glanced over his shoulder. "Looks like the police made good time. I'll stick around and give them a statement."

"Thank you. I appreciate it."

As Kacie waited for the mounted policeman to reach them, a chill swept through her as she remembered those eerie chants: *He's coming for you. He's coming for you.*

What the hell did that mean?

CHAPTER TWO

Alexandria, Virginia

Brennan Sinclair lay on the floor. He'd been here before, more times than he wanted to remember. Bad thing about hitting rock bottom was the grim knowledge that there was no place to go but up. And damned if he had felt like ever getting up again. No, he would've just as soon stayed down in the muck and the grime, wallowing in self-pity. Too bad he'd had the good fortune of having a friend who refused to let him stay down.

"So what's it going to be, asshole?"

The self-satisfied drawl came from the man standing above him. The one who'd just knocked him flat on his ass and was inviting him to get back up so he could do it again.

He was sweaty and had a distinct ache in his ribs, but Brennan knew he had a lot more in him. He cocked an arrogant brow. "Gloating doesn't look good on you, Kelly. Makes a man want to knock the smirk off your face."

"Oh yeah?" came the overconfident reply. "I'd say it looks a helluva lot better than self-pity looked on you."

The man had that right. A few years ago, he'd been so mired in the shit he'd allowed his life to become, a sound beating had been the only way to get him out of his pity party. Justin Kelly, friend, rescuer, and one of the toughest SOBs Brennan had ever known, had gleefully delivered the goods.

But that was then, this was now. Brennan surged to his feet and came at Justin like a lethal bulldozer, slamming one fist into his face and one to his gut, finishing up with a roundhouse kick to his head. In extreme satisfaction, Brennan watched his friend fly halfway across the room and land on the mat with a loud curse and a pain-filled groan.

"Shit!" Justin sat up and shook his head rapidly as if to clear it. "Remind me not to piss you off again."

Brennan grinned down at the man he'd just wiped the floor with. "You've not seen pissed off. Those were love taps. Get back up, and I'll show you a few moves even you LCR guys don't know about."

Justin snorted. "That arrogant attitude of yours will fit in well with LCR."

Grabbing a bottle of water, Brennan tossed it to his friend and then took one for himself. Finishing half of it in one, long swallow, he replaced the cap. "I'm looking forward to meeting McCall. He's not much of a phone conversationalist. Just gave me a date, time, and location to meet. What's he like in person?"

Wiping his face with a towel, Justin twisted his mouth into a wry smile. "About the same. With McCall, what you see is what you get. He doesn't pull punches…calls it like he sees it. If he doesn't like you, you'll know it."

"Good." Brennan liked straight shooters.

"Where are you guys meeting?"

"Some restaurant called Alonzo's Place."

"Yeah. All LCR interviews take place at either a hotel or a restaurant."

Made sense. Last Chance Rescue was one of the most secretive and successful rescue organizations in the world. When lives were at risk, trust couldn't come easy.

And LCR's founder, Noah McCall, was just as secretive as his organization. Few knew where the leader of Last Chance Rescue hung his hat. LCR rescued kidnap victims from some of the most dangerous places in the world. And because of that, rumor had it that McCall had collected some powerful enemies.

"So he knows everything?"

"Yeah...even knows the truth."

Brennan inwardly winced. Even when one knew the truth, that was still a lot of muck to wade through. The good—he was a decent guy. The bad—he'd been an asshole and idiot for a good part of his life. The ugly—he'd done some downright shitty things that he'd give everything he owned to do over.

"With your training and experience, you've got the skills of a seasoned LCR operative. But rumor has it that those things aren't always McCall's top job requirements."

"What do you mean?"

"Let's just say that his interview process can be unique."

Brennan took another slug of water, now more curious than ever to meet Noah McCall. He didn't doubt that he could do the job. He'd been there, done that. He'd clocked numerous successful rescues the last couple of years with another rescue organization and loved his career. However, it was time to move on. Last Chance Rescue was not only the gold standard for rescue organizations, they also had strict policies when it came to privacy, steering clear of public recognition whenever possible. And since publicity was the very last thing Brennan Sinclair wanted or needed in his life, working for Last Chance Rescue would be the perfect job.

CHAPTER THREE

New York City

Her smile frozen in place, Kacie acted as if there was nowhere else she'd rather be than standing before dozens of photographers, talking to people she didn't know, or nibbling on pâté-covered crisps. After today's weird event, the last thing she had felt like doing was going out and mingling with hundreds of people, most of whom she didn't know. Taking a long, hot bubble bath and sipping herbal tea sounded like so much more fun.

At that image, she mentally rolled her eyes. *Really, Kacie? What are you? Ninety?*

This was her charity, with her name on it. It meant too much to her to even consider bailing. Besides, she was already fodder for every gossip rag and online chatter outlet in existence. When you're dubbed America's Sweetheart—not her doing—people seemed even more eager to find something unwholesome about her. Not attending her own charity event might well have qualified.

Her über efficient staff had been working on this event for months. Kacie had hired a limo to carry everyone to the event, and the party had gotten started early. She'd done her best to get into the spirit, and other than a few concerned questions about her lack of excitement that she'd brushed off as nerves, she thought she had covered herself pretty well.

The slight twinges in her shoulder and hip weren't painful, just small reminders of a silly, freaky thing that had happened, nothing more.

"You look a little rough around the edges, my dear." The dry, humorless voice came from behind her. She recognized the speaker immediately and turned, forcing her smile into one of sheer delight.

Tatiana Clark, the cattiest of the online fashion bloggers, seemed to take an almost fiendish delight in tearing into Kacie, from barely veiled insults about her appearance to mean-spirited comments about her sad lack of romance. Tatiana had stated more than once that no one could be that sweet.

Being extra nice to someone who went out of their way to be unpleasant had never been so much fun.

"Thanks so much for coming tonight, Tatiana. You're looking lovely, as always."

One of the many things she'd learned from Skylar was the graceful art of kindness. Complimenting someone who'd just as soon claw your eyes out as look at you was a good way to disarm the enemy. Kacie's kill-them-with-kindness attitude often confused the hell out of people.

Showing that she was tougher than most, Tatiana's brilliant blue eyes narrowed into hard gems of ice. "Too bad about the Oliver campaign. That project could've made you a superstar. Rumor has it that you were never even considered. Sarah March will be the new face of Oliver, probably for years. She's only nineteen, fresh-faced and flawless, whereas you are—"

"Absolutely delighted for Sarah," Kacie finished for her. "She will be a wonderful addition to the Oliver collection. Her face is perfect for them."

"But you—"

Kacie grinned, thoroughly enjoying herself. "Never had a chance, I'm sure."

She waved a donation card in the spiteful woman's face. "Don't forget your donation. I'm sure there are thousands of young women who look up to you and would love to be the next Tatiana."

"What's that supposed to mean? You think someone could replace me?"

"Who could replace you, Tatiana? You're one of a kind."

"You're damn right, I am. I—"

A warm hand grasped Kacie's elbow. "There you are, my dear. I've been looking all over for you. So sorry to interrupt your time with Tatiana, but I wanted to visit with you a moment."

Giving one last friendly, charming smile to Tatiana, Kacie allowed her agent to pull her away. "Thanks. I owe you one," she said under her breath.

"It's what you pay me for, but really, Kacie. Do you have to be so damn nice to the woman?"

"It's too much fun not to be nice."

Edy rolled her eyes and snorted. One of the most prominent agents in the business, Edalyn Brown, known by most everyone as just Edy, had been Kacie's agent for over two years. Without a doubt, Kacie knew she wouldn't have done nearly as well without this savvy woman as her champion.

"Poor Tat looked as though she couldn't figure out whether she was supposed to scratch your eyes out or give you a hug."

"Who knows? Maybe she'll be nicer to the next person she meets."

Edy shot her a droll, cynical look. "Your pay-it-forward nice-ness lost you the Oliver account. You know that, don't you?"

"Sarah is perfect for their campaign. Recommending her just made sense."

"You would've been perfect for it, too."

Edy was ever loyal, which Kacie appreciated. "You're prejudiced."

"No, I'm practical. You keep recommending other people for jobs you're up for, at some point people will think you're in my business."

"I'm getting plenty of work."

Edy huffed out a little laugh. "You have no idea."

"What do you mean?"

"What would you say if I told you that right before I walked in here, I got a call from Julian Montague?"

"I'd say you had a few drinks before you arrived."

"Yeah, well, I did. But I'm still sober enough to negotiate a deal to die for."

Kacie's heart took an excited leap. Julian Montague was looking for a model for his new line of cosmetics and sports and eveningwear. The entire fashion industry had been holding its collective breath to see whom the designer would choose. Not only did Kacie have a great admiration for him, she'd gotten a sneak peek at the new line and had fallen in love.

"Seriously? Montague really wants me?"

"Offer is a two-year contract."

"He's okay with my clauses?"

"Not a problem. Your hometown-girl look is exactly what he's looking for."

That was a relief. Her stipulations on nudity or near nudity were in every contract she'd ever signed. She had several reasons for this, not the least of which she knew she would be a role model for young women and refused to be photographed in anything too revealing. She had developed a reputation for being a prude, but she could live with that.

"There are just a few things we need to nail down. Let's meet tomorrow afternoon and iron those things out. Two o'clock okay?"

"Perfect. I'll—" A burst of male laughter caught her attention, cutting off her words. A shiver zipped up her spine, and she looked around. Where had it come from?

"Kacie...you okay?"

"Yes...I, yes, definitely." Utterly spooked, she turned quickly, almost sure he'd be right behind her.

"What is your problem, Kacie? Who are you looking for?"

"Did you hear that laugh?"

"I hear lots of people laughing. It's a party."

Okay, get it together, Kacie, before Tatiana and her cohorts get a glimpse of the crazy you seem to be flirting with.

"Sorry. Just heard someone laugh and thought it sounded familiar. So...um...yeah, that's great news."

Edy looked at her as if she'd lost her mind. "Hell, I thought you'd be dragging me by my ear to find a place to talk about it tonight, and now you act like I just complimented your nail polish. What's up with you? A year ago you would've been so excited I wouldn't have been able to keep you from screaming the news to the entire room before you demanded the facts straightaway. Is this not what you want anymore?"

"Of course it is. I want this job, Edy. More than you'll ever know. So...two o'clock. Right?"

"Yeah. Sure. Whatever."

Kacie restrained herself from snapping at the woman. Edy sometimes had the ego of a diva, and when things didn't go her way, she had a tendency to pout. Besides, this *was* a big deal. Edy was right. Any other time she would've been dancing like a fiend. But today's weird occurrence at the park, followed by that freakily familiar laughter, had her on edge.

"How about we meet for a late lunch at Marvin's? We'll talk and celebrate. My treat."

Excitement flickered in Edy's eyes but was quickly replaced by doubt. "I called for reservations last week and couldn't get a table for at least four months."

"I know someone. I can get us in."

Looking somewhat mollified, Edy nodded. "Okay. I'll bring the specifics." Her light-blue eyes scanned Kacie's face. "Are you sure you're okay? You're looking kind of washed out."

Oh for an agent who didn't feel she had to call it like she saw it all the time. Delivering the brutal truth was one of Edy's least endearing but most valuable qualities.

"Yes. I'm definitely okay. Just need a good night's sleep."

"Make sure you do that. I don't want Julian thinking you've lost your edge. You have to look as close to perfect as possible from here on out."

Since perfection wasn't possible and sleep didn't always come easy, Kacie merely smiled and changed the subject. "Isn't that Jeffrey Miller standing in the corner? Why don't you go over and say hi to him?"

"Please. As if."

Edy had a longstanding crush on one of the premier advertising executives in the country. Jeffrey Miller, once a top model, now ran his own advertising firm. Still single and in his early forties, the man was considered one of the hottest catches in the world. He was also one of the most arrogant men Kacie had ever met. Edy, on the other hand, couldn't see beyond his good looks.

"I don't know," Kacie teased. "He looks kind of lonely to me."

"You're right, he does." Straightening her shoulders, Edy nodded. "Okay, I'm going in." She took a few steps and then turned back to Kacie. "Don't think I don't know what you just did. However, I'm doing this for a good cause, so I'll forgive the distraction."

"And that good cause would be?"

"He's clearly a misogynist who's dying to be reformed. And I'm the woman for the job."

Kacie laughed, appreciating the woman's confidence if not her goal. "Go for it."

As Edy zoomed toward her target, Kacie eyed her own target—the ladies' room. She smiled, waved, and called out "thank you for coming" greetings as she crossed the room. The event had turned out even better than she had hoped. She gave all the credit to her amazing staff. Without them, she never would have been able to pull this off.

Finally escaping from dozens of eyes, Kacie allowed her smile to slip from her face as she walked down the carpeted hallway to the ladies' room. Five minutes of alone time should give her enough stamina to go back and smile for at least another couple of hours.

She pushed opened the door and was delighted to see that both the lounge and restroom were empty. Quickly using the facilities, Kacie washed her hands and took a moment to freshen her makeup. Okay, maybe she did look a bit ragged…definitely paler than normal.

A quick touch-up helped a little, but what would help the most was a long, uninterrupted, peaceful sleep. After what she'd been through, most drugs repulsed her, which meant she sometimes went without sleep. Even after five years, she often woke up in a cold sweat, the remnants of nightmares preventing her from going back to sleep.

But Edy was right. She had to look her best. Maybe she could find an herbal relaxant. She would call her therapist tomorrow and see if she could suggest something.

Kacie headed over to a cozy-looking chair in the corner. Just a couple of minutes of meditation and she would be ready for round two. She was halfway to her destination when the room went dark.

Releasing a little gasping squeal, Kacie froze. Had the electricity gone out in the entire building? Holding both hands out in front of her, she turned to where the door should be and began to walk slowly toward it. The masculine laughter, slightly high-pitched, took her off guard. It was the same laughter from earlier. The same laughter she heard in her nightmares.

"Hello?" Her voice wavered. "Is someone there?"

Total silence followed.

Her heart pounded hard against her chest as she exhaled terrified spurts of breath. She would not panic. Dammit, she would not panic.

Straightening her shoulders, Kacie took a determined step toward the door and then another. She had a good sense of direction. She knew where the door was. She would get there and get the hell out of here.

The lights flickered on, startling her to a stumbling halt. Her eyes searched her surroundings. No one was around. Had she imagined the laughter? Of course she had. She'd heard it earlier, and her overactive imagination had brought it to mind.

Shaking her head at her ridiculous fears, Kacie took the remaining steps to the door and opened it. Muted voices and laughter could be heard over the classical piano music coming from the speakers in the ceiling.

Everything was normal. It had been a momentary power outage, nothing more.

Working her smile back into place, she strode toward the ballroom, welcoming the sound of normalcy and sanity.

She had panicked for nothing. Everything was fine. And the eyes that she now felt were following her? That was normal. This was her event…of course people were watching.

As Kacie entered the ballroom and began her second round of thank-yous, she ignored the small voice inside her that asked just how long she could keep lying to herself.

CHAPTER FOUR

Hours later, Kacie stood at her office door and debated her choices. Her body was weary, but her mind was restless. After the limo had dropped her off at her apartment, her entire team had continued to party. Even Marta and Hazel, who were both old enough to be grandmothers to the other staff members, had wanted to continue the celebration. The benefit had raised almost twice as much as they'd hoped, and they had just cause to celebrate.

Kacie had cried off, using the excuse of a busy day tomorrow. Amid goodhearted boos and cheerful jeering, they'd waved good-bye to her and went on to their next destination.

And now here she stood, wide awake and more on edge than she'd been in years. After tossing around on the bed for half an hour, she'd gotten up and tried all of her normal remedies for sleep. A hot bath, warm milk, meditation, and reading. None of them had worked. She knew if she got back in bed and tried to sleep again she'd either have another bout of tossing and turning or have nightmares.

What those guys in the park had said today—the creepy, almost monotone chant, as if it were part of some kind of Satanic ritual—continued to replay in her mind. *He's coming for you.*

Was it just some weird street theater, like the officer had surmised, or was it more ominous than that? Had it been some kind of warning she should heed? If so, about what?

Thankfully, no one in the press had caught wind of the assault. That was what money and a world-class publicist like Sandi Winston could do for you. She'd called the woman seconds after giving her report to the police. And somehow, it had gone away. Sandi was a marvel at making bad news disappear and good news shine even brighter.

Kacie eyed the small stack of emails and social media messages on her desk she'd yet to answer. She knew full well she could ask Molly to do them and most people would never know the words hadn't come from her. But since she couldn't sleep, why not knock out a few innocuous emails?

Grabbing the small stack, she headed up to her bedroom. She would read them in bed and then hopefully fall asleep watching television. Who would suspect that one of the top models in the country went to bed alone, often before nine o'clock, and always made sure the television was tuned to something old and comforting? The only thing edgy about Kacie Dane was the clothes she modeled. Everything else was boringly normal.

Barefoot, dressed in her favorite cotton pajamas, her hair pulled back in a haphazard ponytail, she knew she looked less like a model and more like the girl next door. Though much of her appeal as a model was her all-American wholesome girl persona, few people had ever seen her this dressed down. Anyone who saw her this way saw the real person behind the fake life, and only a handful of people were trusted with her secrets.

She pulled back the comforter and sheets and then propped up three of the six pillows against the headboard. Settling back, she clicked the remote till she found a *Friends* rerun and then picked up the pages. Kacie scribbled her answers beneath each message, the soft sounds of laughter from the television a soothing background noise. Her head sank into the pillows as her eyes drifted shut. Myriad colors swirled around her—light, opaque, soothing, then darker colors emerged—thick, evil, vile—as she dived deep, then deeper into her nightmare.

"Hello, my little jewel."

Kacie gasped and tried to raise her head. She couldn't move. She was frozen in place, literally. Her body felt like ice. She was cold and so weak she couldn't work up enough energy to shiver. He had drugged her again. The food she'd eaten, tainted. But if she didn't eat, she would starve.

"Why?" She wanted to scream the word, wanted that small knot of anger lurking inside her mind to force her body up to fight this bastard. Instead of shouting, her words came out on a sigh that sounded breathless...easy.

"Because you're mine...all mine. I shall enjoy you over and over again."

"Cold," she whimpered softly. "So cold."

"Let me warm you." Large hands, hot and slightly damp, roamed her body. Despite the disgust her blurred mind told her she should feel, she relished the warmth, whimpered her pleasure.

"That's my girl. My precious jewel."

"Noooooo!" Kacie shot up in bed.

The lights were on, the television still playing. She drew her legs up, shivering. The nightmares were less frequent than they had been, but sometimes, when her guard was completely down or she was stressed, they would slash at her like a machete.

Taking a long swallow from the bottle of spring water she'd placed on her nightstand, she drew in a trembling breath. She was fine. She had survived. She had overcome and triumphed. Nothing could hurt her...*he* couldn't hurt her. William Harrington III was dead—she'd seen the evidence with her own eyes.

She took in another breath, willing her muscles to relax, her mind to let go of the fear and remembered pain. Leaning back onto the pillows, determined to forget, she picked up another email printout and read:

Hello, my precious jewel.

Jonesborough, Tennessee

Skylar Maddox dropped a soft kiss onto her sleeping daughter's forehead, wishing once again she could stop time. Megan James Maddox was growing up faster than Skylar could ever believe. It seemed like only a few days ago she and Gabe were bringing her home from the hospital, and now she was almost three years old. Where had the time gone?

"She still awake?"

Her heart leaping in joy, Skylar turned to her husband, who stood at the door. "Hey, you. I didn't think you'd be here until tomorrow."

"I took a commercial flight. Shea and Ethan went to Paris to meet with Jordan and Eden on a case. I wanted to get back to you as soon as possible."

Skylar held out her hand, relieved as always at the safe return of her husband. She loved that Gabe was an operative for Last Chance Rescue and saved kidnapped victims all over the world. But when he was on an op, not a day went by that she didn't worry. She knew all too well how quickly happiness could be snatched from a life. She and Gabe had gone through hell to get to their happy ending, and she would never take it for granted.

CHANCE ENCOUNTER | **31**

"She woke up and wanted a sip of water. She just went under again. Come kiss her good night."

Her pulse rose as the gorgeous man who was her husband strode toward her. How was it possible that he was even sexier than he'd been thirteen years ago when she'd first met him? Everything about him was harder, tougher, and as he moved across the room like a sleek leopard on the prowl, her pulse spiked. The sensual gleam in his dark eyes said that he knew exactly the kind of effect he was having on her.

Taking her hand, he pulled her into his arms for a deep, devouring kiss. Skylar wrapped her arms around the love of her life and welcomed him home.

His breath elevated, Gabe breathed against her mouth. "I've missed these lips."

"Oh yeah?" She leaned back in his arms and smiled up at him. "Then I'll just have to make sure you get reacquainted with them tonight."

His lips traveled down her face, to her neck and then her shoulders as his hands delved beneath her blouse. "Hmm. There are several other places I missed, too."

She shivered her delight as his large, callused hands explored. "Why don't you show me which ones you missed the most, and I'll make sure you get reacquainted with all of them."

"Sounds like heaven to me." He stopped and moved his gaze to their daughter. "How's my angel been?"

"Missing her daddy madly. She picked up three books from the bookstore today that she insisted you have to read to her the moment you're home."

He grinned his delight. "Something else to look forward to. I'll get my voices in tune."

Skylar laughed softly. One of the many reasons she loved her husband was the phenomenal father he'd become. He doted on Megan, and every night he was home, they had two hours of uninterrupted father-daughter time.

"She'll be thrilled. I—"

The cellphone in her pocket chimed a familiar ring tone. Ordinarily, she might have ignored it, but it had been almost a week since she'd talked to Kacie.

"Why don't you go chat with Kacie for a few minutes?" Gabe said. "I'll tuck Megan in and grab a shower." He dropped a quick kiss on her mouth. "Meet you in the bedroom in half an hour?"

Anticipation zipped up her spine. "You've got yourself a deal, Mr. Maddox."

As she left the bedroom, she pulled her phone from her pocket and hit the answer key. "Hey, sweetie. I was going to call you tomorrow." Skylar jerked to a stop at the sound of a heartbreaking sob. "Kacie? What's wrong?"

Oh heavens, she couldn't believe she was losing it so quickly. A part of her was appalled at the ugly sounds coming from her mouth. She had to get herself together.

"Kacie? Tell me what's wrong."

Skylar was now sounding frantic. Kacie swallowed her fear and said, "I got a letter from him."

"A letter from whom?"

"William Harrington."

"No, baby. That monster is dead. He can't hurt you."

Kacie stared down at the paper with the vile words printed on them. "I have an email in my hands that says different."

"What does it say?"

"It says, 'Hello, my precious jewel. I've missed you, and I'll see you soon.'"

"Someone's playing a cruel prank on you, Kacie. The man is dead. I promise."

"Who would know, Skylar? Only a few people have that information. And even fewer know what he called me. None of them would do this."

"I don't know, sweetie, but we'll find out." She heard whispering in the background, and then Skylar said, "Gabe wants to talk to you. Hold on."

"Hey, Kacie." Gabe's calm, gruff voice was reassuringly soothing. "Tell me exactly what happened."

She explained about the fan mail she received each day in the form of letters, emails, and social-media comments and how Molly gave her copies of the messages she felt Kacie should see.

"Is there an originating email address?"

Feeling foolish for not checking already, her eyes searched the printout. The instant she saw the address, her blood chilled further. *Oh God. Oh God. Oh God.*

"What?" Gabe barked.

Almost hyperventilating, Kacie answered in a hoarse whisper, "It's HeIsComingForYou@gmail.com."

"Give me your email account information and password. LCR tech people should be able trace the IP address to see where and who it came from."

She quickly rattled off her email account information and password.

"Got it. Now. Is this the first time you've received something like this?"

"Yes. Well…I've had a few nasty messages over the last year or so, but nothing that would remotely indicate it was related to Harrington."

"You still have copies of them?"

"Yes. Molly keeps them on file."

"Okay. We'll want to see them. Anything else?"

Kacie closed her eyes as a fresh wave of tears hit. "Yes… maybe. Probably. I just don't know."

"What?"

"I was in the park today, by myself. Some guys knocked me down and then chanted over and over again, 'He's coming for you.'"

"Are you okay? Did they hurt you?"

"I'm fine. The whole thing lasted only about ten or fifteen seconds. Almost by the time I realized what was happening, they were gone."

"Did you get a good look at them?"

"No. Not really. It happened so fast. They all wore sunglasses and helmets. I think they were young, though. They were on Rollerblades."

"Witnesses?"

"An elderly couple, but neither of them had a good description. They said they were concentrating on me, that the guys were gone before they realized what was happening."

"You called the cops?"

"Yes. They said they figured it was some kind of weird street theater."

"Anything else?"

She felt stupid for bringing it up, but it had freaked her out, so… "Yes. My foundation had an event tonight." She swallowed, suddenly feeling foolish for what she was about to say.

"Tell me, Kacie."

"I swear I heard him laugh. It was this distinctive high-pitched kind of laughter. I hear it in my dreams sometimes, and I—" She shoved a hand through her hair. "I don't know, Gabe. Maybe it's nothing…but still."

"It's best to be safe. Listen, I know your apartment has good security, but double-check your doors and windows. Skylar and I will be there as soon as we can."

Guilt made her protest. "Oh no, Gabe, I'm sure it's—"

"No arguing. It's been too long since we've seen you anyway. I'll call as soon as we know when we'll arrive."

"Thank you, Gabe. I'm sure I'm just overreacting, and I'm sorry for—"

"Let me stop you there. Do not apologize. Anybody would be freaked out by this. You're family. Understand? And we take care of our own. Got it?"

Grateful tears filled her eyes. "I love you guys."

"Try to get some sleep, and we'll see you soon."

"Okay, good night. And thanks again."

Kacie dropped her phone onto the bed and jumped up. She agreed with Gabe that her apartment building security was top-notch. Not only did most visitors have to sign in and be announced to get to any of the apartments, there was a security guard at each entrance. The building housed several well-known celebrities, and though the rent was astronomical, the added security was well worth the price.

Still, it didn't hurt to be extra cautious. She double-checked her front door, noting both deadbolts were secure. She lived on the sixteenth floor, but she had a balcony that looked out over a small park. It had never occurred to her that anyone would try to access her home from such a height, but she supposed the balconies on either side of her could be used to gain access. Although someone would have to be an acrobat, or insane, to try.

Still, she would take no chances. She checked the sliding glass doors as well as all the windows. Everything was locked, secure and tight.

Feeling slightly safer, she went back to the kitchen, poured herself another glass of milk, and traveled back up to her bedroom. Sleeping would most likely be impossible tonight. She settled back onto her bed pillows, sipped her milk, and stared at the email. She didn't know which scared her the most, the words in the email—*Hello, my precious jewel*—or the words used in the email address: *He is coming for you*. Just like those voices in the park.

Harrington was dead. After her rescue, she'd been hurting beyond belief and as weak as an infant, but she'd had one request. No one had been able to talk her out of it. She had wanted to see the bastard's body. She had to make sure—one hundred percent sure—that he was dead.

She had stood in the morgue and looked down at the cold, lifeless corpse. He had been a disgusting piece of humanity, but she had wished at that moment that he would come back alive. She had wanted to tell him exactly what she thought of him, then she'd wanted to be the one to kill him.

William Harrington was burning in hell. That was one thing she knew for certain.

So was this someone's idea of a sick joke? Possibly a blackmail attempt?

Who knew that Kendra Carson and Kacie Dane were the same person? And what more did this person intend to do with that information?

CHAPTER FIVE

Alexandria, Virginia

With the calculated eyes of a man who knew more than his share about human nature, Noah McCall carefully assessed the man across from him. Most times when he was considering bringing on a new operative, he had to dig for information. Spilling one's guts took courage, but when interviewing for an LCR position, it was often a necessary evil. Noah didn't hire people he couldn't trust. And though he couldn't say he always knew everything about everyone he brought into LCR, he knew enough to feel confident about his decision. He'd made the wrong choice only a couple of times. Both had cost him. He didn't intend to ever be wrong again.

Brennan Sinclair was somewhat different from the usual prospective operative. Noah knew everything about the man. Hard not to know when Sinclair's story had been splashed all over newspapers and magazines for what seemed like months on end. Television news reports had devoted hours of airtime dissecting the man's life, revealing his most intimate secrets for all the world to see and judge.

And, oh hell, had they judged him.

Because of the man's history and what he had endured, Noah wasn't going to ask the usual questions. He knew exactly why Brennan Sinclair wanted to work for LCR. Knew the man was more than qualified. And even though Noah had decided to offer Sinclair a job before meeting him, he had his doubts that the man would accept once he heard about his first assignment.

"Tell me about yourself, Sinclair."

"I've got the skills and training. I've got the field time. Numerous successful rescues."

Sinclair spoke with confidence, edging on cockiness. Noah fought a smile. He liked cocky...especially when it could be backed up with irrefutable proof.

"Justin Kelly speaks highly of you. And your skills are impressive. While that's important, I need something more."

"Like what?"

Noah held back a sigh. Just because he was used to cutting open emotional wounds and then cauterizing them didn't mean he enjoyed the process. He liked kicking the asses of evil people and returning kidnapped victims to their loved ones. He took no pleasure in hurting one of the good guys. And despite his concerns, Noah knew Brennan Sinclair was one of them.

As the leader of LCR, Noah had two well-defined priorities for the organization—his employees and the victims they rescued. Meaning he had no choice sometimes but to slice open a life and encourage the spilling of guts.

The first slice was always the biggest surprise. Noah made the jab quick and clean. "Your son, Cody. Tell me about him."

Sinclair couldn't control the flinch of pain. Yeah. Low blows always snuck up on you, stealing your breath and often choking the very air from your body. Just because Noah didn't enjoy the process didn't mean he wouldn't take on the deed.

His jaw clenched tight, Sinclair asked, "What do you want to know?"

Second slice was merely a nick. "You blame yourself?"

A stiff-necked nod was Sinclair's reply.

Third one went a bit deeper. "Why? You weren't even around when he was taken."

Sinclair's green eyes went to shards of hard jade. "And that's exactly why, McCall. I wasn't there for him. I was his dad…I was supposed to protect him. Instead, I was—" Sinclair shook his head. "I was a lousy father."

Noah eased back on the knife, giving Sinclair a little breathing room. "You weren't still at the rehab center, were you? By that time, you were back home, had recovered from your injury?"

"Yes. My rehab was over."

"You were on disability but still with the Jets, right? Quarterback?"

If a jaw could be made from granite, Brennan Sinclair's would make the perfect specimen. The man didn't bother to hide his contempt. "Can't say much for your research skills, McCall, if you have to ask questions that a two-year-old could find the answers to."

Ignoring the man's uncensored jab, Noah said, "And where were your wife and son? They lived in the same house with you?"

"Of course they lived with me. They were supposed to be out of town." He added with a trace of bitter sarcasm, "At Vanessa's parents' house."

"And instead they were where?"

"Still in the city."

"Odd that you would take on the guilt when someone you loved and trusted lied to you."

"Doesn't matter. A father takes care of his children first. I failed him."

"Sounds like it was your wife who failed your son. Not you."

Fire leaped into Sinclair's eyes, and Noah wondered if the guy was going to go for his throat. Instead, he showed an admirable amount of control—a plus in his favor—and spoke through gritted teeth, "Damn you, McCall. You know exactly why I feel guilty."

"Tell me anyway."

Sinclair surged to his feet. "You know what happened. And if you don't, then you fucking suck at your job."

"Sit down, Sinclair. Unless you want to end the interview, that is."

The man slowly sat back down, but the fury remained in his eyes, banked for now.

"Why do you want to work for LCR?"

"I'm not sure I do anymore."

"Now that's interesting. A commitment to rescuing the innocent can be demolished in the span of a few moments? With just a few words?"

"Tell me, McCall. What kind of reaction did you want to see?"

"A truthful one, which I think I got." Noah changed tactics. "You've been trained and worked with some of the best."

"The Carmichael Group. I'm sure you've heard of them."

He'd heard of them, even worked with them. They'd designed the facility in Arizona where he sent all his Elite operatives to train. The Carmichael Group was made up of three former special ops guys, who after their service time ended, opened a training facility in upstate New York. They took only twelve candidates each session, trained the hell out of them and either broke them or made them lethal.

In their spare time they designed facilities for other organizations, which was how Noah first met them. In the last two years, they'd created a name for themselves in both security services and rescuing kidnapped victims.

Sinclair had been with the Carmichaels for three years—first as a student, then a trainer, and now a full-fledged partner. But it wasn't hard to figure out why he wanted to leave them.

There was no doubt that Sinclair's training would be an asset to LCR. But how would the man react when he learned that Noah wanted to throw him to the lions on his first LCR op? Just how strong was Brennan Sinclair's need for privacy? Would it outweigh doing the right thing? He would soon see.

Brennan waited for McCall's job offer, confident that it was imminent. Sure, the guy had pissed him off, picked and dug at a wound that would never heal. His priorities had been screwed up. Cody had paid the price. He understood the reasons for McCall's line of questioning. Didn't like it, but understood.

"Your training is similar to LCR's. You'd be ready on day one to work an operation."

Yeah, he was perfect for the job, and McCall knew it.

"I would want you for the LCR Elite team, which handles the rescue of high-value, hot-target victims throughout the world."

Brennan nodded. Sounded more than challenging and just what he was looking for. Being out of the country for extended periods of time, where few people knew him, sounded perfect.

McCall went on. "However, your first assignment would not be a typical LCR job."

"What would it be?"

"A friend has received some vague threats. She needs protection."

"You want me to be a bodyguard?"

"Yes."

Brennan studied McCall's enigmatic face. He'd hate to play poker with this guy, because he literally had no expression. It was like a blank canvas, unreadable. However, he did know enough about Noah McCall to realize the man wasn't one to play games.

"Okay…I'm listening."

"The name Kacie Dane ring any bells?"

Brennan searched his memory. The name tickled at the back of his mind. Then it clicked. "Model?"

"Yes."

Shit. Shit. Shit.

Brennan held back an explosive sigh. "What kind of threats?"

"Vague at this point. She may or may not have a stalker, blackmailer, maybe both. Or someone is just trying to scare the hell out of her. Either way, he appears to know secrets that could destroy her. I'd like for you to watch over her until we can evaluate the risk."

"The police involved?"

"Not yet. We don't know enough about it to involve them yet. Besides, police means press, and that's something she wants to avoid."

He could definitely identify with that. "Why would she call a rescue organization for something like this?"

"Kacie has a unique connection to several of our operatives."

"She a girlfriend of yours, McCall?"

Though McCall's expression never changed, Brennan knew he'd pissed the man off. "You and I don't know each other all that well, Sinclair, so I'll let that one slide. But yes, Kacie is special to me. She's special to all of LCR."

"If she means that much to you, I would imagine you have plenty of people who could act as her bodyguard. Why me?"

"Avoiding the kind of press a possible stalker would draw is of utmost importance."

Brennan had seen photos of Kacie Dane. Tall, blond, beautiful, but with an intriguing wholesomeness that separated her from the sex-kitten models. When he was playing ball, he'd had more than his share of exposure to various celebrities, including models.

McCall went on. "If the press gets wind that she may have a stalker, they'll have a field day. She has very little privacy as it is already. Understandably, Kacie doesn't want anyone to know she needs a bodyguard, so whoever protects her will need to act as her lover, not her bodyguard."

Brennan closed his eyes briefly. Should've seen that one coming. "And, of course, no one would blink an eye at a former Jets quarterback, who's had more than his share of paparazzi attention, dating a beautiful model."

"You dated several models before you married."

Brennan couldn't decide which angered him more. That McCall wanted him because of his former celebrity status, or that once again he would be subjected to the paparazzi feeding frenzy.

"Isn't Kacie Dane supposed to be the face of innocence? What's it going to do to her reputation when she's seen with one of the most reviled sports figures in the world?"

"People see what they want to see. Some will decide she's even more naïve than they thought. Some will see her as tarnishing her reputation. And some will see her as an angel trying to save one of the fallen."

"And most will see me as the man taking advantage of America's sweetheart...using her to clean up my reputation."

McCall shrugged, making no effort to whitewash the situation. "Yes."

"You know the only reason I want to leave the Carmichael Group in the first place is because of the publicity they're gaining?"

"Yes."

"And yet you want to throw me to the publicity hounds on my first op?"

McCall stayed silent. The question had been rhetorical. There was no question what would happen when word got out that the infamous Brennan Sinclair was dating the fresh-faced, oh-so-innocent Kacie Dane.

"And when the op is over?"

"Then you can sink into LCR obscurity, just as you want."

Though he'd almost rather be stabbed repeatedly with rusty nails and fed to killer sharks, Brennan didn't like backing down from a challenge. And *challenge* was the correct word. Probably the toughest one he'd faced in years.

So what could he say but, "Hell, I'm in."

CHAPTER SIX

New York City

The elevator zoomed up to Kacie Dane's apartment. Brennan had to hand it to the guy—McCall knew how to make things happen. The moment Brennan had agreed to the job, the LCR leader had stood and asked, "You got your go bag?"

That was one thing he never left home without. "Yeah."

"Then let's move."

In less than an hour, they'd been in the air, headed to New York City. LCR's plane had been fueled and ready. Apparently, Brennan's interview and subsequent acceptance of the job had been the only hold up.

As he'd stepped onto the plane, he'd gotten another surprise. Justin and his LCR partner, Riley Ingram, would be on the case as well. Though Justin never talked about specifics of his LCR jobs, Brennan knew he was a member of the Elite team and most of his ops were international. He'd been about to say something when he noticed that Riley winced slightly when she moved to shake Brennan's hand. She must have been recovering from an injury.

It had been the first time Brennan had met Riley, and though she was a pretty, delicate-looking woman, her too-solemn face and expressionless eyes seemed oddly incongruent with the way Justin had described his partner. Something didn't jive.

Once the plane was airborne, McCall had gone into detail about Kacie's ordeal five years ago. Though he'd been vague in his description of what she had endured, Brennan understood enough to know that Harrington had drugged, tortured, and repeatedly raped her. Others had been involved in her abduction and torture, but Harrington had apparently been the mastermind and the rapist.

Harrington was dead, along with three of his henchmen. The last one was in a maximum security prison with no outside access.

Having been hounded by an unrelenting and often heartless press, Brennan could definitely see the reasons behind Kacie's name change. And he could understand her need to keep what happened to her from leaking. The press would have a blast in detailing every horrific thing that had happened to this beautiful woman.

Though the flight had been short, Brennan had used the time to read the background Kacie had created for herself. The official biography on her website said she grew up in Maine, an only child to a single mother who died years ago. No other family was mentioned, other than a vague reference to distant relatives.

According to the bio, Kacie was discovered while working as a makeup consultant at a large department store in Manhattan. She was twenty-six years old and had never been married. She dated occasionally, but wasn't seeing anyone on a regular basis.

Her first few modeling jobs were for clothing catalogs, but as she created a reputation for herself as a serious-minded, dedicated professional, the job offers grew. She was now one of the most recognizable models in the country, and her face had graced the covers of fashion magazines, celebrity magazines, and all the tabloids.

He looked closely at the photographs on several different websites. The description of tall, blond, and beautiful didn't do Kacie Dane justice. She had delicate features, a full, mobile mouth, and a brilliant smile that held no hint of artifice. Her lovely hazel-green eyes looked serene, appearing to have no shadows or secrets. Brennan could definitely see her appeal as the wholesome, hometown girl.

There was an amazing amount of information to read, but almost all of it was superficial, with the exception of one impressive item. Two years ago, Kacie had founded the Kacie Dane Foundation, an organization designed to assist young women who'd been victims of violence and abuse. He admired her for that. She could've just put it all behind her and moved on with her life, but she'd chosen to help other victims. Yeah, that was damn impressive.

He did a quick Web search for Kendra Carson and found the surprising news that the young woman was in a vegetative state in a mental hospital in upstate New York and the prognosis for her recovery was poor.

No doubt about it, when Kendra Carson became Kacie Dane, someone had gone to great links to make the switch permanent. He had a feeling Noah McCall had had a lot to do with that.

Brennan leaned back against the wall and observed two of the other people on the elevator. Skylar James and Gabe Maddox had been waiting at the airport when the LCR plane had touched down.

Years ago, before Brennan had married, one of his friends had tried to set him up on a date with Skylar. He couldn't remember why that hadn't worked out. Seemed like she'd claimed she wasn't interested in dating at that time. Since he'd had a date with a different woman almost every night back then, he hadn't given it a second thought. Damn, he'd been arrogant.

The tall, rough-looking man standing beside her was her husband, Gabe. They'd both mentioned their daughter, Megan, several times, and from the way they continued to whisper and smile at each other, they appeared happy.

Skylar was a beautiful woman with shoulder-length mahogany hair, blue eyes, and a kind smile. Her husband seemed to be her opposite in almost every way. He was broad-shouldered and had dark hair and a perpetual scowl on his face. The only time his expression changed was when he looked at his wife, and the transformation was extraordinary. No doubt about it, the grim-faced LCR operative adored her.

Skylar interrupted the tense silence. "Kacie's only expecting Gabe, Noah, and me. She might feel a bit overwhelmed, but I know she'll be grateful for all of you wanting to help."

The elevator came to a soft, shuddering halt, and the doors swung open. They marched out, one by one, and headed to an apartment at the end of the thickly carpeted corridor.

The apartment building seemed to have good security. He'd check those things out later, after he met his charge. The doorman had looked as tough as any defensive lineman he'd ever encountered on the field, and the two bulky men at the security desk in the lobby had the look of hard-assed, seasoned cops.

Before they could knock on the door, it swung open, and Kacie Dane stood there. Brennan barely got a glimpse of her before she threw herself into Skylar's arms with an enthusiastic feminine squeal.

"It's so good to see you."

He'd seen plenty of photos of her, but it was the first time he'd heard her speak, and he was surprised at the loveliness of her voice. She sounded natural and sweet, without a hint of snobbishness.

Pulling from Skylar's arms, Kacie turned to hug Gabe Maddox, whose grim expression changed once again—this time to one of affection. And then, as if she was used to hugging grim-faced, tough-assed guys, she grabbed McCall and gave him a fierce hug.

"Come in, come in." She laughed nervously. "Sorry to keep you out in the hallway. I'm just so thrilled you guys are here. I—"

As they went through the door, Kacie broke off as she noted there were six of them. She gave a little puzzled smile of welcome to both Justin and Riley, and when she turned to Brennan, he saw a flash of recognition.

McCall introduced Justin and Riley, explaining that they would be in charge of the investigation. He then turned to Brennan.

"And this is Brennan Sinclair."

"It's great to meet you."

As Brennan shook her hand, McCall explained, "Brennan is here to help, too, if you'll agree to our plan."

The sparkle in her eyes dimmed slightly as she took a deep breath. Though she'd been acting as though she was greeting everyone as if they were her honored, invited guests, Brennan realized it had been a façade. The shadows beneath her eyes and the small lines of tension around her mouth told another story. This was a woman on edge.

"Sorry. I was so excited to see everyone, I almost forgot you guys aren't here for a fun social visit." She waved a hand at the three sofas in the large living room. "Have a seat. Would you like something to drink?"

Everyone declined her offer of drinks and took a seat. All eyes went to McCall, who said, "Anything else happen?"

"No. Nothing. Part of me feels as though I'm making this into something bigger than it is. But…"

Skylar was sitting beside her and took her hand. "And that's exactly why these guys are here. To see if there *is* something to worry about. Then we'll deal with whatever it is. You can't be too cautious about something like this, Kacie."

"I know. All these things just seem so slight compared to the other things I've dealt with before."

"We have a plan," McCall said.

"You guys have been so kind, but I know LCR doesn't get involved in—"

McCall held up a hand. "Stop right there, Kacie. You're one of our own. And you're not alone. Got that?"

A sheen of grateful tears brightened Kacie's eyes, and Brennan revised his opinions of both McCall and Kacie. The LCR leader did have a heart, and Kacie Dane was much more like her public persona than he had believed.

"Thank you, Noah." Her eyes fell on each of them. "Thank you all. Since so few know about what happened...back then, I wasn't sure exactly what I would do if this thing escalated."

"And that's where we come in." McCall shot a glance at Brennan. "Sinclair is trained. He can protect and defend you until Justin and Riley can determine if there is a threat and who's behind it."

"So Brennan would be my bodyguard? But I'm—"

"We know how you feel about that kind of publicity, Kacie," Skylar said. "That's why we thought this would be the best way to make sure you're safe without giving any indication to the media that you might be in danger. We—" Skylar's eyes went to Brennan as if her explanation suddenly felt awkward.

Brennan put it as succinctly as he could. "I'm a former celebrity. Few people are going to question why we would be together. None of them would guess that I'm your bodyguard."

"So we're like…supposed to be dating?"

As the cold light in Brennan Sinclair's eyes went below zero, Kacie inwardly cringed at how insultingly that had come out. However, she couldn't truthfully say she was delighted with the idea. Brennan Sinclair was the kind of man she avoided at all cost. He was too big, too austere. Yes, he was nice-looking. Well, okay, *nice* wasn't exactly the right word. She searched for another description—devastatingly handsome, sexy, gorgeous, overwhelmingly male, but only if you were into the tall, muscular, take-no-prisoners kind of guy. Even though she rarely dated, she preferred less intimidating-looking men. Ones who didn't make her forget to breathe.

Don't be silly, Kacie. You won't actually be dating the guy. He's going to protect you.

"I assure you, Ms. Dane, it would be for appearance's sake only."

Now she felt like she'd hurt his feelings, which seemed asinine in the extreme. Still, she needed to make him understand she meant no offense. "Please, call me Kacie. And having people believe we're dating won't bother me at all."

What's a little white lie among friends?

Feeling distinctly off-center, she pulled her gaze from Brennan's dark, piercing gaze and looked over at Skylar. "This seems like a pound of prevention for an ounce of nothing."

"If it's nothing, then that's great," Skylar said. "Let Brennan protect you while Justin and Riley figure out if there is nothing to be worried about."

As if aware she was going to protest again, Skylar added, "For me? Please?"

Turn down the one person who'd saved her life and helped her come back from hell? How could she?

"Okay. I'll do it."

"Excellent," Noah said.

"You said only a handful of people are aware of your story," Justin Kelly said. "We'll need a list of these people."

Kacie nodded. "Of course. I'll put a list together. There aren't that many…really."

"You suspect any of them?" Brennan asked.

Kacie closed her eyes, knowing she had no choice but to bring up a possible suspect, no matter how uncomfortable it made her. "My mother."

Skylar gasped and shook her head. "Why would she do that, Kacie? It would be no benefit to her at all."

"It would if she thought she could blackmail me for more money." She grimaced and added, "It didn't improve our relationship when I cut off my payments to her."

"Recently?" Brennan asked.

"Yes…just this past month."

"You were paying your mother to keep her quiet?" Riley asked.

Kacie thought it odd that Riley picked up on that. Most people would assume she was using her substantial wealth to help her mother.

"My mother and I don't have what you would call a close relationship." She gave a slight shoulder lift, as if that didn't matter to her. "She was more than happy to stay quiet since she looked at my abduction as more of an embarrassment than anything else. The money I gave her just sweetened the deal. She recently got married again, this time to a wealthy man, so I stopped sending her money, and she's angry."

"Then you're right," Skylar said. "I'd put her at the top of my list, too."

"We'll go by and visit with your mother," Riley said. "If it is her, we can…encourage her to stop."

Kacie couldn't help but smile at the thought of Justin and Riley paying Sonia Carson Musgrave a visit. Justin looked tough enough to take on a grizzly, much less her conniving mother. And though Riley was slender and on the petite side, the fierce gleam in her eyes said that she could be just as fearsome as her partner.

Noah stood. "I've got a couple of items I need to see to before I head back home. Kelly and Ingram, keep me informed of your progress. Skylar and Gabe, you're staying in New York a little longer?"

Gabe nodded. "We'll visit with Skye's family for a few hours and then head back home tomorrow."

"Our babysitter is watching Megan," Skylar added as she sent an apologetic glance at Kacie. "I wish I could stay longer, but I've never been away from her for more than a few hours."

"Don't be silly," Kacie said. "I'm just thrilled I got to see you both. If you're available, come back tonight for dinner."

Skylar gave her a warm hug. "That sounds wonderful. We'll catch up then."

Within a minute, they were all out the door with the exception of the tall, unsmiling Brennan Sinclair.

Kacie closed the door and turned to face him. Before she could say a word, Brennan said, "So if we're going to be dating, I guess we'd better get acquainted."

CHAPTER SEVEN

Get acquainted with this grim-faced, tough-looking, gorgeous man? Odd how the idea both excited and terrified her.

She hadn't dated anyone steadily since before her abduction. Dating meant sharing and opening up to another person. Though she no longer considered herself Kendra Carson and felt as though she had almost nothing in common with her, wariness of the opposite sex was something they both shared.

Before her abduction, she had dated plenty. Unfortunately, her selection in dates had been as poor as her decision-making abilities in other things. Kendra Carson's last boyfriend, Calvin Henderson, had been into drugs, both using and selling. She hadn't been a user, not even occasionally. She would have liked to say it was because she had good judgment, but that would be a lie. Her refusal to use illegal drugs had been all about vanity. She'd seen what drugs could do to a person's appearance, especially their teeth, hair, and complexion. Her goal to be a model had trumped any desire to get high.

Kacie checked her watch, thankful she had an excuse to delay the sharing. "I've got to get dressed for a business meeting. I have a two o'clock lunch appointment with my agent. We can talk when I get back."

"Then I guess we need to share quickly."

"This is a business lunch. You don't have to go with me. I—"

"Yes, I do. Remember, that's why I'm here."

"It's just with my agent. It'll look really strange if I bring a date. Besides, I'll be perfectly safe. I'll take a cab there and back."

"I don't care if you're lunching with the pope and riding in the Popemobile, I'm going with you."

"But she knows nothing about you. It'll look odd if you just show up without any warning."

"Can't be helped. Unless you're in the apartment, I'm with you at all times. Understand?"

"But this is a business luncheon."

"And you're my business. Deal with it."

Arguing would do no good, and she didn't have time for it anyway. She gave him a stiff nod. "I'll be back in a few minutes."

Inside her bedroom, Kacie took a few minutes to settle her nerves. She knew she was behaving irrationally, which was the reason she hadn't lost her temper in front of Brennan. He was here to protect her. How ungrateful and churlish of her to be angry with him.

Just because he made her feel things... She swallowed hard as she amended that thought. No, he didn't make her feel things... he made her *feel*. And how scary was that?

Now that she'd left the room, Brennan's mouth tilted in a small smile. If someone could stomp in an elegant, graceful way, Kacie Dane had mastered such a walk. He had pissed her off, and though it might make for some uneasy moments between them, for some reason he couldn't quite figure, he was pleased.

She was clearly having a bad time of it. Anyone could tell that she hadn't slept well. Even as lovely as she was, the shadows under her eyes and the vertical lines at her mouth indicated she was stressed. Maybe that's what pleased him about pissing her off. If she was angry with him, she would focus on that and not some crazed stalker.

While he waited, Brennan took the time to familiarize himself with her apartment. Nicely decorated, nothing fancy. A simple elegance that matched the owner. Eclectic blend of colors, including a fondness for jewel tones. Some good pieces of furniture—expensive but sturdy and durable.

Good-sized kitchen to the left of the large foyer. A small breakfast area just past the kitchen, along with a half bath and a laundry room. No formal dining area. He got the idea that a couple of walls had been knocked down to create a larger, more open living space. A small office on the other side of the living room was both feminine and functional.

He unlocked and slid open the glass door and stepped out onto the balcony. The area wasn't big enough to hold more than a couple of outdoor chairs and a few potted, flowering plants. He imagined that Kacie used it often since it looked over a small park, but he didn't see it as much of a threat to her safety. The apartment was on the sixteenth floor, and at least fifteen feet separated her balcony from the next one. Guy would have to get damn creative to breach her apartment this way.

He went back inside, grabbed his bag, and walked up the stairs. Three bedrooms up here. He was glad to see the smaller one had been converted into a gym that included free weights, a stair climber, and a treadmill. Would make it easier on both of them if she didn't have to go out to a gym every day.

He dropped his bag in the guest bedroom and then headed back downstairs to wait.

A minute or so later, Kacie descended the stairs with grace and confidence, as if she hadn't a care in the world. She had gone through the deepest pits of hell. No one should have to endure what had been done to her, but looking at her now, it was almost impossible to imagine she'd ever suffered any kind of trauma.

"The rest of the world still believes you're in a mental hospital, still suffering from what happened to you. How'd you pull that off?"

She stumbled slightly at his blunt statement but recovered almost immediately. "I see you've done some research."

When he didn't respond, she shrugged and said, "I had a lot of support from some very influential people."

"Which means there are more than a handful of people who know your real identity. Even more than what you supplied Justin and Riley?"

"No, those are the very few who know everything. There are others who might know a small portion."

"I want every name. Even the ones who might know only a portion could've done some digging. We leave no stone unturned."

She chewed on her lower lip for a second. When Brennan realized he was focusing on her mouth, wondering if her lipstick might taste as delicious as it looked on her lips, he pulled his thoughts back to the job. An attraction to Kacie Dane was the last thing he needed.

"Okay, I'll put together another list when I get back." She checked the silver watch on her slender wrist. "We've got to get going. Our reservations are at two."

"Okay, here's the deal. You're with me, no matter what. If you need to go to the bathroom, I'll go with you."

"What?"

She looked so horrified he almost grinned. "Don't worry. I'll stand outside the door."

Looking only a little relieved, she headed to the door. "Let's talk about it on the way. My driver is probably double-parked in front of the building."

They were in the elevator, almost to the ground floor, before she spoke again. "How do we explain our new relationship? Isn't it going to appear strange for us to suddenly look like we're crazy about each other?"

"Keep it as close to the truth as possible. We met through mutual friends. Realized we have a lot in common. Kept it quiet until we'd spent enough time together to think it'll last. Don't make it sound complicated, and it won't be."

The elevator came to a halt, and the door slid open. She was about to exit when she turned to him with a look of horror.

Brennan stood in front of her and stuck his head out, searching for a threat. Seeing nothing, he turned back to her. "What's wrong?"

"Aren't you married?"

Of all the questions she could've asked, this one surprised him the most. Did she really not know his story? Now wasn't the time to get into it, but they needed to talk soon. "No."

In response to his short, stark answer, questions flickered on her face. If she wanted to do research to find out more, that would be disgustingly easy. But damned if he'd go into detail about it right here, right now.

They were seated in the cab, headed to the restaurant, when she said, "I understand not wanting to spill your guts to a virtual stranger, but it's going to look exceedingly weird if I know next to nothing about you."

"I'll give you the condensed version, which should get us through lunch. I'll give you more later. I grew up in a little town outside Cincinnati, Ohio. Got a scholarship to play football at Ohio State. I played professional football for the Jets for two years.

"I'm twenty-nine. My favorite color is green. Favorite kind of food is Italian. My shoe size is thirteen and a half, and my favorite drink is single-malt scotch."

He was grateful when they pulled in front of the restaurant. Just as the driver opened the door for her to get out, she said, "Oh...what about your family? Do they still live in Ohio?"

"I have no family."

Before she could ask another question that would stab him in the heart to answer, he threw out a comment to get her mind focused in a different direction. "And if anyone asks, you can tell them I'm unemployed and living off your generosity. They'll believe that faster than anything else."

Chapter Eight

Kacie scrambled to get her thoughts together. After Brennan's rushed and condensed version of his life, her mind had worked to try to remember all that he'd said. Then, just when she thought he was finished, he'd given that bald, flat statement about his family and then the bizarre sentence at the end. She definitely had some catching up to do.

If she'd had more than a few minutes before she was due to meet Edy, she would have stayed in the car and asked the driver to drive them around for a while. The emotionless way Brennan had spoken told her that the man had been hurt, and quite badly. And though she'd only met him less than two hours ago, for some reason she wanted to comfort him.

She vaguely remembered seeing or hearing something about his past but couldn't honestly remember if it was good or bad. He'd said he'd played for the Jets for only a couple of seasons, but Kacie did have one distinct memory of seeing a photo of him in a magazine. He'd been at some extravagant New York event, but what she remembered most clearly was how incredibly handsome he'd been in a black tuxedo. He'd had a sexy, devilish smile on his face and a cocky confidence that had set her young heart to a quick pitter-patter and her naïve young mind soaring with imagination.

So what had happened to him? To his family, his career? It frustrated her that she didn't know, but finding out more would have to wait. She had a business lunch to get through, contract negotiations to discuss, and a virtual stranger to pass off as her boyfriend. Her agenda was full for the moment.

She took Brennan's hand as she exited the car and flashed a smile at a couple of photographers who called out to her. Marvin's was one of the most exclusive restaurants in Manhattan and attracted numerous celebrities as well as some of the city's wealthiest patrons. Reservations had to be made months in advance, and even then they were almost impossible to get.

As her fame had grown, it had become increasingly easier to get into exclusive places such as Marvin's, but there was still an extensive waiting list.

Last year, the owner, Marvin Lowe, had contacted the Kacie Dane Foundation to request assistance for his fourteen-year-old daughter, Jillian. She'd been sexually abused by a male relative. Though the man was in prison, Jillian continued to have nightmares but had refused further counseling. Knowing his daughter was a fan of Kacie's, Marvin had suggested seeing someone at Kacie's foundation for a reference. Jillian had agreed.

The young girl was still in counseling but, according to Marvin, doing so much better. As a thank-you, Marvin had told Kacie she could make reservations on a second's notice, and he would make sure she had a table.

At first Kacie had balked. Using contacts she'd made through her foundation seemed wrong. When Marvin had insisted, she realized that the man needed to do something. She understood that need. The kindnesses that had been extended to her were immeasurable, and she'd had that same feeling numerous times.

Odd, but when she had recognized that need, she had realized she was on her way to recovery. Wanting to do something for someone else enabled her to get outside herself and her own worries. Gratitude had replaced grief and bitterness.

They walked into the restaurant, and the instant she saw the happiness in Marvin's eyes as he came toward her, she was glad she'd accepted his offer.

Marvin held out his hand. "Ms. Dane, it's so wonderful to see you."

"You, too, Mr. Lowe. And please, call me Kacie."

"Thank you, and you should call me Marvin." He turned to Brennan and blinked in surprise. "Why, you're Brennan Sinclair. I went to every game you played with the Jets."

Brennan nodded and smiled but didn't offer a verbal response.

"I have a special table for you," Marvin said to Kacie.

"I hope it's not a problem that we need a table for three?"

"Not at all. Our tables and booths are extra generous." He flashed them a big grin. "Please, follow me."

As they wove through the crowded restaurant, Kacie recognized at least three Broadway stars, a soap opera actress, and one well-known anchor of a cable news show. She also noted the many shocked expressions when their eyes drifted to her companion. Skylar and Noah had been right. No one would even consider that Brennan was her bodyguard and not her boyfriend.

Marvin seated them at a square, white-cloth-covered table. The instant they were seated, a waiter arrived to hand them menus and take their drink orders.

With one last pat on her shoulder, Marvin wished them a good meal and hurried away.

"Nice place," Brennan said.

"I've never eaten here before, but I've heard the food is fantastic."

"Really? The guy certainly seemed to know you."

Kacie shrugged. She didn't want to go into how she and Marvin had become acquainted.

Before he could question her further, she heard Edy's voice and turned. The woman certainly knew how to make an entrance. She glided toward them as if she was the Queen of New York and those around her were her loyal subjects. She stopped at a table and chatted with a couple.

"There's Edy," she told Brennan. "Just to fill you in, she's been my agent for two years and has been one of my biggest supporters."

"But?"

"She can be a bit...um...assertive."

He gave her a quick nod of acknowledgment. "Thanks for the warning." He stood as Edy finally broke away from the couple and approached them.

Dressed in a cherry-red Dior suit that was both professional and feminine, Edy oozed sexuality. The instant she spotted Brennan, a predatory light glowed in her eyes.

Uh oh. This should be interesting.

Brennan held back a sigh as he watched Kacie's agent coming toward their table. He had known when he accepted this job that he would not only be thrust into the limelight but would also have to deal with certain types of people. This type was the most bothersome. At one time, she was exactly what'd he desired most in a woman. Long-legged, good-looking, and with a gleam in her eyes that said bedroom games were her specialty.

As both a college football star and an NFL player, he'd dated women just like Edy and, before he was married, bedded dozens of them. And damn it all—he'd married one of them, too.

"Darling," Edy cooed. "You didn't tell me we were going to be a threesome." Her lips tilted in a sly smile, making it clear that her idea of a *threesome* had nothing to do with lunch.

"I'm sorry, Edy. Hope you don't mind."

"Not at all. In fact, I'm beyond delighted." She held out her hand to Brennan. "I'm Edy Brown, and you are?"

Brennan took her hand and shook it firmly. "Brennan Sinclair."

"*The* Brennan Sinclair? The former Jets player?"

"That's right."

She sat down in the chair Brennan pulled out for her. "How absolutely…surprising." A questioning gaze went to Kacie and then turned to Brennan. "How on earth do you two know each other?"

Before Brennan could answer, Kacie put her hand over his and said, "Skylar introduced us a while back. We've not been seeing each other that long." She gave Brennan a surprisingly flirtatious smile. "But it's quickly become pretty intense."

Edy grinned. "Is that right?"

When they both nodded, Edy's eyes narrowed into slits. "Seriously? This isn't some kind of gag or publicity stunt?"

"Of course it isn't," Kacie said. "Why would you even think that?"

"For one thing, you've never mentioned seeing anyone, much less the infamous Brennan Sinclair."

"That's because we didn't want anyone to know," Kacie said.

"Also, I was worried about Kacie's reputation," Brennan added. "But she has assured me it won't be problem. Will it?"

Edy didn't answer for a moment, and Brennan realized she was considering the question. He liked that she didn't just give an offhand answer, that she was thinking things through.

"No, I don't think it will. And if I know Julian Montague, the extra publicity will both amuse and thrill him."

The server interrupted them. "Have you had a chance to read the menu?"

After a conversation about house specialties and daily specials, they placed their orders. The instant the server walked away, Edy's speculative gaze went back to Brennan. "So tell me, how long have you and Kacie been dating?"

"Not long," Brennan said.

"We wanted to keep it a secret for a while longer." Apparently getting even more into the spirit of their pretense, Kacie let her fingers trail down Brennan's arm in a delicate caress. "Brennan has been out of town for a few weeks, and when he arrived this morning, I invited him to come along. I couldn't bear to let him out of my sight."

Ignoring the rush of arousal from that electric touch was impossible. And since he was playing the role of the besotted suitor, he took the hand on his arm, kissed it, and then held it in his own.

The flare of awareness in Kacie's eyes was gratifying. He was glad he wasn't the only one with this extraordinary reaction to a simple touch.

"How very romantic. I do hope Kacie's new project won't get in the way of your relationship."

"Not at all. I support Kacie in her career one hundred percent."

"And what about your own career?"

Even though he had been expecting the question, it didn't mean he was going to make it easy for her. If she thought he was taking advantage of Kacie's naïveté and innocence for his own gain—well, so what? "What do you mean?"

"I mean, I know you don't play football any longer, so what do you do?"

Besides take advantage of naïve young women was the implied question.

"I have various investments I oversee."

"Hmm."

"So anyway, Edy," Kacie said, "there's something we need to nail down for the contract?"

Even though it was an obvious attempt on Kacie's part to change the tone and direction of the conversation, Brennan was glad to see the agent pull a thick envelope from her over-sized purse. Hopefully, the distraction of his presence could be swept aside so the real reason for the lunch meeting could take place.

With Edy's focus fully on her client, Brennan ate his grilled prawns and watched the negotiations. As he listened, he became more intrigued by Kacie Dane with each second. He already knew she was an extraordinarily strong person. He knew only the barest of facts about what she had endured at the hands of William Harrington III, and that was enough to tear a hole in his gut. But to look at her now, who could ever imagine she'd had anything but the easiest of lives?

He also liked that she didn't back down. When Edy kept insisting that certain points were non-negotiable, Kacie never balked. She stated her opinion in a firm, calm way. And apparently, Edy knew when to push and when to back off.

They were in the middle of coffee and an incredible chocolate mousse dessert when the final items were agreed upon and the discussion drew to a close. Despite himself, Brennan had been fascinated, not only by the professional way Kacie handled herself but also by the intricate items included in her contract. Who knew that showing certain body parts was negotiable?

Now that business had been conducted, and Edy had accepted his and Kacie's odd and seemingly mismatched relationship, she put the contract away and stood.

"I believe Julian will be very pleased. I'll give his people a call, and if they agree, I'll have them send the revised contracts to you today."

"Thank you, Edy. For everything."

For the first time, Brennan saw a softening in Edy's eyes. The hard-edged agent had a soft spot for her client. He was glad for it. Kacie needed people around her who cared not just about what she could bring to them financially but also about her well-being.

Brennan stood and shook Edy's hand, pleased that she gave him an almost warm smile. "It was a delight meeting you, Brennan. Surprising, but still a delight."

She winked at Kacie. "Take good care of our girl."

The instant she was out of hearing range, Brennan sat down again and turned to Kacie. Out of all the conditions that she and Edy had argued about, one had surprised him the most. "A model who refuses to wear a bikini? Why?"

CHAPTER NINE

Even though it was only a little after five when they returned to her apartment, Kacie was as exhausted as if she'd worked a twelve-hour day. She appreciated and admired Edy beyond measure, but she always wore Kacie out. It didn't help that she was also sleep deprived.

Brennan had been surprisingly quiet on their trip back. His question about her refusal to wear a bikini had come as such a shock, she'd had to scramble quickly to come up with a viable answer. It'd been a while since she'd had to deal with that kind of pointed question. Edy had known what her answer would be when she'd asked about it, which was the reason the discussion on that topic had lasted barely thirty seconds. Brennan had picked up on it, though.

She hadn't been able to tell him the total truth, so she'd given him her standard, albeit truthful, answer. The persona she had created for herself was a wholesome, all-American good girl. No, wearing a bikini was not vulgar, but neither did it scream *sweet hometown girl* either. She didn't mind modeling swimsuits as long as they covered certain areas of her body. A bikini provided little coverage, particularly one area that no one but her doctors had seen since her rescue.

"Kacie?"

Jerked out of her grim thoughts, she looked up at Brennan, who was standing in front of her, looking down at her in confusion and concern.

"What?"

"You okay? You kind of zoned out there."

"Yes. Sorry. Didn't sleep well last night, and it's catching up with me."

"That's understandable. I was asking if you have anything else planned for the day. Anywhere you need to go?"

"No. I'm in for the day. Thought I might take a quick nap."

"I have a couple of errands to run. I was going to suggest calling Skylar to see if she'd come over and stay with you."

"She and Gabe are coming over for dinner tonight. There's no reason for them to come earlier. And no reason for you to be concerned. If you haven't noticed already, this building has excellent security. It'd take a tank to get by those guys."

Those penetrating eyes narrowed, assessing her, and Kacie felt as though he looked into her soul.

"I won't be gone more than an hour or so. Where's your phone?"

"In my purse." She pulled it out to show it to him.

Taking it from her, he punched some keys and then handed it back.

"I put my number in your contacts. Anything happens, even the slightest thing, you call me. Got it?"

She took a breath. As independent-minded as she had become in the last few years, one would think his autocratic tone would be irritating. Instead, she felt cared for, protected.

"And you'd better have this." She pulled out the spare key she'd grabbed from her dresser earlier and had forgotten to give him.

"I shouldn't be long."

"I'll be fine."

With a quick nod, he walked out the door.

Kacie released another explosive breath. He might be over-powering and intimidating, but she couldn't help but be glad that he was here to protect her. That is, if she even needed protection.

Before she did anything else, she was determined to find out more about Brennan's past. Asking him the minute they'd returned to the apartment had felt wrong, like she was being nosy. And okay, looking him up online wasn't exactly less nosy, but at least she wouldn't unwittingly offend him by asking sensitive questions.

Sitting at her desk, she opened her laptop and put his name into a search engine. The instant the results screen popped up, she sat back in dismay. Over two hundred thousand links? She clicked on the first one and began to read. The more she read, the angrier she became. Within ten minutes of searching, she was closing down her laptop, feeling both queasy and guilty. They had massacred him. There were even blogs and websites completely devoted to hatred of him.

He'd been called everything from a child killer to an abuser of women. A loser and a coward. The first nice thing she'd read about him had been on the second page of the results list. A news story reported that he donated the money he collected from his son's life insurance policy to a children's hospital, though the writer pointed out that it still had not been proven that he wasn't involved in his son's death.

She had known the man for less than half a day and already knew that ninety-nine percent of what she'd read was a lie.

But what she truly didn't understand, what she could not begin to fathom, was why it appeared he had never defended himself. In just about everything she'd read, it was suggested that Brennan Sinclair's silence was an obvious admission of guilt. Because, of course, if anyone accused you of doing terrible, hideous things, your first reaction would be to defend yourself, wouldn't it?

Or could he have kept silent because the hurt was too great and the people who believed he could be guilty of such things didn't matter? The people who loved Brennan knew the truth.

Feeling even wearier than she had before, Kacie headed up to her bedroom. As she undressed, the mishmash of information she'd learned whirled in her head. When she settled onto her pillow, her last thought before she dropped into a restless sleep was followed by deep sadness. Brennan had said he had no family. If that was the case, who had believed and supported him during his awful tragedy?

Just over an hour later, Brennan walked back into Kacie's apartment. The errands hadn't taken him as long as he'd feared. He dropped the bags onto the hallway table and was about to head to the kitchen for some water when he heard a muffled scream.

Switching directions, Brennan took the stairs three at a time and sped toward Kacie's bedroom. Pulling his gun from the holster beneath his jacket, he twisted the knob and pushed the door open. The room was dark, and he didn't know where the damned light switch was. Clicking the flashlight on his Glock, he swept it quickly around the room and saw nothing other than a small lump in the middle of the large bed. Turning the flashlight toward the wall behind him, he spotted the light switch and flipped it up. Bright light flooded the room. The small, shuddering woman in the bed hadn't noticed.

Nightmare. He'd had too many not to recognize one.

"Kacie...wake up."

A low whimper, like the sound of a whipped animal, was her response.

He walked to the bed and said in a loud but calm voice, "Kacie. You're having a nightmare. Wake. Up."

He wanted to touch her, shake her from the hell he knew she was reliving, but he feared that would frighten her even more.

"Kacie. Wake up. Now."

Her eyes flickered open, and she blinked up at him in confusion.

"It's me—Brennan. You were having a nightmare."

He saw the fear, the absolute terror, in her eyes. Then, as she realized where she was, who he was, he saw her draw into herself. The fear receded, replaced by a blank calmness.

How many nights had she suffered like this, alone? With no one here to hold her, reassure her? He almost reached out to her but stopped. He wanted to touch her, hold her…be there for her. Shit. How in the hell could he have known her for less than a day and feel this incredible need to comfort her?

She sat up in bed, revealing she wore a white T-shirt. Her perfectly formed breasts showed clearly through the thin, transparent material. Brennan swallowed. Aw hell, he didn't need to see that.

"Have you been back long?"

Her voice sounded slightly hoarse. How long had she been crying or screaming before he arrived?

"I just walked in and heard you…up here."

"Screaming?"

He nodded. "Yeah."

She grimaced and scooted up in bed a little more. "Residual crap. Happens sometimes."

"You've had a few tough days."

"I've had better. But I've had worse, too." She glanced at the bedside clock. "You weren't gone very long."

"I just needed to pick up a few items." Needing to get away from the intimate setting and the totally inappropriate desire rushing through him, he started backing away. "Come into the living room after you get dressed, and I'll show you some things I bought."

At his mention of getting dressed, she apparently remembered she wasn't exactly wearing street clothes. She glanced down, saw how see-through her T-shirt was, and slid beneath the covers again. The tinge of pink blooming on her face was both delightful and charming. Kacie Dane was a paradox of conflicting personalities. And as Brennan walked out of the room, he had the insane thought that he wanted to get to know every single one of them.

CHAPTER TEN

Instead of throwing clothes on and following Brennan into the living room, Kacie took a quick shower and then dressed in a pair of jeans and a white cotton button-down shirt. She not only wanted to wash away the cobwebs from her nightmares, she needed the extra time to settle herself down.

For the first time since before her abduction, she had felt a flash of desire for a man. And even more extraordinary, it had come in response to the heat she'd seen in Brennan's eyes.

Her therapist had told her at some point those kinds of feelings would return, but she hadn't believed her. Having desire for a man, being intimate with him, making herself vulnerable, wasn't something she believed could ever happen again. And though she couldn't say she wanted to just jump in bed with Brennan, feeling the beginnings of arousal was both heady and exhilarating. She clicked a mental check mark next to 'feel sexual interest to a sexy guy' on her list of mental health goals. Progress indeed.

She entered the living room to find Brennan on the sofa and an array of items laid out on her large coffee table.

"What's all this stuff?"

Brennan waved her over. "Come take a look."

Curious, Kacie went to the table and looked at the odd display, trying to figure out why Brennan had bought, among other things, a metal comb, and a curling iron.

"I checked to see if you have a license for a handgun, and you don't."

"No. Not crazy about guns. I do have pepper spray on my key chain, and I've taken several self-defense classes."

He nodded as if he already knew this. "Tomorrow you'll fill out an application to carry a handgun. Then I'm going to take you to a shooting range and help you overcome your dislike of guns. You need to be able to use one without fear."

"I'm not—"

"Kacie."

His voice, patient yet commanding, sparked more heat, and another ripple of arousal swept through her.

"Come sit down and let's talk about these items. They're everyday, ordinary things that can be used to protect yourself in a pinch."

He said nothing more about the gun, and she knew it was because it was already a foregone conclusion. He wasn't going to argue or belabor a point he believed had already been settled.

How did she feel about someone coming in and taking control like that? Her independent *I know what's best for me* spirit was flashing a big stop sign. But surprisingly, another sign was coming along right after it: *proceed with caution.*

She liked that he didn't push her or snap at her to hurry up. He just gave her time to come to terms with his statements. She took a deep breath. Okay, *proceed with caution* had taken over.

Kacie sat on the sofa.

Brennan was surprised at her acquiescence. He had expected an argument. Though he could see she wasn't totally onboard about owning a gun or learning how to use one, he admired her willingness to consider. She didn't seem to be an impulsive person, in speech or action. He'd noticed she sometimes paused a second or two before responding to a question. Had this carefulness to react always been a part of her personality? He had a strong feeling that it hadn't. She had learned the hard way that impulsive behavior could lead to disastrous results.

She picked up a steel-toothed comb and grinned. "Okay, so I'll mesmerize my opponent by combing my long, golden locks and then go in for the kill."

He couldn't resist looking at those long, golden locks. She had gorgeous, silky-looking hair that fell well past her shoulders in thick waves. He gave himself a mental shake. Hell, maybe she was right about being able to mesmerize her opponent.

"Not exactly but almost."

"What do you mean?"

He took her fingers and pressed them against the steel edges of the teeth. "Feel how sharp these are? You could do some damage to a guy's face or throat." He took the comb from her and lightly ran it down his face and across his neck. "Enough for you to get away."

She shivered slightly, and he saw that her amusement had been swallowed by memories. She was remembering her abduction.

"Stay with me, Kacie. That was then…this is now."

She nodded. "Okay. So…what else?" She reached down and picked up a small curling iron. "I'm seeing a theme here."

"You may not carry a purse large enough for that, but if you do, it could do some serious damage to an eye or a throat. Even a groin, if you've got a good angle."

"I've got a couple of good-sized purses I can start using."

He nodded. "My wife had a closet full, some of them as large as my suitcase."

"Your wife?"

Hell, when was the last time he'd mentioned Vanessa in such a casual way? There was something about Kacie Dane that made him let his guard down. He didn't like the feeling.

"Former wife. Remember…she's dead."

Cold, harsh words, but he couldn't have said them any differently. He had learned to forgive Vanessa her infidelity, knowing a good part of that had been his fault. He'd been a self-absorbed asshole, and she'd turned to someone else to get what she needed. He hadn't and didn't believe he could ever forgive her for the other, though. She had ended up taking the easy way out. Even though he'd hated her for what she'd done to their son, he also despised the way she'd handled the aftermath.

Bottom line, they'd both been selfish morons who hadn't appreciated the gift of their son. Cody had paid the ultimate price for his parents' lack of strength and character.

"I'm sorry."

He gave a nod of acknowledgment for her sympathy and then went on to explain the other items on the table. A pen in the eye or throat. Small can of aerosol hair spray to temporarily blind an attacker. Manicure scissors and a nail file to stab.

He held up the hair spray. "Spray this in a guy's face, and he won't be seeing anything until he can wash his eyes out."

"I see you've got pepper spray and mace, too."

"Yes. The more you have, the better your chances of being able to immediately find at least one or two things that can help you."

"So how does a former NFL football player become an LCR operative?"

He was surprised she hadn't asked the question before, although they'd barely had time to talk since he arrived.

The doorbell rang, and he figured that explanation would have to wait a little longer.

She stood. "That's probably Skylar and Gabe. I think they're bringing takeout from the Italian restaurant at the corner."

Only, it wasn't Skylar and Gabe. And from the dread on Kacie's face, it was the last person she wanted to see.

Chapter Eleven

And her day just became infinitely less pleasant. With a frustrated sigh of disgust, Kacie opened the door. Once this visit was over, she planned to have a long, stern talk with front-desk security about who was allowed up to her apartment without her being notified first. This person most definitely was not on that exclusive list.

"Hello, Mother."

Sonia floated in on a wave of Chanel No. 5 and acted as if she belonged there. Her confident stride halted for a moment when she spotted Brennan. Light hazel eyes glinted with speculation. "Now I know why I haven't heard from you. Keeping secrets from your mama?"

Kacie closed the door and resisted an eye roll. She hadn't seen the woman in almost a year and had talked to her on the phone only a couple of times. Her mother knew full well the reasons for the lack of contact. They could barely be in the same room with each other for more than five minutes without Kacie wanting to either toss her mother out the door or throw up from the stress. Or both.

"Mother, this is Brennan Sinclair. He's a…friend."

"I'll just bet he is," Sonia practically purred.

Kacie suppressed a shudder. There was something exceedingly icky about seeing her mother come on to this man—especially when, for all she knew, he could be her daughter's boyfriend.

"Brennan, this is Sonia Carson Musgrave. My mother."

Sonia's eyes roamed up and down Brennan with embarrassing salaciousness. "You look familiar. Are you a model?"

"No, ma'am, I'm not."

Kacie swallowed a nervous giggle at Brennan's respectful answer, knowing her mother would hate it. In Sonia's book, being called *ma'am* was tantamount to being called *old lady*.

"You must call me Sonia. Everyone does."

"All right, ma'am. Thank you."

Sonia's eyes narrowed briefly in irritation before she turned her attention to Kacie. "Friends of yours visited me this afternoon. Honestly, Kacie. It was so rude of you to send them. They questioned me as if I were a common criminal. I didn't appreciate it at all."

"That wasn't my intent, Mother. I've had a few unsettling things happen lately—some threatening messages—and we wanted to—"

"I know what you wanted. You wanted to intimidate me. Well, it won't work, young lady. I know what you're up to."

Completely flummoxed, Kacie asked, "And that would be?"

"You think if I'm frightened, I won't ask for more money. Well, you're wrong. It's the least you can do for all the things you put me through when you were a teenager. Then after you went away with that man, I had to put up with all sorts of questions. Then after you came back…all that nasty media coverage."

It was pointless to remind her mother that she hadn't *gone away* with William Harrington, or that Sonia was the one who had called a press conference and told the world that Kendra

Carson was one of Harrington's victims. Kacie's privacy had been violated mostly due to her mother's need for attention.

"I've given you money for almost three years. Your new husband is very wealthy, and I'm sure he—"

"You leave him out of this." She drew herself up and pointed a long, thin finger at Kacie. "You owe me, young lady. Three years of money is not nearly enough for what I've had to put up with from you."

Yet another reason why she wouldn't see her mother unless she absolutely was forced to. Sonia blamed her for everything. Not once had she held her and tried to console her after she'd been found. Not once had she told her how happy she was that Kacie had survived. Not once had she told her she was proud of her for what she had achieved.

And not once had Kacie been able to defend herself. Since her rescue five years ago, her one act of rebellion against her mother had been last month when she'd cut off funds. It didn't look as though she would be defending herself now either. She opened her mouth to speak, and nothing came out.

Where's your backbone, Kacie?

Brennan did not have the same problem.

"Your daughter just told you she's dealing with some threats, and all you can do is harass her for money that you clearly don't need?" He walked slowly toward her, causing Sonia to stumble backward against the apartment door, where she froze, eyes wide with shock.

"What kind of mother is so obsessed with her own selfish wants that she can't be bothered to give a crap about her daughter's safety?"

Sonia's mouth opened and closed like a fish gasping for air. She stuttered, "You can't t-talk t-to m-me like that. Do you know who I'm married to?"

"About the unluckiest bastard on the planet, I'd say."

"Kendra, are you going to just let him talk to your mother like that?"

Fascinated didn't even come close to what Kacie was feeling. Other than Skylar, no one had ever stuck up for her like that. It was a testament to how very shaken her mother was that she'd referred to her as Kendra. Having friends and acquaintances believe her daughter existed in a vegetative state in a private hospital suited Sonia quite well.

However, it didn't mean that Sonia wouldn't do her best to blackmail her daughter for money if she thought she could get away with it.

She glared at Kacie. "Well, don't just stand there. Tell him he can't talk to me like that."

Instead of replying, Kacie took her mother's arm to pull her away from the door so she could open it. "I don't think we have anything more to say to each other. Please leave."

"You ungrateful little bitch." She cast a wrathful glare at Kacie and then a fearful one at Brennan, as if she thought he might come after her.

Kacie closed the door in her mother's face and then turned to the man who'd defended her. She wasn't quite sure what to say.

Brennan flashed a slightly embarrassed grin. "My mail-order degree in the art of diplomacy should be arriving any day now."

Brennan strapped on his ankle holster and slid in his .38 Colt Cobra. Kacie had emailed her agenda to him, and though the rest of the week looked busy, she planned to stay inside today. Didn't matter, though. He rarely went anywhere without at least one weapon. Even inside the apartment, he planned to be prepared.

Last night, after Sonia had left, he had gone to the lobby to have a talk with building security. Kacie had halfheartedly suggested that she go down, too, but fortunately, Skylar and Gabe had shown up before Brennan had to tell her she didn't look as though she could handle a conversation with an infant. Her eyes had held an empty helplessness that said she had reached her limit.

Skylar had taken one look at her and herded her up to her bedroom. Brennan had suggested Gabe accompany him to discuss who should and shouldn't be on Kacie's approved-visitors list.

They'd learned that though building security was tight, Kacie's list of approved visitors was appallingly long. With Gabe's help, they'd whittled the list down considerably. Brennan had no qualms about doing so. He wasn't denying Kacie visitors, but she damn well would get a warning before someone like Sonia showed up on her doorstep again.

The security guards on duty had been different from the ones he'd seen earlier. Vincent Deavors was a grandfatherly older man who spent a good ten minutes talking about his grandkids. The other guard, Billy Barton, looked barely old enough to have a driver's license and blushed every time they mentioned Kacie's name. Both the men, however, appeared to take their jobs seriously.

After he and Gabe returned to Kacie's apartment, he had noted a definite improvement in Kacie's demeanor. Skylar was good for her.

He had been surprised that his comments to Sonia hadn't come up in dinner conversation but was glad they hadn't. Telling the woman off had not been his finest moment. He actually hadn't intended to butt in, but when he'd seen Kacie's face, nothing could have stopped him. She'd looked crushed, defeated. He had held back—maybe not as long as he should have—waiting for Kacie to defend herself. Instead, she'd stood there as if planning to take whatever abuse her mother doled out.

Considering his own horrendous failure at parenthood, it was laughable that he could criticize another parent. However, for her mother to know what Kacie had endured, to see her not only overcome those things but triumph, and not be proud of her was inconceivable. Hell, he'd known her for only twenty-four hours, and he was in awe of her courage and grit.

The sound of her walking downstairs brought him back to where he needed to be.

Do the job, Sinclair.

He left his room and went downstairs. Hearing her in the kitchen, he headed that way and felt the punch to his gut and then below. He knew she hadn't slept well last night. He'd gotten up a couple of times to check on her, and she'd had the light on in her bedroom, the television on low volume. Yet now she looked as if she'd just come from the spa. Wearing a white skirt that showed off her beautiful legs and a sleeveless yellow sweater, Kacie Dane was the girl next door personified. Fresh, lovely, and innocent.

"Good morning." She flashed him a smile that one prominent magazine had referred to as pure sunshine. "Sorry I wasn't up to offer you breakfast or coffee this morning. I overslept."

"No problem. I got my own coffee and even managed a couple of eggs."

"I'm surprised I had anything in the fridge for you to cook."

"Actually, you didn't. I had some things delivered this morning."

"Oh gosh. I'm so sorry. I'm a terrible hostess."

"I'm not a guest, and you're not my hostess."

Her smile dimmed for a moment as she registered and dealt with that fact.

"You're right." She gave a small shrug. "This is all new to me. I don't exactly know how to deal with a twenty-four-hour bodyguard, much less all the other stuff that's happening."

"There's nothing you need to do about me. I'm here to protect you. I can get my own coffee and meals. When we're out for a meal, unless it's a business thing, I'll pick up the tab to maintain the illusion that we're dating."

"Okay. That helps. I emailed my weekly agenda to you. Did you see it yet? It's a little lighter than usual."

He barely refrained from grimacing at that news. Other than today, she had multiple appointments every day this week. "Any way you can arrange for those meetings to take place here, in your apartment?"

"I guess. Maybe some of them." She nodded after a moment's thought. "Yes, I can do that."

"What's a busy week look like for you?"

"If I'm on location, I stay in a hotel close to the shoot. Depending on the job, I can be tied up from a couple of hours up to twelve."

"Any projects coming up?"

"I'm due in Barbados in a couple of weeks for a shoot at a new resort that's opening."

"If I'm still around then, are they going to be able to deal with an overprotective, hands-on boyfriend?"

"That shouldn't be a problem. I'm working with another model, David Stallings. He always brings along one of his girlfriends."

It wouldn't be an ideal situation. He wouldn't be close to her while they were taking the photographs, but at least he'd be close enough to watch out for her.

"I wanted to thank you for yesterday. I didn't get the chance…" White teeth chewed at her bottom lip as she struggled with her words. "My mother is…difficult."

"I'd say that's an understatement."

She snickered and then sobered immediately as shadows clouded her eyes. "We never had a good relationship, even before… it happened. After…well, it just got worse."

"Seems like a mother would be proud of what you've accomplished. What you've overcome."

The tremble of her lip told him he'd hit his target with bull's-eye accuracy.

As if aware of what she'd given away, she took a shaky breath and straightened her spine. "Anyway, thank you for speaking up for me. No one other than Skylar has ever done that."

"You ever do it for yourself?"

Color heated her cheeks. "I can defend myself against anyone, verbal or otherwise. It's just, with my mom…"

"Your mother is a horse of a different color."

That got a giggle from her, delightful and carefree. His heart lightened as he realized he enjoyed making her smile. But he also wanted an answer.

"You're a strong woman, that's obvious. So why wouldn't you stand up for yourself with your mother?"

"It's complicated."

Yeah, he knew all about complications. Who was he to question her method of handling parents? He hadn't exactly done a stellar job with his own. His parents, however, had been polar opposites to Sonia Carson Musgrave.

"Justin and Riley should be checking in within a few days. We'll see what they've been able to uncover, then go from there."

"You think they might have some leads? The list of people who know the truth isn't long."

"Probably not yet. If they had, one of them would've already called. I did hear from McCall this morning. The IP address came from one of those coffee houses here in the city that provides limited computer time for their patrons. Hundreds use their computers daily…so there's no way to determine who sent the email."

She shivered and wrapped her arms around her waist. "I was afraid of that."

"McCall also double-checked the people who helped with the cover-up…and your name change. He's certain the culprit's not on that end."

"So it's definitely someone here, in New York." She shook her head, her eyes dimming. "Maybe we're exaggerating the threat. It's not like anything major has happened."

Denial was a normal human reaction but also dangerous. Hiring six kids to knock her down and scare the hell out of her wasn't minor. And that might be just the beginning.

"And our job is to make sure nothing major happens. I'll keep you safe, Kacie. Trust me."

"I do. I just—" She gazed around the kitchen, looking lost again.

"How do you like your eggs?"

"You can't make me breakfast."

He almost smiled at her shock. "And why not?"

"I can make my own. Besides, I was just going to eat some fruit and yogurt."

"My mother always said that a good breakfast makes dealing with the rest of the day that much easier." He took a skillet out of the cabinet beside the fridge. "So, tell me how you like your eggs."

"Over easy."

"That's my favorite, too." He opened the refrigerator and took out the eggs, as well as a carton of orange juice." Handing her the juice, he said, "Pour us a couple of glasses to go with breakfast."

"You're eating again?"

"Can't have you eating alone, can I?"

Ten minutes later, Kacie was sitting down at the table to a plate of eggs, a slice of bacon and buttered toast. She lifted her fork to take her first bite, and her stomach growled in anticipation.

Brennan smiled as he dug into his own breakfast. "See? Your stomach is already thanking me."

"I haven't had anyone make breakfast for me in forever. Well, except at a restaurant."

"Easiest meal in the world. Now, when it comes to lunch and dinner, I'm lost."

"Do you live in Virginia, close to LCR headquarters?"

"No…at least not yet. Right now I have a little place close to Glens Falls."

"New York?" When he nodded, she continued. "I've never been there, but I've heard it's beautiful."

"It is."

Silly, but she waited to see if he would invite her to visit sometime. When he continued to eat, Kacie mentally shrugged. It wasn't as if they were actually dating.

"How did you get started with LCR?"

"I knew Justin when we were kids, but we lost touch once he went into the Army. We reconnected a few years back. He told me about LCR then."

"How long have you worked for them?"

He surprised her by checking his watch, and then his words stunned her. "Almost thirty-six hours."

"Seriously? But I thought Noah said you were trained."

"I am…just not with LCR."

Kacie took one last bite of her meal and then thoughtfully sipped her coffee. She knew enough about LCR to know that Noah never would have put Brennan on this job unless he was completely confident in his abilities.

And Brennan had the same kind of look about him that Noah, Gabe, and Justin had. Like they could handle any situation that came their way. She was used to big, hard-faced LCR operatives because she'd been around several, but she had to admit that Brennan made her a lot more nervous than Noah or Gabe ever had. She looked upon the two men as family—like brothers almost. She had absolutely no sisterly thoughts when it came to Brennan Sinclair.

Her phone rang, startling her from her thoughts. Grabbing it, she never thought to check the caller ID.

"Hello?"

"Kendra?"

Blood seemed to drain from her body, and she dropped the phone. Before it could land on the floor, Brennan was around the table to catch it. Holding the phone to his ear, he barked, "Who is this?"

It had been his voice. She would recognize it anywhere. She still heard it in her nightmares. He really wasn't dead.

"Kacie, look at me."

She raised her eyes to Brennan's face. He was crouched in front of her, and the anger on his face felt good, bracing.

"What did you hear?"

She took a calming breath. "It was a man…Harrington's voice. He said 'Kendra.'"

"Anything else?"

"No, I…when I heard his voice say my name…did he say anything to you?"

"No. The line went dead. I'm going to call LCR and see if McCall can get his tech people to trace the call."

She nodded numbly. Yes, that was the sensible thing to do. Find out who had placed the call and from where. She swallowed a small sob. Were there phones in hell?

"Listen to me." Brennan shook her shoulders to get her attention. "Someone's playing a cruel trick on you to scare you. Don't give them what they want. We will find this bastard, and we'll put him away."

When she nodded and whispered a soft, "Okay," Brennan stood and started talking on his cellphone.

Kacie went about clearing the table of their meal and then cleaned up the few dishes in the kitchen. The task calmed her nerves. Brennan was right. This was just someone trying to scare her or extort money from her. She imagined that soon she would be getting a call or letter demanding money to keep the truth of her identity quiet.

And if it isn't?

When she was a kid, she'd feared the boogeyman. Her mother, never the most patient person at any moment of the day, had been even less so late at night when Kacie would go running into her room. Occasionally, when she didn't have company, Sonia would allow her to sleep in her bed. Most of the time, she'd sent Kacie back to her room. Kacie had eventually outgrown the phobia, realizing her fears had been groundless.

But what if they hadn't been groundless? What if she had been wrong? What if there really was a boogeyman…and his name was William Harrington?

CHAPTER TWELVE

Brennan lay on his bed and fought every instinct he had to go to Kacie. To say she'd had a stressful day would be an understatement. After hearing that freak's voice on her phone, she'd closed in on herself. He understood her need to do that—he'd definitely done same in the past. Didn't mean he liked it, though. He wanted to talk to her, reassure her. Unfortunately, things had gone downhill from there.

McCall had informed them that the call had come from a burner phone that couldn't be traced. LCR tech people were able to narrow it down to the New York area, which helped not at all. They'd barely gotten that discouraging news when Kacie's phone had chimed with a text. Another *He is coming for you* message. She'd received three more texts with the same threatening words. All were from different burner phones that, of course, could not be traced.

Whoever was doing this obviously wanted to emotionally torture her, but what else did he want? What was his end game? Blackmail…or something more evil?

Brennan had no doubt that he could protect her until they discovered who this bastard was. And he knew LCR would leave no stone unturned in finding the man and stopping him. But just how much more could Kacie handle before she fell apart?

He knew from experience that stress brought out the demons at night. Those bloody bastards delighted in creeping into your mind when you were at your most vulnerable. Their intent was both evil and cunning. Slice into your insecurities, pound away at your sanity, and then dance on your wounds with vengeful glee.

He'd been the victim of his own demons for years. Sleeping soundly had been impossible. Either he had nightmares that made him imagine the last moments of his son's life and what he must have gone through, or he would wake up and realize his nightmares were reality.

Thank God his friends and family hadn't let him destroy himself. Didn't mean the demons no longer attacked. They were always lurking, always ready to pounce. But he had learned that beating the hell out of a boxing bag or running long distances was a hell of a lot more cathartic than letting the past devour him into darkness.

How did Kacie handle her demons? He'd been around her only a short while, but he'd already discovered that she didn't like drugs and last night had drunk only half a glass of wine with dinner. What did she do to battle against the memories of what had happened to her?

Telling himself he was a fool didn't stop him from leaving his bedroom and heading toward hers. If the lights were off and she was asleep, he'd turn back around.

He was halfway to her room when he heard the sobs. His feet sped up, and without giving it a second thought, he walked into her room.

The lights were dimmed but not off, which made him wonder if she had trouble sleeping in the dark. She was in bed, and from the wrecked look of the sheets and comforter, she'd been having some violent nightmares. He cursed himself for not coming sooner.

Another sob escaped her, heartbreaking in its sadness.

"Kacie, you awake?"

No answer.

Not wanting to frighten her by just appearing at her bed, Brennan stood in the middle of the room and spoke firmly. "Kacie, it's Brennan. Wake. Up."

She shot upright in the bed as if on springs and let out a loud scream.

Cursing softly, Brennan quickly flipped the switch behind him, and bright light flooded the room. Turning back to her, he stood several feet from her bed and said again, "Kacie. It's Brennan."

"Brennan? What's wrong? Are you okay?"

"I'm fine. I heard some noises in here. Thought I'd better check on you."

She dropped down onto her pillows. "Just my typical nightmares. Nothing new. Sorry I disturbed you."

Brennan snorted his disgust. "Don't be ridiculous. I—" Shit. Was he about to berate her when she'd just had a nightmare? Tenderness and compassion had never been his strong suits, but if anyone deserved them, it was this woman.

"You didn't disturb me. I came to check on you and heard you. Figured you were having a nightmare."

She shrugged. "Same old, same old."

"You need something? Milk? Hot tea?"

She smiled, and Brennan wondered how anyone could look so washed out and still be so incredibly beautiful.

"Thanks. I'll be fine."

He nodded, figuring that was her way of telling him to leave. She surprised him, though.

"I know this is an awful imposition, but would it be too much trouble for you to just stay awhile and talk?"

"Not at all." He eyed the bright lights and went to the wall switch. "Let me get the lights. If you get sleepy, you can drift off, and I'll tiptoe out of here."

"Okay, but not all the way off." She gave an embarrassed little grimace. "I'm a wuss. Still can't sleep in the dark yet."

No, she wasn't a wuss. She was a traumatized woman still recovering from a horrific event.

He turned the dimmer switch. "How's that?"

"Perfect. Thanks."

He picked up a chair that she'd placed beside the window for looking out over the park. Setting it a few feet from the bed, Brennan eased into it.

"You know, you're awfully sweet for a football player."

He barked out a rusty laugh. He didn't think anyone had ever thought of him as sweet. "You've met a lot of mean football players?"

"Well…actually, just one. He's a former player, too. After he left that career, he became a model. Kind of a jerk."

"Jerks come in all professions."

"Yeah, I guess."

"Mind if I ask you a question?"

"Not at all."

"Why modeling?"

"You mean after what happened?"

"Yes." He didn't say it, but the more he thought about it, the more he had to know. She had been pursuing what she thought was a modeling job when she'd been abducted.

"Just seems that you wouldn't want to do anything related to what happened to you."

She didn't answer for a long time, and he wondered if she was angry or uncomfortable with the question.

Finally, she answered, "I think, more than anything, it was to prove something to myself."

"How so?"

Again, she was quiet, and it struck him again that this was her way. She gave careful thought and consideration before answering a question.

"When I was younger, I wanted everything and I wanted it right then, right now. And that's how and why I was abducted. I thought I'd found the easy way in, that I wouldn't have to work at it like other girls.

"My plan was to shoot straight to the top and bypass all the trials and tribulations of real effort.

"What I endured…what I went through, I wouldn't wish on anyone. After I was rescued, I blamed everyone, especially Skylar and myself. It took months for me to accept that, if anything, Skylar was the one who kept me alive and sane during that time. It was her influence, her voice inside my head, that kept me going. And I knew she was doing everything she could to find me.

"Once I accepted that it was in no way her fault, I had no one else to look to…I had only me to blame. It took a long time to forgive myself. My stupidity and blind ambition had gotten me into the situation. But once I did forgive myself, I finally began to heal.

"When I was stronger, ready to decide my future, I realized I had something to prove to myself. I had wanted something without being willing to work for it. I needed to know if I could work for it and actually achieve it, on my own. Not just because I wanted to reach my goal. I needed to know if I had it inside me.

"I told others that I was fine…that I had recovered, but how could I know for sure if I didn't try? So I did it the right way…

the hard way. I borrowed money for a photo shoot and modeling classes. I went on interviews, sent my photos everywhere. Took the rejections, the lost jobs, the disappointments."

"That's one of the reasons you changed your name, isn't it? Because of the press coverage, your real name would have gotten you notoriety and attention. Probably even opened some doors for you."

"Exactly. Believe me, having doors open to me because of what happened was the last thing I wanted. Besides that, how would I know if I actually did this on my own? Have to admit, though, I learned a lot more than I bargained for."

"In what way?"

"Like no matter how hard a person works, success can't be achieved without assistance and help. No matter how much I want to say it was all me, I can't."

Brennan nodded to himself. Having achieved several goals in his life, he could attest to that fact and knew exactly what she meant. Every opportunity and good thing he had achieved had been, in either small or large part, because of another person.

"No man is an island."

"Exactly. There were women who were more beautiful, younger, more photogenic, had better smiles, longer legs."

"So why do you think you made it?"

"Luck. Making the right contacts. Being in the right place at the right time."

"And sheer dogged determination."

"Yes, that, too."

"Is it what you thought it would be? As exciting or fulfilling?"

"Yes and no. I love the clothes, the traveling. But there's also a lot of hard work involved and a whole lot of boredom. Sometimes I just don't feel like smiling. My feet hurt, head hurts, back hurts.

And, dammit, sometimes I just want a fricking cheeseburger and fries."

He chuckled at that. Having once had a strictly regimented diet, he could totally identify.

"Something else I learned the hard way was that my mother wasn't always wrong."

That one meeting with her mother made him want to disagree fervently. Still, he wanted to know exactly what the woman might have been right about. "About what?"

She laughed softly. "I can hear the doubt in your voice. Admittedly, she doesn't make a very good first impression.

"But she told me time and again that I would never appreciate fame or success if I achieved it but didn't earn it myself. She was right. If the ad I answered had been what I thought it was, if I had soared to stardom overnight, I never would have fully appreciated it. I would have been dissatisfied and unhappy but probably wouldn't have been able to figure out why.

"Having worked to achieve my goals, I can appreciate them so much more."

He was beginning to get a clearer picture of why she'd said that her relationship with her mother was complicated. "That's one of the reasons you helped her financially. Isn't it?"

"What?"

"You didn't give her money to keep her quiet. You gave her money because you care."

She was quiet for several seconds and then sighed. "You have to understand. I was not an easy kid to raise. I didn't like to follow rules, thought I knew better than anyone else. Got mixed up with the wrong crowd. Dated the wrong guys. My mom actually tried in the early years, but she just couldn't handle me any longer. I gave little thought to her feelings, what she was going through trying to raise a kid on her own. I guess, after all that, I felt I owed her."

"And you wanted her to be proud of you."

"Childish, huh?

Brennan shook his head, liking this woman more and more. "Human."

"Maybe so."

"So why did you stop sending her money?"

"Because I realized I was trying to buy her love. That made me angrier with myself than with her. She's never going to be proud of me or love me. We're never going to have a close mother-daughter bond."

He couldn't see her face, but he saw her shoulders move in a small shrug. "It was time for me to let her go and move on."

"She seems to disagree."

"She likes the money."

He wished he could argue. Wished he could tell her that her mother might still come around. It would be a lie—one that Kacie would easily see through. Whatever Sonia wanted, it had nothing to do with having a relationship with her daughter. Kacie was better off without her.

"I don't believe she could have anything to do with what's happening now, though."

He didn't think so either, but not for the same reason. The woman simply didn't strike him as bright enough to carry off the kinds of taunts Kacie had received.

She shifted against her pillow. "It suddenly occurs to me that you know everything about me, and yet I know almost nothing about you."

He went so silent that Kacie figured he'd frozen, even stopped breathing. Perhaps it was unfair to ask him. It wasn't as if knowing personal things about him would stop him from doing his job. He was here to protect her, not be her friend and confidant. But there was something about him that called to her. Something in his eyes matched an emptiness that she often felt inside herself. Almost like they had a connection.

She already knew he'd lost his wife and son. She'd learned that much from her brief search on the Internet. In between the vitriol and the hatred, she'd gleaned that his son was murdered, and then a few weeks later, his wife mysteriously died.

She knew she could go back to the Internet and probably find the truth behind the lies that had been spewed about him. But if he didn't want her to know, what right did she have to find it out for herself?

She started with something easy. "You said you live close to Glens Falls. How'd you end up there?"

"I did some training at a facility there. It's a camp run by former special ops guys. After my training, they asked me to stay on as an instructor."

"Wow. You must be pretty good at it."

"I enjoyed the challenge. When they started a security and rescue operation, I went onboard as an operative."

She propped up on her elbow so she could see him better. "You've worked as a rescuer already? Why change over to LCR?"

"They're the best."

"Is that the only reason?"

Again, silence.

"Sharing is really hard for you, isn't it?"

"I'm sure you already know what happened, so I'd think you would understand why I'd want to work for an organization like Last Chance Rescue."

"I actually don't know what happened. I'm sorry...it must be horrific to have lost both your wife and son."

"You don't know?" His laugh was jagged...humorless. "You're about the only person on the planet who doesn't."

"Well," she said reasonably, even a little cheerfully, "others might not know if they were going through their own trauma at the same time."

"Ah, Kacie...shit." He blew out a harsh breath. "I'm sorry."

"Don't worry about it. I just thought...I don't know. I thought it might help to share."

"Maybe someday. Not tonight."

"Okay, no problem."

"You're sounding a little weary. Think you can get some sleep?"

She knew he wanted to get away from her, from any more questions. She could understand that. Having others ask for details about her ordeal had always made the nightmares worse. Did Brennan have nightmares, too? Probably.

"Yes, I think I can sleep now. Thanks for staying with me."

"No problem."

He moved the chair back to its place beside the window, said a soft, growling good night and closed the door behind him.

Kacie settled back into her pillow and thought about the little she'd learned about Brennan Sinclair. Noah McCall trusted him. Even if she didn't know more than that, it would be enough for her to trust him, too. But in the two days he'd been here, he had shown her more with his actions than he ever could have with words.

He had defended her against her mother. He had prepared breakfast for her. Today, with the phone call and texts she'd received, he had been furious on her behalf. He also noticed small things about her—like how she took her coffee. He'd bought groceries and even helped her clean up in the kitchen after dinner.

In two days' time, he'd done more for her than all her former boyfriends combined. Well, except the physical part.

Kacie rolled over and put her head under her pillow. That was something she hadn't thought about in so long, she barely acknowledged its existence. She could look at a man and see certain characteristics she found attractive, but since her assault, the thought of a man touching her in any kind of sexual way sent shivers of revulsion through her. Her therapist had told her that her need for physical intimacy would return at some point. And now...with Brennan...maybe she was getting closer to believing it.

She fell asleep wondering how it would feel to have Brennan's lips on hers.

CHAPTER THIRTEEN

Tonight, they would make it official—their first public appearance as a couple. The news that beautiful model Kacie Dane was dating former Jets player Brennan Sinclair would finally be revealed. Brennan had looked forward to tonight's event as much as he would a root canal without Novocain.

Except for the lunch with her agent the day he arrived, they hadn't been seen together in a social setting. They'd been out almost every day, but no one would have recognized them. Maybe because they had so many secrets, they were both excellent at disguising themselves.

With Kacie's shoot next week in Barbados, it was bound to come out. Revealing their new relationship at a time and place of their choosing was not only expedient but would look natural. Kacie had claimed this was a low-key event and the perfect forum to reveal their relationship to the public.

It had been several days since the freaky phone call and the texts, and nothing since. They were both feeling the tension of waiting for something without having any idea what they were waiting for. If nothing else, he hoped this event would take her mind off the worry.

"Just wow," a soft voice whispered behind him.

He looked over his shoulder, and while his mind repeated the same exclamation, it also added a few extra superlatives. He'd seen her look beautiful before but never like this.

Turning slowly to face her, he took in the beauty of Kacie Dane. Standing about five-eleven in her bare feet, the heels she wore put her well over six feet tall. He hadn't given much thought to his own height since his football career ended, but tonight he was glad of his six-foot-six frame. Her head would fit perfectly beneath his chin if they danced. And just how bizarre was it that he even thought about dancing?

But Kacie made him think of things he had never considered before.

The gown she wore, an eye-popping red, flowed around her like a rippling river of scarlet. It had some kind of shimmering jewels sewn into the material, and when she moved the slightest, even breathed, she glimmered. Her pale, creamy skin glowed, and the golden-blond waves of her hair were caught up in some kind of intricate knot, revealing a long, slender neck and elegant shoulders.

Without a doubt, she was the loveliest woman he'd ever seen. And having been around hundreds of attractive women, he considered himself an expert.

His eyes roamed over her body before he caught the wary expression on her face. Hell, here he was salivating like a starving man at a smorgasbord. She saw lust in men's eyes every damn day, she sure as hell didn't need to see it in the man who was protecting her.

Clearing his throat, he said, "Nice dress." He winced. Not only was it a lame compliment, but his voice sounded more like a predatory growl.

"Thanks. It's a Montague. Even though we're not announcing until next week that I'll be their new model, Mr. Montague wanted me to wear it for speculation purposes. It'll set the busy-bodies of the fashion world all a twitter, wondering if I'm wearing it as a statement of intent or something else."

They would definitely be talking about her and the dress. And, hopefully, the fact that she was now dating the infamous Brennan Sinclair would be secondary.

"I doubt I'll be seen as anything other than a backdrop for your beauty."

She laughed softly and shook her head. "You apparently haven't looked in the mirror then. You look stunning."

He glanced down at the black tuxedo and grimaced. He hadn't worn one of these in years. The designer wasn't one he'd ever heard of, but when Kacie had handed it to him, she promised that it would not only be a perfect fit but would look fabulous on him. He wasn't quite sure about the fabulous part, but he had to admit the suit fit as if it'd been made for him.

"So how does this thing work? You said it's a birthday party?"

She nodded. "For Eleanor San de Voy."

"And she would be?"

"One of the oldest living designers. Her dresses once graced the elite of Hollywood actresses. It's her ninety-fifth birthday, so it's a relatively small affair."

"A three-hundred-fifty-person party is a small affair?"

"Comparatively speaking, yes. However, there will be between fifty and a hundred photographers there, too. They wanted to use a nostalgia theme, so it'll be like the Academy Awards. We'll arrive in a limo, walk down the red carpet, pose for a few shots, and then head inside."

"Interviews?"

"No. Photographers only. This is Eleanor's party, and she insisted that her guests were not to be harangued by reporters."

"I like this woman already. Do you know her well?"

"In a way, but not really. Remember how I told you that a lot of people have helped me? Well, she's one of them. She saw a group shot of me and a dozen other models for a sportswear event a couple of years ago. She called a friend of hers, who knew Edy. And in turn, Edy called me. That's how I managed to get her as an agent."

"But you've never met Eleanor?"

"Actually, I did meet her once, but it was before—" Her eyes went dark, and she lost her smile. "I went to an event with Skylar and was introduced to her. I'm sure she doesn't remember me. I've changed a lot since then, but I'm incredibly thankful for her help."

The buzzer at the door sounded, and a young male voice announced, "Ms. Dane, your car is here."

Drawing in a deep breath that made her dress shimmer like a million diamonds, she held out her hand to him. "Let's go announce to the world that Kacie Dane has caught herself a really big one."

Laughter burst from him, and he took her hand. "I'll take that as a compliment."

Realizing what one might infer from her words, she blushed a pretty shade of light rose and cleared her throat. "On that embarrassing note, let's go."

Kacie was grateful she'd learned to smile even when her nerves were frazzled. This wasn't the first time she'd attended a high-profile function with a man at her side. Convenience dates were her specialty. But never had she attended a function with a man who both fascinated her and scared her into a breathless dither.

They'd talked little on the way to the party, each seemingly lost in their own thoughts. The instant the limo driver opened the door, she felt Brennan's body go rigid. Had she made a mistake in announcing their relationship this way? Even though there would be a lot of people in attendance, this party would be a much more laidback affair than any other upcoming events she would be attending.

Once they were out of the car, she took his hand and gave it a squeeze, letting him know she was right beside him. The bemused look he gave her almost made her laugh. Yes, she knew he was here to protect her, but that didn't mean she couldn't shield him, too.

As promised, a red carpet had been laid out, leading up the stairs and stopping at giant glass doors. Photographers lined both sides of the carpet, and lights flashed like manic fireflies as they competed for the best shots of the night.

An odd, palpable silence descended the moment she and Brennan were spotted, and then, like a massive lightning storm, cameras flashed in a frenzy of clicks. Even though questions had been prohibited, several people were bold enough to shout some out.

With a smile of confidence and serenity, she waved as if she were the happiest person on the planet. Brennan didn't bother with a smile, but that was okay. No smile was better than a fake one. She had been trained to make even her fake ones look real. Brennan hadn't. Besides, that seething, sexual energy he exuded didn't call for anything else.

They made it inside without the least blunder. Once the doors closed, she turned to him. "See, now wasn't that fun?"

"You ever have a root canal?"

She laughed, getting his meaning. "I promise, the rest will be much less painful."

She glanced around. The glitter of thousands of diamonds gracing the necks of New York's wealthiest women competed with the brilliance of giant chandeliers. Everything sparkled and dazzled. It was the perfect ambience for the grand dame of classic Hollywood fashion.

"Let's grab some champagne and go wish Eleanor a happy birthday."

Kacie was used to stares and whispers, so she wasn't put off by the small groups of people who were blatantly gossiping about her chosen companion. Still, the moment she spotted Eleanor in the middle of the room, she zeroed in on her target. She hadn't realized her grasp on Brennan's arm had gotten increasingly tighter until she felt him grip her hand and squeeze it gently.

She threw him an apologetic look. "Sorry. Guess I'm a little more tense than I thought."

He gave her a small smile, his first since they'd left her apartment. Though it was clearly forced, she appreciated the effort. Feeling somewhat better, she slowed to a stop and accepted a glass of champagne from a nearby waiter.

She took a small sip and sniffed delicately.

"Why do you drink champagne if you don't like it?"

"How do you know I don't like it?"

Surprising her, he gently touched a spot between her eyes. "When something displeases you, a tiny little line appears right here."

Kacie stood frozen, mesmerized by the touch, by the dark, penetrating eyes that seemed to see inside her the way no one else ever had before. This man who both fascinated and frightened her made her more aware of herself than she'd ever been. Even as heat flooded through her, goose bumps sent shivers up her spine.

Someone burst out singing *Happy Birthday* and jerked Kacie from her trance. She looked around the room, almost shocked that she was in the middle of a large group of people. She'd been so lost in Brennan's eyes she had completely forgotten her surroundings.

She took a breath, the mixture of expensive perfume and cologne another bracing reminder of where she was. These people were the elite of the city. Perhaps if they changed their perception of Brennan Sinclair, the rest of the world would follow suit.

"Let's go wish Eleanor a happy birthday, and then I'll introduce you around."

They made their greetings to the guest of honor and then began to mingle with the rest of the crowd. Things were going so smoothly, so incredibly well, it only made sense that it all would crumble at her feet without any warning whatsoever.

"Kacie, you look lovely."

Turning at the sound of Edy's voice, Kacie's smile froze when she saw the man standing beside her agent.

"You know Carlton Lorrance, don't you?" Edy asked.

"Yes, I do." Hoping to maintain a polite demeanor, she worked to sound only mildly curious. "I thought the press was barred from the party."

To refer to Carlton Lorrance as *the press* was laughable. The man was one of the most infamous celebrity and fashion bloggers in the country. He had a huge following, and though he had never posted anything horribly negative about Kacie, she had seen him tear down and destroy more than one well-known celebrity with only a few words. Why on earth had Edy brought him here tonight?

"Never hurts to have a little preliminary speculation before the official announcement. With Carlton as my date, no one blinked an eye." Edy winked. "You wearing the only Montague at the party will be the most-talked-about fashion news for days until the official announcement."

"Great." Maintaining her smile with effort, she nodded at Carlton. "It's good to see you, Carlton. Let me introduce you to—"

"I'll be damned. Brennan Sinclair."

Kacie could see this going downhill extremely fast. Brennan had been an excellent, attentive companion so far, making polite conversation and the occasional amusing comment. How was he going to react to this, though?

"Yes, I'm Brennan Sinclair."

A giant grin split Lorrance's face as a speculative gleam sparkled in his eyes. He glanced at Kacie, then back at Brennan. "You two are together?"

"Oh, that's something I forgot to tell you, Carlton," Edy said. "Kacie and Brennan just recently started dating. It's all very mysterious and romantic."

"I think I watched every Jets game you played in."

His jaw set to granite, Brennan nodded but didn't speak.

"When you just walked out that day, I was pissed."

Brennan's silence seemed to egg Lorrance on. "Bet you've regretted that every second of every day since."

"No, can't say that I have." Brennan looked down at Kacie. "I'll get us another drink."

Like a wild animal sensing an easy meal, Carlton went in for the kill. "You know, some people still speculate that you had your son kidnapped and killed for the sympathy so you could get your job back. Bet that rankles."

Kacie could only gasp and stare at the vile accusation. What kind of person would say something like that? Even for a jerk like Lorrance, it was over the top.

Brennan turned slowly, the ice in his eyes both scary and sad. She saw the hollowness and pain beneath the coldness.

"I think we need to leave, Brennan." She glared at Lorrance, then at Edy, who, though she looked horrified, had been clueless enough to bring him. "Your rudeness, Mr. Lorrance, is not only out of line but in very poor taste."

As if he hadn't just said the vilest thing possible to a complete stranger who could easily knock him into another orbit, Lorrance ignored her and gave Brennan an easy, oily smile. "It'd be a pleasure to interview you so you can set the record straight."

"Carlton, stop," Edy said. "That's not why I brought you here."

"Yeah, I know, but this is so much juicier."

Kacie took Brennan's arm and tried to tug. He was an immovable boulder. No way was she going to get him to budge until he was ready. She could feel the bunched muscles and knew he was holding himself back with extreme difficulty. They needed to get out of here fast, before he threw the slimy blogger through the ice sculpture a few feet away.

"Brennan, please. He's just trying to make a name for himself."

"I know exactly what he's doing, Kacie." His eyes, cold, hard, and unforgiving, stared down at her. "This makes for some good publicity. Right?"

"What do you mean?" Did he think she had something to do with this?

Instead of answering, Brennan returned his gaze to a smirking Lorrance. "Here's what you can say in your sleazy rag tomorrow, Lorrance. The day I give a fuck about what your useless readers think is the day I'll slit my own throat."

With that, he turned and walked away. She would have liked to tell the guy off, too, but didn't want Brennan to be alone. Yes, he'd hurt her with his accusation, but she knew what it was like to have the rug pulled out from under you like that. In the heat of the moment, you said things you didn't mean.

He paused at the door, waiting. The moment she drew near, he whipped it open for her, then followed her out.

A few photographers jumped to attention, and though she wanted to tell them to get away from her and Brennan, she knew better. Brennan might not act as if he cared what others thought about him, but she wasn't about to give them more fodder that they could distort. She smiled, waved, and all the while hung on to Brennan's arm as if everything was just as lovely as when they'd entered the building only an hour earlier.

The man at her side acted as if the photographers didn't exist, as if she didn't exist. He stalked down the wide, carpeted steps toward the street. Miraculously, the limo she'd rented for the evening eased up in front of them, and without missing a step, as if this had all been planned, Brennan opened the door, and she slid inside. Brennan came in behind her. The car door slammed, shutting out prying eyes and flashing cameras and closing her up with one very pissed-off bodyguard.

CHAPTER FOURTEEN

"Brennan, I'm sorry. I—"

Brennan held up a hand to stop another apology. If he said anything right now, it'd be the wrong thing. The plan was to get her home, safe and sound. Then and only then would he allow himself to implode.

Kacie huffed out a frustrated breath. "Fine. You can be as angry as you want, but that's not going to stop me from apologizing for what happened. I don't know exactly what Lorrance was talking about, but—"

"Will you just be quiet for a moment?"

She blinked in surprise, and then a glimmer of hurt showed in her eyes before they turned cool and blank.

He figured that at some point he'd regret the words, but not yet, not now. All he felt now was this gut-aching need to slam his fist through the glass partition in front of him.

Silence filled the interior of the limo. Traffic was a stop-and-start, curse-inducing, horn-blowing, mangled mess. He wanted to get out and run until he couldn't breathe, couldn't think. He couldn't. His first priority was taking care of his client. He would not leave her alone, no matter how gutted he felt.

Horns blared. A symphony of various kinds of music blasted around them as New Yorkers enjoyed the warm night by lowering their car windows and sharing their playlists with the rest of the city. He heard the noise as a distant hum. Inside his mind was a voice—sweet, childish, innocent.

Daddy, can you come play ball with me?

Daddy, read me a story.

Daddy, can I come with you?

Daddy, please do what the bad man says. Please come get me.

Brennan closed his eyes against the memories, the regret. But they never went away, never left him. Until the day he closed his eyes for the last time, he would hear his little boy's voice asking, begging…pleading.

His hands clenched into fists, and he held them stiff and still, willing the violence within him to subside. He didn't often get this way anymore. Stupid not to have anticipated this. He should've been ready. Being blindsided and unprepared had exposed the one vulnerability that would never go away.

Something soft, gentle, touched him. Brennan opened his eyes to see a slender, delicate hand covering his clenched fist. Kacie's hand. Gently but firmly, he removed her hand from his. He didn't want her comfort. Didn't need it. Definitely didn't deserve it.

"Brennan, I had no idea he—"

"I know you didn't. That doesn't mean your agent didn't. She saw an opportunity, and she took it."

Anger and shock glinted in her eyes. "That's not true. There's no reason for Edy to do something like that. She—"

"Don't be naïve. There's every reason. The more you're in the news, the better for your career. To hell with anyone else's life."

"That's extraordinarily unfair, on top of being untrue. Yes, Edy can be ruthless when it comes to negotiating contracts, but for her to arrange something like this would be ludicrous."

"Then tell me how one of the most vicious and spiteful celebrity stalkers happened to be her date?"

"He doesn't do that anymore. He's a blogger, for fashion and trends."

"Tigers don't change their stripes, Kacie. Take off your rose-colored glasses."

"I don't wear rose-colored glasses, Brennan. I know better than anyone that there are bad people in this world. I'm just saying people can change."

Part of him admired her spirit and goodness, another part pitied her incredible naïveté.

"You keep your idealistic dreams, sweetheart. I live in the real world, where shit happens and then you die."

"I'm sorry you feel that way."

Turning his gaze to the mass of humanity outside his window, Brennan blanked his mind to everything but his job. He was here to protect Kacie Dane, physically if need be. Trying to change her attitude about life wasn't in his job description. Besides, if she was happier living in a fantasy, who was he to deprive her?

The rest of the trip passed in a tense, grim silence. Her cell-phone rang twice. He didn't look at her, but assumed she rejected each call and perhaps then put it on silent. He was sure Edy would call and apologize, all the while gleeful at the outcome of her setup.

At last the limo pulled up to the front of Kacie's building. Brennan opened the door to get out. Kacie pulled on his hand, stopping him.

He looked down at her hand, then into her compassionate eyes. His heart did a weird leap and then thudded inside his chest. No…just no.

He pulled away from her, got out of the limo, checked for anything or anyone suspicious, then helped her from the vehicle.

In silence, they walked toward the building. A young doorman opened the door for them and wished them a pleasant night. Brennan could only manage a nod, but he heard Kacie's friendly greeting.

Once inside, Brennan nodded at the big man at the security desk. Kacie threw out a, "Hey, Frankie, have a good night," as she walked to the elevator with Brennan at her side.

Once the elevator doors closed, Kacie turned to face him. "Okay, we're alone and trapped for a few seconds. Now you have to listen to me. I had nothing to do with that man being there. And I know Edy. She only meant to drum up publicity for this deal we've made with Julian Montague. Media speculation is gold in our business. That's all she intended."

She looked so sincere, so worried about him, that he wanted to say something reassuring...even kind. Maybe later. For right now, he just needed to be alone.

When he didn't answer, her shoulders slumped slightly, and she nodded. "Fine. I'll leave you alone."

The elevator doors slid open. Brennan went out first, checked the hallway to make sure it was clear, then motioned for her to come out. They walked together to her apartment.

He took five minutes to search the apartment, all the while aware that she stood in the middle of her living room, watching him. Assured that there were no intruders and she was safe, he said, "Good night," and went to his bedroom.

The instant the door closed, Brennan ripped off the ridiculous bow tie at his neck and opened the collar of his shirt. Now he could breathe...now he could let go.

He went to the window and looked out into the darkened night. The only thing he saw was his reflection—harsh, unforgiving, bitter. He closed his eyes against the familiar sight, but the instant he did, he saw Kacie's face…her hurt and her compassion.

Hell, he could've said something to make her feel better. Probably should've. After he'd been an ass to her, she'd tried to comfort him. He almost laughed at that thought. Comfort? There was no such thing. Not when it came to this kind of gut-ripping, soul-destroying pain.

Yeah, he knew what the experts would say. Move on, come to terms with what happened and live your life. And he had for the most part. Rescuing kidnapped victims fed his soul unlike anything else he'd ever experienced. None of them was his son, but he'd seen the relief and happiness in a parent's face when a child came home. Each rescue had healed a little bit of his soul. But the pain would never be gone, completely healed. How could it?

The soft knock on his door should've surprised him but didn't. Kacie had a tenaciousness about her that refused to give up.

He didn't bother answering, knowing it would do no good. She would come in whether he wanted her to or not.

Sure enough, seconds after she knocked, the door opened and she peeked inside. "Hey, I made some hot chocolate. Do you want marshmallows or whipped cream for your topping?"

He answered without the slightest hesitation. "Whipped cream."

Her smile was so bright and engaging it took everything he had not to smile back. How in the hell did she do that?

"Be right back."

Less than a minute later, she was back with a tray holding two mugs of hot chocolate topped with whipped cream and a plateful of chocolate-chip cookies.

"Sometimes there's no better comfort than chocolate with a side of chocolate."

Setting the tray on the table beside his chair, she handed him a mug and then took one for herself. He was about to get up to offer her his chair when she pulled a large throw pillow from the bed and sat on the floor in front of him.

He took a swallow from his mug and made an appreciative noise.

She waited until he'd had his second swallow before she said, "I really am sorry for what happened tonight. I don't know the details of your son's death, but—"

"Why don't you?"

"I told you that I—"

"I'm not talking about when it happened. Why haven't you looked it up on the Internet? Are you not the least bit curious?"

"Of course I am." She grimaced and confessed. "I did look you up the first day you came. But I didn't really find what I was looking for."

"What were you looking for?"

"The truth."

She said it so simply, he had the wild urge to grab her up and hug her.

"Then I started feeling guilty and decided if you wanted me to know, you'd tell me."

And it was as straightforward as that, for her. To most other people, it would just be a matter of wanting to know something. But Kacie saw it as an invasion of privacy.

He couldn't look at her, couldn't face the compassion he heard in her voice. There was something so incredibly gentle about this woman, and he wasn't a gentle man. She was his to protect, to keep safe. She couldn't be more.

She did, however, deserve an explanation.

He drew in a breath, let it out slowly, and began. "I got hurt midseason of my second year. Busted my leg. Had surgery and went through rehab. And I—" He swallowed past a dry throat. "I lost myself. Got so caught up in me and what I thought I should be doing. I told myself that providing for my family was my most important role. To do that, I had to get better, get back out on the field. That was my only focus.

"Vanessa, my wife, said I was obsessed. She was right…I knew she was right, but I kept telling myself that once I got back into the game, my life would straighten out. Instead, it went to hell, and then it went farther."

When Brennan went silent again, all Kacie could do was wait him out. He was finally sharing his pain with her, and she wouldn't push him. Had he ever talked to anyone about what happened, or had he kept it all inside?

While she could identify with the agony in his eyes, his pain seemed almost too fresh. As if he hadn't recovered or come to terms with his tragedy. Not that she knew anything about being a parent or coming to terms with losing a child. But she did know that talking helped. She hoped he would continue.

After several long minutes, he said, "I was at home when the call came. Things were about to get better for us. I'd finished all my rehab, and I was one hundred percent again. I was due back at training camp the next day, ready to show everyone, my coaches, the owners, that I was fully recovered and ready to retake my position.

"When the phone rang, I figured it was Vanessa wishing me luck. She'd taken our son, Cody, to visit her parents in Florida. We weren't exactly on speaking terms at that point, but again, I'd told myself when I got my job back, things would be better.

"The call wasn't from Vanessa. It was a ransom call. The man said that he'd kidnapped Cody and if I didn't do what he said, he'd kill my son."

He stopped to pull in a ragged breath, and Kacie put her hand over his and squeezed it, in sympathy and support.

"He demanded $3.2 million. I asked questions, kept insisting I had to talk to Cody."

He stopped, rubbed the middle of his forehead, then said, "I got to talk to him…my son…maybe about five seconds. Just enough for me to confirm it was Cody…just enough for me to hear how terrified he was.

"The guy came back on the phone, refused to answer any questions. Just told me if I contacted the cops, my son would die.

"As soon as he hung up, I called Vanessa. She was in hysterics, said that she'd stopped at an ATM for money and had left Cody in the car for just a few minutes. When she came back to the car, he was gone.

"I told her about the ransom call, what the guy wanted. She told me I had to pay it. Told me if I called the cops and the guy killed Cody, it would be all my fault." He shook his head. "So I didn't call anyone. But I didn't have access to that much money either. At least not anymore. A few days before that, I'd bought a vacation home in Colorado. Was going to surprise Vanessa and Cody. I wasn't exactly broke, but I didn't have easy access to a lot of cash. I had some stocks and short-term investments I could sell, but it wasn't going to be quick.

"When the man called back, I agreed to do whatever he said but told him it would take a few days for me to get that much cash together. He screamed at me, told me he knew I was lying.

"Things got heated. I swore to him that I was telling the truth. He hung up and I went crazy. After I calmed down, I knew I had no choice but to call the police.

"When they arrived and interviewed me, they asked me a lot of questions. Some really weird ones. The more they asked, the more it got me to thinking. Why such a specific number, $3.2 million? Why not four million or just three? Who but my wife knew how much we had in savings?

"And why would Vanessa leave Cody in the car when she'd had a fit more than once when she saw other parents do the same thing."

"Oh no," Kacie whispered.

"I know Vanessa never intended for Cody to be hurt. Her intent was to get all the money she could from me. Then, once Cody was back home and safe, she would file for divorce. Since I was gone a good part of the year, she figured it'd be easy for her to get full custody."

"But why not get the money in a divorce settlement? Why make it so complicated?"

"We had a prenup. Very simplistic, which, funnily enough, she was the one who insisted we have one. When we got married, her career was on the rise, and she believed it was only going to go higher. So if our marriage ended, she would keep what was hers, I would keep what was mine."

"But that's not what happened, is it? You began to make more money...she made less. But this way, she could get your money and hers, too."

"Yeah...at least that was her plan. Something she didn't consider was the guy she'd hooked up with was certifiable. When I told him it'd take me some time to get the money, he figured Vanessa had lied to him." Brennan swallowed hard. "So he freaked and ran."

"What did he do to Cody?" she asked gently.

"Tied him up, force-fed him sedatives, and left him to die in the trunk of a car."

Kacie closed her eyes against the tears. How any person could hurt a child was incomprehensible. And this had been so deliberate, so very cold-hearted.

"What happened to the monster who did that?"

"Police found him at his parents' house outside Lexington, Kentucky. Had a shootout. He's dead."

"And Vanessa? Was she with him?"

"No. Vanessa came home, acted innocent. The police grilled her, and she denied everything. It was when they found Cody that she broke down. Blamed me for making her have to go to such extremes to get my attention. Said that's what it'd all been about.

"She was arrested and charged with kidnapping, accessory to murder. She was staying with her parents, awaiting trial when she decided she'd rather not. So she took a load of pills and never woke up."

Kacie couldn't decide which was more sickening, Vanessa's blind greed or her exceedingly poor judgment. Not that it mattered now. A child was dead, and his father was broken.

She wanted to reach out to him, comfort him in some way. Hold him if he'd let her. She knew he wouldn't. So she sat, continued to hold his hand, and listened.

"I don't think she could ever forgive herself. And neither could I."

He gave a jagged, humorless chuckle. "Lorrance was right about one thing. A lot of people did think I was in on it. That I'd arranged the whole thing so if things didn't work out with getting my position back, the sympathy would put me back on the team. Some even speculated I was responsible for Vanessa's death, too."

"That's absolutely absurd. No one with any sense would believe that."

"Vanessa's parents had a lot to do with their thinking."

"How so?"

"First they were grieving for a grandson, then defending their daughter. And then grieving for her, too. It only made sense that they blame me. My in-laws had a lot of influence with their local paper. It got picked up and spread like wildfire. Guess it was easier for them to blame me than come to terms with what their daughter had done."

"Can I ask you a question?" Afraid he would say no, she asked anyway, "Why have you never defended yourself? I didn't do a lot of research, but from what I did see, you never granted even one interview."

"At first I didn't give a damn. I'd lost my son, and even though the law never considered me a suspect, I blamed myself. I couldn't talk about it to anyone, not even my parents.

"I went back to work…had no problem earning my position back. But I had nothing left to give. I was empty inside. So, I just quit."

"But the fans wouldn't forgive you?"

"Lots of people take their football seriously. They'd wanted a championship and thought I was their best bet. People were pissed."

From what she'd read, that was a major understatement. The *I hate Brennan Sinclair* bandwagon was still alive and well even after all these years.

"Maybe if you gave an interview…explained what happened, they would—"

"Would what, Kacie? Like me again? Do you think being liked matters to me now?"

"No, I don't. But seeing you treated the way that Carlton Lorrance did today makes me sick."

"Why?"

She jerked back, surprised at the ridiculous question. "Because it's not fair."

"Why do you care?"

Oh, that was a subject she wasn't even close to being ready to discuss. This man brought out so many feelings and emotions in her—feelings she'd never experienced and emotions she'd never believed she'd be able to have.

Instead of telling him that, she told him another truth. "I don't like to see good people get hurt. And in spite of that gruff, growly exterior of yours, you are a good person."

"How the hell does someone who's been through what you've endured stay so sweet?"

She gave him a sad smile. "Staying sweet was never in the cards. Before Harrington, I don't believe I had a sweet bone in my body. But after..." She shook her head. "I still don't think I'm sweet, but I do like to smile, be happy.

"I know that sounds simplistic and kind of trite. I don't mean it that way. It's just I was so miserable for so long, I had to make a conscious decision that I was put on this earth for a reason other than to feel sorry for myself. I survived. There had to be a reason."

"What do you think that reason was?"

"I know what you're thinking. Being a model, wearing gorgeous clothes, making a lot of money isn't exactly Mother Teresa behavior."

"I don't think you have to be a nun to do good things."

"Exactly. I told you I wanted to be a model to prove that I could actually do it, but I also realized that I could have an incredible influence on young women this way. Skylar was a great example of that."

"Is that why you went with the girl-next-door persona?"

"Kind of but not totally. When I went to modeling classes, my instructors kept referring to me as the fresh-faced one. I thought, why not? It's different from the sexy, sultry models. And in this business, different can make a splash if it's done right. So, when I started getting my portfolio ready, that's the look I told the photographer I wanted.

"Young girls are bombarded daily about what's sexy or attractive. I wanted to be a different kind of beautiful." She shrugged. "I like not having to wear tons of makeup or show a lot of skin. And I like that young girls are able to see that simplicity can be even more beautiful than overt sexuality."

"What do you do in your spare time?"

"I spend a lot of time with my charity. I occasionally do speaking engagements. Last year I taught a class at NYU on modeling."

"I meant for fun, to relax? I'm assuming you don't have an actual boyfriend since I haven't heard his name yet. From what I've read online, your name isn't connected to any one specific guy."

The lack of a social life was a sore subject. Even Skylar, who understood and knew how driven she was, had cautioned her about it. And it wasn't as if she didn't get asked out. There were plenty of men inside the fashion world, and outside it, too, who had asked her out. She turned most of them down, telling herself that getting serious with anyone at this stage of her career would be foolish. But in her heart of hearts, she knew there was another, darker reason.

"I'm guessing this isn't a favorite topic."

"Are you a mind-reader?"

"No, but you have a very expressive face. Easy to read."

She grimaced. "I spent hours upon hours practicing to make sure no one could read me."

"If it makes you feel any better, I've spent hours upon hours practicing how to read people."

She laughed. "We should practice on each other."

"And you're evading the question."

Darn it, he was persistent. "No, I'm not dating anyone." There, that was short, succinct, and the truth.

"You don't owe me an explanation, Kacie."

The compassion in his voice almost made her weep. "Why couldn't I have met a nice guy like you years ago instead of getting involved with one loser after another?"

Sadness darkened his green eyes. "I wasn't such a nice guy years ago. Barely am one now, but I see things a lot differently than I did then."

"Life will do that to you," she said softly.

"Yeah."

She squeezed his hand one last time and then went to her feet. "It's getting late."

"Justin and Riley should be here sometime tomorrow morning. Hopefully, they'll have some good leads."

She nodded, then took the tray with the empty mugs and now empty plate and headed to the door.

"Sleep well."

"Kacie?"

She stopped and turned. "Yes?"

"Thanks for letting me unload on you. Sorry I was an ass before."

"You don't need to apologize. I would've felt the same way and been just as angry."

"Yeah, but you would've been nicer about it."

"Just more devious. I might've spiked your hot chocolate with a laxative."

"Now that *is* evil."

She walked out the door, laughing. Hard to believe that a couple of hours ago, both of them had been miserable. Amazing what a little chocolate and spilling of the guts could do for a soul.

CHAPTER FIFTEEN

Kacie stood in the middle of the living room, waiting and on edge. Security had just alerted her that Justin Kelly and Riley Ingram were on their way up. Would this end today? Though the thought that someone wanted to blackmail her to keep quiet about her real identity was terrifying, even more horrifying was that someone wanted to torture her about it. Either way, she refused to be cowed. Kendra Carson had been a victim; Kacie Dane was not.

It had been days since that phone call and those texts. Maybe whoever it was had gotten scared. Perhaps Justin and Riley's questioning had made this person realize how much trouble he could be in if he continued. Even though it was a lame attempt at hope, she couldn't resist grasping on to it.

"We'll deal with it, whatever happens."

Brennan came to stand beside her, and even though he wasn't touching her, she felt his comfort. Amazing that she had known this man for so short a time, and he'd already become a major influence on her life.

If this was over, if the LCR operatives had discovered there was no real threat, what would happen with Brennan? Would she ever see him again?

The doorbell rang, and she jumped an inch off the floor.

Surprising her further, Brennan wrapped an arm around her shoulders and squeezed gently. "I'm here."

But for how long? It was on the tip of her tongue to ask. She swallowed past a sudden lump in her throat. "Thanks." Straightening her shoulders, she said, "If you'll let them in, I'll get us all some coffee."

His eyes darkened with both concern and curiosity. Great, the last thing she needed to do was let him in on this silly, irrational crush.

"You okay?"

Putting on her brightest smile, she nodded toward the door. "I'm fine. Really. Let them in. I'll be right back."

Brennan watched as she exited the room. One minute she'd been standing like a valiant soldier, bravely waiting for Justin and Riley to arrive to either give her good news or tear her world apart again, the next she'd had the appearance of a frightened deer. What had set that off?

He headed toward the door. Hopefully, they would hear good news today, and this could all be put behind her. Just as he was about to open the door, his mind flickered back to what had just happened, and then it clicked. She'd started looking both worried and sad when he'd put his arm around her. Dammit, he never should have touched her. After what she'd been through, a man touching her, especially one she didn't know very well, probably brought back all sorts of bad memories. He needed to be careful not to do that again. He was here to help her, not terrify her.

He double-checked the peephole, confirming that it was indeed Riley and Justin at the door. His gut clenched with dread. The ominous expressions on their faces did not bode well.

Kacie hurriedly poured coffee into a carafe. Pleased that Brennan had been thoughtful enough to include some pastries in his grocery order, she placed several on a plate and added them to the tray. The instant she entered the living room, all doubts that this would soon be over halted.

She stopped in the doorway. "What's wrong?"

Instead of answering, Brennan solemnly took the tray from her hands. "Sit down."

She shook her head. "No…tell me. Now."

"Do you remember Dr. Julia Curtis?"

"Of course. She was my psychiatrist at the hospital. I haven't seen her since I left, but I—" A sick feeling flooded through her. "Why? What happened?"

"She was murdered a few months back."

A flash of pain went through her. Dr. Curtis, with her no-nonsense but compassionate attitude, had been enormously helpful during her recovery.

"How? What happened?"

"Her office was broken into while she was there, by herself. She was killed, her office ransacked."

"I'm sorry to hear that, but how do you know this is related to me? She's probably had hundreds of patients in her career."

"That's what made the investigation especially difficult. The police had reached a dead-end, until we showed up and started asking questions. Now they're revisiting the case."

"Why?"

Brennan had placed the tray on the table. She barely noticed when he took her hand and led her to the sofa. Then, as if they'd known each other for years, he sat beside her and put his arm around her shoulders.

"They only checked the doctor's current files. Didn't even think to go into the archives of her former patients. When we insisted they check on your file, they realized it was missing."

"But...maybe—"

Justin shook his head. "The only one missing was yours."

Someone out there knew everything she'd told Dr. Curtis. Kacie closed her eyes. Oh God, not only had she revealed the humiliating and revolting things Harrington had done to her, she'd also shared her secret shame.

"Excuse me. I think I'm going to be sick." Pulling away from Brennan, she dashed into the hallway bathroom and slammed the door behind her.

"Shit," Brennan said softly.

"Sorry," Justin said. "Wish we had better news."

"What about the other people on the list? They check out?"

"Yeah. For the most part."

Riley snorted, her disgust of her partner's assessment clear.

"Sounds like you have reservations about someone, Riley," Brennan said.

Riley shot a fuming look at Justin. "Kelly doesn't agree with my assessment, but the mother is a..."

"Piece of work," Justin admitted.

"She's out to get as much as she can from her daughter. Blackmailing her would be damn easy."

Before Brennan could speak, Justin explained why he didn't agree with his partner. "Blackmailing someone for money, as despicable as it is, is a far cry from murder."

"It might be, but she could easily have hired someone. Sonia Carson Musgrave is a—"

"You think my mother is behind this?"

They'd been so focused on their discussion, no one noticed that Kacie had slipped back into the room. Her face was bloodless, her eyes dull, almost vacant.

Brennan went to her and pulled her into his arms. He couldn't have stopped himself from touching her if a tank had been in his way. He forgot his promise to be careful with her. Forgot about who else was in the room. His only aim was to comfort her and try to wipe the devastation from her face.

She felt fragile in his arms, her body shuddering. Even though he hadn't been able to keep from touching her, he was surprised and encouraged at how she burrowed into his arms as if she belonged there.

He whispered, "It's going to be all right. I promise you."

Her voice was muffled against his shoulder. "I'm okay. Really. Just need a moment."

She raised her head and gave him her famous smile, only this time, her eyes said something else. She was scared.

Pulling away much sooner than he would have liked, she turned and faced the LCR operatives. "Sorry about that. So…" She released an explosive breath. "Where do we go from here?"

Riley gave her a nod, as if approving of her determination to move forward. "Let's review the list of the people you gave us, just to get that out of the way. Then we'll talk about some other things."

Taking her arm, because hell, now that he knew she wouldn't flinch from him, he couldn't stop touching her, Brennan led her back to the sofa. As she settled onto the cushion, he poured her a fresh cup of coffee, sweetened it the way he knew she liked, and handed it to her.

Though he'd noticed the surprise and questions in Justin's eyes, he ignored them. Was he acting out of character? Hell yes. Could he explain what was going on with him? Hell no.

"We ran a background on everyone on your list. Talked with everyone with the exception of Dr. Curtis, of course," Riley was saying. "Your private nurse, Nancy Wyatt, checks out. Her financials are stable." She shot a glance at Justin. "Kelly and I both concluded that she can be eliminated."

"I remember her," Kacie said. "She was stern but incredibly compassionate."

"The only other person at the hospital who knows the truth is the administrator, John Weeks. Financials are a little shaky for him, but after talking with him, we don't see him doing this either."

"I don't remember much about him, but I trust your judgment."

"Of the other two on your list," Justin butted in, as if to get ahead of his partner, "your current therapist, Dr. Ramona Crenshaw, checks out as well. Financials are in excellent shape, and our conversation with her was satisfying. Her number one concern is you and what you're going through. We didn't go into detail with her…just that we were investigating some possible threats against you. She's seeing you in a couple of weeks?"

"Yes." After seeing Dr. Crenshaw weekly for almost three years, Kacie now saw her therapist once a month or on an as needed basis.

"Neither Ingram nor myself saw any indication that she isn't one hundred percent legitimately on your side."

"And that leaves your mother," Riley said.

"Ingram and I have argued this extensively. I have to admit, her attitude was not only combative, but also—" Justin broke off as if realizing that what he'd been about to say wasn't something a daughter would want to hear.

"Go ahead and say it," Brennan said. "Kacie has no illusions about her mother."

Instead of Justin answering, Riley did it for him. "She seemed happy that you're having these problems. In fact, she said"—she looked down at her notepad—"'About time the little slut got her comeuppance.'"

Kacie's response was a small flinch in her expression and then another straightening of her shoulders.

"Sorry to be so blunt," Riley said, "but what kind of mother says that about her daughter?"

"Not the good kind," was Kacie's wry reply.

"We checked her financials," Justin said. "She's got money, but she spends a lot, too."

"I'm sure the money I was sending her is being missed already."

"Makes sense she would want to get back at you," Riley said.

"Possibly...probably. But why would she have anything to do with Dr. Curtis's death?"

"Perhaps she was preparing, just in case. Having your file would give her the security."

"True," Brennan said. "But she's got to know that if she were to release information from that file, she'd be incriminating herself in a murder."

"Could be she's not bright enough to get that."

"Do you think your mother's capable of murder?" Brennan asked.

"I don't know. I'd like to think she isn't. But she is a greedy person, and if there's money to be had, who knows if she'd let a little thing like murder stop her?"

"Then she stays on the list," Brennan said.

"So now what?"

"Even though she's on the list, we need to consider that there might be someone else out there who knows your real name and either wants to blackmail you or ruin you."

Kacie gave a small, husky laugh, but Brennan heard the stress beneath it. "So basically we have no clue. It could be anyone."

As if realizing or regretting her earlier roughness, Riley gave her a sympathetic smile. "I think we can narrow it down a bit, with your help."

"How?"

"We need a list of your employees, closest associates, and friends."

"But I—" She shook her head. "No one close to me would do something like this. I trust all of my employees and associates implicitly."

Brennan could understand and appreciate her defense. It was hard as hell to accept that the people you had given your total trust to had betrayed you. He knew that feeling well. And he also knew that betrayal happened every damn day.

"All too often it's the one we never suspect," Brennan said. "We don't have a choice but to suspect everyone until we can eliminate them."

Kacie took a long swallow of her now cold coffee. Hard to believe that only days ago she'd been sure of her path and the brightness of her future. Today, she felt as if a boulder was hanging just above her head. The likelihood of it falling and crushing her was becoming increasingly certain, and there wasn't a damn thing she could do to stop it.

She took in Justin and Riley's expressions. They had a job to do and had every intention of carrying it out. She couldn't fault them for that. The fact that this was a difficult situation was understood, but that wouldn't lessen their resolve to move forward.

Glancing at the man beside her, she saw that same resolve but something more, too. There was compassion, worry, even tenderness. How could he have become so important to her in such a short amount of time?

At that thought, Kacie gave herself a mental ass-kick. As astounding as this incredible knowledge was, now was not the time to be getting all starry-eyed over a man. Someone out there wanted to ruin her. That someone had killed to get information on her. And that information could destroy not only her career but also her sanity. She needed to get her ass in gear and help find out who it was before it was too late.

Standing, she said, "Even though I do trust my employees, I figured you'd want to check them out, too, so I've already made a list of everyone. I'll get it for you."

Aware that all eyes were on her, she exited the room with dignity. She'd been trained to keep her poise, maintain a smile even in extreme stress and physical discomfort. She told herself this was no different. But it was a lie.

Dr. Curtis had been murdered. A horrifying indication that whoever was behind this would go to great lengths to get what they wanted. If they had killed once, how easy would it be to kill again?

Chapter Sixteen

Sweat poured down her face, and though her legs were beginning to feel like overcooked pasta, she refused to quit. If she did, that meant she had to make a final decision, take that final, inevitable step.

After Riley and Justin left yesterday, she'd retreated from Brennan. Even though he'd been extraordinarily kind to her, she hadn't wanted to hear his reassurances or advice. She had needed to think, and think hard.

She had stayed in her room most of the day and had come out only when he'd pounded on the door and insisted she eat something. She hadn't been hungry, but neither was she looking to make herself sick by not eating. So she'd sat across the table from him and eaten what he'd put in front of her. The instant she could say that she'd made a decent dent in her meal, she'd thanked him, told him to leave the dishes in the sink and she would clean them later. Then she'd returned to her room.

Last night she'd alternated between pacing the floor and trying to get some sleep. She had been much more successful at the pacing. This morning, she'd walked out of her bedroom and headed straight to the small gym she'd set up in her spare bedroom. Physical exhaustion felt much more productive and healthier than mental fatigue.

"Dammit, if you don't stop, you're going to pass out."

Brennan's furious voice grabbed her and threw her back into a reality she'd been trying so hard to avoid. Dressed in jeans and a black T-shirt, he stood before her, beautifully male and thoroughly pissed. Those vivid green eyes fascinated her, as they seemed to change with every mood. When he was angry, they darkened to a brilliant emerald. And, oh man, were they jewel-hard now.

Before she could detect his intent, Brennan reached over and slammed the off button on the treadmill. Kacie came to an abrupt, stumbling halt. And then, because her legs were limp noodles, they collapsed.

Brennan caught her before she hit the floor. Holding her in his arms, he carried her to a chair. Instead of dropping her into it, he sat down with her, cradling her against him.

"Let me go. I'm all sweaty and wet. You'll—"

"Just. Shut. Up."

She knew she should protest his rudeness, but she was too tired and dispirited to even try. Besides, being held in his muscular arms, pressed up against his hard chest, with her head against his broad shoulder, was the best feeling in the world. When was the last time she'd felt this safe?

And so she lay there, saturated in perspiration and weak as a sick kitten, enjoying being in a man's arms. Despite all the fear and angst over the last few days, plus the dread of what lay ahead for her future, Kacie allowed herself this small moment of joy and triumph. She was in Brennan's arms, and she wasn't scared or revolted. In fact, she was just the opposite. Imagine that. With a sigh that sounded like surrender, Kacie closed her eyes and reveled in this newfound feeling of safety.

Brennan told himself he shouldn't be holding her. He'd come in to check on her and watched for almost half an hour while she'd pounded away on her treadmill. He'd known she was in shape—she was slender, but her body was taut and sleekly muscled. He hadn't known just how physically fit she was. He'd timed her. A six-minute mile was damn impressive, especially since he knew she'd been running well before he walked into the room.

After a while, he realized that she wouldn't stop until her body gave out. That'd pissed him off, though he probably could've figured out a way to stop her without scaring the shit out of her. Definitely could've simply supported her when she fell instead of holding her. And without a doubt, he should've deposited her into a chair and let her go. Instead, he was holding her in his arms and wasn't quite sure when he'd be able to let her go.

She wasn't fighting him. In fact, if the small smile curving her full lips was an indicator, she was enjoying being in his arms as much as he liked holding her.

They needed to talk, make some decisions. Yeah, he knew it wasn't his business. He was here to keep her safe, not give her personal advice. But she'd had over twenty-four hours to ruminate. He might not know everything about her, but what he did know made him think she wasn't one to bury her head in the sand and hope things got better. She would want to act.

Resisting the urge to taste the smile still curving her lips, he said quietly, "Ready to talk?"

She blinked up at him as if she'd been asleep, and Brennan wanted to laugh. He'd feared scaring her, but he'd put her to sleep instead.

"Yes."

"Let's get you hydrated first." With great reluctance, Brennan stood and deposited her in the chair. He grabbed a bottle of water from the small fridge across the room, twisted the cap off, and handed it to her.

She downed the entire bottle in one long drink, and he didn't think he'd ever seen anything sexier. Watching her slender throat work as she swallowed, seeing the bliss of enjoyment on her face. *Hell.* He turned back to the fridge on the pretext of getting another bottle. If she saw the erection he was starting to sport, he'd lose her trust.

"I'm going to tell Edy. Who I am…what's going on."

He took a swallow of the ice-cold water and then turned back to her. The misery on her face demolished his desire, replacing it with the need to shield and protect.

"She'll need to let Julian Montague know. If whoever is doing this leaks the truth, he'll be caught unaware. That's not right, and it could damage his company…definitely hurt sales. He's planning to make the announcement about me in a few days. I need to inform him as soon as possible so he can select another model.

"Also, Edy's put a lot of time into my career. She deserves to know the truth, too, in case she wants to dissolve our agreement."

This was all so damned unfair. After finally getting her life back, and achieving her goal, someone wanted to take it away from her. If they could only understand this person's motivation, it'd make it a lot easier to know how to proceed.

"You think Montague will renege on the deal?"

She lifted her slender shoulders in a weary *who knows?* shrug. "The reason he chose me is because of my wholesome, fresh-faced look. Being the drugged-out slut for a wealthy pervert doesn't exactly say pure and untouched, does it?"

Fury zoomed through him, and Brennan didn't think, he acted. Striding across the room, he pulled Kacie up by her upper arms and shook her, hard. "Stop that right now. You damn well will not take that attitude. You. Were. Raped. Not your fault, and anyone who sees it differently is a fucking idiot and not worth your time."

Hell, she should have slapped him. He wasn't exactly being the kindly counselor she probably needed. Instead, she gave him a sweet smile. "Thank you, Brennan. I needed to hear those words."

He should've backed away, should've said he was glad she saw the light. Instead, he did something so incredibly stupid… so damn impulsive and very unlike him. Still holding her arms, he pulled her to him and kissed her. Slowly, gently, he savored the softness of her lips, the sweet taste of her mouth. Brennan groaned and deepened the kiss. Damn, she tasted good.

Kacie knew her heart would burst open any moment. Not only was she being kissed for the first time in years, he hadn't given her any kind of warning. If he had, she would've backed away from him. And wouldn't that have been a crying shame, because…

Oh my stars, the man kisses like a dream.

Tenderly ruthless, he ate at her lips with a gentle insistence that defeated every fear and replaced them with a need she'd never felt. Unable and unwilling to stop the invasion, Kacie opened her mouth, and Brennan accepted her invitation with a sexy growl. Delving into the depths of her mouth, his tongue swept across hers, tangling, tasting. He plunged deep, retreated, thrust again. It was as close to the sex act as she'd experienced since before Harrington, and while a sane part of her told her she needed to back away, she shushed that voice and went with what the rest of her wanted.

Since he held her just with his hands on her arms, and his mouth, Kacie was limited in where she could reach him. She didn't give it too much thought, though. Her hands literally ached to touch him, feel him. She put them on his waist, and her first thought was that she'd never touched anyone so hard and unyielding. He was like a solid, brick wall without the slightest give. Why did that make her go even hotter?

Needing to feel naked skin, her fingers went beneath his T-shirt. His skin was a tactile delight for her senses—smooth, hot, hard, velvet roughness with a touch of silk.

Oh my.

Abruptly, and much too soon, Brennan lifted his head. Kacie had to look at him, had to see if he was feeling even a small percentage of the wonder she was. There was definite heat, which matched her own. But the longer she looked at him, the more she saw something else—something she never wanted to see. Regret and remorse washed away the desire in his brilliant green eyes.

"I'm sorry, Kacie. I don't know—"

Unable to withstand either his rejection or his apology, Kacie pressed her fingers to his mouth. *Oh...* No wonder his mouth had felt so glorious on hers. His lips were soft but with an underlying firmness that matched the rest of him.

"Please don't... I—" She halted, embarrassed. How do you tell a guy that not only did you enjoy his kiss, but you really wanted him to do it again, plus a few more things?

If you're Kacie Dane with zero confidence in your sexuality, you apparently stammer and say something incredibly stupid. "So...um...was that part of LCR's new services?"

Like the flip of a light switch, his expression went blank, and his eyes went to an icy green. He dropped his hands and backed away. "Again, my apologies. It won't happen again."

She wanted to apologize, tell him it was the most delicious kiss she'd ever had. Anything to get that look off his face. Instead, like a tranquilized zombie, she watched him as he disappeared out the door. The minute it shut behind him, she wilted, dropping to the floor with a thud.

The best thing to happen to her in years, and she'd ruined it.

CHAPTER SEVENTEEN

Edy arrived the next day, promptly at ten—a rarity for her. She'd heard the seriousness in Kacie's voice and knew something had happened. Most times when they met to discuss business, Kacie would either go to Edy's office or they'd have lunch together. With Kacie's invitation to her home, Edy had apparently realized this was a meeting like none other.

Yesterday had been the most awkward day in Kacie's memory. After that mind-blowing, life-altering kiss, then her incredibly stupid, inept response to his apology, Brennan had avoided her as if she had a contagious disease.

She'd been in the kitchen, grabbing a yogurt, when he'd walked in, gotten a bottle of water without so much as looking at her. At the door, he'd turned and coolly informed her that if she needed to go out, she should knock on his bedroom door and tell him so he could accompany her. Then, he'd shut himself up in his room and hadn't come out once.

Kacie had roamed around her apartment. Working was out, as concentrating on anything significant would have been impossible. Not only was her life unraveling once again, she was dealing with a boatload of tumultuous emotions about Brennan.

She was all over the board on how she felt. One moment she was telling herself that getting involved with someone when she clearly still had intimacy issues was insane. The next moment it was all she could do not to knock on his bedroom door, apologize for her asinine remark yesterday, and ask him to kiss her again, longer, deeper.

Ugh. Insanity, plus one!

Thankfully, Edy's arrival put her in a different frame of mind. Not a happy one, but at least she was concentrating on something besides her adolescent-like crush.

She should have guessed that even though Brennan wasn't visible, he was more than aware of what was going on in the apartment. The instant Edy walked in, he'd come downstairs and nodded a greeting. He didn't speak, didn't stay. It was more of a *Kacie is not alone in the apartment* kind of warning.

Before he could disappear up the stairway again, Edy said, "I'm sorry about the other night, Brennan. I had no idea that would happen."

His expression never changing, he gave her another nod, acknowledging her apology, and then left them alone.

Settling herself on the sofa across from Kacie, Edy nodded toward the steps where Brennan had been. "He's both terrifying and exhilarating, isn't he?"

That was an excellent description of Brennan Sinclair.

"Before we get started," Edy said, "let me apologize to you, too. I'd totally forgotten that Carlton Lorrance used to be one of the paparazzi. His shenanigans at the party didn't set well with Eleanor. Now he'll be scrambling to repair his own reputation. I'm just sorry I was the one who brought him inside."

"I know it wasn't purposeful, Edy. Carlton is a sleazebag who has apparently been hiding his dark side. I doubt that we'll be hearing from him again."

"I hope not." Edy took a sip of her coffee and then pinned her client with a narrow-eyed, calculated gaze. "So, tell me what's wrong."

Thankful she had an agent who wasn't one for chitchat or inane conversation, Kacie went for the heart of the matter. "I have to tell you something, but before I do, I need your promise that, other than the people I authorize you to tell, this will remain strictly confidential."

Irritation flashed in Edy's eyes. "Everything my clients tell me is confidential. I take my responsibilities very seriously."

"I know that—I just feel the need to reiterate since this is a very sensitive topic."

"Okay. You have my promise. Shoot."

She took a breath and expelled it on a giant rush of air. "I wasn't born Kacie Dane, nor did I grow up in Maine. My real name is Kendra Carson."

Kacie waited a moment to see if the name would trigger Edy's memory. She was sure most people had forgotten her name, and many had forgotten the incident that had brought her name to the public's attention.

Instead of looking surprised, Edy's face held both puzzlement and concern. "Why does that name sound so familiar?"

"Because a little over five years ago, I, along with several other women, was kidnapped. William Harrington III held us captive. He drugged and raped me repeatedly."

Recognition clicked. "Holy. Shit."

"After we were rescued, I was in the hospital a long time. Almost a year. When I emerged, I wanted nothing to do with my name. Wanted to forget what happened. I knew if I didn't change my name but pursued a career, I'd always be that girl who got kidnapped and raped by the wealthy William Harrington.

"I asked some well-connected friends for help. They assisted me in changing my name and creating a new background for me.

"As far as the rest of the world is concerned, Kendra Carson remains in the hospital, comatose and unresponsive."

Edy had been around the block too many times to be completely surprised about anything for long. She nodded, as if in approval. "Why are you telling me now? What's going on?"

"Several weird things have happened lately that lead me to believe someone has found out my real identity and plans to either blackmail me or try to ruin my career."

Comprehension clicked quickly. "You're concerned about Montague."

"Yes. If this comes out while I'm his spokesmodel, it could damage his sales. Not only would it be unethical not to let him know beforehand, I want to give him a chance to choose someone else if that's what he wants."

"I want to say it won't matter, but I really don't have a clue how Julian will react."

Kacie appreciated Edy's honesty. Instead of giving platitudes and telling her she was sure everything would be okay, her agent gave her the bald-faced truth.

"I know that, but in all good conscience, telling him is my only choice."

"I agree. Much better to lose the contract now than to have him pull out publicly if the worst happens."

Next, Kacie approached what might be an even more delicate situation. "I also wanted you to give consideration about our partnership, Edy. You're a well-established agent, but this could have negative impact on your career. I totally understand if you'd rather part ways."

Temper sparked in Edy's eyes. "I won't even dignify that insulting remark with an answer. You're my client, and I care about you, and now that I know the truth, I admire you even more. And no self-serving, asshole blackmailer or perverted fiend is going to scare me away from you. Got that?"

Grateful tears flooded Kacie's eyes. She had hoped that Edy would feel that way and was heartened by her support. "Thank you, Edy. You've been one of my biggest champions from the beginning."

"Now don't go getting all sentimental on me." She leaned forward, determination stamped on her face. "So, listen up. Here's what we're going to do."

Brennan rubbed his tired, grit-filled eyes. There was an endless amount of information related to how to deal with intimacy after a rape. For the last twenty-four hours, on minimal sleep, he'd been doing research. Trying to figure out how to handle a situation like this was tantamount to tiptoeing around landmines.

One thing for sure—he sure as hell hadn't handled yesterday correctly. First, he never should have kissed her. That'd been way out of bounds for a bodyguard. Second, he never should've kept kissing her. Just because she'd tasted so damn good might be the truth, but it was a piss-poor reason all the same. And lastly…oh hell, he'd seen the heat and the desire in her eyes, felt it in her body, but when she'd gotten flustered and blurted out what she'd said, he'd responded with all the grace and dignity of a twelve-year-old. She'd been uncertain, scared, excited, and vulnerable. And he'd handled it with the finesse of a lumbering ox.

So he'd done the only thing he could do until he learned how he should have handled things. Then, he'd go from there.

Hell, after the way he'd acted, she might not have any interest in doing anything other than calling McCall to request his immediate removal. Couldn't blame her. Not that he would listen. Whether Kacie wanted him to stay or not was no longer her decision. He didn't quit when the going got rough. Someone wanted to hurt her. Someone who was capable of murder. Even if Brennan had to protect her from a distance, he'd make sure she stayed safe until the asshole was caught.

With everything she had on her mind, that ill-timed kiss probably was the least of her worries. Not only did she have some sicko trying to destroy her life, she was being forced to make incredibly difficult decisions about her career.

The soft knock on his door was a pleasant and welcome surprise.

Clicking off the link to a rape victims' advocacy blog, Brennan went to the door. The instant he opened it, his heart shattered. Her eyes were swimming in tears.

Ignoring all the curses he'd thrown at himself because of yesterday's screw-up, Brennan grabbed her arms. "What's happened? What's wrong?"

"Edy was insulted that I would even think she would want to drop me."

His opinion of Edy Brown went way up. After the party the other night, he hadn't been impressed with Kacie's agent. Now he was quite sure he might like her quite a lot.

"And she called Montague. He doesn't want to pull me off the campaign. He said that he'll stand behind me, no matter what."

"That's great."

"Yeah, it is." And then, as if yesterday's awkward words had never been exchanged, she threw herself into his arms.

Brennan closed his eyes, determined to not mess this up again. Her easy hug... her ability to touch him without fear, was a gift.

"I've missed you," she whispered against his chest.

"I thought you might need some space."

She pulled back and faced him bravely. How the hell did she do that? "I said something really stupid because I was so nervous. I'm sorry."

"You don't owe me an apology, Kacie. I never should have kissed you."

"You didn't like it?"

"Oh, hell yeah, I liked it. Too much."

"Good. I did, too." And before he could explore that extraordinary confession, she said, "I'm dying to get out of the apartment for a while. Want to go grab some lunch somewhere?"

Her mercurial moods were one of the many things he found so charming. "Sounds good."

"Let me grab my purse."

Shaking his head at the odd turn of events, Brennan strapped on his ankle holster and tucked in his gun. This unusually optimistic mood was a dangerous thing. In his experience, it was almost always a precursor to disaster.

Hours later, he learned how much he hated being right.

Chapter Eighteen

She wouldn't go so far as say it was the best day ever. After all, she still had some major hurdles to overcome, and they loomed in the distance like a faraway thunderstorm. However, Kacie firmly believed that today was in the top three of best days ever.

She wasn't so sure that Brennan felt the same.

Contrary to what her employees liked to believe, Kacie wasn't yet a totally recognizable public figure. Sure, some people recognized her, but many on the street going about their daily lives didn't know her face from Adam's housecat. On the other hand, Brennan Sinclair's ruggedly handsome face was once splashed all over televisions and newspapers. That might have been years ago, but New Yorkers liked their football. Plus, Brennan had the kind of face that was impossible to forget.

They'd walked only two blocks before he was recognized. Knowing how he felt about his former fame, Kacie didn't know what to expect when a street vendor selling NYC memorabilia called out, "Hey, Brennan Sinclair! You were the greatest. Can I have your autograph?" He held out a Jets cap and a black pen.

Brennan stopped at his booth, gave him a quizzical smile. "You going to sell it if I do?"

"No way, man. It's going up on my shelf at home."

Brennan took the cap and pen, scrawled his name across the top of it, and gave it back.

"Gee, thanks, man." The vendor held it to his chest as if it meant a lot to him.

Brennan nodded, took Kacie's arm and started walking. Three more times, before they could make it to the Chinese restaurant seven blocks away, they were stopped for autograph requests. Once for Kacie, twice for Brennan.

The instant they entered the restaurant, she could feel Brennan's shoulders relax, and it occurred to her that even though he'd been gracious and kind to everyone who had stopped him, he had definitely not enjoyed the attention. But instead of acting like a horse's ass, which some celebrities seemed to have no problem doing, Brennan had taken it in stride.

It was early afternoon, so the restaurant was filled with the lunch crowd. They managed to get a small table in a secluded corner, and Kacie couldn't think of a better place to be. Here they could sit in relative anonymity and pretend they were just a guy and a girl getting to know each other better.

While they dined on dim sum, kung pao chicken, and Mongolian beef, she settled down to learn all she could about the real Brennan Sinclair.

"We both seem to know about the worst times in each other's lives, but tell me about your best day."

The instant she said it, she wanted to take it back because she already knew what his answer would be, and she knew it would make him sad again.

"The day Cody was born."

"Yes."

"Can you talk about him? Tell me what he was like? Did he look like you?"

"He was a miniature of me. Green eyes, black hair, stubborn little jaw. Had a sweet disposition though…was easy going. Had the cutest little laugh." His voice went husky. "When I was home, he was like my shadow…would follow me everywhere."

She reached across the table and briefly touched his hand. "I'm sorry, Brennan. I didn't mean to bring up something painful."

"Memories of my son don't make me sad. I only get sad when I remember what kind of parents he had." His face went granite-like. "He deserved a helluva lot better."

He leaned back in his chair, and though his eyes remained solemn, he smiled and said, "What's Kacie Dane's best day?"

She'd be revealing too much if she said that this was one of them. Instead, she remembered the day she got her first modeling gig. "I got the call when I was still working at Macy's. I didn't get to return the call until I was on my lunch break. When I was told I got the spot, I swear the whole store heard me scream."

"Who was the first person you called to tell?"

"Skylar. Hands down, she's been my biggest supporter. My mentor. My best friend."

"And did you call your mother?"

"Not for a couple of days. I knew she would have something sarcastic and demeaning to say, so I waited."

"And did she?"

"Of course. By then it didn't matter."

"She's jealous of you, you know."

"That's what Skylar says, too. Hard to understand a mother being jealous of her own daughter."

"You have youth and beauty on your side. She's losing both. And you've got a bright future ahead of you."

"Still no reason for her to be jealous." She shook her head. Talking about her mother was a sure prescription for putting her in a bad mood. "Let's talk about more-pleasant stuff."

"Like what?"

There were so many things she wanted to know about him. If she started bombarding him with questions, though, she figured he'd clam up like he had before.

"What do you do in your spare time when you're not protecting damsels in distress?"

He looked so completely blank for a moment that she knew she had caught him off-guard.

"Would you believe scrapbooking and knitting?"

She tilted her head, as if considering his question. "Scrapbooking? No. But I could definitely see you with some knitting needles."

He grinned. "That's because they can be lethal weapons."

"Exactly."

He shrugged. "I don't have a lot of downtime, but when I wasn't on an op, I taught a weekly self-defense course at the local Y. Sometimes even the smallest amount of knowledge can save a life."

She nodded, completing agreeing. After her recovery, she'd taken self-defense courses and classes on how to spot a predator. She would never be unprepared again.

Brennan didn't like that look on her face. She'd been relaxed, carefree, until he'd caused bad memories to return. He wanted her to be aware and ready when trouble struck, but today he wanted to see her relaxed.

"You ever been to the Empire State Building?"

Her brow furrowed. Yeah, it'd been a one-eighty turn in the conversation, but it worked.

"Of course I have. Haven't you?"

"Yeah, but a lot of New Yorkers haven't. Thought you might want to play tourist today."

Her nose scrunched in a cute way. "Too many people. You'd be recognized by every other person. We'd never make it to the top."

He still couldn't believe he was still so recognizable to New Yorkers. Whenever he looked in the mirror, he saw a completely different person than he'd once been. Even harder to believe that no one had yelled obscenities at him today. That'd been refreshing.

"How about a walk in the park? We can work off the meal we just consumed."

"Sounds perfect."

After paying the check, they walked out the door. As if they were just like any other couple, he took her hand in his and began to stroll down the sidewalk.

Kacie gave him a quick, smiling glance and then started talking. She told him silly, nonsensical things that made him laugh. Made him wish that today wasn't an anomaly, that it could be this easy every day.

But he had the darkest feeling in his gut that this day was the calm before the storm.

CHAPTER NINETEEN

Kacie went through the main door of her apartment building feeling as though she could conquer the world. Brennan still held her hand—as he had almost the entire day. They'd talked and laughed like nothing scary or unusual was going on in her life. And for a few hours, she managed to forget that they'd both seen horror and sadness. Or that a new horror might well be around the corner.

The instant they entered, Vincent stood to welcome them, his smile good-humored and kind. "Good evening, Ms. Dane, Mr. Sinclair."

"Hey, Vincent. How's your day been?" Kacie asked.

"Perfect. My youngest grandson walked for the first time today. My wife said there's video on my phone, but I'm going to have to wait to get home to watch it."

"Why?"

His big shoulders lifted. "I can't get it to play."

Before she could offer, Brennan said, "Want me to try?"

"That'd be great."

He handed his phone over and watched while Brennan clicked a couple of buttons. Seconds later, the video of a wobbling toddler appeared on the screen.

Vincent's eyes lit up, and then he beamed like a proud grandfather. "Thanks, Mr. Sinclair."

"You're welcome. He's a good-looking boy."

"Takes after his mother."

Brennan took Kacie's hand again and headed toward the elevator. Just as the elevator dinged, Vincent called out, "Oh, Ms. Dane, I forgot to tell you that Ms. Greenfield came by earlier. Said she left something for you to take a look at."

"Okay, thanks," Kacie said as she walked into the elevator.

A thoughtful frown appeared on Brennan's face. "How many people have a key to your apartment?"

"Other than me, just two. Tara Greenfield, my personal assistant, and you."

"Your secretary doesn't?"

"No, Molly never comes to my apartment. She works in our offices in Midtown."

"She works for the Kacie Dane Foundation?"

"Yes, both she and Tara work for the foundation and have offices there, but they also work for me personally. Tara is my right-hand person...I don't know what I'd do without her. And Molly handles a lot of my personal correspondence."

"Molly's the one who sent over that note that sounded like it was from Harrington?"

And the honeymoon was officially over. Even though Kacie had known reality would have to intrude eventually, she hadn't been ready for it to arrive so soon. She could see where Brennan was going with this line of questioning, but it was unthinkable.

"There's no way Molly would have anything to do with that. She's barely old enough to vote."

"What does voting have to do with any of this?"

"Nothing. It's just my way of saying she's a young girl who would have been way too young to know anything about Harrington."

"They're teaching kids to read quite early these days."

Kacie rolled her eyes as she inserted her key into the lock. When the door swung open on its own, she swallowed her sarcastic comeback.

In one effortless move, Brennan pushed her behind him and pulled his gun from his ankle holster. "Stay here."

Gun at the ready, Brennan stepped into Kacie's apartment. Reaching behind him, he flipped the switch at the wall and watched carefully as light filled the main floor. Nothing looked out of place.

He went from room to room, checking closets, under beds, behind furniture, but found no one and nothing out of place.

Brennan went back to the front door and found Kacie with her back against the wall, pointing her can of pepper spray directly at the door. Though her face was pale, her eyes blazed with resolve. This was one woman who was determined to never be caught off guard again.

"Looks okay. Can't find anything out of place either, but I want you to go through the rooms with me, just in case I missed something."

They went from room to room together, and as he had the first time, they found nothing wrong.

"Tara must've forgotten to lock the door."

"Is she irresponsible like that?"

"No…she's incredibly mature. She's never let me down."

"Why don't you call and ask her?"

She pulled her cellphone from her purse and punched a speed-dial number. When he heard Tara answer, Brennan mouthed, "Put her on speaker."

Though she frowned slightly, Kacie didn't argue and punched the speaker key. "Hey, Tara, it's Kacie. Did you come by my apartment today?"

"Yes. I left you some ideas for the commercial we wanted to run during Domestic Violence Week. They're on your desk." She paused a second, then said, "Did you not see them?"

"I haven't had a chance to look yet. Listen, do you remember locking my apartment door?"

"Yes, I'm sure I did…I…well, I can't say I remember exactly, but I'm sure I did. Why?"

"The door was open when we got back. We thought someone had broken in."

"Oh no, Kacie. I would never…I—" She stopped abruptly. "I did have my hands full, though. You asked me to take that gown you wore to the party the other night for cleaning, plus I had my bag and a cola in my hand." She paused for a second and said, "I'm sorry, Kacie. Now I'm not sure."

"It's no problem, Tara, No harm done."

"I'll be extra careful next time. I promise."

"No worries. I just wanted to check and make sure that's what happened. I'll see you soon."

Kacie ended the call and dropped her phone back into her purse with a gusty sigh. "That's a relief."

"If that's what really happened, yeah, it is."

"What other explanation could there be? No one else seems to have been here, nothing's missing or out of place. It was a simple mistake on her part."

Brennan wasn't so sure, but he'd reserve judgment until he could check for himself. Though Kacie swore her employees had been thoroughly vetted, he was glad that Justin and Riley would do a more thorough search on them.

"Now that the excitement has passed, I just realized how tired I am." She flashed him a shy smile. "Thanks for a lovely day. It's exactly what I needed."

"I enjoyed it, too."

He wanted to say something else, keep her there for a few more minutes. Wanted the right to kiss her, hold her close. But no matter how much both of them had enjoyed their time together, today hadn't been a date, and he sure as hell wasn't her boyfriend.

He nodded, backed away. "Good night."

He came to an abrupt stop when she whispered, "Brennan?"

"Yes?"

"Would it be too out of line if I asked you to kiss me again?"

Hell yeah, it'd be out of line. And totally unprofessional and inappropriate if he complied. So then why was he walking toward her, standing in front of her?

She was easy to read. He saw the anxiety, but more than that, he saw the hope, the need. "I don't want to frighten you again."

"You didn't frighten me…" Her smile was uncertain, almost shy. "You made me really nervous…and—"

"And?"

"You made me feel something I haven't felt in a very long time. Wasn't sure I ever would again."

"Like what?"

A pretty, pink flush washed over her face. "You made me want."

She left him breathless with her sweetness, her honesty and courage. Even though every masculine instinct told him to take her, hold her, devour that sweetness, Brennan held himself still. Everything, including the smallest of gestures, must be up to her. She'd had too much taken from her already. Damned if he would demand something she wasn't ready to give.

He could, however, give her this. "I've never wanted to kiss anyone more than I want to kiss you."

Her eyes lit up. "Really? Skylar told me you dated a Miss America contestant and a Miss World in the same week."

He liked that she could tease him, that she felt comfortable with him.

When he did nothing, she bit her lip slightly, tilted her head. "So, you going to do it or not?"

"No, you are."

Anxiety again, but it was almost immediately replaced by excitement, curiosity. Stretching up on her toes, she leaned into him, put her mouth on his, and then instantly raised her head, looking somewhat disappointed.

"That the kind of kiss you wanted?" Brennan asked.

Darn him. He knew it wasn't, but he also wouldn't take anything she wasn't ready to give. After yesterday's near fiasco, she couldn't blame him for his caution.

Kacie wanted to growl her frustration. She'd never asked a guy to kiss her before, never had to. And now, she wanted this man's kiss more than anything, and he expected her to do it on her own?

"Okay…let's try it again." She put her hands on his shoulders, her mouth on his and pressed a firm kiss onto his unsmiling lips. That was better but still not what she wanted.

Taking a breath, she wrapped her arms around him, pressed her body against his, and put her mouth back on his. Still nothing.

She spoke against his mouth. "You know it takes two to tango."

She was so close she felt the smile curve his mouth against hers.

"You're doing good…keep going."

She might've given up if it wasn't for the fact that she was pressed against his chest and could feel the rapid beat of his heart. He might be playing it safe, but he wasn't unaffected.

Feeling empowered, Kacie put her mouth against his again, moved softly, caressing. He responded, but too slowly, too careful. She wasn't about to give up, though. She pressed deeper into him and licked his lips, then took a nibble at his sensuous lower lip. A deep growl started in his chest. Progress, at last.

Continuing the assault, she nibbled, sucked, and also added the occasional tongue caress. That lasted for several seconds until, with a deeper growl, Brennan took over. His mouth opened, and he drew her into a soul-devouring, heart-stopping melding of his mouth to hers.

Kacie halted all efforts to control the kiss as she let Brennan sweep her away into the most delicious moment of her entire life.

Minutes later, he raised his head and said softly, "Good night, Kacie."

Every part of her body throbbed with need, and though she knew she'd never wanted anyone the way she wanted Brennan Sinclair, she also knew she wasn't ready to take this any further.

Pulling away from him, she said softly, "Good night," and made her exit before she could change her mind.

She felt his eyes on her as she walked up the stairway. If she turned and went back down, she knew she could have more of those delicious kisses, plus other things. She didn't have the courage to try, though...at least not yet.

Feeling as though she was dancing on air, Kacie prepared for bed. Her usual ritual of face washing and teeth brushing were done automatically as she relived those moments in Brennan's arms. How wonderful he had tasted, and while she'd felt safe and cared for, she'd never experienced such off-the-edge excitement.

It was like freefalling from an airplane but knowing that you would land safely and securely.

She pulled on a favorite pair of pajamas, short shorts, and a tank top, pulled back the covers, and settled down to sleep. By habit, she'd left the light on in the bathroom, but she was almost sure that very soon it would no longer be a necessity. Even though someone out there possibly wanted to ruin her, she actually felt safer than she'd ever felt in her life. How incredible was that?

Sliding her hand under her pillow to position it more comfortably, she paused when her fingers touched something odd. Puzzled, Kacie sat up and picked up her pillow. She squinted in the dim light. Flat, shiny, and square, it appeared to be a photograph of some kind.

Flipping the light switch at the top of her bed, she looked down again. A moan escaped her, and then she couldn't breathe. Breath rasped from her lungs in loud, ugly gasps. A dim part of her mind told her she was hyperventilating, but she couldn't stop, couldn't think.

Oh God, how had—

Practically falling out of bed, Kacie stumbled to the door, opened it and was at Brennan's door in a second. She barely managed to wait until she entered his room before she sobbed his name.

CHAPTER TWENTY

Brennan shot out of bed and was holding Kacie before she'd finished screaming his name. She was plastered against him, but he needed to know if she were hurt. He tried pushing her away, but she refused to let him go.

"Tell me, Kacie."

Instead of answering, she buried her head against his shoulder and let out a keening cry of grief.

Shaking her slightly, he growled, "Dammit. Tell me what's happened."

"P-P-Picture."

"Picture? Where?"

"Under my pillow…can't look at it again. Take it away… take it away."

Since there appeared to be no immediate threat, Brennan took the time to calm her down. He sat on the edge of the bed, pulled her into his lap, and held her close. She cried silent tears for a long time as her body continued to shudder.

Several minutes later, she huffed out one last sob and raised a tear-drenched face from his chest. "He really does want to destroy me."

"Who?"

"Harrington. He'll never let me go."

"The bastard is dead. And whoever is doing this will not destroy you, Kacie. I promise you that."

She didn't look like she believed him, but she nodded and said, "You're right. I just don't know what to do."

"Okay...you ready to tell me about the photograph?"

"It was under my pillow...in my bed."

"If I leave you here, will you be okay?"

"I—" She closed her eyes. "I don't want you to see it." She buried her face against his chest. "I'm so ashamed."

He was getting a clearer picture of what the content of the photograph might be, and a gut-clenching anger built up inside him. Someone had photos of her time with Harrington. The bastard had drugged and raped her, starved her half to death. McCall had mentioned that everything had been recorded, but all of the DVDs had been destroyed. Had there been still shots, too?

He shook her slightly, gently. "There's nothing to be ashamed of, Kacie. You're smart enough to know that. And whoever is doing this, we will find him. I promise you."

Standing, still holding her in his arms, he laid her gently on his bed. "Stay here. I'll be back in just a second. Okay?"

She nodded, keeping her eyes closed. Unable to do anything else, Brennan pressed a comforting kiss to her forehead.

He went into her bedroom and spotted the photograph on the floor. Before picking it up, he looked under all the pillows, then under the bed. No more photos. Hopefully, this was the only one.

Taking a tissue from the box on her nightstand, Brennan picked the photo up by the edge and then looked at it.

A much younger Kacie lay spread-eagle on a bed, her limbs tied to the four corners. She was nude, and the expression on her face gave the impression she'd been satiated by her lover. Her eyes, however, were glazed, the pupils dilated, indicating she was drugged and probably not even remotely aware of what was happening.

Brennan wanted to wad up the photograph and burn it. He couldn't. Whoever was doing this not only knew that Kacie Dane was Kendra Carson, they had physical proof. This offensive, disgusting photo was a shot across the bow.

It was only the beginning.

Kacie lay in Brennan's arms. After he'd returned to his room, he'd asked her if she wanted him to hold her. She hadn't been able to speak, just moved into his arms. He had eased down beside her, as if afraid of frightening her, then held her close. He hadn't offered platitudes, false hopes, or even assurances. He'd just held her and made her feel safe again.

Amazing how just two hours ago, she'd felt so incredibly optimistic, and now she knew that this would never be over. Whoever was doing this wouldn't stop until she was totally destroyed.

"You'll feel better tomorrow if you can get a little sleep."

Like midnight silk, Brennan's deep voice spoke in the darkness, smooth and comforting.

"I know, but my mind won't shut down. I keep trying to figure out who would do this, and why."

"We'll figure it out together. I'll call Justin and Riley in the morning. Then we'll sit down and go over each person who could even remotely be a suspect."

"You're angry."

"You sound surprised."

She raised her head to peer up at him. The lighting in the room was dim, but she was close enough to see the grim set to his mouth. The mouth that only a few hours ago had kissed her with a passion she'd never known before.

"Thank you for being here, Brennan. I know it's your job, but—"

He squeezed her tight against him. "There's no place on earth I'd rather be. Now go to sleep. I'll be right here if you need me."

That reassurance was like a warm comforting blanket allowing her to close her eyes and drift off.

Brennan held her for several more moments, making sure she was deeply asleep. He hadn't been able to do anything while she was awake. Now that she slept, he needed to get to work.

Shifting her gently against the pillow, he watched, waiting to make sure she didn't wake. She had to be exhausted after everything she'd gone through the last twenty-four hours. Hopefully, she'd get the rest she needed, because his gut told him she was going to need all the strength she could muster.

Rising, he grabbed his cellphone by the bed and silently went out the door. The instant it closed behind him, he punched a speed-dial button.

"Hey, man, what's up?"

It was just after two o'clock in the morning, but Justin sounded wide awake.

"We've got problems."

As Brennan relayed the events of the past couple of hours, he did a more thorough search of the apartment. When he'd checked it before, he'd been looking for an intruder or missing items. Now he was looking for things that might have been left—more threats that the asshole wanted Kacie or someone else to find.

He opened the cupboard where she kept her coffee cups and whispered, "Shit."

"What?"

Brennan's stomach roiled. "Another photograph. It was taped to the inside of the cabinet. Hell, there's no telling how many this bastard has."

"I'll grab Riley, and we'll be there as soon as we can."

"Okay... I—"

"What?"

"I don't want to tell her about this other one. And there may be more."

"Do a thorough search. We'll be there as soon as we can." He paused and added, "Would you want to be kept in the dark?"

"I'll see you soon."

Brennan slid the phone into his jeans' pocket and then searched for more photos as meticulously as a surgeon looking for bullet fragments in a gunshot victim. He found three more photos. One was behind a sofa cushion, another in the folds of a magazine sitting on the coffee table. The last had been rolled up and placed inside the deli tray of the refrigerator.

Sick freak.

Each photo was different. Each was a different perverted act of sexual violation. And each one had the ability to unveil Kacie's identity and destroy her carefully rebuilt life.

After a glance at each photo, Brennan preserved them in plastic freezer bags he'd found in the pantry, just as he had the one that Kacie had found.

He returned to his bedroom. Kacie's steady, shallow breaths told him she was still sleeping. After quietly searching his room for any more photos and finding none, he stored the photos in a folder to give to Justin and Riley. He had his doubts they'd get any fingerprints off them, but it'd be stupid not to check.

For now, he wouldn't tell Kacie about finding more. Maybe once they got the bastard, he'd let her know before he destroyed them. But there was no way in hell he'd tell her now that there were so many different ones.

Wanting to make sure security wouldn't buzz the intercom when Justin and Riley arrived, he called the desk and requested they be allowed up as soon as they arrived. Within fifteen minutes, he was at the door, letting them inside.

"Sorry to pull you guys out this late." He spared a quick glance up the stairway. "Kacie's asleep."

"How is she?" Riley asked.

"Understandably freaked out."

Justin followed Riley and Brennan into the living room. Kacie might be freaked out, but Brennan was something else. Justin hadn't seen his friend this furious since the day he buried his son. While he was glad to see that much emotion in Brennan's eyes, he couldn't help but worry. Kacie Dane and Brennan Sinclair didn't live in the same world, at least not anymore. Brennan had given the celebrity life up years ago because it had destroyed him. He sure as hell didn't need to be dragged back into it.

As soon as he and Riley sat down on the sofa, Justin said, "Okay, let's go over it again."

"Kacie and I went out for the day. When we returned, security told us that her personal assistant, Tara Greenfield, had been up to her apartment. When we got to the door, it was unlocked, slightly open."

Obviously struggling to keep his rage barely in check, Brennan told them everything that had happened since he and Kacie had returned from their day out.

When he was done, his jaw was even more rigid. "I want the life of every person she's connected to turned upside down. If someone's even looked at her sideways, I want to know—"

Justin held up his hand. "We've got the best researchers in the world. We can take care of that. My concern is this person's end game."

Brennan nodded. "If he's capable of murder, he's capable of anything."

"He?" Riley asked.

Brennan shrugged. "Just a generic term—could be either gender."

Justin didn't agree. "I don't see a woman for this. Dr. Curtis was strangled. Damn hard to kill a person that way…takes a tremendous amount of strength." He didn't add that he knew this from personal experience.

"There are some women who are just as strong as a man," Riley said. "Don't discount a female just because you think we're too weak…or too sweet."

This wasn't the time, but he was damn well going to figure out what his partner's issues were when it came to women. Within seconds of meeting Kacie's mother, Riley had pinned her as the culprit. Admittedly, the woman was a piece of work, but it just didn't play that she would do this. Kacie was her meal ticket, and while he could see Sonia anonymously blackmailing her daughter for some big bucks, he didn't see her involved in murder. And destroying Kacie would gain the woman nothing. Just made no sense.

"We'll agree to disagree about this, Ingram. Right now, we've got more than enough suspects."

"Like who?"

All eyes turned to Kacie, who stood at the door. She knew she probably looked like three-day-old roadkill but couldn't bring herself to care. They were here to discuss her case. They were talking about her life. She deserved to be in on this conversation.

Brennan stood and went to her. Her indignation at him for not including her in their discussion fizzled and disappeared. His eyes, bloodshot from lack of sleep, blazed with a need to protect and comfort. Being angry would be selfish and counterproductive. If he hadn't been here when she found that photo… She really had no clue what she would have done without him.

"Sorry to sneak up like that. I woke up, and you weren't there."

The instant she said the words, she regretted them. Both Justin's and Riley's eyes widened at the knowledge that she and Brennan had been sleeping in the same bed. She thought about explaining that Brennan had offered comfort and safety—not sex. Then she decided against explaining anything. It really wasn't anyone's business.

Brennan stood beside her and held out an arm. The way he did it gave her a choice of either taking his hand or going into his arms. For Kacie, there was no choice to be made.

Strong arms wrapped her in warmth and comfort, and Kacie gave little thought to how it looked to the two LCR operatives on the sofa. She pressed her face against Brennan's chest, drawing strength.

Finally, she lifted her head, straightened her shoulders. "Okay. Where do we go from here?"

CHAPTER TWENTY-ONE

Brennan stood under the hot pulsing beat of the shower, hoping it'd give him a few more hours of upright time before he crashed. He had a mountain of things to do today, and sleeping needed to be last on the list.

Kacie was doing some work in her office. With the hollow look in her eyes, though, he wondered just how much she could get accomplished. Still, anything that could get her mind off the shit that was happening for even a few moments was good.

Yesterday had passed in relative quiet. After the night she'd had, Kacie had held up amazingly well and had even managed to get in a couple of naps during the day. Surprising since he'd had a security company there for hours installing a security system and new locks for her doors. With this sophisticated system, even the most experienced intruders would be deterred. And with only he and Kacie having a key to the apartment, she was as safe as he could make her.

Her personal assistant, Tara Greenfield, had stopped by early this morning, and Brennan had taken a few minutes to talk to her. Questioning her without revealing what was going on gave him the leeway to talk to her in a friendly get-to-know-you manner, as opposed to grilling her like she was a suspect.

Tara was young, attractive, with a lively intelligence in her warm brown eyes. Didn't mean she wasn't guilty. Normal-looking people did incredibly abnormal deeds every damn day.

She seemed open to all his questions and even teased him that her grandfather had never forgiven Brennan for leaving the Jets. But when Brennan had asked about why she'd left college her senior year and moved back home, she'd given an evasive answer that she'd been homesick. He wasn't buying it, but without outright accusing her of lying—which he might well do at some point—he couldn't proceed beyond an understanding nod.

Kacie had insisted on being in the room with them, and while he had no problem with that, as she was Tara's employer, he had warned her to stay quiet. She'd given him a fiery look, and he'd been so glad to see the flash of temper, it was all he could do not to kiss her soundly. Thankfully, Tara had shown up before he'd gotten too stupid.

As steam loosened the tight muscles in his neck and back, he thought about Justin's words as he and Riley were leaving the other night. His friend knew him better than anyone. He'd seen the way Brennan was treating Kacie and was concerned. And because they were friends, he'd give Justin latitude he wouldn't give anyone else. However, when the man had lambasted him for getting too close to a client, it'd taken every ounce of strength not to knock him on his ass.

Getting too close to a client? Shit, yeah, he was close. But that didn't mean he had feelings for Kacie beyond his job. A young woman who'd done nothing wrong other than to try to live her life and overcome a horrendous event was being tortured by some asshole for unknown reasons. He was pissed and wanted the creep's ass in a sling. Anyone would.

It was nothing more than that.

A knock on the door barely registered before he heard Kacie calling his name. Whirling around, he was stunned to find her in the middle of the bathroom. Modesty had never been a big concern for him. Hell, he'd been in too many locker rooms with a bunch of sweaty jocks to even think twice about baring it all. Not to mention the stupid-assed underwear ad Vanessa had talked him into doing when he'd been with the Jets.

But there was another reason modesty had no issue here. Kacie had come searching for him. If it was important enough to barge in while he was showering, something major had happened.

"What's wrong?"

"I got another message."

"From the same email address?"

"No, this was sent to my Twitter account. Fans or whoever can send me direct messages or tweet me. Most of them are answered by Molly, occasionally by Tara…a few by me.

"What did it say?"

"'Hey, KC. Did you like my gift?' With a hashtag about getting what I deserve."

"Okay, let me dry off and let's take a look."

As if she'd just become aware that'd she barged into the bathroom at an inopportune time, her eyes moved from his face and roamed over his body.

Biology was a helluva thing. A gorgeous woman was standing before him, the appreciation on her face a sight no man could ignore or resist. There wasn't a damn thing he could do about his body's physical response to the heated interest in her lovely eyes.

A delightful tinge of color rose in her cheeks, and she swallowed hard. "Uh…sorry about barging in…I, um…thought you'd want to know."

Brennan swallowed a painful laugh, instinctively knowing his amusement would irreparably harm her confidence. If he hadn't been painfully hard before, he sure as hell was now, because instead of leaving in embarrassment, she continued to stand there and stare. Torn between the need to laugh out loud and the even greater need to pull her close and answer that heat in her eyes with his own, he growled, "Is there something else?"

Going an even deeper shade of red, she took one last lingering all-over-body glance and quickly shook her head. "I'll...just go."

The instant she closed the door, Brennan took a second to knock his forehead against the damp tile of the shower, hoping it would pound some sense into him. As pissed as he'd been by Justin's warning, Brennan knew his friend was right. Getting involved with a client was a dangerous thing to do. And Kacie wasn't just any client. She had a boatload of hang-ups and fears that he felt ill-equipped to handle.

Now if he could just convince his heart, mind...oh hell, his entire body.

Kacie raced back to her office as if her feet were on fire. But hot feet weren't her concern, it was other places. Secret places she had tried to pretend no longer existed were coming back to life.

She was around nearly naked men several times a week, so often that she rarely paid attention anymore. Occasionally, she'd appreciate a well-built body or impressive eight-pack abs, but she felt no physical impact. After what happened to her, she had assumed that part of her was dead.

"So let's have a look."

She'd been so deep in her thinking about Brennan and her stunning reaction to his body, she hadn't heard him behind her. Telling her nerves to settle was easier said than done. Not only did she have some lunatic wanting to destroy her, her frozen libido was melting like an igloo in the desert.

Unable to say anything remotely coherent, she twisted her laptop around so he could read the message.

Hey, KC! Did you like my gift? #Finallygoingtogetwhatyoudeserve

"Interesting hashtag, huh?"

She tried to sound calm and unaffected. She failed miserably. Questions whirled around in her head, all clamoring for answers that she could not fathom. Had this person actually killed Dr. Curtis? Where did he get the photograph? What did he want to do other than torment her? Ruin her? Extort money? Kill her?

"I didn't mention this to you before… Noah may have already told you. Harrington recorded everything. What he did to me, what others did to me."

"Yes, McCall told me."

She turned to face him, unwilling for him to think she was a coward. "They told me all the recordings were destroyed. They promised me."

"Who promised you?"

"Skylar. Noah. They all promised."

"Then they told the truth. Do you remember anyone there taking still shots?"

An unexpected sob broke through her calm façade. She hadn't even realized she was this close to breaking down, and now here she was about to become a sobbing mess.

Brennan reached out for her, but Kacie backed away from him. If he held her, she'd totally lose it.

"That's the thing…a blessing, they said. I remember almost nothing. They kept me so drugged I could barely function. Half-starved…drugged. I was delirious." She shook her head. "That vile picture. I remember nothing about it."

"Then that is a blessing. I—"

At his hesitation, dread almost consumed her. Was he going to ask about the photograph? About what it revealed?

"Listen…I wasn't going to tell you this because you've had to deal with so much, but you deserve to know. I found more photos than just that one."

Instead of more alarm, she felt irrational relief. "How many more?" she said weakly.

"Five total. They're all being checked for prints."

"They were different…than the one I found?"

"Yes."

She appreciated Brennan wanting to protect her, but appreciated even more his need to be honest with her.

"Thank you for telling me."

His eyes gleamed with something like pride. "You're handling it well."

She turned away before he could see the truth. One, or a hundred. Did it really matter when a single photograph could destroy her? The one photo she'd seen was hideous, vile, and revealed something about her. The one thing she did remember. The one thing she had never been able to share, even with her therapist. Not even Skylar knew her secret shame.

As if he knew she was trying to hide something from him, Brennan came to stand in front of her.

"Something my mom used to say to me, when things were so dark, was, 'This too shall pass.' Which means it will get better."

Her mouth twisted in a small smile. She appreciated his effort. "Did it help?"

He didn't answer for a second and then huffed out a laughing breath. "No, not really. Guess it made her feel better to say it, though."

"Okay…all right." She straightened her spine. "It's being dealt with. Lots of bright, talented people are on the case, trying to find this person. I've got the Montague press conference today. And then, tomorrow, we leave for Barbados."

"About that…don't guess there's any way to delay that shoot, is there?"

"None. It got canceled last month because of a tropical storm. Weather's supposed to be perfect. I have a contract…and unless I'm dead, I'm going."

"Don't talk like that," he snapped.

"Sorry, poor choice of words." She shook herself out of her unhelpful melancholy and focused on what she could control. "Before I forget, you do have a passport, right?"

"Yeah."

"Okay…good. We're set then. So, I'm going to get to work on hiding the dark circles under my eyes. And I'll let you and the other professionals figure out who's trying to destroy me." She gave him her brightest, most practiced smile—projecting a cheeriness she in no way felt. "I think we both have our work cut out for us."

Brennan sat offstage, behind curtains, watching the press conference on the closed-circuit television he'd requested ahead of time. If he'd shown his face, questions that had nothing to do with Kacie's new job would have been asked. He was here to protect her, not add fuel to the firestorm of gossip already raging about them.

She sat behind a table along with cosmetic and fashion icon Julian Montague, several of Montague's executives, and Sandi Winston, a gray-haired, pleasant-faced woman Kacie had introduced as her publicist.

So far the announcement had gone off without a hitch. In broad, sweeping terms, Montague described his vision for his company and how Kacie Dane would be the new Montague It Girl, hopefully for years to come. The newest fragrance, Innocence Revealed, had been designed with Kacie in mind. The newest clothing line, Sweet and Sassy, would carry the tag *A Kacie Dane Exclusive by Montague.* The new line of cosmetics was created with the intent to make fresh-faced and wholesome a fashion trend.

Montague was putting a lot on the line. Brennan understood why Kacie had insisted she had to alert Montague about the threats against her and the possibility of exposure. Even though Kacie had been an innocent victim, the media could spin what happened to her in a thousand different ways. Brennan knew from bitter experience how one tiny thread of doubt could be woven into an entire blanket of cruel innuendos and suppositions.

He admired the way Julian Montague stood behind Kacie when he learned about her attack, and her real name. That said a lot about the man and his integrity.

Other than what he'd read online, Brennan knew very little about Montague. The man was purported to be a genius, and not only in designing, and was reportedly very hands-on with the daily operation of his many businesses.

He remembered that Vanessa had tried to attract the designer's attention years ago and failed. Just one of the many failures that had led to so many damn problems for them.

Brennan studied the sea of faces in the audience. He'd been trained to detect danger in expressions and body language. Always expecting shit to happen gave him a hyper-alert sensitivity.

No one stood out as being evil or bent on any agenda other than learning about the Montague campaign and Kacie's upcoming location shoots. Brennan allowed his shoulders a small, incremental easing. Keeping one ear open to the questions being asked and his eyes focused on the audience, he let his mind wander to the coming meeting he and Kacie had later today.

The Kacie Dane Foundation was located in Midtown. Kacie had told him she worked out of the center infrequently, preferring to stay behind the scenes, allowing her excellent staff to handle the day-to-day operations of the charity. Though she was the driving force behind it, and unapologetically used her celebrity status to garner attention as well as funding, she'd freely admitted that she had absolutely no training in regards to how to run a charity or how to counsel the young women who came to the center. She'd told him that being a victim of physical abuse and rape didn't qualify her to know what to do to help others.

He liked that about her. Liked that she understood her limits but did everything within her power to help others any way she could. There were way too many things he liked about her. Probably the only thing he didn't like was that she was a successful, sought-after model who was only going to get more famous. Brennan didn't belong in her world, and the minute he knew the danger was over and she was safe, he was out of here. This was not the kind of life he ever wanted again.

And there was another reason he and Kacie could never match. He would be hell on her career. Yeah, he'd found a few people in New York who didn't hate his guts, but he was still one of the most disliked sports figures in the country. He'd made the mistake of reading an article not too long ago that had included a poll ranking the most hated athletes in the sports world. He'd been number three on the list.

It didn't matter that he had never even been a suspect in the kidnapping and death of his son. Because he had refused to give interviews or even discuss what happened, the media had called in "expert" after "expert" to analyze his state of mind, posing hypotheticals that put him at the center of the kidnapping plot. Added with Vanessa's parents' claims of abuse and neglect, and Brennan couldn't have ended up looking more guilty.

No, he liked Kacie way too much to taint what would be— once the lunatic tormenting her was caught—a long, successful, and scandal-free career for her. He was here to do a job, then he'd be out of her life forever.

Today's meeting would give him the chance to personally meet her staff. Along with his specialized training, he had an ingrained bullshit detector. If he met the person behind these "attacks" on Kacie, he felt sure he'd be able to perceive something off. And even if he couldn't, he wanted to get a look at her employees. Each person, no matter how small their connection to Kacie, was under scrutiny. No one was above suspicion.

A slight, sudden movement in the audience caught his eye. Was someone sitting behind that tall woman, second row from the back? Brennan leaned forward. Yeah, he definitely saw movement, but the person appeared to be hunkered down in his seat. Why would anyone do such a thing unless he was there for nefarious reasons?

Brennan stood, about to head to the back of the conference room. If he could, he would extricate the guy without too much disruption. If he couldn't, so be it. Kacie's safety trumped causing a scene.

A hand shot out from behind the woman, and Brennan went for his gun beneath his jacket. He stopped in mid-movement when he realized the man had his hand up to ask a question. Still not convinced that there wasn't a threat, Brennan kept his hand on his Glock. The guy was acting strangely.

The moderator called on the man, and the instant he stood, Brennan knew why the prick had been hiding. *Carlton Lorrance.* Hell, he couldn't shoot the guy for being an asshole, could he?

"Congratulations on the new gig, Kacie. In light of your reputation as being the face of wholesome innocence, I was wondering why you're dating a man many people believe murdered his son and his wife?"

Shit. Shit. Shit.

Kacie wanted to groan, loud and long. It had all been going so well. The announcement had gone off like a dream, and the questions being asked had been as smooth as if Julian Montague had written them himself.

Now this. What was this guy's problem?

She glanced over at the fashion mogul, who wasn't bothering to hide his fury that his press conference had been hijacked by a petty, malicious man who clearly wanted to make news that had nothing to do with fashion.

Before she could come up with an appropriate comeback, Julian gave a response that any diva worth her salt would have loved to have come up with.

"Excuse me, but what does that have to do with my designs? This conference is to talk about me—not Ms. Dane's private affairs. Am. I. Clear?"

Carlton Lorrance shrank back into his seat as if his legs had given out on him.

Julian glanced over at the moderator. "I'll allow one more *pertinent* question."

Thankfully, someone up front asked a question about the timing for the first magazine ad. Julian answered the question, and at last the press conference was over.

Kacie pulled the mic off the collar of her dress and stood. Though she loved many things about her chosen profession, press conferences were one of her least favorite tasks. She understood the necessity for them and certainly appreciated good press when it came her way. However, she always worried about what might be asked. Especially since she had more than enough secrets to fill every tabloid for months if they were ever discovered.

"Well, other than that small bit of unpleasantness near the end, I believe that went quite well," Julian said.

What a pleasure to work with someone who was not only brilliant but a genuinely kind person, too. The minute she'd seen him today, she had thanked him again for his support and not withdrawing his offer because of her past. He had shushed her immediately and, with a twinkle in his eyes, told her he was just glad she had survived so she could wear his masterpieces.

Kacie shook his hand, about to apologize for Lorrance's disgusting and inappropriate question, when Brennan came to stand beside her. She halted abruptly when he caught her elbow and looked down at the designer, who was an inch or two shorter than Kacie. Brennan's overwhelming presence would've intimidated most people. Julian Montague wasn't one of them.

"Mr. Sinclair, what a pleasure to meet you."

"It's good to meet you, too, sir. I apologize for the question about my past."

"You owe me no apologies. That man is a hideous toad and will not be invited back to any of my press conferences."

"You got that right," Brennan muttered softly. He said it so quietly she knew Julian hadn't heard him, but she had, along with his tone of satisfaction.

As he continued to talk with the designer, his voice pleasant and friendly, she knew a moment of amazement. He sounded as relaxed as any man talking football with another guy, but she felt the tension in his body—he was positively vibrating. He was furious, and she suspected he'd done something about, or to, Lorrance, but he was somehow able to control the anger. That kind of control was both fascinating and scary. And okay, a little hot, too.

"We'd love to have dinner when we return. Wouldn't we, darling?"

Brennan squeezed her arm, reminding her to stay in the moment. Julian had asked them to dinner at his house when they returned from Barbados.

"Yes, thank you. We'd love to come."

"Fine…fine. I'll have my assistant set it up." He glanced down at his watch. "Now I must go. Meetings to go to, people to devour." He grinned at his own humor, air-kissed Kacie, shook Brennan's hand again, and then was gone.

The instant she was sure no one could hear them, she asked, "What did you do about Lorrance?"

"Let's get out of here."

Making it clear she wouldn't get anything else from him until they were alone, he took her elbow and gently but inexorably guided her to the exit.

Chapter Twenty-Two

Brennan ushered Kacie into the elevator and pressed the button for the fifteenth floor, where her foundation offices were housed. He'd answered her questions about what he'd done about Carlton Lorrance as best he could under the circumstances. She didn't need to know just how ruthless he could be. Soon, Carlton Lorrance would have much more to worry about than an exposé on a former sports figure. He'd be too busy trying to cover his own ass.

"You have six employees working here. Correct?"

Kacie nodded. "Five full-time, one part-time. When we have a major fundraiser, like we had a few weeks ago, we bring in temps."

"How many temporary employees did you bring in for that?"

"I'll have to check with Molly, but I think maybe about ten."

The list of suspects continued to grow. Even though most of them could be eliminated fairly easy, it was still a time-consuming process that could take time away from focusing on the most likely suspects. McCall had said that he was devoting substantial manpower hours to discovering the identity of this dirtbag.

Another thing to admire about McCall. Rescuing kidnapped victims might be LCR's main focus, but when their help was needed elsewhere, he held nothing back.

"Listen, Brennan," Kacie was saying, "I know everyone needs to be checked out, but I thoroughly vetted these people. Even the temporary employees have to go through a stringent background check. I don't do that just for me—I do it for the charity. There are too many people willing to exploit others for their own gain. I make sure my employees always have our clients' best interests in mind."

"Your background check is extensive—I've seen it, and it'll be helpful in ruling everyone out. However, you have certain parameters...lines you can't cross."

She frowned up at him, and despite his best intentions, Brennan couldn't resist using his fingers to smooth the cute little line that appeared at the bridge of her nose. Damn. Had he ever touched skin this soft and silky?

"Brennan?"

The frown deepened, but her eyes glinted with the same heat he'd seen the other day when they'd kissed. It was all he could do not to bend down and take those luscious lips with his own.

Mind on your job, Sinclair.

Dropping his hand, he turned from temptation, facing the elevator door again. "You're looking for a good, dependable employee, so your focus is on that. I'm looking for someone with criminal intent. Our perspectives differ."

He didn't add that he had ways of digging deeper than most people knew was possible. And based on what McCall had said, they could dig deeper still. Because of their combined resources, Brennan felt sure that they'd find this asshole soon. Problem was, would it be soon enough?

The doors slid open, and Kacie stepped out, Brennan close behind her. It had been a long time since she'd had anyone get this close to her, either physically or emotionally. But with Brennan, it had happened extraordinarily easy. Odd, since he wasn't exactly an easy man. Those dark, brooding eyes saw through even her most practiced façade.

They walked into the office and were instantly greeted as if their visit had been anticipated.

"Kacie, I saw the interview. It was so awesome! You did a great job and you looked great, too."

She smiled at the effervescent young woman standing before her. What Molly Rowe lacked in age and height, she made up for in efficiency and skills. Though Kacie had been a little hesitant hiring someone so young, Molly had more than proven her worth.

"Thank you, Molly. It went very well." She turned to Brennan. "I'd like you to meet Brennan Sinclair."

In her cheerful, straightforward way, Molly took a step forward and held out her hand to Brennan. "It's great to meet you. I'm not one for football, but my foster dad is a huge fan. Would it be too much trouble to get a photo of us together?"

Brennan returned her handshake. "It'd be my pleasure."

"Gosh, thanks." She called over her shoulder. "Hey, guys, he's here."

Like a gaggle of excited geese, five people exploded from the conference room, practically falling over themselves to be first.

Kacie laughed at their enthusiasm. "Now, why is it you guys don't act that way when I show up by myself?"

Tammy Peterson, their computer and technical wizard, snorted inelegantly. "You're just a world-famous model. Brennan Sinclair is a legend."

"Then allow me to introduce you to a legend." She turned to Brennan who, she was pleased to see, was taking their slobbering adoration in stride.

"Brennan, this brood of over-excited juveniles is the office staff for the Kacie Dane Foundation.

"This is Tammy Peterson, our computer genius and self-proclaimed goddess of all things mechanical. And Marta Croft, our accountant and self-proclaimed princess of numbers."

She nodded her head to the middle-aged man to the right of Marta. "This is Stewart Lakes, our adman and…" She stopped and frowned. "What's your unofficial title?"

He grinned and answered in a bullfrog-gruff voice, "King of All I Survey." The grin widened. "It's a work in progress."

Kacie looked at the elderly woman standing beside Stewart. "And this is Hazel Johnson, the office manager who keeps everyone in line and on point."

Brennan shook Hazel's hand. "And what's your self-proclaimed title?"

Her watery gray eyes twinkling, she said, "Why, I'm Duchess of It All, of course."

Kacie proudly took in her small group of employees. The foundation had come a long way from one woman's vague goal of *I've got to make a difference* to this small but incredibly dedicated group of employees. She loved them all and felt fortunate to have them on her staff. The charity ran like a well-oiled machine, and it was all due to them.

Tara appeared at the door of the conference room and said, "We're ready for you."

"Ready for me?" Her eyes took in the small group. They were practically dancing with excitement. "What's up?"

"Come this way."

Molly led her to the conference room and opened the doors. Kacie gasped as she took in the décor. It was filled with balloons, and the instant she stepped inside, confetti dropped from the ceiling, swirling slowly around her like tiny, glittering stars.

"Surprise!" Voices shouted from behind her.

Kacie whirled around. "What on earth? It's not my birthday, is it?"

A goofy, sweet smile appeared on Tara's face. "You didn't think we were going to just pretend this Montague deal was just another job, did you?"

"You guys...this is so sweet."

"We're so excited for you, Kacie," Molly said. "There was no way we were going to pretend this wasn't a big deal."

"Lunch is here!" Stewart called out.

Everyone gathered in the conference room while workers from one of Kacie's favorite Italian restaurants brought in a catered lunch.

Kacie sat between Tara and Marta, answering questions and chowing down on delectable lasagna and breadsticks. Brennan sat across from her, between Molly and Stewart. Kacie couldn't decide who was asking him the most questions. But he was taking it all in stride, seeming to enjoy himself just as much as everyone else. Another thing she liked about Brennan was his ability to blend into whatever scenario he faced.

"I've been meaning to tell you that I brought those items from the drugstore you asked me to get."

Tara's soft voice reached only Kacie's ears, for which she was glad. After that amazingly hot kiss the other day, Kacie couldn't stop thinking about the possibilities of going further with this newfound sexual need Brennan had uncovered inside her. When she'd talked to Tara a few hours later, she'd asked her to pick up a few things at the pharmacy, including condoms.

Not having been in a physical relationship since before her attack, the need for birth control had never been on her radar.

Although Brennan hadn't repeated those delicious kisses, and might not want her in that way, she couldn't stop thinking about all the possibilities. For the first time in years, she wanted intimacy with a man. She wanted his mouth on hers, his hands roaming all over her body. She wanted that hot, hard male part of him she'd felt pressing into her bottom the other day. She wanted to taste him, feel him inside her.

"I put some in your bedroom nightstand, his nightstand, your office, the weight room, and in the kitchen."

"The kitchen?" Kacie practically squeaked. Glancing around to make sure no one had heard her, she whispered, "The kitchen? Seriously?"

"Yes, in the drawer where you keep your candles." Tara laughed. "You never know where you'll be when the mood might hit you. Best to be prepared for wherever."

A vivid image of Brennan lifting her up on the kitchen countertop and Kacie wrapping her legs around his waist while he—

"Why Kacie Dane, are you blushing?" Tara's teasing voice pulled her from her lust-filled thoughts.

"It's a little warm in here, don't you think?"

"Ha. Only when you're looking at six and a half feet of manly gorgeousness." Her voice went even softer. "If you want to cool down, take a look at Stewart."

Kacie did, then inwardly winced. Stewart had never done or said the least inappropriate thing, but she'd caught him more than once with a puppy-dog expression of adoration on his craggy face. She hoped it would never materialize into anything more than a crush. She would hate to lose him. Stewart was a brilliant adman who'd had a successful career at one of the most prestigious advertising companies in New York. He had retired early and claimed he wanted his second career to really count for something.

Molly stood. "Attention, everyone. I just wanted to say how very proud we are of Kacie, and"—she looked at Kacie—"I know I speak for everyone here when I say that we're blessed to know you. And, as I'm sure Kacie and Brennan probably want to go have a little celebration of their very own, let's cut the cake."

A beautiful six-layer cake with butter cream icing was rolled in, and Kacie oohed and aahed. The surface of the cake had one of her favorite photos from a jewelry commercial she did last year.

"This is just too much. I can't imagine working with brighter, more talented, or kinder people than you guys."

Before she could go all teary-eyed again, Kacie cut large slices of cake, and Tara passed them out. Though she was stuffed, she took several small bites so no one would be offended.

"We'll wrap up some to take with you," Molly said.

"Thanks, Molly." Kacie stood and was about to issue another round of appreciation when a hand grabbed her arm. She looked down at Marta, who had an unusually solemn expression on her face.

"What's up?"

"Can we talk a few minutes…privately?"

"Sure thing." She glanced at Brennan, who'd apparently heard the request. He shook his head slightly and stood, too. Outside her apartment, he wouldn't let her go anywhere without him, and while she appreciated the protection, she didn't agree with his need to be in on a meeting with her sixty-eight-year-old accountant.

"I'll be fine, Brennan. Stay here and visit with everyone. We'll be right back."

Silly her had forgotten whom she was dealing with. With an arrogant arch of an ink-black eyebrow, along with a *remember what we talked about* look, Brennan said, "That's okay. I'll be glad to come, too."

Making a big deal out of it would cause both concern and speculation, neither of which she wanted. So, putting her smile in place, she said, "Sure, come right along."

The three of them went out the door, and Kacie was pleased that the party conversation continued, without any seeming disruption or questions.

The instant the door closed behind them, Marta said, "I don't want to worry you, Kacie, not when you have so much on your mind, but I have something I need to show you."

Her irritation with Brennan was completely forgotten. The look on Marta's face gave her a grim warning that, once more, a day that had been going so well was about to turn sour.

Brennan apparently agreed, because he took her hand and squeezed it gently. "Steady. It might be nothing."

She nodded and, still holding Brennan's hand, she followed Marta into the office she shared with Stewart.

Marta closed the door and then went to Stewart's desk. "I was looking for a black pen this morning—mine are all red, for some reason. Anyway, I know Stewart keeps an assortment in his desk and figured he wouldn't mind me borrowing one. I opened his bottom drawer and found these."

She opened the drawer and withdrew a folder. "I wouldn't have even opened it except one of the photographs slid out, showing half your face. I recognized you immediately."

Placing the folder on the desk, she opened it to reveal dozens of photographs—all of Kacie. Some were of her jogging, a few of them had been taken at parties. At least a dozen of them were from a campaign she'd done last year for a swimsuit designer. The photos were neither explicit nor distasteful. But whoever had taken them had been at the shoot. These weren't professional pictures from a talented photographer, but candid shots.

Kacie's mouth went dry. Was Stewart stalking her? Was he responsible for all of this? Did he somehow find out she was Kendra Carson and planned to blackmail her? If so, how had he gotten still shots of her with Harrington? And was he honestly capable of murdering Dr. Curtis?

Kacie shook her head. "This makes no sense. Stewart just isn't a stalker kind of person."

"We'll discuss later what a stalker kind of person looks like," Brennan said, "but for now, tell me which photograph is the latest one that you can remember."

Taking a breath to steady her jittery nerves, Kacie went through each shot, able to identify by the outfit she was wearing where and when it had been taken. Most of them seemed to be from last year. She came to the last one, and her breath hitched.

"What?" Brennan asked.

Holding up a photograph by the corner, she said, "This is the latest one."

"When and where were you?"

"It was the day I was attacked in the park. The first time I heard the words 'He's coming for you.'"

Chapter Twenty-Three

Brennan hustled Kacie into the waiting taxi. After Marta had shown her the photographs in Stewart's desk, she'd been noticeably subdued. Since he didn't want anyone questioning why, he'd suggested they leave immediately. The excuse that they had to pack for Barbados was as good as any. Apparently, no one had detected anything off. They'd all waved cheerfully as he and Kacie headed into the elevator.

Marta seemed to have perked up once she'd revealed her discovery. After Kacie assured her that it was most likely a silly crush that Stewart would get over, Marta acted as if she totally agreed and there was nothing to worry about.

Brennan knew differently. Stalkers were unpredictable. Could this really be just a silly crush? Was Stewart just a lonely older guy who'd developed an affection for a beautiful, vivacious woman?

Kacie said the photograph had been taken before she was assaulted by the skaters. The photo had shown her with a hot dog and soda in her hand, headed to a park bench. So it was possible that while Stewart might be stalking Kacie, it didn't necessarily mean he was the asshole torturing her. But just how coincidental was it that one of the photographs was of Kacie in the park right before she was knocked down by the skaters? Not bloody likely.

On the way back to her apartment, he'd texted Justin with the information they'd discovered and the instructions to turn the lives of every one of Kacie's employees upside down. In a very short while, he expected to know everything, including underwear size and if they recycled their plastic.

No, Kacie wouldn't like it, and he had no intention of telling her just how far he'd go to get information.

She believed in her staff, thought she knew everything she needed to know. And while they all seemed supportive and proud of their employer, *seemed* was the operative word. It was easy enough to maintain an act if you had a different agenda.

They got out of the taxi, and Brennan placed his hand on Kacie's lower back as they went into her apartment building. Giving a nod to Gregory, the security guard at the desk, Brennan ushered Kacie into the elevator and then into her apartment. She'd been quiet on the drive back, and he wondered if the shock of finding Stewart's photos was about to wear off.

She stood in the middle of the apartment as if unsure of her next move. He wanted to come up with something reassuring. She deserved none of this trouble, and he wanted to fix it for her. Take care of all these issues so he could see her smile that sweet, innocent smile without a hint of worry in her eyes.

"It may not be him for all of this."

She whirled around. "You really think so?"

Brennan winced. He rarely said impulsive things, and he'd only said that because he wanted to make her feel better. She was searching for a reasonable explanation and a way to exonerate Stewart. Brennan didn't have one, and no matter how badly he wanted her to feel safe, he wouldn't lie. Besides, burying her head in the sand was not Kacie's way. She would want the truth, straight up.

"I don't know, Kacie. Sometimes the people we trust the most are the ones who end up tearing our guts out."

Warm compassion on her face, Kacie stepped forward and took his hand. "I'm so sorry you were hurt like that."

Rarely without words, Brennan found himself speechless. Here she was dealing with the nightmare of possibly having all of her secrets revealed, her life torn apart again, not to mention the extreme likelihood that one of her employees was stalking her, and she was trying to comfort him.

Unable to be this close to her and not hold her, Brennan pulled her forward. He watched for any sign of fear or unease and saw only anticipation and desire. Telling himself he was a crazy, insane, stupid fool didn't stop him from lowering his head and covering her lips with his.

Holy sweet hell, she tasted better than he remembered. Like a fantasy inside a dream. He wanted to devour her sweet mouth and then move down until he'd tasted every sweet, sexy inch of her.

Brennan didn't know if he had ever held something so exquisite in his arms. Kacie was lovely inside and out, and he wanted to cherish her in the way she deserved. He'd read up on how to handle a sexual-assault victim and didn't want anything to trigger those memories. But she had told him she remembered nothing about the assaults and torture she had endured. If that was the case, could he go further without scaring her?

Long, slender arms wrapped around his body as she moved in closer. He heard her moan, and when he pulled his mouth from hers and trailed a kiss down her neck, she released a soft, sighing breath. Everything told him she was right there with him. He hoped to hell he was reading the signs right, because he definitely didn't want to stop.

Heated and needy and so incredibly aroused, Kacie could barely think straight. Every sexual experience she'd ever had couldn't have prepared her for this want and desire. She blocked her mind to that other horrific event. It didn't belong here, and she wouldn't allow it. Brennan's mouth, both hot and tender, moved over her neck and then pressed soft kisses to her bare shoulders. He was going slow...too slow. She was burning with need and had a feeling that until she got him inside her body, that heat would continue to build.

"Brennan?"

"Hmm?" he said against her neck.

"Take me to bed?"

Before she got her entire sentence out, he was lifting her into his arms.

"Hold on," he said.

Wrapping her arms around his neck, she held tight and never moved her eyes from his face. Earlier, she had admired his extreme control, but judging by the grinding of his teeth and the working of his jaw, that control was being sorely tested. She loved that she could do that to him.

He carried her up the stairway and then down the hallway to his bedroom. Never once did he act as if he strained to carry her weight. His strength and endurance boded well for a glorious night ahead.

He stopped just inside the door, and she saw his expression change.

"What's wrong?"

"I don't have any protection. I'm clean...I know that, but if you'd rather—"

She pressed a finger to his mouth, feeling quite pleased and mature that she had taken care of that herself. "Condoms are in the drawer of the nightstand."

The fire in his eyes went to a blaze. Striding to the bed, he laid her across the spread and then followed her down. Covering her mouth with his again, the kiss began sweet and light. Brennan played gently with her lips, then licked the seam of her mouth with a slow, sensual glide. Kacie gasped at the surge of arousal from that erotic caress. As if that was his cue, his tongue delved deep into her mouth, twisting and tangling with hers. They devoured each other's mouths for endless, delicious minutes. Just when she thought she would go wild with need, Brennan pulled back, and Kacie was relieved to see that his breath was coming much faster, too.

His eyes roamed over her face and then followed her body all the way down to her feet. "You are without a doubt the most beautiful, most sensuous woman I've ever seen."

Kacie raised her hand and caressed his strong jaw, loving how his five o'clock shadow tingled against her palm. "I've never wanted anyone the way I want you."

His eyes were like glittering dark emeralds. "Kacie..." He dropped his mouth against the hollow of her neck. "You're unbelievable."

Wanting and needing to feel his skin next to hers, she began to unbutton his shirt. He'd worn a white shirt beneath his suit jacket, but she was relieved there was no tie she had to deal with. Buttons were hard enough for her nervous fingers.

With a sexy, knowing smile, Brennan covered her fingers with his and helped her. When at last his shirt was undone all the way to where it disappeared inside his pants, Kacie spread his shirt wide and sighed with delicious relief at the hot velvet silk of his chest. A sprinkling of dark coarse hair went down the middle of his chest and, like his shirt, disappeared behind his pants. She'd once heard that called a happy trail, and she could certainly see the reasoning. It would make her exceedingly happy if she could follow that trail wherever it led.

Brennan sat up and tugged his shirt from his pants. She heard shoes dropping. Before she could think about kicking hers off, his hands were there, taking them off for her. She hadn't worn any kind of tights on her legs, and she heard an appreciative hum when his fingers discovered that. Hard, callused hands, both rough and tender, caressed her legs, from ankles to her knees and then behind one knee, up one thigh.

Kacie wiggled a little, surprised to discover this particular area seemed to have a direct connection to her sex, which had been on a slow throb that was now increasing in tempo.

"Like that?"

"How did you know?"

"Your eyes went wide with surprise. I like that you don't hide your desire from me." He stopped caressing and said, "Let's get you out of that dress."

Kacie went to sit up, and Brennan pressed against her shoulders to keep her still. "Just turn slightly so I can get to your back."

She did what he asked and heard the slight rasp of her zipper, along with a cool wash of air over naked skin. He then pulled the dress off her shoulders and slid it down her body, leaving her in only her bra and a thong. "Oh holy, holy hell." he whispered.

She smiled at the reverence in his voice that was also a little shaky. She truly felt beautiful in his arms, even cherished. No man had ever made her feel so wanted.

"Kacie, look at me for a second."

She looked up at his face and knew a moment of trepidation. Was he about to stop?

"What's wrong?"

"If at any time I do something that scares you, you'll let me know. Right? I'm trusting you with that."

"Absolutely. But everything feels wonderful."

"I'm glad. But if I go too fast or say or do something that you don't like, I want you to say so."

Wanting him to stop worrying, because she really was completely fine, Kacie reached for this belt. She heard his gasp and knew she'd surprised him with her boldness. She liked surprising him, throwing him off guard, and she was delighted that she was comfortable enough with him to be bold. She unbuckled the belt, unbuttoned the front button, and then slowly unzipped his pants. Her fingers brushed against the hot, hard length straining for freedom, and she couldn't resist tracing the thick bulge lightly with her finger.

"Oh..."

"You like that?" she asked softly.

"Give me twenty—thirty minutes, and I'll answer you."

Laughing with satisfaction, she cupped him in her hand and marveled at the heat, the hardness. And then she swallowed hard, slightly nervous at his size.

Brennan surged to his feet and stripped off his pants and underwear in one sweeping move. Kacie's eyes went wide, and she gulped again. Okay, that was a little bit bigger than she had anticipated.

Brennan laughed. "You keep looking at me like that, I'll get a big head."

"Um, well, you already have a big..." She couldn't finish the sentence, suddenly ridiculously shy.

Joining her on the bed, Brennan leaned over her and said, "I'll make sure to go slow. And I'll make sure you're so ready for me, I'll slide right into you without causing any pain."

The husky, raspy promise caused an amazing response to her sex. Could a person climax from words alone? She had a feeling that if anyone could make that happen, this man could.

And, of course, Brennan would make sure she was ready to take him. He had shown time and again how extraordinarily gentle he could be, and he always took care of her when she was frightened. She couldn't exactly say she felt fright, but she did feel a bit of alarm that he might not exactly fit inside her. She knew she could stop him at any time...trusted him not to hurt her.

Brennan saw the relief on her face and felt his own relief. If he did anything to scare her, to break the bond of trust that they'd established, he'd never forgive himself. He unsnapped the front closure of her bra and then pulled the material apart. Never had he seen anyone lovelier—she was a variety of different shades of pink and cream. Like a beautiful, delicate confection, and he wanted to devour every sweet, silky inch of her.

She was perfectly proportioned, with an elegant neck that sloped down to soft, gleaming shoulders. Her breasts were actually a little larger than he had guessed and were, like the rest of her body, beautifully shaped. He cupped them and marveled at how well they fit in his hands. Her nipples were a light rose color, and when his thumbs raked over them, they stood to attention and went even rosier.

Dying for a taste but determined to first get them both bare, he reluctantly left her breasts and moved his hands down her flat, smooth stomach. His fingers slid under the band of her thong, and he watched her carefully as he pulled until it was around her ankles. When she wiggled to get it completely off, Brennan's fear disintegrated. She wanted this just as much as he did, was just as eager.

Unable to wait another moment, he pulled her against him just so he could feel her naked body against his. It was better than any fantasy he'd ever entertained. "You feel so damn good," he growled.

"You do, too." She wrapped her arms around him. "I can't believe this is happening."

Releasing her slightly, he looked down at her. "Still okay?"

"More than okay. I feel like I've been asleep for years and am just waking up."

"Then let me kiss the sleeping beauty to wake her up even more."

He made this kiss more carnal, hotter, deeper. To arouse, to prepare. His tongue matched the movements that his cock would soon be making inside her.

With a moan of approval, Kacie returned the kiss with just as much carnality and heat. Even though he wanted to be inside her, Brennan didn't want to rush it either. He wanted her so needy, so wild with desire, that coming together would be the only thing she could think of to satisfy that need.

Starting back at her neck again, his mouth traveled a familiar route, but when he got to her breasts, he had to stop, to taste… to adore. As he sucked a nipple deep into his mouth, one of his hands held her head and the other smoothed down her torso and stopped just short of her sex. He released her nipple with a pop and then raised his head to look at her. With deliberate intent, his eyes watching for any sign of fear or negative feelings, he delved his fingers between the folds of her sex. What he found shook him to his core. She was wet and hot, so incredibly aroused he knew a moment of insanity. Frozen, his mouth clenched, he fought for control. The need to slide into that hot, tight channel was almost more than he could handle.

When his eyes went to her face again, that control was won. The trust in her expression steeled his resolve.

She kept her eyes on him, letting him see she wasn't scared, that she was in the moment with him. She wanted this just as much as he did. Using his fingers, one, then two, he sank deeper to rouse her even more. Her eyes flickered closed as she became wetter, and then she began to undulate against his fingers. As much as he wanted to be inside her, he wanted Kacie's pleasure first. Seeing her come apart would be an incredible sight.

She rode his fingers, her hips rising, twisting. She was close, right on the cusp. Just when he knew she was at the edge, a half second from letting go, her eyes went wide with shock, horror. All motion stopped, and she rolled onto her stomach with a small, keening cry.

What. The. Hell?

Kacie sobbed into her hands, hiding her face from Brennan. Oh God, she couldn't believe she'd let that happen. Couldn't believe she had panicked like that. What must he think of her?

"Kacie...talk to me." A hand tentatively touched her shoulder. "Let me help you. What did I do that scared you?"

No, no, no. She couldn't stay here and listen to this. He thought he was the one at fault, and it was all her. She was the dysfunctional, screwed-up weirdo. She was mortified...humiliated.

Unable to look at him, she quickly slid across the bed to the other side.

"Where are you going? What—"

Feeling lower than a slug, she whispered hoarsely, "I'm so sorry," and ran from the room.

She made it to her bedroom in seconds and locked the door, because if she didn't, he'd barge in and want to talk. She didn't think she'd ever be able to face him again, much less talk to him. How could she have let herself get carried away like that? She hadn't known how it would affect her, but she should have suspected.

How was she ever going to explain this to him?

The knock on the door was inevitable.

"Kacie, talk to me. Are you okay?"

"I'm fine." She grimaced at how very unfine her hoarse, quivering voice sounded. Clearing her throat, she tried again. "I'm fine, Brennan, really. And you didn't do anything wrong. It's me."

"But I—"

"Can we talk in the morning? It's been a really long day."

"Yeah…sure. I…" He huffed out a breath. "For what it's worth, I'm sorry. I shouldn't have…" Another harsh breath. "I'm just sorry."

Kacie heard his footsteps as he walked away and finally gave in to the tears that were bursting to be set free. Beneath the harsh sobs of a heartbroken woman, she heard the hideous words she told herself she'd never hear again: *You'll never belong to anyone but me, my precious jewel. I'm never going to let you go.*

And he had been right.

Brennan jerked on a pair of jeans and paced around his bedroom. Calling himself every vile name that'd ever been created would never alleviate the guilt of what he'd just let happen. After knowing what she'd gone through, how could he have let himself believe she was ready to be intimate with a man?

He knew about PTSD. Knew even odd, obscure things could trigger a horrific memory. After what she'd been through, it only made sense that sexual intimacy, especially the first time since her ordeal, would bring memories to the forefront.

It didn't matter that she had assured him she was okay. It'd been his responsibility to take care of her, and he had failed miserably.

And that hadn't been all he'd discovered. He now knew the reason she didn't wear bikinis. There might be truth to her claims that wearing more modest suits went better with the persona she'd created for herself, but that wasn't the biggest reason. He'd seen that reason as she'd raced out his bedroom door. A tattoo at the base of her spine. The writing had been small, but when she'd gotten to the door, the light had been on her back, and he'd read the words. *Precious Jewel.*

Why the hell had she never had it removed? He knew that tattoo removals could be painful, but hell, could it be more painful than the constant reminder of what she'd endured?

She lived with that every day. Saw it whenever she looked in the mirror.

Shaking his head at how very messed up everything was, he grabbed his cellphone and made a call he didn't want to make. It was the right thing to do.

McCall answered on the first ring. "Sinclair, what's up?"

There was no point in hiding behind his pride—Kacie's emotional well-being had to come first. "I screwed up. Kacie may not want me to guard her any longer."

"Explain."

"We got…intimate. She freaked out—my fault."

"Freaked out…how? Do I need to send someone over there to calm her down…be with her?"

That would probably embarrass Kacie even more. "No. I think she's okay." Brennan closed his eyes. But what the hell did he know?

McCall huffed out a breath, and Brennan couldn't help the mortification that swept through him. It had been a long time since he'd been called on the carpet by an employer.

His first job with LCR—one that so far hadn't involved much more than escorting a beautiful woman to a few events—and he'd messed it up. He was a trained professional and knew better than to become involved with the primary. It was not only unethical, it was a sure path to disaster. Having his focus on anything other than keeping Kacie safe could put her in more danger.

"Did she say she wants you to go?"

"No." Not yet, anyway.

"Then let's wait. I know she's talked to Skylar and Gabe several times and had nothing but good things to say about you. And from what I've heard from Kelly and Ingram, she seems to trust you."

"Yeah…until tonight."

"Don't beat yourself up, Sinclair."

Before Brennan could say thanks for the surprising support, McCall added, "I'll be doing that myself if anything happens to Kacie. Got it?"

Brennan grunted out a surprised laugh but knew the man spoke the truth. "Yeah…got it."

"Kelly told me about the photos you were shown at her office—apparently taken by one of her employees."

"That's the story."

"You have your doubts?"

"Seems too damn convenient. However, this Stewart guy does have a crush on her. That's not something he even bothers to hide."

"If he's not hiding it…everyone knows about it. Yes, seems like he'd be a convenient scapegoat. What do you think about the woman who showed them to you?"

"She's mid-sixtyish. If she's involved…" Suddenly weary, Brennan wiped his hand down his face. "Hell, I don't know. People can do all sorts of shit for all different kinds of reasons."

"You got that right. We'll dig deeper into everyone and see what we can see."

"We're leaving for Barbados tomorrow afternoon."

"Will be interesting to see if things die down until she gets back."

"Yeah. She's not taking any of her people. Be a good test."

"Update me when you have something."

"Will do. And McCall, thanks for…" For not firing me or telling me what an asshole I am. "Just, thanks."

"We've all been there, Sinclair."

And with those enigmatic words, the LCR leader ended the call.

CHAPTER TWENTY-FOUR

Kacie braced herself for what lay outside her bedroom door. After hiding out all evening and overnight, she was sick of the four walls but mostly sick of herself. She knew for a fact that Brennan blamed himself for what happened yesterday, and none of it was his fault. Now she just needed to find the guts to apologize.

With one last breath for courage, she opened the door. The apartment was quiet, but he was still here. Not only would he never leave her alone without telling her, she could feel his presence. Brennan had such a strong personality that even when he wasn't in view, his overall aura could still be felt.

As she made her way downstairs and into the kitchen for coffee, she rehearsed again what she would say to him. He probably thought she was a neurotic basket case. Last night she had been. Today she was something else.

"Good morning."

She jerked around, sloshing coffee onto the counter.

"Careful."

She'd barely registered that the hot liquid had landed on her hand and burned her skin before Brennan was holding her hand under cold water at the sink.

"Does it hurt?"

"No…it's fine."

"Sorry I startled you." He took a deep breath. "The last thing I want to do is hurt you, Kacie. You know that. Right?"

Gently pulling her hand from his grasp, she turned off the water and then dried her hand on the dishtowel beside the sink. Handing him the towel, she said softly, "You haven't hurt me, Brennan. I'm so ashamed for the way I acted last night. I—"

He held up his hand to halt her apology. "Please do not apologize to me. I should never have pushed you like that."

"You didn't push me. I wanted you so much." She closed her eyes for a brief moment. "I just…I don't know. I just panicked."

"Which is understandable. With everything that's going on, the last thing you need is some random guy trying to get you into bed."

Her mouth lifted in a sideways smile. "You're as far from 'some random guy' as the earth is from the sun. And you did nothing I wasn't one hundred and fifty percent onboard with. Got that?"

He gave her a smile, but his eyes still held shadows. "Got it."

She cleared her throat. "So…in light of all that's going on, I thought it might be a good idea to talk to my therapist before we leave. I called her last night, and she's kindly agreed to come by this morning."

"I'll stay out of your way. I just—"

"What?"

"I need you to tell me the truth about something."

Her heart took a giant leap into her throat. Did he suspect what her real issue was? She froze, waiting for her bitter humiliation to be complete. Or was it something less excruciating but still painful? He had to have seen her back—and the tattoo. Was he going to ask why the hell she hadn't had it removed?

"Would you rather I leave and let someone else take my place? I'm not saying I want to leave, but if it would make you more comfortable, I will."

The question took her completely off guard and pushed her own messed-up issues aside. "Absolutely not."

She had the sudden need to touch him, have a physical connection to him, to make her point. Placing one hand on his arm, she cupped his strong jaw in her other hand and looked directly into his eyes so he could see her sincerity. "I do not want you to leave, Brennan. Please."

He nodded, and even though he was as hard to read as a philosophy book printed in ancient Greek, she was sure she saw a flicker of relief in his eyes.

Feeling slightly better, Kacie pulled away and said, "Dr. Crenshaw will be here in about ten minutes."

"I'll make myself scarce and finish packing."

"The Talbot Company, the group that owns the resort where we're going, is sending a car to take us to the airport. Should be here at one o'clock. We'll be traveling in a private plane, which will be nice, but David Stallings and his girlfriend will be on the flight, too."

"You don't like them?"

As she envisioned Brennan's reaction to David and his current girl of the week, she perked up. It would make for a couple of entertaining hours if nothing else. "You'll see."

Kacie opened the door and gave a warm greeting to Dr. Crenshaw. She'd been seeing the therapist for several years now, and thanks to her, Kacie was tremendously better. Not completely well, though, or last night would have had a very different ending.

After quickly introducing Brennan as her friend, Kacie led her therapist into her office. Though she hadn't told Brennan her plans, she was going to explain to Dr. Crenshaw all the things that had been going on. Perhaps those things had helped trigger what had happened last night. In her heart of hearts, she knew that to be a lie, but the thought was a brief, if false, comfort.

"You're looking lovely as ever, Kacie, but you have shadows beneath your eyes that you didn't have last time we met."

Perceptive as always, the well-put-together Dr. Crenshaw could detect trouble on a patient's face as easily as Kacie could spot a shoe sale. It was a gift.

Even though Riley and Justin had talked with Dr. Crenshaw already, Kacie knew they hadn't gone into detail with the doctor about what was going on with her. "Some really weird things have been happening."

"Like what?"

Kacie started from the beginning, describing everything: the attack at the park, the threatening messages, the phone call with Harrington's voice, the Twitter and text messages, the break-in at her apartment, the photograph she'd found, as well as the pictures they'd found yesterday in Stewart's drawer.

"Well, my goodness, no wonder you have shadows. Just one of those things would cause endless hours of worry for someone. But with your history, I'm surprised you look as calm as you do."

"Brennan has helped."

"Tell me about him. Last time we talked, you weren't seeing anyone. And now, if I'm not mistaken, he's staying here?"

"Yes…" Kacie shrugged. She didn't mind spilling her own guts, but revealing Brennan's real role felt instinctively wrong. For many reasons, LCR preferred complete anonymity. Not telling the doctor he was an LCR operative would make no difference in the issues she intended to discuss.

"We started seeing each other recently, but with all these crazy things happening, I just feel safer if he's here."

"Totally understandable. And your relationship with him? When you called last night, you said you'd had a flashback. Did it have to do with being intimate with Brennan?"

"Yes…and no."

"How so?"

This was probably one of the hardest moments she'd ever had in therapy, and it was her own damned fault. If she'd just come out and told the doctor years ago, they might've gotten her past this issue, and last night could have been wonderful instead of just the opposite.

"Take your time, Kacie. I know this is hard, but remember, there's absolutely no judgment when we're together."

She nodded, closed her eyes, and began. "When I told you I remembered almost nothing of my…time with Harrington, it was true. What I didn't tell you was I do remember one specific thing, something I barely let myself acknowledge."

A shudder of a breath, and then she said the unthinkable: "Pleasure."

"You mean you had an orgasm while you were being raped?"

Kacie opened her eyes, expecting to see censure or, at the very least, surprise at her confession. All she saw was compassion and understanding.

She stumbled through the explanation. "He gave me something each time he…" She tried to swallow, but her mouth was too dry to do so. "He wanted me compliant… unable to fight. But whatever he gave me loosened my inhibitions. It didn't matter that he was a perverted freak of a man…

didn't matter that I didn't want it to happen. I felt pleasure...I climaxed repeatedly."

"That's not all that unusual. Surely you know that. In addition, you were drugged and had no control over your body."

"I feel like I betrayed myself...my body, my emotions... my intellect. I should've fought him...done something to make him stop."

"The mind is a powerful thing, Kacie, but even so, when under the influence of certain drugs, you have no control over your mind or your body. Harrington gave you drugs to inhibit your free will, take away your choice. Rape is not just an assault on the body...it's an assault on the mind."

"But I shouldn't have enjoyed it."

"When your mind is blurred, your thoughts of right and wrong, good and bad, are compromised. Your body, not in tune with your mind, felt pleasure and responded accordingly. On top of that, he may have given you an aphrodisiac as well."

"Those things really exist?"

"Yes...legal and illegal ones. What I'm trying to say, Kacie, and which I believe you know in your heart, you were not responsible for anything that happened with that man. Not for the abduction, for the rapes and also not for any perceived pleasure your rapist instigated against your will."

"I do know that, but—"

"But...Brennan?"

"Yes. We tried to—I mean I tried—" She shook her head. "It was a disaster."

Showing just how perceptive she really was, Dr. Crenshaw cocked her head. "All of it was a disaster, or just one part?"

"The kissing part was wonderful. Having him hold me... being close to him, even without clothes on was—"

She blushed a deep red as she realized she was becoming heated just thinking about Brennan's body and how good he'd felt.

"Anyway…all of that felt really good. But then—"

"He moved on top of you…slid his penis inside you… said something?"

"No…that wasn't it."

Comprehension came and was followed instantly by gentle compassion and understanding. "He gave you pleasure."

"Yes. I was on the verge of a powerful orgasm, and then it hit me that I'd felt that way with Harrington. I thought I was going to be sick. I felt so much shame."

"So everything worked fine up until that pivotal moment?"

"Yes, it was…sublime." She laughed softly. "I was even a little assertive, which I didn't expect from myself, especially in bed. But Brennan…I don't know. He made me feel comfortable…safe, as if there wasn't anything I could do that was wrong or out of place."

"Kacie, I don't think you're looking at this in the proper perspective. You have come so far in your recovery, and I'm extraordinarily proud of you."

Kacie blinked her surprise. She had assumed Dr. Crenshaw would see this as, at the very least, a setback, if not a total relapse.

"But why? I failed…miserably."

"No, my dear, you did not fail. You admitted that being intimate with a man felt good and right. That's a huge achievement. You need to celebrate that."

"But I didn't get to that pinnacle. And I most certainly didn't get Brennan to it." She winced inwardly and then blushed as she remembered how hard and erect he'd been. The least she could've done was give him pleasure even if she couldn't take her own.

"Do you know how long an orgasm lasts?"

"Um…no." That was one area of research she'd never considered conducting.

"On average, about eighteen to twenty seconds."

"That's really…"

"Short. But the journey to get there is…" She cocked her head again. "To use your word…sublime."

"So you think…?"

"I think you need to enjoy that journey, and you'll get to the destination. But let me ask you something we've not talked about. How did Brennan react to your response?"

"He blamed himself, which made me feel terrible. None of it was his fault. I told him that, but—"

"So you explained why you stopped him?"

"Well…no. I just told him it wasn't his fault."

"Do you hope to continue seeing him? You certainly seem to care for him."

After this was over, would he be interested in continuing to see her? As an LCR operative, he might be out of the country for months at a time, but when he was available, would he want to be with her?

Kacie didn't know the answer to that but could say with one hundred percent certainty, "Yes, I definitely want to continue seeing him."

"Then don't you think you need to share this with him? He deserves to know, don't you agree?"

Of course he did, and if she hadn't been such a sniveling coward last night, she would have—

"No…none of that, Kacie. I see the guilt on your face, and you need to get over that right now. You had just cause to react the way you did, and your embarrassment in explaining it to Brennan is understandable. However, don't you think he deserves to know?"

"Yes...of course, you're right."

Dr. Crenshaw glanced at the clock and stood. "I know you're getting ready to leave for your trip, so I'll take my leave. But first I wanted to tell you how very happy I am at your progress and that you have a young man who seems to care for you. You deserve only the best."

"I so appreciate your help. And thanks for coming to my apartment, and on such short notice."

"That's not a problem. One other thing, I encourage you to open up a strong line of communication with Brennan. If he's as wonderful as you believe, then this will only make your relationship stronger."

Kacie nodded, and after thanking the doctor once again, she said good-bye.

Now, she just needed to figure out how to get up the courage to take the good doctor's advice.

Chapter Twenty-Five

Brennan had never experienced a giggling headache before, vicarious or otherwise. Hadn't known such a thing even existed until he met David Stallings and his incredibly well-endowed girlfriend, Britney. And he certainly had never known that a grown man could even giggle.

Now he knew why Kacie had given him that little secret smile earlier. She knew exactly what they were in for.

She looked better than she had when she'd come out of her bedroom this morning. There was still that tiny line of worry at the bridge of her nose, but she seemed to be more at peace. He hoped like hell he wasn't just seeing what he wanted to see to make himself feel better.

The flight had taken off on time. They'd been greeted by the pilot, co-pilot, and a flight attendant, and within minutes were off the ground. The instant the captain alerted them that they were free to move around the cabin, the two giggle boxes had unbuckled their seat belts, accepted cocktails from the flight attendant and, in between giggles and occasional guffaws, proceeded to make out on the sofa across the aisle.

"Having a good time?"

Brennan twisted in his chair to look at Kacie, appreciating the view much more than any sight out the window. She looked fresh and lovely in a light blue sleeveless dress and matching sandals that showed off her slender, elegant feet with light pink polish on her toenails.

"You've traveled with this couple before?"

"Not as a couple, but I've traveled with David several times. He always has a different woman with him."

"And they all…giggle?"

She laughed softly, and he had the silly, poetic thought that her laughter was like a warm, soft breeze floating across wind chimes.

"Every single one of them. David is known for his giggling girlfriends."

"Didn't he do a cologne commercial where he was a bull-riding cowboy?"

"That was him. Why?"

Brennan shook his head. "I just have preconceived notions about a bull rider, and none of them involves giggling like a ten-year-old girl."

"Then you'll be doubly disappointed to learn that Britney plays a neurosurgeon on the soap opera *To Live for Tomorrow*."

"That doesn't surprise me in the least. Every neurosurgeon fantasy I've ever had looked exactly like Britney."

She grinned. "I'm glad at least one of your notions held up."

"You look like you're feeling better about things."

"Yeah, I am." She lowered her gaze for a moment and then raised her head again and said with more confidence, "I really am."

"I'm glad."

Since neither of them wanted to try to have a serious discussion while in the presence of the overamorous giggle twins, he said, "So tell me about the shoot. It's for a new resort. Right?"

For the next half hour, she described the new Rosalina resort and what the shoot would entail.

"We won't have a lot of free time during the day, but other than a few photographs of us decked out in dinner duds dining on..."

She halted, and with a grin Brennan helped her out, "Dungeness crabs and Diet Dr Pepper."

Showing her appreciation of his humor in a surprising way, she leaned over and hugged him. "Thanks. Most people don't get my corny sense of humor."

Instead of moving away from him, she let her head stay on his shoulder as if it was the most natural thing in the world. Brennan was humbled by her trust and ease with him, especially after the disaster of last night. And when he realized she'd fallen asleep, the ice around his heart cracked just a little more.

Kacie stood in the unbelievably beautiful bungalow of the Rosalina resort, Brennan beside her. The limo driver quickly deposited their suitcases, thanked Brennan for the tip and left.

She was still groggy from the plane. Waking up on Brennan's shoulder had been a shock, but in the best way possible. It had been a long time since she'd felt comfortable enough in another person's presence to fall asleep like that. And he hadn't seemed to mind. She'd apologized, and he'd given her a slow, sexy smile and said he'd gladly act as her pillow anytime.

The giggle twins, as Brennan referred to them, were thankfully on the other side of the resort. She didn't know how that happened and wasn't going to ask. She was just grateful for the privacy. Especially since this new dilemma had presented itself. The bungalow was beautiful, elegant, and had all the amenities. It also had only one bed.

Casting a nervous look up at Brennan, she said, "I guess when I told them I was bringing my boyfriend with me, they assumed we'd be sleeping together."

"Not a problem. I'll sleep on the sofa."

Together, they looked at the sofa, and Kacie shook her head. "There's no way your six-and-a-half-foot frame is going to fit on that five-foot sofa."

She turned so she could look up at him. She'd yet to explain about last night, so he was understandably wary. Now wasn't the time to go into it.

"Listen, we're adults. We can sleep in the same bed without anything happening."

"You're sure?"

"Yes…very sure."

Relieved that the problem had been settled so easily without an argument, she took her bag and headed into the bedroom. "I don't know about you, but I could eat half the fish in the ocean about right now."

"I'll split them with you."

"Then let's change clothes and go find something scrumptious."

There were a helluva lot harder jobs than sitting beneath a giant umbrella, downing some sort of froufrou fruit juice drink, and watching one of the most beautiful women in the world frolic in the waves. The only thing ruining Brennan's view was the damn photographer.

They'd been here for two days and the most strenuous thing he'd had to do was hold back his desire for Kacie. That was quickly becoming an unstoppable force of nature.

The first day, after a surprisingly relaxing and delicious meal of fresh sushi, grilled trout, and crème brûlée, he and Kacie had walked around the resort. Though it wasn't officially open yet, he was surprised by the number of people staying there. One of the things he liked about it was the fact that, though there were a lot of people around, it didn't feel crowded or too commercialized.

Yesterday Kacie had met with the photographer, the other model, Stallings, and the resort's publicity department. Brennan had insisted on attending as well and figured he was viewed as a cross between an overbearing, controlling boyfriend and a humorless cyborg. He did nothing but stand in the background and maintain an expressionless if somewhat threatening demeanor.

He'd thought sleeping in the same bed might pose some problems, especially for Kacie. That hadn't been the case. Both nights, by the time he'd finished showering, she was already deeply asleep and, from what he could tell, didn't move a muscle.

This morning, she'd gotten up early for a spa treatment she'd said Francois, the photographer, insisted on for all his models. Even though Brennan didn't expect trouble here, he refused to take any chances. And while he wasn't in the spa room for whatever treatments Kacie had to endure, he sat in the lobby and waited. Yeah, he probably looked like a jerk, but that didn't bother him in the least. If everyone knew up-front that they'd have to go through him to get to Kacie, it just made things easier.

Now Kacie played and laughed in the waves as if she were having the time of her life. Fortunately, Stallings seemed to have overcome his giggles. Brennan didn't know where his other half was but sincerely hoped she stayed away.

The ring of the cellphone lying on the table before him was a reminder that a world beyond this paradise existed and someone in it wanted to hurt Kacie.

Grabbing it, he clicked answer and heard Justin's growling voice. "How is it your first job with LCR has you protecting a beautiful model and slurping down some kind of pink drink under a big umbrella?"

The description was so accurate, Brennan looked around him. "Damn, are you here?"

"No, that was just a guess." His tone got grumpier. "Hell, is that what you're doing?"

"Of course not." He laughed and added, "You know I hate piña coladas."

"Piña coladas aren't pink."

"Do you have something, or did you just call to whine and talk about froufrou drinks?"

"Got a few things to give you, but nothing that'll point to a specific person...at least not yet."

"What do you mean?"

"I've gone a half-dozen layers deeper than what Kacie did for her employee background check. I can go deeper, but it'll take me a few more days."

"What've you got?"

"We'll start with Stewart Lakes. Single but divorced three times. Has two grown children with his first wife; none with his second; a five-year-old with his third. Is consistent on child support, no back taxes, no priors, or outstanding warrants. Lives in a small house in Queens. Eats Raisin Bran for breakfast every morning and orders from the same Chinese restaurant every Friday night."

"Nothing in his background on stalking?"

"Not that I could find. He made a good living at his old advertising job...invested wisely. This job he has with the Kacie Dane Foundation pays about a quarter of what he used to make."

"Is he being altruistic, or is there an ulterior motive?"

"That's going to take more digging."

"Okay…what about Marta, the accountant?"

"Now, she's a much more interesting character."

"How so?"

"Lives in an upscale neighborhood on Long Island. House is completely paid for. Never been married. Goes to Vegas at least once a month."

"Gambling problem?"

"Maybe, but if so, it's a lucrative problem. She's come out ahead just about every time."

"Cheating?"

"I've got a call into a few of my contacts in Vegas. I'm thinking she's a card counter, but not sure. Whatever her deal is, she's good at it."

"Seems unlikely she'd have an ax to grind with Kacie."

"I agree."

"Still, keep digging. There may be something more to her than just questionable gambling practices."

"Will do." Keys clicked on a keyboard, and then Justin continued, "Next up is Hazel Johnson, the office manager."

"What's her deal?"

"I don't think she has a deal, at least not one I've been able to uncover. The woman is a saint. When she's not working at the foundation, she's either volunteering at a food pantry close to her home, or she's visiting a nursing home where her mother stays."

"She sounds a little too good to be true."

"I haven't even gotten started. She sings in her church choir, went to Liberia a couple of years ago to help with an outbreak of Ebola and, in her spare time, volunteers at the animal shelter. If all this is true, when Hazel passes on, St. Peter's going to insist she come to the head of the line."

It seemed ridiculous, considering the woman would barely have time to sleep much less torture Kacie, but still Brennan said, "Keep digging."

"Will do, but if I find out anything more on this woman that's good, I'm going to ask her to adopt me."

Brennan snorted. "She'd kick you out the first day."

"Yeah, but she'd probably bake me cookies before she made me leave."

"What about the other three?"

"Tammy Peterson is your typical geek…but not. Family is überwealthy, but she lives in a one-room apartment in Yonkers. Graduated high school when she was fifteen and eschewed all the scholarship offers, plus job offers from tech companies. She apparently prefers the simple life.

"She's an only child, never been married, and has two cats, Theo and Otis."

"Sounds harmless enough. But…"

"Yeah, I know, we'll keep digging. Next up is Molly Rowe, who is almost too young to have a past. Her parents died in a house fire when she was twelve. She went to various foster homes before she found a good one when she was sixteen and stayed there till she graduated high school. Her foster mom passed away a couple of years ago. She's close with her foster dad, goes to see him every Sunday.

"She went to a community college for one year and got a certification to be an executive assistant. Apparently couldn't afford to keep going in school and started looking for a job. Kacie's her first employer."

"How old is she?"

"Nineteen. Doesn't date. Lives with three other girls in an apartment in Brooklyn. Looks spit-shine clean."

"Yeah…hell, keep looking just in case."

"Okay. So I saved the best for last."

"Tara Greenfield? Kacie's personal assistant?"

"Interesting woman."

"How so?"

"She gave you the goods when you first met her, and you said you thought something was off."

"Yeah…maybe a little."

"Okay, here's what I've got. She grew up in Brooklyn Heights. Got a full scholarship to Stanford. The woman's got a one hundred forty IQ, a freaking genius. Went three and a half years to Stanford. Had a 4.0 grade point average until her last semester when she just up and quit. Moved back home. Lives with her mother in a tiny apartment in Queens.

"Has no siblings. Doesn't date. Kacie pays her a good salary, but her credit cards are almost maxed out. She has a second job at a diner two blocks from the foundation. Works there three nights a week and weekends."

Tara was the only employee of Kacie's that Brennan had been around for more than just a quick meet. His first impression was of a bright, young woman with a cheerful outlook on life and a gentle heart. But some people were born actors.

"What about her mother? What does she do?"

Justin sighed. "Apparently nothing. At least outside the home. She's occasionally seen looking out the window of the apartment, but that's about it."

"Dig deeper on her. Something's not right."

"I agree."

"And we're sure…one hundred percent sure, that the other assholes who helped Harrington are accounted for?"

"Yes. The only one still living is in prison…has no access to the outside. No way he could be doing this."

"Okay. What about Harrington's family? He had some kids, didn't he?"

"Yeah, four. They're spread across the country. The oldest girl is a Wall Street guru. Doing very well for herself. There's a son who's a plastic surgeon in Boston. Another son who apparently wanted nothing to do with the family and lives in a commune in Idaho. The youngest, a girl, is a vet tech in Florida."

"And the mother, Harrington's wife?"

"She died a couple of years ago—booze and painkillers."

"Yeah…that'll do it to you every time. Anything else?"

"Not much more. Riley's been digging into the backgrounds of the other girls that Harrington kidnapped. McCall's kept tabs on them through the years, but nothing extensive other than to give them some help when they needed it."

McCall had mentioned the same thing to Brennan. The women had only glimpsed Kacie from a distance when they'd first been taken.

"Has Riley gotten anything on them yet?"

"No. They all seem to be doing okay. Nothing on the radar that would fit this MO. Three of them aren't even in New York any longer."

"What about the friends Kendra Carson had?"

"Kacie told us about two roommates who don't live in New York any longer. One lives in Juneau, Alaska, and works for an oil company. The other lives in Madisonville, Wisconsin, and is the mom to triplet boys."

"Okay…what about the ex-boyfriend? He sounded like a loser."

"He was. OD'd on heroin a couple years back."

"Well, at least we can eliminate one from the list." Brennan shoved a frustrated hand through his hair. "So many damn suspects and almost none of them is stronger than any of the others."

"Yeah. So, how's it going with Kacie? You guys getting along okay?"

No way in hell was he going to tell Justin what had been going on with them. That was between him and Kacie…and McCall, too, of course.

"Going fine. I admire her courage."

"That's all it is? Admiration?"

"What else do you think it is?"

"I don't know, man, you tell me. When we were there the other night, she apparently had been in your bed."

"She had just found that damn photograph under her pillow. No way in hell was there anything else to it."

"Okay…okay. Don't get your nose bent out of shape. Just expressing concern for my friend. Nothing more."

"Appreciated but unwarranted. Let's move on."

"There isn't much more. We're still digging into other people with direct contact with Kacie, like her agent and publicist. So far, other than they may eat their young for breakfast, I don't see either of them involved in this."

Brennan agreed. The better Kacie did professionally, the more money for them. However, stranger things could happen.

"Keep digging…just in case."

"That's the plan. How's the weather there? Isn't it monsoon season?"

"Not a cloud in the sky."

"Asshole," Justin growled as he ended the call.

Placing his phone on the table in front of him, Brennan looked up to see Kacie headed toward him. Wrapped in a cover-up, her blond hair slightly mussed, and a healthy glow on her cheeks, she was the epitome of a lovely all-American woman.

Brennan gripped the edge of the table to keep himself from going to her, lifting her in his arms, and tasting those smiling lips. No one around would think twice about it—after all, they were supposed to be lovers. Kacie would be the only one who would be surprised, and probably not in a good way.

When she was within a couple of yards of him, Brennan stood. "You through for the morning?"

"Yes. Francois wants to get some shots of us on a sailboat after lunch. But for now, I'm all yours."

The instant she said the words, two things happened. Kacie blushed like a teenager, and Brennan pulled her to him, lowered his head, and spoke against her mouth, "Oh yeah? Good to know."

Chapter Twenty-Six

It was a kiss like none other he'd given her. As if he had a right to her lips, to her body. As if she was his to do with what he wanted. He wasn't kissing her like she was damaged, or a victim. He took her lips like a man staking a claim.

She loved it.

Wrapping her arms around Brennan, Kacie gave in to the desire. Every fear, every doubt disappeared. His mouth drew on hers, his tongue delved deep, sliding in and out, while his hands cupped her bottom and brought her closer to him. She could feel his arousal, thick and heavy, against her belly. With only his jeans and the thin barrier of her swimsuit separating them, she could feel every hard inch.

She wanted every inch inside her.

"Get a room, you two."

Reality crashed around them as Brennan pulled his mouth off hers. And despite David's amusement, she was grateful for the interruption. She'd been so far gone, so deep into the need and want of Brennan that she'd been ready to let him take her here.

Loosening his hold, Brennan said, "Kacie...I—"

Fearing an apology, she pressed her fingers against his mouth, loving that they were moist and hot from their kiss. "No, don't apologize. That was surprising…delicious. Exactly what I wanted and needed."

He looked startled for a moment, and then the heat returned. "Then maybe we *should* get a room."

She laughed, and as if she had every right and did this every day, she reached up and kissed him, this time just a quick one, in case they got carried away again.

"We can discuss that later. For now, I've gotta eat."

"You know, for someone I can do this to, you have an incredibly healthy appetite."

"Do what to?"

"This." In another surprising move, Brennan lifted her into his arms as if she were a child. "Where to?"

Who was this man? She was used to a grim, solemn Brennan. This man bore only the slightest resemblance to her too-serious bodyguard.

Her eyes narrowed. "What have you been drinking?"

As if he realized how bizarre his behavior was, he grinned down at her. "Fruit juice. Has a remarkable influence on a man's attitude. Well, that and a beautiful woman telling me she's all mine."

After Brennan had literally swept her off her feet, Kacie thought things might be a little awkward for them at lunch. She was delighted that, instead of awkwardness, their conversation flowed as if the other night had never happened.

Brennan had carried her only a few feet to the restaurant door and set her down. Then, while she dined on delicious lobster salad, he devoured a cheeseburger and fries. When he caught her staring covetously at his fries, he picked one up and held it to her mouth.

Unable to resist the temptation, she opened her mouth, and he slid the salty, crispy fry inside. Her mouth closed around it, and then her tongue swept out to remove the salt from her lips.

Making a sound of appreciation, she chewed the fry and was about to thank him when she saw the look in his eyes. Breath caught in her lungs, and a flush that had nothing to do with the ninety-degree weather swept through her body. Many men had given her lascivious, lustful looks before, but she'd never once wanted to return it with one of her own.

As if he realized that things were getting a little more heated than he'd intended, he flashed her a quick, easygoing smile. "What comes after the sailing photos this afternoon?"

"Supposed to be a full moon tonight. Francois wants to get some shots of a midnight picnic on the beach. I probably won't be finished until late."

"No worries." He gave her a rare, sexy smile and added, "I can wait."

Somewhere down the line, insanity must run in his family. That was Brennan's only explanation for what had happened with Kacie earlier today. The minute she whispered those words—*I'm all yours*— he had felt like a different person.

And now, as he watched while Francois insisted on another round of shots with the beautiful couple enjoying a midnight picnic on the beach, Brennan knew he was going to have to reel himself in. Kacie wasn't ready for what he wanted from her.

Okay, the way she'd been responding would lead anyone to believe otherwise, but he'd witnessed her breakdown the other night during their foreplay. No way was he going to put her through that again.

"Thank you, my darlings. That's a wrap. See you tomorrow afternoon."

Dressed in a short, white, sleeveless dress that seemed to drink in the moonlight, Kacie was a vision as she slowly came toward him. Brennan stood as she reached him. Despite the stern lecture he'd just given himself, he was about to tell her how beautiful she looked when he noticed that she was walking with extreme care.

The instant he saw her eyes, he knew something was wrong. "What's wrong?"

"Headache." She closed her eyes and mumbled, "Really bad one."

"Okay…take it easy." For the second time today, Brennan swept her up into his arms. This time, very carefully.

Instead of protesting, she showed him exactly how ill she felt by leaning her forehead against his chest and closing her eyes.

Ignoring the curious looks of the crew, Brennan headed toward their bungalow, which thankfully wasn't too far away.

Within minutes, they were inside, and he was laying her on the bed. She moaned briefly but didn't open her eyes.

"Kacie, do you have anything to take?"

"Cosmetic case on the bathroom counter. Blue and white bottle."

With rapid strides, Brennan located the bottle, read the directions of the proper dosage, and then filled a glass with water.

Taking them to her, he was alarmed to see her standing and swaying as she tried to unzip her dress.

"Here. Take these. I'll take care of your clothes."

"Thanks." She took the pills, swallowed them down with the water, and returned the glass to him.

Brennan put the glass on the nightstand and said, "Just stay still for a sec, and I'll get you comfortable."

With quick efficiency, he unzipped her dress and let it fall to her feet. Ignoring the fact that she wore no bra and barely there panties wasn't easy, but concentrating on taking care of her trumped desire by a long shot.

"Want me to get your nightshirt?"

"No. Just want to lie down."

Sweeping back the comforter and sheets, Brennan lifted her up, laid her on the bed, and then covered her up.

"Need anything else?"

"No…thanks. Just need to sleep it off. I'll be better tomorrow." She opened her eyes slightly. "Sorry to ruin our night."

Placing a soft kiss on her forehead, he switched off the bedside lamp, and whispered, "Get some sleep."

Her eyes closed again. Brennan knew he should leave but couldn't make himself do it. Instead, he used his fingertips to massage her temples.

"Mmm. Feels good. Where'd you learn to do that?"

"My mom suffered from migraines. When my dad was home, he'd massage her temples. If he was at work when she got one, I did it. Seemed to help."

"It does…thank you." Her last words were slurred, telling him she was dropping off to sleep. He continued to massage her for several more moments and then quietly stood. He recognized the pain pills from some he'd taken before. They were powerful and should put her out for several hours.

Brennan went to the bathroom to get ready for bed and then pulled on a pair of running shorts. Sliding in beside Kacie as silently as possible, he allowed her even, shallow breaths to lull him to sleep.

Kacie woke, instantly aware of three things: Her headache was gone, she was in desperate need of the bathroom, and someone was holding her hand.

Turning slightly, she looked beside her and marveled at the sight. Brennan Sinclair was sprawled out before her like a Greek god. Pushing aside her need for the bathroom, Kacie sat up, gently slipped her hand from his, and then took the time to fully appreciate waking up next to the sexiest man she'd ever known.

With the exception of the black running shorts he wore to bed, all six and a half feet were hers to appreciate. Her eyes started at his head, taking in the thick black hair, only slightly mussed and incredibly sexy. Her gaze moved to his face. When his eyes were open, their piercing intensity either made her quake with a delicious kind of fear or want to hide because he seemed to see too much. With his eyes closed, she felt infinitely safer to enjoy the scenery. His silky black lashes were so ridiculously long and thick, they would make any woman envious, and he had the kind of cheekbones that would make a photographer ache to capture. When he was angry or upset, they looked as though they were set in granite.

His nose would probably be considered his biggest facial flaw—the slight bump in the middle indicated it'd probably been broken at least once. However, it suited him and allowed a slight imperfection in an otherwise perfect face.

His mouth… Kacie held back a sigh. She had never fully appreciated a man's mouth before, but Brennan's was quite the most delicious mouth she'd ever encountered. His lower lip was larger than his upper lip and had a sensuous, sexy tilt to the edges. And from experience she knew how very soft and delicious his lips could taste.

Reluctantly leaving his face but wanting her eyes to experience even more wonders, she moved her perusal downward. His neck was thick and muscular and melded into broad shoulders and muscular arms that looked as though they could squeeze the life out of a person with little effort. But all they'd ever done to her was hold her gently or passionately.

His chest had a light sprinkling of hair that led to hard abs that she could only describe as magnificent. The trail of hair followed beneath his shorts, and she had to grip her hands at her sides to resist temptation. What would he taste like? She remembered his size. How much would she be able to take into her mouth?

She had never done that before, never wanted to. And then Harrington. No, just no. That perverted pig had no place in her thoughts.

Resuming her visual exploration, she shifted her gaze lower. Long legs, covered in black hair and bountiful muscles, flowed to big, narrow feet. Size thirteen and a half, he'd once said—they matched the rest of him.

All in all, Brennan Sinclair's body had seemingly been packaged to create what any sane person would describe as utter male perfection.

She moved her gaze back up his body, intending to stop on her favorite parts for a second, maybe longer, look. When she reached his shorts, she swallowed a gasp. One part of his body had made a sizable change and was apparently ready for action.

"Enjoying yourself?" The raspy voice, with a touch of smooth velvet, held slight amusement.

Fire burned through her, and Kacie figured she had three choices. She could pretend she hadn't been staring at his body like a starving woman over an all-you-can-eat dinner buffet. She could just get up and walk away without saying anything at all. Or she could move those shorts aside and let her curiosity about his taste take control.

Instead, she opened her mouth and made the most inane, irrelevant statement she'd ever uttered. "You have ugly feet."

He snorted a laugh. "They get me where I need to go."

Of everything she could have said, why did she say that?

"I take it you're feeling better?"

She forced herself to look at his face, a little surprised that his eyes were still shut. "Much. Thank you for taking care of me."

A slight smile curved his beautiful mouth. "My pleasure."

She cleared her throat. "I…um. I guess…"

"Kacie?"

"Yes?"

"Kiss me good morning?"

Brennan kept his eyes closed, wondering if she would take him up on his offer. He had been awake for several minutes, aware that she'd been staring at his body like it was some sort of statue she was trying to figure out. He hadn't planned on saying anything, wanting to see just how long she would stare at him and what she might do. His morning wood, along with her heated perusal, halted that plan. He was now so hard that he was clenching his jaw to keep himself in check.

He wanted her to feel comfortable with him, which meant she needed to take the initiative. If she wanted, she could get up and he'd never say anything else. But, by the look in her eyes, she wanted something else, and he wanted to give her that opportunity to take it.

It seemed to take an eon for her to make that decision. At last, he felt a soft, sweet press of her lips against his. He smiled, and he could feel her lips smile back. Seconds later, she was off the bed and headed to the bathroom, leaving Brennan harder than ever with no relief in sight.

After a light breakfast, she and Brennan took a long run on the beach and then used the weight room for a quick workout.

Since she and David had worked late last night, Francois had been gracious enough to give them a long break. They were due back at four o'clock for another boat ride for snorkeling photos. Tonight they'd have to be photographed enjoying an elegant dinner, which meant another hour or so at the spa for Kacie.

Neither of them had mentioned the good-morning kiss or what had led up to that offer. She was grateful for that but also couldn't wait to see what else might happen.

She finished a set of upper-body lifts and then wiped her face with a towel. She glanced over at Brennan, who was finishing up a set with some massive barbells. No wonder he had no issues with lifting her as if she weighed nothing.

He was a man of great strength, both mentally and physically. He was also a man of action.

"This assignment is probably the dullest one you'll ever have."

In the middle of lifting a large barbell, Brennan finished and then replaced the weight with impressive control. "Guarding a beautiful woman in paradise? Most guys dream of this kind of assignment."

"You're not most guys, though, are you?"

His face took on a seriousness as he said, "There's no place I'd rather be than here with you."

She wanted to melt at that sweet answer. When she'd first met him, his gruff, grim demeanor had been off-putting and downright scary. Now she realized that, though he was more serious-minded than lighthearted, he possessed a strong element of kindness, too.

She sat on a workout bench, took a breath to steel her nerves, and said, "Can I ask you a question?"

"Yes."

"What's going on with us?"

He dropped down to another bench across from her. "What do you mean?"

Okay, he was going to make her come out and say it, and she was so not experienced at this. "I know we're attracted to each other…I just don't know where we go from here."

"Where do you want to go?"

"You know, it'd be real helpful if you would stop answering my questions with questions."

"I don't know what you want me to say, Kacie. Am I attracted to you? Most definitely. I don't think I've ever been more attracted to anyone. But I'm your bodyguard, not your boyfriend. When this thing is over, we'll probably never see each other again."

Exhilaration and heartbreak in one swift, compact answer. But he was right. He was here to guard her while LCR found out who was trying to hurt her. She was a job to him.

Yet she had never felt more comfortable with another man before.

"Can I ask you another question?"

He nodded.

This was going to take quite a bit more courage, but she had to take the chance. "Even though we might not see each other after this is over, would you…could we…" Crap, this was harder than she had imagined.

Apparently realizing where she was headed, he leaned forward and took her hand. "When we tried before, I scared you. I never want to do anything like that again."

"It wasn't you that scared me…it was—" Oh hell, how do you tell a man that you want to make love with him but that you'd really prefer it if he didn't give you an orgasm?

"What, Kacie? You know you can tell me anything. Right?"

"I just…" No, she didn't have that much courage. "Could we try it again? I know that doesn't sound very sexy, but—"

"Stop right there. There's nothing that's not sexy about you. Hell, you take a deep breath and I get a hard-on."

"Really? That's…wow. Guess I'd better start breathing deeper more often, then."

"Don't you dare. It's damn uncomfortable to walk around like that."

"So…would you? I mean…could we…?"

Still holding her hand, he pulled her until she was close and then settled her onto his lap. And she discovered that, despite her very unsexy proposal, he was very hard.

Without worrying whether he would like it or not, she wrapped her arms around him and kissed him. Despite her attempts to seduce him with her mouth, he kept the kiss light, teasing her mouth, easy and sweet.

And Kacie knew, no matter what happened tonight, whether she was able to go through with it or not, Brennan wouldn't judge her. He would keep her safe.

If he had the patience to try once more, then she should have the courage to try, too.

CHAPTER TWENTY-SEVEN

He had been on edge all day. In fact, Brennan didn't know if he'd ever been more nervous in his entire life. At least not about something that had to do with sex. Since losing his virginity at age sixteen, sex had been easy, and when he'd been playing ball, from high school all the way to the NFL, it had been available to him in abundance.

Having a beautiful woman ask him to make love to her would be a fantasy by most men's standards. It had happened to him many times. And before he was married, he'd said yes numerous times.

But when it came to Kacie, she was more than just a beautiful woman. She meant more to him than anyone he'd known in a very long time. If he hurt her, or damaged her trust, he'd never forgive himself.

What courage she had, though, to come out and ask him if they could try it again. That kind of grit humbled him and made him more determined than ever that she would enjoy tonight. He didn't care if it took all night long to help her overcome her fears, didn't care if they had to stop and talk about it. He'd always been a man of patience and control, and he'd prove that tonight.

He'd spent the afternoon on a giant cruiser watching Kacie and David snorkel and pretend they were having a blast. He'd never been on a photo shoot like this one before, his short stint as an underwear model notwithstanding. A three-day shoot had to be exhausting, but Kacie took it all in stride. Even when he figured she was exhausted and would much rather be lounging by the pool, when Francois told her to smile, she gave him a genuine, sunny one.

What Brennan would consider torture, she honestly seemed to find enjoyable.

Now, as he watched her have a romantic dinner with David, he struggled with what would happen when they went back to the bungalow. He admired her determination to pursue this when she was still obviously terrified that she would panic again, but he wondered how far that resolve would allow her to go.

She had visited with her therapist the morning after their first disaster, so maybe the doctor had suggested something that would help her overcome her panic. One thing for sure, they'd have a long talk before they even got naked. Seeing the horror in her eyes was a sight he never wanted to see again.

Having a seemingly intimate and romantic dinner with one man while your mind was on sleeping with another man wasn't as hard as it sounded. Whenever David smiled, leaned in to touch her with a tender caress, she simply superimposed Brennan's face onto David's.

Of course, poor David would be insulted if he knew the truth, but it worked wonderfully. And when Francois called it a wrap, he excitedly proclaimed that he'd never seen a couple so attuned to one another, nor had he photographed a more romantic evening.

Kacie thanked everyone for the lovely few days and said good-bye. It was hard to believe they would be headed home tomorrow. Harder still to acknowledge that she'd been literally living in a fool's paradise. Going home meant facing whatever and whoever was trying to destroy her.

"You ready?"

At the sound of Brennan's deep, sexy voice, she pushed all of that aside. Tomorrow was soon enough to worry about that. Tonight was hers and Brennan's. Oh, and that big giant elephant that would soon join them in the bedroom that she had aptly named in her head: Orgasm Terror.

She held out her hand, and he took it, bringing it to his mouth for a soft kiss. One romantic gesture from this man would put an entire week of fake romance to shame.

"I think so."

He gave her a tender, heated smile. "There's no pressure, Kacie. No timetable. No rules." He drew her in for a sweet, lingering kiss and then whispered against her mouth, "Only pleasure."

How could she tell him that unfortunately, *that* was the problem?

The flicker of doubt in Kacie's eyes was the last thing Brennan wanted to see. He was about to suggest they go to one of the bars for a nightcap, hoping to show her he was in no rush. A jagged streak of lightning followed by a loud clap of thunder changed his mind.

He had a bottle of wine waiting for them, and even if it took all night, he planned for her to know that tonight there was absolutely nothing to worry about, especially from him.

Taking her hand, he pulled her along with him toward their bungalow. They ran the last few steps, and the minute they stepped inside, the heavens opened.

The rain hitting the roof made a rushing, almost thunderous sound—the perfect accompaniment for the hot blood thundering through his veins.

"Want some wine?"

She whirled around and saw that he'd ordered not only wine, but a variety of sliced fruits. "Wow, you've been busy."

"Yes…well, watching a gorgeous woman have a romantic dinner with another man leaves little time to myself, but I manage."

She winced. "Sorry…can only imagine how boring that must've been for you."

"Boring?" He pulled her into his arms, pressed her into his body. "Boring is the last word I would use."

"Oh yeah?" she said softly. And then, in a bold move that both surprised and delighted him, she grabbed his hips and rubbed her sex against his hardness. "What word would you use to describe it?"

"Why don't you tell me?"

"Hard," she whispered against his mouth. "Hard. Thick. Long. Beautifully male."

"Hmm. Are we still talking about the job?"

"What job?"

He growled, "Exactly," and covered her mouth with his.

Somehow, kissing Kacie was always better than he remembered. Her taste, so fresh and pure but sensual, wrapped around him, and he wanted to devour every single morsel in one long swallow. Brennan ate at her lips, loving the feel of her surrender, her passion. When Kacie kissed, no matter how fearful she might be, she put everything into it. Her passion, need, and heat transmitted to him like an electrical charge.

Drawing away so they could breathe, he said, "Now about that wine."

"Can we drink it later? After?"

He almost said yes. Almost, because he wanted her so much, and she seemed so willing and eager, but the anxiety in her eyes said something else. No, they weren't going to rush this.

"How about I take a shower and you pour us a drink? I got a little heated watching you tonight."

She grinned. "I plan to get you a lot heated."

"Good." He kissed her nose. "Would you mind bringing me a glass?"

She nodded, and he stepped away from her. Maybe it was a mistake to cool down the intensity since she had seemed so eager, but quick, hard sex, especially with Kacie's history of abuse, seemed so damned wrong.

Brennan pulled off his shirt on the way to the shower. He hadn't lied. Just thinking about what would happen later had gotten him so heated at dinner, he'd requested ice water. Watching Kacie smile and simper at another man wasn't the most enjoyable way to spend an evening, but his imagination had taken him away from that scene.

Dropping his pants to the floor, Brennan turned on the shower and let the cool, pounding water give him the relief he needed. He turned at a sound and saw Kacie holding out a glass of wine, wearing nothing but a sexy smile.

He groaned and went rock hard in a second. So much for going slow.

Kacie hoped the wine she was holding didn't spill. It had taken all her courage to strip and walk in here. Now she was shivering, though not all from nerves. She was ready, really ready this time to give herself to this man. But she couldn't deny the nerves, along with anticipation and a volcanic kind of heat that felt as though it could erupt and spill over any moment. This heated need was one that only Brennan could quench.

Brennan stepped out of the shower and took the glass of wine from her hand. He took a long swallow and then held the glass to her mouth. She took a sip, and as the fruity merlot flavors of red grapes and black cherries hit her tongue, the need rising inside her went even higher. Taking one more swallow of the wine, Brennan set the glass on the countertop and then pulled her into the shower with him. As water cascaded over them, their mouths melded into a devouring, tongue-tangling connection. His hands roamed everywhere, and Kacie delighted in them, even as her hands did the same. He was so incredibly hard. Everywhere she touched was a tactile, sensual experience.

His chest rubbed against her breasts, making her nipples achy and needy. When he lowered his head and covered one with his mouth, she almost sobbed at the glorious feeling. His hands touched her hips and then cupped her butt, pressing her sex into his. Unable to stop herself, Kacie stood on her toes so she could rub his hard penis against the top of her sex.

Oh... Heat swamped her, need overwhelmed her. She could feel arousal pulsing, begging for release. She wanted it so badly she almost screamed at the incredible, delicious, overwhelming intensity. One second more...one last pulse and...

An image of Harrington came into her head.

Oh no. Oh no. Not now. Please not now.

Brennan wanted to cry with her. She was crouched in a corner, sobbing, and he didn't think he'd felt this helpless since he'd lost his son. His arousal completely gone, Brennan knelt down beside her. "Kacie...baby. It's all right."

She raised her head, and he didn't think he'd ever seen such stark pain. "No, it isn't, Brennan. It really isn't. It'll never be all right."

The water that had felt so good a few minutes ago was now chilling them both. Standing, he turned the shower knobs, halting the water, and then turned back to the devastated woman in the corner. He wanted to fix whatever was wrong, but how in the hell could he do that when he had no idea what her issues were. Okay, yes, he knew what they stemmed from but why was she able to get to a certain point before she freaked out? He was messing this up but had no clue how or why.

He tucked his hands under her arms and pulled her to her feet. She went into his arms so sweetly, so beautifully, he knew it wasn't him she feared. They had almost made love twice now, and each time she'd been right there with him until...

Oh hell. He'd been so damn blind. The photos that had been left in her apartment. In every one of them, she'd looked obviously drugged and...almost blissful, as if she had no idea what was happening to her, as if she'd been a willing participant in an act that had resulted in...

Oh damn, damn, damn.

The two times she'd flipped out with him had happened right when she'd gotten close to getting off. Right at the moment when...

Harrington. That fucking, perverted, son of a bitch, sadistic bastard. He had drugged her into submission, drugged her until she had no idea who she was, much less where she was, and then he'd used her body against her, messing with her head in unimaginably sick ways.

Had she climaxed while she was being raped? Is that how she equated sexual pleasure? With what that perverted piece of shit had done to her?

Kacie's shiver brought him back to his surroundings. His anger was washed away with his concern for her...his need to help her. Now that he believed he might have the answer, he needed to figure out what he could do about it.

Pushing open the shower door, he took Kacie's hand and led her out of the stall, snagging a large bath towel on the way to the bedroom. Kacie needed to get dry, and she needed to be comfortable. He led her to the bed and pushed her down. She had stopped crying but was looking at the floor, her shoulders slumped in defeat. This was not going to be an easy conversation.

First, he dried her thoroughly, rubbing her vigorously enough so that her body should be zinging with life. He then took a few swipes at himself and threw the towel across the room. Then, lifting her in his arms, he sat on the bed and scooted till he was leaning against the headboard. Her long, lean body was draped over his like the loveliest of blankets. He took a moment to savor the feeling.

Long moments later, he said quietly, "Harrington made you orgasm, didn't he?"

Her body stiffened in an instant, and she buried her faced against his chest.

"That's why you stop me every time you're close."

She nodded.

Well, at least the mystery was solved. Now how to deal with it. "Did you talk to your therapist about it?"

"Yes."

"And?"

"She said there was no shame in that. It was forced upon me...just like the rape."

"And you don't believe that?"

"Yes...I know it was, it's just..."

"When you feel the pleasure building, you have a flashback."

"Yes." She raised her head and looked into his eyes, her expression so sincere. "I love making love with you...but I thought maybe...if you wouldn't mind, you'd let me..." Her face went beet red. "You'd let me pleasure you. I'd really like to."

"So you want me to orgasm, but you don't want to. Is that right?"

"Yes. But even if I say stop, you don't have to. I just really want to get past this."

"Kacie, first and foremost, when a woman says stop, she means stop. I'm not going to go forward until you're giving me the go-ahead, no matter how much you want to get past it. Got it?"

"I know...but—"

Cutting her off, he continued, "And letting you give me pleasure, but not giving it back? Sorry, I don't roll that way either. Sex, to me—especially with you—has got to be a mutual giving of pleasure. I can't just take from you without giving back."

"But it would make me happy... Giving you pleasure would make me happy."

"And you don't think me giving you pleasure would make me happy?"

Her eyes flickered with surprised confusion. "Well...yes."

"But you'd hoped I would overlook that small detail?"

Her eyes filled with tears again. "I don't know that I can give you that kind of...happiness, Brennan."

"Can we try...one more time? Do you trust me enough?"

"I trust you more than I've ever trusted anyone."

A lump developed in his throat, and the last of the ice that had encased his heart melted under the warmth of this woman's sweetness.

Rolling her over until she lay beneath him, Brennan proceeded to kiss her and tease her again, heating them both to a slow simmer. His mouth moved from hers and traveled down her neck, then settled onto a breast for some slow, sweet suckles. When her nipple tightened into a taut, little bud, he scraped his teeth over her and delighted in her gasp of arousal.

Moving to the other one, he gave it the same treatment, all the while his hands roamed up and down her body. Heat and need once more took over Kacie's body.

Brennan's hands and mouth seemed to be everywhere at once. He was willing to try this again, and she intended to give him everything she could to make that happen. His comment that it would make him happy to give her pleasure had struck a strong chord within her. If giving her sexual release would make him happy, then she wanted so very much to give him that happiness.

"Kacie, look at me."

She opened her eyes to see Brennan staring down at her, his beautiful eyes both hot and tender. "Who am I? Say my name."

"Brennan Sinclair."

He smiled, took her hand in his, and kissed her palm gently. Then, surprising her, he took that same hand and brought it down onto her sex.

"Wh-what are you doing?"

"Since orgasms are taboo for you, I'm assuming you haven't pleasured yourself in a long while?"

Her face now hotter than a Texas summer, she shook her head. "I've never…you know."

"Never?"

"No…that's, uh…no."

"Then it will be my distinct pleasure to be with you the first time."

"You want me to make myself orgasm?"

"Actually, we're going to do it together."

Oh wow. That was so hot and, well, scary, too. Before she could ask him exactly how that might work, he took her fingers and pressed them to the top of her sex, where she was already achy, needy, and swollen.

"Rub back and forth...yes, just like that."

While she did what he asked, she watched his eyes. He had said he would get pleasure from this, and she could see it was true. As they continued to rub, his fingers still guiding hers, she felt arousal rise fiercely once again. She could feel herself getting wet, then wetter. The glide of her fingers against her sex became easier. She squirmed on the bed, her legs opening wider.

"That's it, sweetheart. Feel how wonderful you feel. You're wet...hot...so beautiful in your arousal."

Her eyes closed on a strong surge of need.

"Kacie, keep your eyes open. Look at me. Who am I?"

She blinked up at him, focusing on his beautiful face. "Brennan," she said softly.

"Whose fingers are inside you right now?"

"Brennan's...and, well..." She smiled. "Mine, too."

"Exactly. Now keep your eyes on me, and let's make both of us happy."

Her eyes locked with his, her fingers slid inside her wet heat as his hand guided her, plunging, retreating, rubbing. In and out, easy and hard. Again and again.

"That's good, sweetheart."

"Brennan...I..."

"Shh. Just let it happen. I'm right here with you. Say my name. Who's with you, Kacie? Who's got you, baby?"

"Brennan…Brennan…Brennan." His name began as a chant in her mind and then she whispered it aloud as the tension built… rising higher…then higher. Her eyes still locked on Brennan's, she felt the explosion upon her, throwing her up into heights she'd never known existed. She hung there for several seconds, suspended in exquisite pleasure, and then like a beautiful rainbow exploding in the sky, she swirled slowly down, disintegrating into the most beautiful colors she could ever imagine.

Brennan pulled Kacie into his arms, holding her tight against him. He'd never felt prouder or more humbled in his life. This beautiful, sensuous woman had given him a gift he had never experienced, allowed him to share in a moment he would never forget. And though he was harder and aching more than he'd ever been before, he was somehow satisfied. This had been for Kacie, and it had been one of the most glorious sights he'd ever witnessed.

She lay panting in his arms, and even though he wanted to hold her for eternity, he needed to make sure she was still okay. Pulling slightly away, he looked down into her face. "Hey… everything okay?"

"More than okay. Thank you, Brennan. That was a delicious, mind-blowing, phenomenal experience."

He smiled. "My pleasure."

"And now…" Showing that she still had quite a bit of confidence despite her insecurities and fears, she sat up and rolled him to his back. "Let's find pleasure together."

"Kacie, you don't have to."

"Oh yes, I most definitely do, Mr. Sinclair. Tit for tat."

He burst out laughing. "I sincerely hope that just because you have tits, you haven't named something I have tat."

She looked down at the long, hard length of him that reached almost to his navel. "I definitely don't think *tat* would fit."

"Want to see if you fit?" he asked softly.

"Yes...I do."

Awed by her courage, Brennan reached for a condom he'd placed on the nightstand. Ripping it open with his teeth, he was about to slide it on, when she took it from him. Brennan stopped breathing and watched as she slid the protection over his length.

Then, gifting him with a sexy, confident smile, she rose up and then slowly lowered herself onto him. He stopped breathing again.

Kacie bit her lip as she concentrated on taking him inside her body. Even though she was impossibly wet, he still didn't slide in as easily as she'd hoped.

"Take me slow, baby. No race...no hurry. Stay focused on me, Kacie. Eyes on me. Okay?"

"Okay," she whispered.

Showing her once again that his control was incredible, Brennan took her hips in his hands but did nothing but hold her while she worked on taking him inside her, inch by deliciously slow inch. When at last he was seated as deep as she felt he could go, she took a moment to savor the fullness.

"Kacie?"

"Yes."

"Who's inside you?"

She smiled dreamily. "Brennan Sinclair."

"Who's going to make you come again so hard that your eyes will cross?"

She grinned down at him. "Umm. Tat?"

When he laughed again, his body surged up, and he went even deeper.

"Oh…" she gasped.

"Still okay?"

"Yes."

"Ready for more?"

She stared at him, now more than a little worried. "There's more?"

He grinned. "I mean ready for more action?"

Relieved, she said, "Ready, willing, and able."

Taking her at her word, Brennan pushed her hips up until he was only halfway inside her and then brought her down again. Kacie caught on to the rhythm and began to ride him, slow and then fast. She watched his face, saw the tension, the absolute need to give her more pleasure, and that made her want to give him hers, along with his.

Pressing her hands against his chest, she concentrated solely on giving them both what they wanted. And, like a surging tidal wave, another climax washed over her, this time in a slow flush of ecstasy.

And Brennan, seeing that she had indeed come again as he'd planned, gave himself permission to let go.

Surging deep inside her, he held her in place, and Kacie felt him pulsing as he found his own release. Satiated and incredibly relaxed, Kacie fell over on to his chest, kissing him softly.

Hard, muscular arms closed over her, and peace washed through her. Here, safe in Brennan's arms, was the only place she wanted to be...for the rest of her life.

Chapter Twenty-Eight

She lay so quietly in his arms, Brennan wondered if she'd fallen asleep. After the emotional night they'd had, he was weary to the bone, but he was also exhilarated. He'd never had a closer, more intense connection than this in his life. It would be a memory he'd carry with him forever.

Kacie snuggled deeper into his arms.

"You asleep?" he whispered, just in case she was.

"In between." She sighed. "I can't believe we're going home tomorrow."

"Are you anxious to get back?"

"Yes and no. I'm looking forward to working with Montague on his new lines, but the other…I just wish it could be over."

"We'll find out who's doing it soon. I know we will. Have faith."

"I do…in you and all of LCR. You guys saved me once…I know you'll save me again."

He pressed a kiss against her forehead, hoping against hope that her trust was not in vain.

"Can you tell me about the tattoo?"

She drew in a deep breath. "Hard to hide something like that when you're naked."

"I know where it came from. I just—"

"You're wondering why I've never had it removed?"

"Yeah. I've heard tattoo removals can be painful, but—"

"If it were that simple, believe me, I would have had it removed the day after my rescue." She took his hand and pressed it to the small of her back. His fingers moved over something that felt like ridges.

"What the hell?"

"He had some kind of branding pen used on me first, then the tattoo went over it."

"Son of a bitch," Brennan growled. "So even if you had the ink removed…"

"Right. It would still be there. I didn't see the point."

"Another reason why you won't wear a bikini for a photo shoot."

"It would be hard to explain."

She had that right. No wonder she felt that Harrington would never let her go. Every time she looked at her naked back in a mirror, she saw the reminder of what he had done to her.

She shifted in his arms to get more comfortable. "Enough about me. Tell me about Brennan Sinclair's early years."

"You mean, before he screwed up so badly?"

"No," she said softly, "before he was hurt so badly."

Unable to stop himself, he took another kiss, slow and thorough. She was so sweetly addictive, he could kiss her a million times and never get tired of her lips.

Settling her back into his arms, he said, "I had a great childhood…wonderful parents. My dad was the hardest-working man I've ever known. He was a cop, and on his days off and every other weekend, he was a bartender at a pub not far from our house.

"My mom was a stay-at-home mom, but not really. She was a CPA, worked out of the house. But she was always home when I got in from school…always had cookies or something waiting for me.

"I was an only child, but our house was always the house where all the kids congregated. Everyone felt at home with my parents."

"They sound wonderful."

"They were. I started playing football in junior high school. It came so easy for me…too easy. Played through high school. Did so well that I got recruited all over the country. I wanted to stay close to home, though, so I accepted a scholarship from Ohio State…played there for three years.

"I started getting highly recruited from the pros. My parents wanted me to finish my degree, but I didn't listen to them. The money, the fame, everything was so damn enticing. I was going to make millions. I was arrogant…so incredibly full of myself. No one, not even my parents, could talk me out of it."

"I remember hearing once that you were one of the youngest quarterbacks ever to play for the NFL."

"Yeah…too damn young. Twenty years old and still wet behind the ears…knew nothing about life and so damn cocky I thought I knew it all. Got picked up by the Jets…didn't figure I'd play much for a year or so. I was having a good time hanging out with my buddies and dating as many women as humanly possible.

"I met Vanessa that first year. It was lust at first sight for both of us. She was a few years older than me. She was already making a name for herself…commercials, a few small parts on Broadway, but she had her sights set on bigger things."

"You?"

He squeezed her. "No, not me. She was ambitious. More than I ever knew. She wanted us to get married, said then we could both focus on our careers. We flew to Vegas one weekend and did the deed. Broke my parents' hearts. But they got over it and did their best to like Vanessa. Unfortunately, it never took for either of them.

"After we were married, we saw them less and less. Not long after that, Todd Fulton, the Jets QB, broke his leg, and I had my chance. I took full advantage of it. I played, had a good time. Focused on what I wanted to do."

"What was Vanessa doing?"

"She was focusing on her career…or at least she was until she found out she was pregnant. I convinced her it would be okay, that she could have the baby and still have her career, too.

"By that time, the charm had kind of fallen off our marriage. We were both so into our own selves, it didn't leave us much time to focus on anyone else."

"And then a baby was coming your way."

"Yeah." Brennan tried and failed to control the still-crushing pain of what came next.

"I was happy to be a dad…adored my son. But my job… my life was still football. I told myself that I was a hard-working man, just like my dad. That it was my responsibility to care for my family. But that was a damn lie. Everything I did, I did for me. My dad never let himself forget that we were his priorities. Nothing got in the way of his family.

"Everything I did, I did for Brennan Sinclair. No one else. And Cody…my perfect, precious boy, had a lousy father. When I was home, I'd pay attention to him, but not like I should have. Certainly not the way my dad did with me.

"I took him for granted…took everything for granted. And then it was gone."

Kacie hugged him gently. She had started this conversation because she wanted to know more about him, and now that she understood what drove him, it broke her heart.

"So I'm guessing Vanessa wasn't exactly mom of the year?"

"No. She resented Cody. Hated me. Blamed both of us for ruining her career. We got a nanny so she could go back to work, but the offers didn't come. She became more despondent. I didn't realize how bad it was until—"

He blew out a harsh breath. "That's the kind of wake-up call no one ever wants. After Cody…I was so mired in regret, in pain. God, I hated myself. Hated Vanessa. I should've stepped up and finally become the man my parents raised me to be. Even though she had been a party to what happened to Cody, it was never her intent that he should die. I couldn't forgive her, though. And she never forgave herself. Then, it was too late.

"I went back to work…thinking that would be the solution. Still stupidly believing that work was the answer. Football was all I had…all I'd ever done with my life. Brennan Sinclair was nobody unless he played football."

"But then you just walked away?"

"Yeah. Walking off the field in the middle of the biggest game of the season wasn't my finest hour."

"Bet that caused you a lot of problems."

"Yeah…and a lot of money. By that time, I didn't care…not about the money, the fame. Most definitely not about me. I was lost for a very long time."

"How did you come back?"

"Not overnight, that's for damn sure. It was a long, slow process, and every time I thought I was on the road back, I got slammed again."

"You never played ball again?"

"No. Not that anyone would've had me. I was a very bad risk. A twenty-four-year-old has-been. Besides, I didn't have the desire to pick up a football, much less play.

"But it took my mom getting cancer before I dug myself out of my pity pool."

Oh no, she'd feared something like this when he'd mentioned his parents as if they'd already passed.

"I still had some money...got more by selling all the properties, cars, and junk I'd amassed. I'd bought my parents a house my first year with the Jets, but it was nothing compared to what they'd done for me. I had to do something, so I contacted the most respected cancer doctor in the US. Flew him to where my mom was being treated. It was too late. She hadn't told anyone, even my dad, how long she'd been feeling ill.

"We had her a few more months, and then she was gone. My dad..." He swallowed hard, and she held him tighter.

"My dad died only a few months later. Heart attack supposedly, but...I just don't think he wanted to live without my mom."

Kacie's heart broke for him. He had lost everyone he'd cared about...and blamed himself for most of it.

"I was so full of self-pity...so full of guilt. And so damn sick of myself. I'd been given some powerful painkillers when I was injured, and for several months, that was my escape. Then, one morning I found myself on the floor of the bathroom. Had no idea how I got there...no memory. And I guess you might say I had a come-to-Jesus meeting with myself. I threw every pill I had away. Even aspirin.

"I realized no matter how much I wanted to die, it would be just another selfish act. And I was so damn tired of all the selfish acts I'd committed throughout my life. I decided I had to do something with purpose. Do something that really mattered, but I had no clue what that was.

"About that time, I saw Justin again. He's a couple of years older than I am, but we went to the same high school and were friends. He kicked my ass back into shape and introduced me to the Carmichaels."

"Who are the Carmichaels?"

"The meanest, toughest, baddest guys you could ever meet. Three former Navy SEALs who opened a kick-you-in-the-ass-or-kill-you training facility in Glens Falls. I went there to get trained and then stayed to be a trainer. Then about a year or so ago, they started a security and rescue branch.

"Then Justin got me in touch with McCall and…"

"And now here we are."

"Never expected you."

That might possibly be the sweetest thing anyone had ever said to her.

CHAPTER TWENTY-NINE

Brennan figured he'd remember this day for the rest of his life. It had happened before. Not this exact thing, but something like it. One moment you were happy, feeling like nothing, no matter what happened, could destroy you. And then disaster.

They were on the plane, headed back to the States. David Stallings and Britney had decided to stay a couple of extra days at the resort, which was a welcome relief to Brennan. Two hours of the giggle twins would put anyone in a sour mood.

Kacie hadn't gotten much sleep last night, so he'd teased her about it and told her to take a nap, that she would need her strength for later. To see the confidence and happiness on her face was unlike any feeling he'd ever had.

Everything took a back seat the instant his cellphone rang. Before Brennan could get in a hello, McCall cut in, "We've got a problem."

"What?"

"There's a sex video online of Kacie."

His eyes immediately went to Kacie, who was already deeply asleep. Thankful for small favors, Brennan stood and went to the back of the plane.

"With Harrington?"

"Yes. It's not a clip…not photos put together. Lasts twelve minutes, forty-seven seconds. Even though she's older and looks different, she's easily recognizable as Kacie.

"And before you ask, yes, we were one hundred percent certain that those recordings were destroyed. No one has a clue how this one got past us."

"Can you shut it down?"

"Our tech people have already taken care of it. Thankfully, it was only on one site. We monitor the web twenty-four/seven. The video was posted three minutes and six seconds before we found it. We got it down in a matter of seconds."

"Any idea who posted it?"

"No, not yet. That might take a couple of days to track down, but we think we can find where it came from. But if it's like the other online shit, this freak is traveling all over the city and using other computers to do his dirty work."

"Then it's likely it'll get uploaded again. Possibly on more than one site next time. We're one step behind each damn time."

"Yes… Till we can find the creep and stop him for good. You think she's going to be able to handle it? Will this destroy her?"

Tamping down his rage, Brennan took time to consider the question before he answered. Kacie was so damn courageous… but this…

His gaze went to the sleeping woman on the sofa. Slender, delicate, vulnerable. Strong. Yes, that was the key. She was unbelievably strong.

He answered McCall with complete assurance, "No, it won't. It's going to hurt her, but she'll survive. She's come too far… overcome too much. She's strong…a fighter."

"Skylar wanted to call her, but I'd like for you to be the one to tell her. She needs it done quickly and unemotionally. Tell her before you land. If any paparazzi are waiting for her, she needs to be prepared."

"Will do. You know what this means, don't you?"

"Yeah, whoever is doing this knows her schedule, knows she's coming back today. Have Justin and Riley come up with anything more?"

"Not yet."

"Keep me in the loop."

"Will do."

"Let Kacie know we're here for her and will leave no stone unturned until we find this bastard."

Brennan ended the call and then leaned back against the doorframe. He'd told McCall that this wouldn't destroy her, and while he believed those words, Brennan also knew that it would crack open the fragile self-assurance she'd only recently gained.

McCall had been right about delivering the news quickly and unemotionally. She needed to see this as a small setback. A bump in the road, nothing more. Hell yeah, it was a damn big bump, but he believed in her. She would weather this storm, too.

He glanced at his watch. He had about an hour to tell her, allow her to adjust to the news, and then buoy her back up before the plane landed.

Feeling as though he'd aged a decade in a matter of minutes, Brennan pushed away from the wall. Best get started.

A soft, delicious kiss on her lips woke her. Kacie blinked her eyes open and looked up into the greenest, most beautiful eyes in the universe. Brennan was on his knees, leaning over her. She felt like Sleeping Beauty gazing up at the charming, handsome prince.

Smiling, she said softly, "Now that's the best way to wake up. Far better than an alarm clock."

"Did you sleep well?"

"Yes, it was heavenly." She looked around. "Are we already home?"

"Not yet...still have about an hour to go."

She frowned, not only surprised that he'd woken her but also by the seriousness of his tone. "What's wrong?"

Instead of answering, he rose to his feet and then scooped her up in his arms. Sitting back down on the sofa, he just held her for a few minutes.

She told herself he was just being romantic. But warning bells were clanging in her head, telling her to pay attention. She was no princess, and her life was most definitely not a fairy tale.

"Talk to me, Brennan."

"McCall called. There's been a new development."

A new development sounded so innocuous, almost boring. She knew better. New developments, especially these days, meant something horrendous. Fearing the worst, she whispered, "Another murder?"

"No...nothing like that."

Thank God for that, but it had to be bad, or he would've already blurted out what had happened. Holding herself still, she braced herself.

"A video appeared online... McCall's already had it taken down, but it was out there for a few minutes."

Her heart thudded like a wild thing against her chest. "A video? Of—" She couldn't say it, couldn't think it.

"One Harrington had made."

She shot straight up in his arms, her mind whirling with horror. "No...no, no, no, no..."

"Kacie, listen to me. It's gone. They've taken it down. And they'll find out who uploaded it. It'll lead us to the creep who's doing this."

She threw herself out of his arms, unable to sit still, unable to think rationally. "Oh, well, why didn't you say that up-front?" Bitter sarcasm and tears were all she had left. "That makes it all better. Maybe when we find him, we can thank him for putting it up there and making it so easy for us."

She looked around like a cornered animal looking for escape. A sob built in her chest, and she wanted to let it out, wanted to scream, to cry. Instead, only a small whimper came from her.

Brennan wrapped his arms around her, trapping her against him, and she fought him. She didn't want him to see her like this, didn't want his compassion and his kindness. She was furious, and she wanted to take that fury out on anything and everything.

"Let. Me. Go."

He wouldn't budge, wouldn't let her go. She jerked, tried to escape. He held tight.

"Dammit, let me go."

"No, no way in hell."

Dragging her back to the couch, Brennan kept his arms around her torso, confining her. When she tried to stand up, he solved that problem by wrapping one of his legs around both of hers.

She felt powerless, helpless... So very close to the way she'd felt during her time with Harrington.

He leaned his forehead against the side of her head, growled into her ear, "I'm not going to let you shut me out, Kacie. You've got so much courage, so much strength. You will fight this with everything within you, and I'll be right here beside you." He shook her slightly. "Understand? We're in this together."

She held herself stiff for several more seconds, grinding her teeth and glaring at the wall of the plane. And then she wilted. Collapsing against him, she buried her face against his chest and let herself give in to the sobs tearing through her body.

Brennan held her, spoke softly, encouragingly. He told her again how strong and brave she was, how proud he was of her, how she had triumphed, and how she would again.

Several minutes later, feeling drained and empty but much calmer, she lifted her head and asked hoarsely, "What now?

"We don't know yet who, if anyone, saw it. McCall's people monitor the Internet twenty-four/seven. They caught it a few minutes after it showed up and managed to delete it immediately."

"Noah thinks they can track it down somehow. That's good, then." She closed her eyes, leaned against his shoulder again, suddenly too tired to think. "When will this be over?"

"I don't know, baby, but soon. We'll make it happen, soon. I promise."

It was there between them, but neither mentioned the fact that when it was over, Brennan would be gone, out of her life forever.

If this nightmare never ended, it would destroy her life.

But if it did end, Brennan would be gone, and it would break her heart.

Either way, she lost.

CHAPTER THIRTY

New York City

The bitch was coming back today. And she would pay...
pay...pay!

She danced around the small room, so delighted with her
work she couldn't sit still. She had everything ready, everything
in place. One click of a button, and the whole world would
know Kacie Dane's real name. They'd know what a slut she
was. Little Miss Innocence with her golden-blond looks and
simpering smile, acting like she was something special ...
something better.

She was a dirty slut whore who had seduced and taken
advantage of an old, mentally frail man. But did anyone know
that? Of course not. That information got buried beneath the
avalanche of shit. Made it appear that William Harrington was
at fault. But she knew the truth, knew what no one else wanted
to admit.

It was time to expose that truth to the world. Time to reveal
the guilty party. Time to punish the wicked for her sins.

One click, just one click, and every news outlet in the world
would see Kacie Dane for what she really was.

Brennan hustled Kacie into the lobby of her apartment building. He wanted to get her upstairs as soon as possible. Who knew what this freak hounding her would try to do next?

As usual, Kacie had other ideas.

She stopped at the security desk. "Hi, Vincent. How's everything going? Were you able to get off work to watch your grandson play in his baseball game?"

"Sure did, Miss Dane. It was a sight. Little bugger got a home run and made it to second base twice."

"That's great!" She presented a wrapped gift. "This is just a little something I picked up while I was away. Hope you like it."

"Why thank you, but you didn't have to do that." He winked at her and then Brennan. "The wife already thinks I have a crush on you."

Kacie laughed. "Have her come talk to me, and I'll set her straight. I'll tell her how you're always bragging on her."

"I might just do that." He held up the gift. "Thanks again, and welcome back."

Acting as if she hadn't a care in the world, Kacie thanked him and then headed to the elevator. The instant the doors closed, her smile disappeared, and the haunted look returned to her eyes.

"Why do you do that?"

"Do what?"

"Give gifts, smiles, when I know it's the last thing you feel like doing?"

"It takes very little effort to be kind."

Yet another reason he found this woman both enchanting and fascinating.

Brennan opened the door to her apartment, stepped inside and handled the security panel on the wall.

Kacie closed the door, then stood behind him, her arms wrapped around herself. "I hate not feeling safe in my own home."

"The new locks and security system should make you feel safer. With no one but you and me having door keys or the security code, there's no way in hell anyone could come in now."

"I know you're right. I just…I'm not sure I'll ever feel safe again."

His arms went around her again. "You will, Kacie. It'll just take time."

She nodded against his shoulder and then pulled away. "I'm going to take a quick shower and then make some hot tea."

"You shower, I'll make the tea."

"Have I told you lately how much I appreciate you? Thank you for being here."

Pressing a kiss to her forehead, he said, "No thanks needed. Want me to bring your tea up to your room?"

"Thank you. That would be wonderful."

Weariness was revealed in every step as Kacie went up the stairs. Brennan watched her, felt impotent and helpless…useless. He could spout meaningless platitudes, hand out hugs and kisses, give her smiles of reassurance, but that didn't make any of this shit go away.

Cursing his frustration, Brennan went to the kitchen to make the tea. Hell, at least it was something productive.

Setting the kettle on the stove, he was about to turn the stove light on when he heard her scream.

Nausea clogged Kacie's throat. She wanted to throw up but had no place to go. They were everywhere. *He* was everywhere.

A thundering sound behind her and then the door crashed open. She turned to see Brennan, gun in his hand, searching for the threat. But there was no one here except for the trauma-tized, horrified woman standing in the middle of her bedroom and staring at walls covered in photographs of Harrington raping her.

Brennan's arms came around her, and she pushed him away. No, she didn't need sympathy or comfort, didn't need him telling her everything would be okay. She wanted this stopped. Right. Fucking. Now.

As if accepting that his comfort wasn't what she needed, Brennan went around the room, staring at the photographs. A small voice inside her said she should be ashamed, mortified that he was looking at the most horrific moments of her life. She was tired of the shame...the degradation was not hers. It belonged to that pervert Harrington and the sick freak torturing her for some unknown reason.

Brennan turned to look at her, and in the back of her mind, the thought came that she should be terrified. She'd never seen such fury in a person's eyes before.

He took out his cellphone, punched a button, and then held it to his ear. "Did you give your security code to anyone else, Kacie? Any friends, employees? Anyone?"

"No. No one but you, me, and the security company knows the code."

"Then how— Justin, you and Riley need to get over here. We've got a—"

Kacie couldn't believe Brennan could get any angrier, but whatever Justin said made his face harder than ever.

"Right. I'll see you soon."

Brennan dropped the phone back into his pocket and then rubbed his forehead.

"What?" Kacie snapped. "Did another video surface?"

"No. But McCall gave Justin the IP location for where the video was uploaded."

"And?"

"It came from your apartment, Kacie. From your computer."

"No…that's not possible—"

"Whoever has access to your apartment would have access to your laptop."

She turned away from him and closed her eyes. Was nothing she had safe anymore? How many more ways could she be violated?

"Let's look around the apartment and then I'm getting you out of here."

She took a breath, then his hand, and they began their search.

An hour later they sat at the kitchen table, holding hands and drinking hot, sweet tea. Justin and Riley had arrived a few moments ago, and if they thought it strange that he and Kacie were holding hands, they were wise enough not to mention it.

Brennan didn't know if he'd ever be able to let her go. Her scream had awakened a fear inside him, similar to the fear that he'd felt when his son was taken.

"How many photos in total did you find?" Riley asked.

"Sixty-nine," Brennan answered grimly.

"If it weren't so perverted, it would be funny."

The calm way Kacie said this fooled no one. And none of them needed to ask what she meant. The photographs revealed just one sex act.

"And they were just in Kacie's bedroom and bathroom?"

"Sixty-seven were. We found two others. One glued to a framed photograph of Kacie on the bookshelf in her office. The other was on my pillow in my bedroom."

"This framed photograph of you, Kacie. Any special significance?" Justin asked.

"Yes…" Her answer was hoarse, husky. Clearing her throat, she tried again. "Yes, it was my very first magazine cover."

"It's definitely a woman," Riley said softly.

"Shit, Ingram. Don't start that again."

Riley shook her head, her mutinous expression saying she wasn't backing down. "You've got this weird, blurry view of women, Kelly. You think they can't come up with perversions just as well as men? Think again."

"Not saying that at all. I'm just saying don't go jumping to conclusions based on your bias against women."

"Oh, for the love of…I don't have a bias. You do. I know men and women are both equally capable of evil acts."

"Why do you think it's a woman?" Kacie asked.

"Jealousy factor," Riley said. "A man might post those photos on your wall, desecrate your underwear drawer with…well, use your imagination. But a woman will be more subtle, more willing to go the extra mile. Because she—"

"Knows how to twist the knife where it would hurt the most," Kacie finished.

"Exactly."

Brennan didn't know, didn't care. He just wanted the bitch or the bastard found and strung up by whatever method would cause the most pain.

But first he or she had to be identified.

"Justin, you and Riley check out the lobby security feed. When you get back, check for fingerprints, any evidence he or she might've left behind." Brennan turned to Kacie. "Good thing you didn't unpack. We're going to a hotel for a few days."

"No. That pervert is not going to force me out of my home."

"It's just for a few days. I'm going to have security cameras installed inside the apartment."

She swallowed. "Everywhere?"

"Just in the common areas. I'll be the only one with access to the feed."

Even though she still didn't look all that thrilled, even with the knowledge it would just be him, Brennan didn't care. Until this shit was over, her personal freedom would have to be limited.

She opened her mouth, most likely to argue, but stopped when Riley and Justin stood.

"We'll go watch the feed. Who knows? Maybe he"—Justin looked at his partner—"or she left a clue this time."

Kacie stayed seated as Brennan led the LCR operatives to the door. She was more exhausted now than she would be after a full day of shooting. It was almost impossible to believe that she had felt the least bit optimistic that this would be over soon. Whoever was doing this would stretch this out for maximum pain.

"Want me to help you up?"

The question rankled, and judging by the gleam in Brennan's eyes, he had said it intentionally to get a snarky response. But Kacie was fresh out of snark. She was just so damn tired.

"Get your pretty ass up, Kacie Dane. We've got places to go, rat bastards to catch."

"Some rats can't be caught."

"This one will be. Now get up."

Before she could respond, Brennan was at the table. He pulled her chair out and then lifted her up and put her over his shoulder.

"Dammit, put me down. I don't need you to carry me anywhere."

"Apparently you do, my love, or you would've gotten up on your own."

My love.

Had he actually called her *my love*? Was that a slip of the tongue? Maybe he called everyone *my love*. They'd known each other for a few weeks now, and she'd been around him almost twenty-four/seven. He wasn't one to use casual endearments, and she'd certainly never heard him call anyone *my love*.

Energy surged through her. Okay, so she had some sadist who was torturing her, wanting to ruin her or worse. So she might possibly lose the career she'd worked so hard for. And so she would suffer extreme and total mortification if any of those photos or the video got out to the public.

So the hell what?

She had met an amazing man, who through his enduring patience and kindness, had helped her in numerous ways. And he had called her *my love*.

Shimmying her body, she said, "Let me down."

He apparently heard the need in her voice, because when he dropped her feet to the floor, he was looking at her as if he wanted to devour every inch of her.

Leaning forward, his intent was clear. He'd just touched his mouth to hers when a cellphone rang.

Sighing deeply, he pressed a quick kiss to her lips. "Remember where we left off."

He answered the phone, his eyes going from warm and sensuous to ice cold in a flash. "We'll be down in a minute."

Shoving the phone back into his pocket, he said, "Let's go."

"Where?"

"Midtown."

"Why?"

"Because that's where we'll find the rat-bitch who's doing this."

CHAPTER THIRTY-ONE

"Let me do the talking. Understand?"

"I have a right to ask questions, Brennan."

"Yes, you do, but I'm compromising the interrogation just by letting you be in the room."

"You have no right—"

Brennan twisted around in his seat and glared down at Kacie. They were in the backseat of Justin's SUV. Riley sat up front with Justin, and they were both getting an earful.

"I have every right. This is my job. Understand? When the time is right, you can ask her all the questions you want. Until then, you keep quiet."

Okay, yeah, he probably could've been a little more diplomatic, but he was so furious he was just glad he could speak a coherent sentence. After all Kacie had done for the bitch, for her to repay her like this…

"You're one hundred percent positive it was her, Justin?" Kacie asked.

"No doubt about it," Justin replied. "Saw her face clearly. She walked into the elevator and came out about fifteen minutes later. Plenty of time to post the pictures."

"I don't understand any of this," Kacie whispered. "What could have happened to make her hate me like this? And where on earth did she get those pictures? Or the video? How did she even get into the apartment?"

"We'll get our answers, then you'll get yours." Seeing the pain reflected in her eyes, Brennan softened his tone a bit as he amended, "Fine. You can ask her first. But after what she's put you through, she doesn't deserve your compassion."

They didn't speak for the rest of the ride to Midtown. Brennan knew Kacie was probably going over every conversation she'd ever had with the woman, trying to find that one kernel of information that would explain her behavior. Unfortunately, and all too often, there wasn't an explanation, at least not a reasonable one any sane person would accept.

Justin found a parking space a half block from the office building that housed the Kacie Dane Foundation. Vigilant until the end, Brennan, Riley, and Justin surrounded her as they walked the short distance to the building.

They walked inside, and Brennan gave a cursory nod to the security personnel, and then the four of them loaded onto the elevator. All were quiet, each in their own world, their own thoughts. Brennan's were about getting to the truth and getting justice for Kacie. And if he knew the kindhearted and gentle woman beside him, her mind was still whirling with the whys.

The elevator dinged and slid open. As a group, they headed down the hallway. Brennan pushed the door open and walked in. Kacie was behind him. Behind her were Justin and Riley.

The instant they entered the small waiting area, several doors opened. Stewart and Marta walked out of their office at the same time that Molly, Tara, Hazel, and Tammy came from their offices.

"You're back," Tara squealed with glee and headed toward Kacie. Molly was right behind her, asking, "When did you get back? Did you have a fabulous time?"

Marta, Stewart, and Hazel moved slower, but they headed her way, too. The only one who hung back was Tammy, who gave a bright, enthusiastic smile and said, "Welcome back."

No one seemed to notice that Brennan stood in front of Kacie, shielding her. Tara moved to go around him, and Brennan caught her wrist. "Hold on a sec."

Even though everything inside him was urging him to act, take down the bitch immediately, he would stick to his agreement and give Kacie the moment she'd wanted.

"It's great to see you guys, and I have loads to tell you, but..." Her eyes went to the woman standing beside Brennan. "Tara, can we talk with you for a moment?"

As if she had nothing to hide, Tara turned back to her office. "Want to go in there?"

"Fine," Brennan said. "Let's go."

"What's going on?" Stewart asked.

Kacie threw the rest of her employees a reassuring smile. "We'll talk about it later."

Brennan wrapped his hand around Kacie's arm as they followed Tara into her office. Riley and Justin came in right behind them.

The instant the door shut, closing them in Tara's office, she said, "What's going on? Uh oh, what did I do?"

"Why, Tara? Why would you do this?" Kacie asked softly.

"Why what? What do you think I did?"

"Okay, enough." Gently nudging Kacie away, Brennan stood in front of Tara and glared down at her. He'd been trained by some of the meanest coaches in football, but nothing could top the training three Navy SEALs had given him on intimidation tactics. If this look didn't scare the shit and the truth out of her, nothing would.

"Why are you guys looking at me like that?" She tried to look around him to see Kacie. "Kacie, what's going on?"

When Kacie didn't answer, tears filled Tara's eyes. "I don't know what's happening here, but I refuse to let you try to intimidate me. I deserve better."

"Like hell you do, you—"

Kacie put her hand on Brennan's arm. "Brennan, no...wait—"

"Riley, would you escort Kacie into the another office and stay with her until this is over?"

"No, dammit, I'm not leaving."

Riley was smart enough not to argue. She took Kacie's arm and urged her forward. "This is what we do, Kacie. Don't worry. He won't hurt her."

Kacie spared one last look at Tara, who was now sheet white and had tears flowing down her face. The look of betrayal seemed completely incongruent with what she was being accused of doing.

Kacie opened the door and walked out to the lobby area. Surprising her, Riley stood at the door and watched her.

"Aren't you going back in to help question her?" Kacie asked.

"No. Brennan and Justin have this."

"But you—"

"Trust me, the way I'm feeling right now, Tara's much safer with those two than with me."

At a loss as to what she should do right now, Kacie stood in the middle of the room.

"Kacie," Molly called from her office. "Is that you?"

Molly came to the doorway. "Hate to ask you, but while you're here, would you mind taking a look at some of the mock-ups for next year's funding gala? If we can get them to the printer this week, they'll give us a ten percent discount."

It was better than just standing here, feeling useless.

She went inside the office and sat in front of Molly's desk.

Handing her a folder, she said, "I like the third one from the top the best, but all of them have potential."

Her mind on what was going on in the outer office, Kacie opened the folder, barely paying attention to what she was looking at. Several things registered at once. The door lock clicked, Molly laughed softly, and Kacie found herself staring down at photos of Harrington raping her.

Molly!

Chapter Thirty-Two

Brennan was getting a bad feeling about this. Not only was Tara not breaking, she seemed realistically appalled at what she'd been accused of doing. He'd seen liars before, could usually spot one within a minute or two of interrogation. The answers he was getting didn't feel like lies.

"Okay, let's try this a different way. Why did you go to Kacie's apartment while she was gone?"

She blushed guiltily and looked down.

At last he was getting somewhere.

"I…was going to borrow one of Kacie's dresses." She jerked her head back up, an earnest, pleading look in her eyes. "I was going to get it dry-cleaned and have it back in her closet before she got back. I swear I was."

"How did you get into her apartment? You don't have a new key or the security code."

"But I didn't go in. Kacie didn't tell me she'd changed the locks. When I got to her door and realized I couldn't get in, I left."

"Why did it take you fifteen minutes to figure that out?"

"What?" She frowned for a second, and then her brow cleared. "Oh. I got a call on my cellphone. Talked for several minutes in the hallway before I went back down."

It all seemed reasonable, but this woman appeared to have multiple secrets.

"Why did you give up your scholarship at Stanford and come back home before you graduated?"

She huffed out a furious breath. "Not that it's any of your business, but my mother has dementia. I didn't have any choice. I had to come back home and take care of her."

Brennan glanced over at Justin, who looked as uneasy as he felt. This just didn't feel right.

"What about—"

He looked up when Riley opened the door. "We've got a problem. Kacie went into Molly's office to talk to her about something. As soon as they went in, the door was closed and locked. No one answers when I knock."

"All this time it's been you, Molly? But why?"

The sweet girl with the twinkle in her eyes and apples in her cheeks was gone. Evil and malice gleamed in her eyes, and her smile had a maniacal twist.

"Because you deserve to pay for what you did. You got off without paying for your crimes."

"For the love of... What crimes, dammit?"

"For what you did to William Harrington."

This was the most surreal conversation she'd ever experienced. "I was kidnapped, drugged, beaten, starved, and raped repeatedly. Tell me exactly what my crime was."

"You seduced him, made him do those things to you."

"How did I seduce him?"

"You flirted with him at that party. I saw you."

That day, almost six years ago, had always stood out in her mind as the beginning of the end of the life she'd once had. Skylar had invited her to a party, to introduce her to some influential people. While Skylar had been away, William Harrington III had approached her. Having never been around anyone so distinguished looking, she had been both intimidated and excited, and when asked what she wanted to do with her life, she had blurted out her ambition to be a famous model. Harrington had seemed so interested in her career goals.

A few days later, she'd been both delighted and surprised that he'd called her and told her about an ad he'd seen for an open call for models. Kacie had gone to the location the ad had mentioned, and that's when she'd been snatched. That's when her true nightmare had begun.

"How could you have seen anything? You would've been just a child."

"I was at the party...with my parents. I saw exactly what happened."

"I don't know what you think you saw, but I did not flirt with that perverted piece of garbage."

"Don't you call my daddy that!"

Oh, hell...hell...hell. "William Harrington is your father?"

"He *was* my father. But he's dead now, thanks to you and your friends. And now, bitch, you're going to pay for every second of agony you put my family through."

"The agony *I* put *your* family through? What about me? What about the other girls he raped? The girls he sold into slavery? Your father was a sick, perverted—"

A drawer slid open and a gun appeared in Molly's hand. "I suggest your choose the rest of your words more carefully, Kendra."

"My name is Kacie Dane. Your father destroyed Kendra Carson."

"Not like I'm going to destroy her." She nodded at her laptop. "Guess you figured out already that the video I posted came from your computer. I cloned your computer in preparation for this."

"Why now? Why did you wait—" Realization came. "The Montague deal. You wanted to wait until I had something like that."

Molly grinned. "Maximum exposure, maximum fun."

"What do you plan to do now?"

"With one tiny click, every news outlet from here to the smallest village in Australia will receive the video of you seducing my father."

"He. Raped. Me."

"Because you wanted him to, you slut!"

Was this woman so delusional that she had no idea that what she'd just said was a complete contradiction?

"No woman wants to be raped."

"Don't lie to me. I saw the video. You liked what he was doing to you."

"He drugged me."

"You let him."

This was getting them nowhere. While poor Tara was being grilled like a criminal, here she sat with the real thing. Without a doubt, Molly would shoot her if she screamed or tried to leave. Kacie had mace in her purse, but she'd dropped it into a chair on the way inside Molly's office.

There had to be a way out of this.

To distract her, Kacie said, "How did you become Molly Rowe from Brooklyn with a foster dad?"

Molly giggled. "You think you're the only one who can create a fake identity? It's amazing what a hefty trust fund can buy these days. I couldn't get to the money until I was eighteen, but by that time, I already knew exactly what I was going to do with my daddy's hard-earned money."

"But your other family…"

"My mother died a couple of years ago…of a broken heart, I might add. My sister and brothers were never close. It was easy enough to pay to get a new identity and then wait patiently until I was ready for the big reveal."

"Molly, or whatever your real name is, you were just a child when this happened. I understand that you loved your father, but he was—"

"My father was a wonderful man, a wonderful father. So he had a weakness for young girls. Lots of people do. He didn't deserve to die for it."

Never in a million years would Kacie regret that William Harrington was dead. However, she was smart enough not to say that to his demented daughter.

"Did you kill Dr. Curtis?"

"Don't be ridiculous. Strangling a complete stranger is so not me. I did, however, hire a very competent fellow to do the deed."

"But why have her killed?"

She gave a grimacing smile as if it was just a bit of embarrassment. "Truthfully, I didn't plan for her to die. She caught the guy in the act of stealing your file, and he had to keep her quiet. I didn't pay him to kill her, so he didn't get any extra money for that."

"So what now?

Before Molly could answer, someone pounded on the door. "Kacie, are you in there? It's time to go."

"Oops," Molly said cheerfully, "totally forgot." She clicked a button at her desk.

Kacie heard the smooth glide of something mechanical. Turning around, she saw a steel door slide from the wall and across the wooden door. It hit the other side of the wall with a loud thud.

"See, that's the nice thing about being charge of an office, Kacie. I get to order all sorts of neat things, and no one questions me. My daddy had one of these in his office. Of course I paid for the door with my own money. Had to pay extra for them to install it during the weekend, but it was worth it.

"Now, we're all alone. For real."

Chapter Thirty-Three

Brennan glared at Hazel Johnson. "You got a key to this door?"

Apparently more terrified by him than by the circumstances, she kept her distance as her trembling hand dropped the key into his palm.

Even though he'd heard the sound and had already figured out what he would face, Brennan unlocked the door and pulled it open. Exactly what he had expected. A steel wall. Didn't have a keyhole, no access whatsoever.

He probed around the edges, feeling more and more desperate as time went on. What the hell was going on in there?

"Here." Riley handed him a phone. "I called the number. See if she'll answer."

The phone rang for what seemed like forever. Just when he was about to decide to hand the phone back to Riley, Molly answered.

"Kacie Dane Foundation. May I help you?"

"Molly, it's Brennan. I'd like to come inside. Would you please open the door?"

"Oh hey, Brennan. Sorry. No can do. Kacie and I are having a girl chat. You know, giggles and boy talk."

"Dammit, Molly. How the hell do you think you're going to get out of there?"

"Who said anything about getting out of here, Brennan? This thing with Kacie has been brewing for a long time. You really think I'm going to let a little thing like no escape stop me from taking care of business?"

His jaw clenched so tight he figured it might break, he said in a controlled voice, "Can I talk to Kacie?"

"Um, not right now. She's a little busy. Maybe later. Ta…ta."

The line went dead, and it was all he could do not to throw the phone across the room. They'd been so damn sure of Tara's guilt, they had completely missed any clues Molly might have given off.

He took a breath and turned. "Riley, get on the phone with McCall. See if he can dig deeper than we've already gone on Molly Rowe. Find out what we fucking missed."

He turned back to Hazel, who seemed to have gotten her composure back. "Is there any other entrance into Molly's office?"

"No…well, there's the window, but we're fifteen stories up."

Superman he was not.

He turned to Justin, who was in the process of examining the door. "You think we can ram it?"

"Doubtful. Damn thing is at least a couple inches thick."

"What about a drill?" Stewart asked.

"Hell, it's worth a try. You got one?"

"No, but I've got a friend working construction a couple blocks away. I'll give him a call."

"What can I do?" Tara's soft voice penetrated the tense silence.

Brennan turned to her. They owed her an apology, but right now all he could concentrate on was saving Kacie's life.

"Unless you can figure out a way for me to break this door down, nothing."

"Maybe if I talked with her," Marta offered. "Molly and I have always had a special bond."

"Hell, it's worth a try." He hit redial. Clicking it on speaker, he said softly, "Try to get her to agree to let me come in and talk to her."

She nodded, and when Molly answered in the same professional tone she had before, Marta said, "Hi, Molly, it's Marta."

"Hey, Marta. I'm kind of busy right now."

"I know, dear, but I thought maybe if we talked, we could figure something out."

Molly laughed. "Oh, you dear, sweet old lady. Snickerdoodles aren't going to fix this problem. But I do have good news for you. Kacie said you and the other office staff can take the rest of the day off. Isn't she like the bestest boss ever?"

The line went dead.

"Shit." Brennan strode to a window and looked out. Fifteen stories. Even if he could climb out of the window above Molly's office, how could he—

His eyes moved to the windows he could see, and an idea sparked to life.

"There are small balconies on several of the windows. Is there one at Molly's window?"

"I...don't know." Tara looked at Hazel, then Marta and Stewart. "I've never paid attention."

Hell, it was better than any other idea he'd had lately, which wasn't saying a helluva a lot.

He glanced over at Riley, who seemed to be in deep discussion with McCall. He caught her eye, and she nodded. Apparently, she'd heard him.

"Justin, come with me."

They walked into the hallway together and then ran to the stairwell that would lead them to the floor above. On the way, Justin let his thoughts be known.

"You know this is a damn foolish idea, don't you?"

"You gotta better one, I'm all ears."

A minute later, they were on the next floor and running toward the office that should be right above Molly's. They burst through the door, and Brennan let Justin explain the situation to the indignant man who'd been sitting at his desk.

Brennan ran to the window. Sure enough, there was a small balcony. Thankful this was an older building with windows that still opened, he lifted it and looked out. The balcony was really just thin black railing, obviously intended for ornamental purposes only and not to hold a two-hundred-forty-pound man.

He leaned farther out... But as he'd hoped, there was a balcony attached to Molly's window, too. So if the balcony held up, he could hang from the bottom of it and swing himself onto the one below.

"Shit." Justin stood beside him. "I doubt if that thing would even hold Riley."

"You got any other ideas?"

"What about the ventilation? We're too big, but Riley might fit."

Apparently getting into the spirit of what they were trying to do, the man behind them said, "I don't know how small this Riley is, but the last time the building inspector was here, he made a comment about how narrow the vents are."

"Then we have no choice," Brennan said.

"Even if you make it, how the hell are you going to get in? The window will be locked."

"I'll shatter the glass, swing myself in." He felt the thinness of the windowpane. "Shouldn't be a problem."

"Molly will likely have a weapon."

"Yeah, that had occurred to me," Brennan said dryly.

Justin was silent for a half second more and then huffed out a breath. "Ah hell, let's do this then."

Taking his gun from his ankle holster, Brennan debated, then stuck it in his waistband at the small of his back. He gave a nod to Justin and then climbed out the window.

Kacie hadn't been able to stay seated. Fortunately, Molly didn't seem to have a problem with her hostage moving around, so Kacie took advantage of that and roamed the office, looking for anything she could use to defend herself.

The office wasn't large, holding only a desk, a credenza behind the desk, and a bookshelf. Since Molly sat at the desk, Kacie's only option for searching for a weapon was the bookshelf, which held an odd assortment of tiny stuffed kittens and a few graphic novels. Not exactly weapon material.

Kacie turned and considered her opponent. Molly was shorter but outweighed Kacie by at least fifty pounds. Still, Kacie had taken several self-defense courses and felt sure she could take Molly in a scuffle. Problem was, how to get to her without getting shot?

The gun was pointed directly at her. If Kacie rushed her, she had little to no chance of surviving. So the only thing she knew to do was talk until either Molly got up and Kacie could take her down, or Brennan figured out a way to muscle his way inside.

"Did you set Tara up, make her look guilty?"

"But of course I did. Worked like a dream."

"Not exactly, since we now know it was you all along."

"All in my plan. You and your friends think you're so smart."

"And the photographs of me in Stewart's drawer?"

She grinned. "I admit that was a bit of a gamble. Bet you didn't know that Marta has a tendency to go through other people's desk drawers. I knew she would find them eventually."

"How did you get into my apartment to post those...photos?"

The gleam in her eyes showed both triumph and insanity. "You shouldn't leave your purse just anywhere, Kacie. Last time you were here, I stole your password from your password book and made a putty mold of your apartment key."

"Where did you get the recording?"

She blinked innocent eyes at Kacie. "You mean the one of you seducing my father?"

Kacie was well past arguing about what this woman thought of her. But she did want to keep her talking. The longer she delayed her, the better the chances of rescue.

Molly's voice changed from sweet to hard in a second. "I asked you a question, bitch."

Blowing out a silent, weary sigh, Kacie said, "Yes, the one of me seducing your father."

As though she'd just won the lottery, Molly pounded a hand on her desk with obvious glee. "That's what I'm talking about. Finally, the slut speaks the truth. But to answer your question, it was as if my daddy was speaking to me from heaven. That night, when those evil bastards killed him, I went to his office, like I did sometimes when he wasn't there. He didn't like us going in there without him, which made me all the more curious. When I was going through his desk drawer, I found a DVD."

She shrugged. "I couldn't resist. I took them."

No wonder this girl was so screwed up if, as a child, she watched a recording of her father raping a woman.

"I didn't even look at the DVD for a few years. We found out that same night that he had been murdered. I forgot all about it until I was about sixteen and found it when I was going through some of my old stuff." Her eyes went bright again. "Imagine my surprise to see up-and-coming model Kacie Dane doing the deed with my daddy. I knew then that I had been meant to find that recording, to redeem my father's legacy and to show the world who you really are."

"So all this time, you've been—"

Kacie swallowed a gasp, disguised it as a cough. Were those legs hanging outside the window? Yes, and they were Brennan's. She'd recognized those long legs anywhere.

"Been what?"

Act natural, don't change your expression. If she sees what's happening behind her, she'll turn and shoot.

"Been planning to ruin me?"

"It's been my only focus for years. In a way, I guess I should thank you. I had no real goals or ambitions until I saw the recording. It was like an epiphany. I knew what I had to do."

Brennan dropped down onto the small balcony at the window. Kacie knew it couldn't hold him—that railing was for decoration only. She had to do something.

Molly was frowning, her focus on a framed photograph on her desk. The reflection showed Brennan behind her!

With the gun in her hand, Molly swung around in her chair. Kacie flew across the desk and landed on top of her. The chair tipped over, crashing them both to the floor. Molly's shrieks and curses drowned out most of the other noises, but Kacie heard the sound of shattering glass. Had Brennan managed to get inside?

A fist to her temple refocused Kacie's thoughts. Grappling on the floor with Molly, she tried to avoid another fist as she pinned the woman down, but wasn't successful. Her head ringing, she tried to flip Molly over and work her knee into her back. But the crazed woman wasn't going down without a fight. Kacie dodged another blow to her face. Where on earth was Brennan?

Kicking with all his might, Brennan finally created a big enough hole in the window to swing through. He ignored the thousands of cuts and nicks his body took as he went through the jagged-edged window frame. He landed on his feet and twisted around. Kacie and Molly were rolling around on the floor, grappling for the gun that was inches from Molly's hand. Brennan went for the gun, kicking it into the corner.

Trying to get around Kacie's body to get hold of Molly was another matter. He shouted at Kacie to ease up, but she either didn't hear him or wasn't going to let Molly up until she'd subdued her totally. Even though Kacie deserved her pound of flesh, and a whole lot more, if they continued to fight, there was a chance she could get hurt worse than she already was. Molly was not only much heavier than Kacie, she was also a lunatic bent on destruction.

Seeing no other choice, Brennan picked Kacie up off Molly's struggling body. The instant he had her in his arms, he placed his foot on Molly's back. With his size thirteens pressing into her spine, all the woman could do was beat her feet and hands against the floor like a toddler having a temper tantrum.

Kacie fought him like a wildcat, but he held on and spoke calm, precise words. "Kacie, it's me. Stop struggling."

At last, she grasped the concept that she was no longer fighting the enemy. Her breath coming in panting gusts, she found her footing and gasped out, "My God, Brennan, you're bleeding."

For a man who'd just crashed through a glass window, Brennan figured he'd gotten off pretty easy. He might have a few places that needed stitches, but the bitch was on the floor, and he was standing upright. And, most important, Kacie was alive.

Keeping his foot on the woman whose squeals of outrage had turned to sobs, he said, "You know how to get that door open?"

"I think so." Going to Molly's desk, she pulled out a drawer and pressed something. Like magic, the steel wall slid back into place, and the door was open.

Justin ran inside, Riley right behind him.

"You guys okay?" Justin asked.

Before Brennan could answer, Kacie said, "Call 911. Brennan needs help. He's bleeding everywhere."

Looking down, he was surprised to find that she was right. Though one foot was still pressed into Molly's struggling body, the floor around him appeared to be a sea of red.

"Here, buddy." Justin moved Brennan slightly and, with quick efficiency, zip-tied Molly's hands behind her back.

A chair appeared beside him. "Sit before you fall."

That was Kacie's voice, and she sounded close to tears. Since he was feeling surprisingly lightheaded, he decided to take her advice, though he didn't so much as sit as fall into it. Damn, what was his problem?

He looked down to see both Kacie and Riley kneeling in front of him, pressing something against his legs, his arms, and his side. Shit, that hurt.

Kacie gratefully accepted all the towels that were being handed to her and Riley as they tried to slow the bleeding. Everywhere she looked on his body, blood seemed to be flowing.

"Ambulance is on the way," Tara called out.

Wrapping a towel around a bloody gash in Brennan's thigh, Kacie looked up at his face. He was pale, his eyes slightly glazed, but the most amazing smile was on his mouth.

"What on earth are you smiling about, Brennan Sinclair?"

"I'm thinking that you are the loveliest, gutsiest woman I have ever known."

The tears came then, but Kacie managed to stop their flow. "And I think you are the most foolhardy and heroic man I've ever known."

He grinned. "Match made in heaven."

She heard the roll and clank of a gurney, and then, in an amused voice, Justin said, "Okay, you lovebirds, let's get you fixed up."

Kacie stepped out of the way, letting paramedics take over Brennan's care. From what she could tell, the bleeding had slowed, but oh heavens, he had what seemed to be a thousand cuts all over him.

"You bitch, you think this is over?" Molly gave a maniacal, coarse laugh, the sound scraping across Kacie's skin like a cheese grater. "I'm just getting started."

Molly was now sitting in a chair, her hands still locked behind her back. She was helpless, powerless. Though a policewoman stood at her side, reading her her Miranda rights, Molly had eyes only for Kacie. Hatred, spite, malice, and everything evil were revealed on her face. A woman who had once looked innocent and sweet had transformed into something almost demonic.

Kacie turned back to Brennan. She would deal with the fallout of whatever news might leak later. For now, this man was her only concern.

"Hey, stop!" a man shouted. "Somebody grab her!"

Kacie turned to see Molly running at full speed, straight toward her. Though her hands were still secure, the expression on her face told Kacie that she would do whatever she had to do to hurt her enemy. And with Kacie standing right in front of Brennan, Molly could hurt them both.

Brennan apparently surmised the same thing. Grabbing Kacie by the waist, he jerked her aside. Instead of landing on Kacie,

Molly rammed into the open window. Both of them shouted at her to stop, tried to catch her.

Revealing what Kacie had known all along, the ornamental railing gave way. Molly's screams echoed as she plummeted to the ground and then stopped abruptly.

CHAPTER THIRTY-FOUR

Brennan opened his eyes to a sight he'd remember forever. Kacie sat in a chair beside his bed, sleeping. Her delicate hand held tight to his, as if even in sleep she feared letting him go.

He'd never been in more awe of anyone in his entire life. No doubt in his mind that she'd saved him from death. In that instant when he'd seen what Molly was going to do, he'd worked like hell to break through the glass before she could get her gun on him. And Kacie, realizing what was about to happen, had thrown herself onto Molly, taking her down.

She might look like a fragile, delicate flower, but Kacie Dane was made of guts, courage, and so damned much heart. His throat clogged when he thought of her—what she had gone through, what she had overcome. How in the hell she could still have goodness in her after all that?

"You're awake," she said softly.

"Yeah, but you should have gone home. You must be exhausted."

"I didn't want to leave, at least not until I was sure…"

Her voice had gone thick, and he knew she was fighting back tears.

"I'm fine. Just a few nicks."

Her inelegant snort was completely incongruent with her beauty, but she was pulling no punches. "Seventy-seven stitches to close up those little nicks. One so close to an artery they thought they were going to have to do surgery to repair it." She went to her feet and leaned over him. "You scared me so much, Brennan Sinclair. But thank you for saving me."

He appreciated the words, but she needed to understand exactly what had gone down. "You're the one who saved me, Kacie. If you hadn't tackled her, she would have shot me point-blank in the gut."

She shook her head. "What were you thinking? That balcony wasn't sturdy enough to hold two pigeons."

"Which Molly found out all too painfully."

"When I saw your legs dangling, I almost passed out from shock."

"But instead, you kept your head and saved both of our lives. Well done, Kacie Dane. You're my hero."

She snorted again, this time a little softer. "Hero, shmero. I was terrified."

"And yet you stepped up and took down a monster."

"She was an emotionally damaged and mentally ill young woman. I can't imagine what it was like for her, having her entire world ripped apart like that when she was so young, her father accused of something so hideous.

"I never gave any thought to what his family endured, the innocents who were hurt."

Now it was Brennan's turn to snort, and it wasn't nearly as polite. "It wasn't your place to care about that bastard's family. He's the one who destroyed their lives, just like he tried to destroy yours."

"I feel empty...and so incredibly sad for her. She was a sick, twisted little girl."

"Who would've done everything within her power to kill you." Maybe it was his hardened heart, but he couldn't find it anywhere inside him to feel the least bit sorry that the woman was dead.

"How the hell did she get away with it?" Brennan asked.

"Apparently, she had plenty of money to do what she wanted."

"We dug deep into the family. How—"

Kacie squeezed his hand. "Her family hid what was going on with her. She'd been in and out of mental hospitals since she was an early teen. Tried to kill herself twice before." A sad smile stretched across her mouth. "I think when she realized who I was, that gave her something to live for."

"Torturing and killing you."

"Looks like. I can't believe it's really over."

"Fill me in on everything she told you."

So relieved to hear him so coherent, with that commanding tone back in his voice, Kacie had to clear her throat before she could continue. She had been so very scared.

"She admitted everything. The break-ins, sending the emails, planting the photographs, uploading the video. She cloned my computer, so it was easy to make it seem that it had come from my laptop. She told me she was set to send the video to every news outlet in the world. And she spoke the truth. Riley went through her laptop and found the link. With one click, my dirty little secret would have been known by everyone."

Brennan had to stop her there. "First, it's not your *dirty little secret*. It was a disgusting crime perpetrated by a perverted piece of scum upon an innocent young woman. Even if the entire world knew about it, there's not a sane person alive who wouldn't see it for what it was. Got that?"

She smiled, appreciating his defense. But she had been giving a lot of thought to what would have happened if the whole world had discovered her identity and knew what had happened. It was something she planned to think about much more when she wasn't so tired and her head was clearer.

"What about Dr. Curtis?" Brennan asked. "Molly was a physically strong woman, but I don't see how she could have choked another person to death."

"She told me she hired someone to break into the doctor's records room. She hadn't intended for Dr. Curtis to be killed, but apparently, the guy got caught and felt he had no choice."

It saddened and hurt Kacie that the doctor who'd been so kind to her had died because of her. And unless Molly left some kind of clue somewhere about the person she'd hired, that man would go unpunished. Sometime soon, Kacie planned to reach out to the doctor's family and offer them what she could.

"What about those street thugs? Did she admit to that, too?"

"We never got around to talking about that, but I'm sure it was."

"And the press? What's being reported?"

Kacie shrugged. "I see no reason to drag the family of Molly, whose real name is Sally, by the way, back into the mud and spotlight. They've endured enough. The press is reporting it as a suicide, nothing more. Tragic but nothing more dramatic than that. Hopefully, that'll satisfy the vultures."

"I need to apologize to Tara."

"I've apologized for both of us, several times. However, Tara, being Tara, said there was no need. She's just glad we're okay."

"Did you know about her mother having dementia?"

"I had no idea. When I hired her, all Tara would tell me was she had been homesick and decided to leave school. Now that I know what she's been dealing with, I'm going to see what I can do to ease her burdens."

"I'm glad." He frowned. "How'd Molly get into your apartment to plant those photos? The security cameras in the lobby should have—"

Kacie shook her head. "Remember Billy Barton?"

"The kid at the security desk in your apartment building?"

"Yes. He's admitted to looking the other way when she came by, showed her where the blind spots on the camera were so she wouldn't get filmed. Apparently, she slipped him a few extra bucks. The police are questioning him and will probably charge him."

"How'd Molly know your security code? Get a key to your apartment?"

She blushed guiltily. Even though she'd told herself she had no reason to have suspected any of her employees, she still couldn't believe she'd been so careless.

"I made the mistake of leaving my purse out where, apparently, Molly helped herself to my password book and made a putty mold of my key."

"Guess it's too late for me to lecture you about keeping your password book at home, not in your purse?"

She grinned. "Lesson learned."

Brennan's eyes began to glaze over again, and though she didn't want to stop talking with him, Kacie knew he needed his rest. There would be plenty of time to talk when they were both a little less traumatized.

Standing again, she pressed a soft kiss to his forehead. "Sleep. I'll be here when you wake up."

She wanted him healthy as soon as possible, because if there was one thing she had learned from all of this, it was that she wanted Brennan Sinclair in her life forever. She just had to work up the courage to tell him.

"What do you think she meant?" Brennan asked.

Justin and Riley were sitting in chairs on either side of the bed. Though they hadn't said so, Brennan got the distinct impression that they'd had an argument. Anger seethed beneath the surface, causing a heaviness in the atmosphere. That, along with the fact that they'd yet to look at each other, even when talking to each other, made him sure of it.

"What who meant?" Justin asked.

"Before Molly jumped out the window, she said it wasn't over, that she was just getting started."

"She obviously intended to continue to hurt Kacie," Riley said.

"Then why kill herself?"

"Maybe she thought when it was revealed who Molly really was, Kendra Carson would be exposed, too," Riley said.

"Or it could be that you're trying to apply logic to a woman who had none," Justin said. "She was delusional on top of being insane."

"And you're certain, other than the kid at the security desk, no one else was in on this with her? Her family? They might all feel they have an ax to grind if they know who Kacie really is."

"We're sure her family knew nothing about this." Justin finally looked over at Riley. "Wouldn't you agree, Ingram?"

As if agreeing with her partner went against her better judgment, she simply said, "Molly's family doesn't know about Kacie. They don't know why she was in the building and have no idea that the office window she jumped from belonged to the Kacie Dane Foundation."

"You're sure?" Brennan said. "Maybe I should talk to the oldest brother."

"If you do," Justin said, "you'll stir up suspicions he doesn't have. The police have been extraordinarily cooperative because they don't want a media frenzy any more than Kacie does.

"Molly, Sally, or whatever the hell she wanted to call herself, is dead by her own hand. Everyone in the room saw it happen. No one wants to have to explain how a handcuffed woman threw herself out a window and killed herself."

He could see where that would cause some problems. And maybe it was his own paranoia at work. He'd been worried for Kacie night and day for weeks. It was hard to let go of the idea that she wasn't completely safe.

And it would be a million times harder to let go of Kacie. But let her go, he must.

Chapter Thirty-Five

It was a scene set for seduction. Her very first. Brennan had left early this morning to meet with the police. Noah had arrived to smooth out the rough edges from last week's bizarre event. She had offered to meet with them, too, but Brennan had assured her it was more of a diplomacy meeting than anything else.

So with a day to herself and no appointments, what was a girl to do but get ready to seduce her man? She'd spent a couple of hours at the spa, getting a much-needed facial, all-over body scrub, and a mani-pedi. She was now polished from the top of her head to the tips of her toes.

While she had been gone, the apartment was cleaned, thanks to her wonderful cleaning service. And since premade salads, Greek yogurt, or PB&J sandwiches—her repertoire in the kitchen—didn't say sexy in any language, she'd ordered a delicious meal to be delivered from one of her favorite restaurants.

Candles were glowing, the wine was opened and breathing, and Kacie was wearing one of her favorite summer dresses. Off-white, with lace shoulder straps, the dress landed about three inches above her knees, showing off her still-glowing tan to perfection. Finishing off the ensemble were delicate-looking sandals that highlighted her perfectly painted toenails.

She'd washed her hair this morning, blow-drying it till it was poker straight, but before applying her makeup, used a curling iron to create sexy, soft waves. Her makeup was light, her perfume subtle, her jewelry understated and classy.

Everything was perfect, everything was set. She was missing only one other ingredient for her perfect night, the most important one. Where was her man?

Brennan sat across from the LCR leader. They'd walked out of the police station with everything tied up as neatly as something like this could be tied up. Outside the station, Justin had slapped him on the back and told him he'd see him soon. Riley had given him one of her grave smiles and said good-bye. They'd walked away, presumably to handle another case.

McCall had nodded toward a bar in the distance and invited him for a drink. Hard to believe a hard-edged man like Noah McCall could soothe ruffled feathers and indignant feelings, but that's exactly what he'd done. Brennan was still new enough to LCR to be unfamiliar with its protocol when it came to local authorities, but McCall seemed to have a good relationship with the NYC Police Department. The LCR leader's diplomacy skills would do a US ambassador proud. After an explanation about the circumstances, including the need for privacy for one of their own, the case was now closed.

Molly/Sally's body had been claimed by her older brother and laid to rest. According to McCall, the family had drifted apart, and Sally had suffered the most. In and out of mental hospitals since she was fifteen, she'd tried suicide twice. The last time they'd heard from her, she was working as a veterinarian technician in Jacksonville, Florida. But none of them had made any real attempt to see her in a couple of years. Maybe that was another reason why the young woman was screwed up. No one seemed to really give a damn.

"So you've completed your first LCR operation and did a damn good job."

Brennan grimaced. "Not exactly a smooth op. Accused the wrong person, while the real perp almost succeeded in killing the primary. And instead of being able to put the criminal away, I let her commit suicide.

"And the one guy we can pin something on is so pitiful looking that even my less-than-compassionate heart has issues with putting the kid away."

Poor Billy Barton had been a pawn in Molly's sick game. He swore he hadn't known what Molly was up to, or even that Kacie was Molly's intended target. She'd given him extra money, which he'd sorely needed for a band he was trying to put together, and that was that. When he'd learned exactly what was going on, the kid had broken down and blubbered like an infant.

"I'm just damn lucky it turned out as well as it did," Brennan said.

"I've never expected perfection from my people. Both Justin and Riley thought the same thing you did, that Tara was Kacie's stalker. And while Molly's death is regrettable, she made that decision herself. Something I learned a long time ago is that you can't force someone to be evil—it's innate. She showed that, and while a lost life is always regrettable, she made her choice.

"Protecting Kacie was your primary goal, and you did an admirable job."

Brennan gave a nod. While he appreciated McCall letting him off the hook, he wasn't feeling quite so stellar about his job performance. Not only had Kacie been locked up with a lunatic, Brennan had slept with the woman he was protecting.

As first jobs went, he couldn't say he was all that impressed with himself.

McCall's mouth tilted a little, as if he was aware of Brennan's thoughts. His words confirmed it. "I talked with Kacie a few days ago. Not only did she insist that you were an excellent bodyguard, she wanted me to know the relationship you two developed has had an amazing effect on her self-confidence. She said you've helped her heal."

Before Brennan could scramble with an appropriate response, McCall leaned forward and added, "You're human, Sinclair. And Kacie is a vibrant, beautiful woman. However, I do not want her hurt, so let me ask you this—how do you feel about her?"

Of all the conversations he thought he might be having with McCall, talking about his feelings for Kacie wasn't one of them. In his world, a guy didn't share things like that with another man. Especially one who was his boss.

But McCall looked upon Kacie as family, so Brennan could understand his concern. Didn't make talking about his fascination for Kacie any easier to discuss. In fact, it made it harder.

"I care about her, McCall. Of course I do. I just—"

Hell, he what? She was a model, heading toward super-stardom. He was a hated has-been, a former celebrity with an ax to grind with the press. Brennan had no desire to step back into the limelight. Kacie was in the news constantly, whereas he wanted to smash every reporter's face into a wall.

He and Kacie were like oil and vinegar. They blended well for a while, but once things settled, they would have to separate. It was only natural.

McCall's eyes revealed an odd sadness, but he nodded. "I understand. So, since the doctor has released you, I have another job for you."

The LCR leader stood, threw down several bills for their drinks, and said, "Be at the airport at six in the morning. I'll send you the details."

McCall disappeared, leaving Brennan staring sightlessly into space. A grinding, hollow sensation had settled deep in his gut, a feeling he feared would never go away.

She sensed something was wrong the moment he walked into the apartment. They'd been living with each other for weeks, and other than sleeping, had been with each other almost every moment.

Though they hadn't made love since before his injury, she had slept beside him every night. And in the dark, before falling asleep, he'd held her and they talked…about anything…everything. She knew this man. His expressions, his body language, even the little twitch in his right eye when he wanted to say something but restrained himself. And now, though there was no discernable twitch, his eyes held a sadness she wasn't used to seeing.

Standing in the middle of the foyer, she waited for him to tell her what was wrong. They'd come so far, been through so much in such a short time. She trusted him with every secret, every fear. He had to know he could trust her, too.

Instead, an instant after she sensed his worry, his expression changed to that wickedly sexy grin that made her knees weak and every erogenous place in her body come alive.

"Hello, beautiful. What did you do today without your giant shadow hounding your every step?"

Kacie took a breath. Okay, so he wasn't ready to talk about whatever it was that was bothering him. He'd had a long day. While she'd been pampering herself, getting ready for a big date, he'd been doing some actual work. A good meal, a little wine, some sweet loving, and he'd be in a more talkative frame of mind.

Instead of telling him the truth, that not seeing him all day had made her feel empty and sad, she gave the smile that had earned her multiple million-dollar contracts. "A little of this, a little of that." She added some sexiness to her smile. "Are you hungry?"

There was the heat and need she wanted to see in his eyes. "Famished," he said softly and held out his hand.

She went to him. Aware that her feelings were written all over her face. She couldn't hide them from him any longer. Even if he didn't feel the same way, this man who had given her so much needed to know how much he meant to her.

Pulling her into his arms, he held her tight, almost too tight. Then, as if he realized it, he loosened his arms and looked down at her. "You look good enough to eat, but is that chicken Parmesan that I smell?"

Pleased to see the teasing light in his eyes, she grinned. "It is."

"You managed chicken Parm on top of everything else you did today?"

"I can't take credit for that, but I did toss the salad."

"Amazing woman." He dropped a tender kiss on her lips. "Is dinner ready, or do I have time to shower?"

"You have plenty of time to shower."

His eyes roamed over her. "If you didn't look so damn perfect and delectable, I'd invite you to shower with me."

Remembering their last shower together, she almost said yes simply because she wanted a good memory to replace the bad one. Of course, what happened after that had been one of the most amazing nights of her life, so maybe it wasn't too bad of a memory.

Before she could answer him, he dropped a quick kiss to her nose. "I'll be back in a flash."

Releasing her, he stepped around her and headed up the stairs, his long legs taking the steps two at a time.

Kacie stared up the stairway long after he had disappeared. The sad but resigned look in his eyes that last second had told her what was bothering him. A heaviness, along with a deep, aching hollow spot in her heart, settled inside her.

She knew what was coming, knew what was wrong. Now she just needed to figure out how to deal with it.

CHAPTER THIRTY-SIX

She had gone all-out. The whole time he'd been showering and then dressing, he'd been gearing himself up to tell her he was leaving. In fact, he'd been set to leave tonight and grab a hotel room somewhere till morning. But that was before he realized how much she had done. She had wanted tonight to be special, and for the life of him, he couldn't find the words he should've said.

Instead, he complimented the table setting, the wine, the candles, and music. She'd even bought flowers and placed them in the middle of the table. Sure, he'd had plenty of women do all sorts of things to try to impress him, but none had been so damn sweet or meant so much to him.

"How'd you know that chicken Parmesan is my favorite Italian meal?"

She blushed and dropped her eyes. "I looked it up online." Raising her head, she said, "I know I said I wouldn't snoop on you like that, but I just wanted you to have your favorite meal."

He couldn't resist teasing her. "I suppose that means we're having pecan pie for dessert?"

Eyes wide with panic, she glanced toward the kitchen, where he figured a chocolate cream pie was sitting in the fridge waiting to be sliced.

"You know you can't believe everything that's online, don't you?"

"I know that, but this site really seemed to know you. So maybe your second favorite is chocolate cream pie?"

He had to laugh, unable to keep up the pretense. "Actually, chocolate cream pie is my favorite. I just wanted to see how you would react."

"Not nice at all. I was all set to run down to that new Southern restaurant ten blocks away."

"So is anybody saying anything good online? I know there's plenty of garbage." He grimaced. "You already know all that, plus the truth."

"Well, let's see." She grinned wickedly. "When you were a kid, you had a stuffed toy turtle named Mean Joe Green. You once walked naked down 5th Avenue in December because your teammates told you the coach makes all new players do this. And, oh…" Her eyes went wide with delight. "In college, a girl tied you up and poured a jar of honey all over your naked body."

He grinned, pleased that there were some fun things among all the bad. "Let me set the record straight. First, it was a stuffed rhino, not a turtle. Second, it wasn't 5th Avenue, it was Times Square, and I was allowed a jockstrap and a pair of shoes."

"Oh my." She exaggeratedly fanned herself. "And the honey?"

Leaning close, he took her hand and dropped soft little kisses on the back of it. "It was the other way around. I tied her up, poured honey on her naked body, and…" His tongue licked up her hand to her wrist as he said softly, "I licked it all off."

"Oh…" She breathed out softly. "Really?"

He was elated to see the flush of heat in her face and the obvious interest in her eyes. He could almost guarantee that not that long ago she would have been appalled at the thought of something like that.

However, he couldn't take credit for something that never happened. "No. If my parents had heard about me doing something like that, I don't care how big or old I was, I would've had my ass whipped by both of them."

"You had great parents, didn't you?"

"The very best."

There would always be a stab to his heart when he thought about his mom and dad, not just because he missed them so much, but because he hadn't been the best son when they were alive.

He took one last bite of his dinner and pushed the plate away slightly. "That's about the best chicken Parm I've ever had."

"I'm glad you liked it. Ready for dessert?"

If he answered the way he wanted, he'd have her spread out on the table before him like a feast. But if that happened, then he wouldn't be able to say the things he needed to say.

"Sounds good." He stood and took both their plates. "I'll do cleanup while you get that ready."

Though they hadn't eaten many meals at the apartment, other than breakfast, they'd gotten into a routine. When he'd been married, he had hated kitchen duty. Of course, except for the occasional salad, Vanessa hadn't been one for the kitchen either.

Since there was very little to clean up, by the time he rinsed the dishes and loaded the dishwasher, she had sliced the pie and poured coffee.

Kacie felt like she was on a seesaw that might go wild any moment and fling her across the room. One moment Brennan was seducing her with a hot look or an erotic gesture, and the next he was acting like she was his friend and nothing more. She'd gone hot and cold so many times over dinner that she feared her body temperature would be permanently out of whack.

Taking a tray with two slices of pie and the coffee, she headed toward the living room. Before she got two steps out of the kitchen, he was taking the tray from her.

"Where to?"

Oh, how she wanted to be confident enough with him to grab the jar of honey out of her pantry, and say, *Follow me*, and lead him straight up to her bedroom. The conversation earlier had her thinking some delicious and wickedly sticky thoughts.

But since she was far from the confident sexual being she wanted to be, she said, "Follow me," and led him to the living room instead.

Brennan placed the tray on the coffee table and waited until Kacie sat down before he handed her a piece of pie. She thanked him and waited till he'd served himself before she took a bite. The chocolate hit her tongue, and the sound she made would've made any porn star envious.

Judging by the heated look Brennan gave her, he thought so, too.

He raised a brow. "Good pie?"

Dark red wasn't her best color, but she was sure it was the exact shade of her cheeks.

"Try it."

He did and made a similar noise. Although his sound was decidedly masculine and, to her ears, much sexier.

"Told ya."

"My favorite meal, my favorite pie. Are you trying to seduce me, Ms. Dane?"

"Are you seducible, Mr. Sinclair?"

"Darling, all you have to do is look at me to seduce me into doing anything for you."

Like staying with me forever?

But of course she couldn't say any such thing. She had no real clue how Brennan felt about her, beyond sexual desire. Did he want to continue seeing her? How would that work with his job as an LCR operative?

"Kacie, I—"

She stood, cutting him off. She couldn't do it. By the look in his eyes, she was about to get a standard, albeit gentle, *Well, it's been fun* shutdown, and she quite simply did not have the courage to face that tonight. Tomorrow would be soon enough to deal with the hard stuff.

Taking destiny into her own hands, she stood before Brennan and unzipped her dress. It slid to the floor, leaving her in a pair of white minuscule panties and nothing more.

"Holy hell," Brennan breathed. "What are you doing?"

"I'm trying to seduce you."

Turning her down never crossed Brennan's mind. If he lived to be a hundred, he would never forget the sight of this lovely, courageous woman standing before him, offering herself.

He stood, bringing their bodies within inches of each other. She gave him the smallest of smiles...so incredibly sexy, and said, "Want to follow me somewhere else?"

Even though he'd much rather pick her up and carry her, this was her show, her seduction. "I'll follow you anywhere."

She took his hand and led him up the stairs to her bedroom. Wearing only those tiny lace panties and nothing else, she was like every dream, every fantasy he could ever have. Her skin almost shimmered beneath the lights, and her hair fell in soft, thick waves to her lower back. How could anyone be so lovely and still be mortal?

Brennan walked into her bedroom, determined to show her, if not with words, then with his body, what she meant to him. He couldn't possess this dream forever, but he could have it tonight.

Pulling her into his arms, he kissed her, softly, tenderly, his mouth worshipping hers. He wanted to ravage her, savor her, devour her whole. Breaking away from the kiss, he looked down at her face. He had to make sure she was with him all the way. Only a short time ago, she'd been unable to let herself completely go and enjoy pleasure. Damned if he would push her into a setback by going too fast or being too demanding.

"Why did you stop?"

"Just wanted to look at you…see you."

"How about I see you, too?"

Together they unbuttoned his shirt. He started with the first button, she followed with the second, and so on. While she pulled at his shirt, he tugged his shoes off and started on his pants by unbuckling his belt. Before he could unzip, her fingers were there for him. As she pulled down his zipper, a small, confident smile played around her mouth. She was teasing him, torturing him. He loved it.

When at last his pants and underwear were on the floor, Kacie pushed him backward toward the bed. He dropped down onto it and watched. Even though every cell in his body told him to take over, claim her, make her his, he reminded himself again that this was Kacie's show. If she wanted to tease and torture him all night long, then he'd let her. He might die from it, but damn, it'd be a fun way to go.

She went to her knees in front of him and took one of his feet, pulling the sock off, then lifted the other and repeated the action. "Can't believe I said you have ugly feet."

He grinned. "So now you think they're pretty?"

"Well...not exactly pretty." She kissed the top of one foot. "But they brought you to me, so I think they're perfect."

This woman was going to break his heart.

Pulling her up to stand, he slowly removed her last piece of clothing. And when she was bare, he lowered his head and kissed her at the top of her sex. She gasped and grabbed his shoulder. Stopping for a moment, he looked up to make sure she was in the moment with him, not back in the past. The simmering heat in her eyes was a sight to behold. She was definitely right here with him.

Reassured and wanting to taste her more than he wanted his next breath, Brennan twisted her around until she lay on the bed and he was standing over her. Taking one of her feet, slender, narrow, and perfect, he slipped off her sandal. He kissed the top of her naked foot gently, and then, still holding that foot, took the other one, removed the sandal, and kissed it as well.

"You know, some people have foot fetishes," she said.

"If all feet looked like yours, I can understand why." Taking those beautiful feet, one in each hand, he pushed them forward until she was fully exposed to him. She was waxed, her sex totally bare, and colors from the palest of pinks to a deep shade of rose enticed him, enthralled him.

"What are you doing?"

"Looking at you."

"But why?"

"Because you're beautiful everywhere...and because I want to kiss you...everywhere."

"Oh..." She said the word on a soft, sexy sigh.

Before lowering his head, he checked her face. Her eyes were half-closed and still glittering with heat. Her perfect mouth was slightly open, as if in anticipation.

Putting his mouth to her, he licked delicately. Tasting her like this for the first time was an experience he wanted to savor, prolonging his pleasure and hers, too. She tasted as delicious as he had imagined. He kissed her, licked again and then, no longer able to wait, slid his tongue inside her and devoured her sweetness.

Heat consumed her, want overwhelmed her. Brennan's mouth on her was unlike any other feeling in the world. His tongued swept inside her, consuming, devastating her senses. Unable to control herself, she arched her body up to take him deeper. When he groaned, the vibration of his mouth sent her to the very edge.

"Kacie...look at me."

She looked down at him. His eyes were glittering with heat, unbelievable desire. Awash in her own need, she could barely keep her eyes open.

"Kacie," he said again.

She opened her eyes. "Yes?"

"Whose tongue is about to make you come?"

"Brennan...only Brennan."

Giving her a sweet, albeit hot smile, he said, "Damn straight. Only Brennan," and then put his mouth on her again. This time he didn't go slow, didn't go softly. His tongue lashed at her, then thrust deep inside, and he sucked greedily at her clitoris. Lights flashed behind her eyes. Brilliant, vibrant shades of every imaginable color swirled around her, and she soared to the highest peak, hung in ecstasy for several seconds, then fell softly back to earth.

When she opened her eyes, Brennan was standing over her again, his eyes questioning, wanting to make sure she was okay.

Mere words could never describe just how very okay she was. Wanting to show him, make him understand that there was nothing he could do with her or to her that would scare her ever again, she sat up and took him into her hand. Marveling at the silky, hard heat of him, she tenderly caressed him as she brought him to her.

Stopping her for a second, he quickly grabbed a condom from the nightstand and slid it on. Then he leaned over her again and once again let her set the pace. But this too controlled, too caring man needed to know that he could take her as hard and deep as he wanted and she would be right there with him. She trusted him, and she needed him to know that.

"Brennan?"

"What, baby?"

"You don't have to be so careful with me. I won't break."

"I don't want to scare you."

"I trust you, Brennan. Everything you do to me only makes me feel wonderful, powerful…beautiful. Forget about who I am, what I've been through. You're a man, making love to his woman. Take me and make me yours."

Something hot and wild flashed in his eyes, and Kacie felt a thrill of sheer, unadulterated excitement. With a rough, needy growl, Brennan took her hand that held him and, together, they pushed him inside her. When she let him go, he lay on top of her and plunged deep, retreated, and then went deep again. Then, setting up a rhythm that left her both breathless and crazy with need, he pounded into her as if he couldn't get enough. All Kacie could do was hold on and ride out the storm. This was what she wanted, what she needed. He wasn't treating her like a fragile flower or a victim, but as a sexual partner. As his woman.

Brennan could no longer hold back. He'd seen the heat and need in Kacie's eyes. They matched his own. She had given him permission to let go, and he was taking it, taking her. Claiming her as he'd never claimed another woman in his life.

As she tightened around him, her body telling him she was near release again, he leaned over her and covered her mouth with his, his tongue plunging ruthlessly into her mouth as deep and hard as his cock was thrusting inside her. His release tore through him, and he almost shouted at the explosion bursting through his body.

Kacie throbbed and pulsed around him, setting off another spark of release he'd never expected. Holding her hips still, he thrust again and then once more.

To avoid crushing her, he rolled her over until she lay on top of him, boneless and limp.

"Okay?"

"Okay?" She sputtered out a laughing breath. "Try spectacular."

Brennan tightened his arms around her, treasuring and savoring, glorying in the incredible experience of having this bright, beautiful, courageous woman in his arms. How in the hell was he ever going to let her go?

He held her quietly, gently, for a long while, reveling in the closeness. He wouldn't allow himself sleep. Wanted to treasure every moment...every single second. Every soft breath, every sweet sigh. The memory of holding this woman in his arms tonight would have to last him a lifetime.

She'd been silent for so long, he figured she'd fallen asleep and was surprised when her soft voice whispered, "Brennan?"

"Hmm?"

"Did you like tasting me?"

Arousal slammed through him at her words. His satiated body instantly on alert, he answered truthfully, "Yeah...I liked it, a lot. You're sweet, salty. Delectable."

"Better than chocolate cream pie?"

Smiling, he rolled her to her back and leaned over her. "Much better." A tender kiss to her lips, then another. "Deliciously addictive."

"So...I was wondering what you might taste like."

He went hard in an instant. Imagining her luscious mouth wrapped around him was enough to stop his heart and then bring it back to life in a thundering gallop.

While he was trying to deal with his imagination and just how he'd be able to handle a sexually curious Kacie, she decided to take things into her own hands. Her slender fingers wrapped around him, holding, caressing...

Brennan's strangled breath produced an incredibly sexy laugh from her. And then she gently pushed him onto his back. He had seen Kacie with many emotions and expressions, but he had never seen her like this. Her face showed resolve. Her eyes glittered with intent. She had an agenda.

Needing to touch, to taste her, too, he reached for her, but she pulled away from him. "No...let me. Please."

And he knew what she meant. What she wanted. This was Kacie in her element. Taking her sexuality back, taking her power back. What was a besotted, overly aroused man to do but lie there and allow it to happen?

An adventurous and sexually confident Kacie Dane showed him exactly what making love was all about. Every place she touched, every part of his body her mouth landed on zinged to life. She started at his neck, trailing soft kisses down his torso and across his stomach. Brennan sucked in his breath, barely moving.

She teased, explored. She savored. When she reached the part of him that was hard and aching for her, she slowed down and began to explore more thoroughly. Caressing, kissing, her lips and hands both curious and incredibly arousing.

Barely breathing, Brennan's entire body was stiff as he fought for control. Those soft, sweet kisses and long, slow licks were going to be the death of him.

"Kacie, I…" Hell, he didn't know what he was about to say. Coherent speech was beyond him. And then she took him into her mouth. Moist heat surrounded him, and then she took him deeper.

Known for his control, his incredible restraint, Brennan lost it all. Grabbing her shoulders, he pulled her up and rolled with her on the bed until she was beneath him. He checked her expression, just to make sure he hadn't scared her. The hot gleam in her eyes, the triumphant smile on her face said she knew exactly what she'd done to him.

And then she whispered words he figured he'd hear in his dreams for the rest of his life, "I like your taste, too."

With a growl, Brennan showed her that his famous control meant nothing when it went up against a sexually confident Kacie. Thinking rationally for one more second, he grabbed a condom. Tearing the packet with his teeth, he slid the protection on quicker than he ever had in his life and then thrust deep inside her.

Kacie's arms came around him, her legs wrapped around his waist, and she held on tight for a hot, fast, no-holds-barred moment of sexual frenzy. Brennan let loose, devouring her sweet mouth even while his body drove into her over and over, the harsh sounds of his breathing a perfect accompaniment to Kacie's own frantic gasps. Then, like a meteor falling to earth, release crashed into him with the mind-blowing, life-altering force of a tsunami.

CHAPTER THIRTY-SEVEN

He lay there gasping, still coming down from the incredible high, the sweat had barely dried on their bodies, when she said softly, "You're leaving."

Brennan tightened his arms around her, wanting to prolong the sweetness just another moment and then sighed. No use putting off the inevitable. "Yes."

"When?"

Turning slightly, he glanced at the alarm clock beside the bed, surprised how quickly the night had passed. "Couple of hours."

"Where are you going?"

"Have no idea. McCall said he'd text me details."

"Would it do any good if I asked you to stay?"

"Kacie…don't."

Her hurt was a palpable, painful presence, but she still had the courage to ask, "Will I see you again?"

"I think it would be best if you didn't."

"Best for whom?"

"For both of us. We live in two different worlds. You can't come into mine, and I sure as hell can't be in yours."

She sat up and looked down at him. Though it was dim in the room, he had no problem seeing the glint of tears in her eyes.

Dammit, he shouldn't have stayed the night. He should've grabbed his clothes, given her a peck on the cheek, and left. Staying had only made leaving a billion times more painful.

"Why can't you be in my world?"

"Because it's a world I despise. And one that despises me."

He hadn't meant to be so blunt, but he had to tell her the truth. He hadn't done her career any good by being seen with her. He would damage it even more if he stayed.

Sitting up, he leaned against the headboard and stated his case. "When I left the limelight a few years back, I swore I would never return. This kind of life eats at you from the inside out. It corrodes and corrupts."

"You see me as being corroded and corrupted?"

Out of everyone he'd known in his life, save his mother, she was the least corrupted person he'd ever met. "No. You're neither. And maybe it's because you have an innate goodness in you that can't be penetrated by all the shit surrounding you."

She snorted. "I'm no saint, Brennan. I just choose to believe that this world, and the people in it, have more good in them than bad."

"I hope you always believe that, sweetheart. But I know different."

"I can understand why you would feel that way. You were treated horribly when you should've received compassion and help."

"You think the shit people said about me was what turned me off to this life? It wasn't. It was what I allowed it to do to me. If I hadn't been so corruptible, I would've been the kind of father my little boy deserved."

He held up his hand. "And before you try to defend me by saying Vanessa should've looked out for his well-being, let me just say that even though she should have, the responsibility was still mine. I was a bad husband and an even worse father. I got what I deserved."

Kacie closed her eyes against the threatening tears. Brennan made it impossible to be angry with him. He beat himself up worse than anyone else could. But she could hurt for him. Hurt for the man who'd made mistakes and couldn't take them back. Hurt for the man who would've made a wonderful father if circumstances had been different and he had been older, and wiser. Hurt for a man who had been unjustly judged and never fought to redeem himself because he didn't care enough to try.

Yes, she hurt for him...and she hurt for them. Because, despite the fact that they were good together and she knew he cared deeply for her, it was clear he saw no future for them.

The ache in her chest was an agonizing pain, unlike anything she'd ever felt before. Tears threatened to explode, pounding against her eyelids, and she fought them for all she was worth. She would not give into the pain right now. Not yet.

She went back into his arms, cherishing the last few moments she would have with hm. Part of her wanted to scream at the injustice of at last finding love only to have it denied her. But Kacie knew too much about loss not to appreciate what she had been given. Meeting this man, getting to know him, making love with him, had been a gift. He had saved her life, freed her sexually, and treated her as if she was something special.

She refused to sully those gifts with a temper tantrum or waste precious moments in tears. She would appreciate this time, and when he said good-bye, then and only then, would she allow the grief to take over.

But she had to make him understand. Had to make it clear how she felt. She raised her head and pressed a soft kiss to his mouth. "I won't try to convince you to stay, but I do think you're wrong. You…we…can have everything if you just let us have it. We don't have to live in the limelight. We can work all that out, make a private life for ourselves."

The dubious expression on his face told her he didn't believe it. Wasn't buying it.

"Fine, I'll drop it. But I want you to know that you'll always be welcome in my home, and in my arms."

"Kacie…don't. I don't deserve—"

"You deserve everything good and fine, Brennan Sinclair." She pressed another kiss to his hard, unsmiling mouth but pulled away before she got carried away or became a sobbing, emotional mess. "While you pack and dress, I'll make coffee."

"You don't have to do that. I can grab something when I get to the airport."

She didn't argue but got up and walked out of the room. Yes, it was cruel. She was completely nude, and though she felt she had plenty of flaws, she knew what her naked body did to Brennan. It turned him on, and she knew if she turned around, he'd be aroused.

So, yes, perhaps it was unfair of her, but since she didn't cry, throw things, or have a temper tantrum, this was her way of protesting, of saying, *You could have this if only you were willing to fight for it.*

Sadly, she knew he wasn't.

Brennan stood at the door. He didn't want to go. Leaving her felt like he was leaving a body part behind. And in a way, he was, because she now possessed his heart, whether she realized it or not.

"Even though there's no crazy woman after you, I want you to be careful, Kacie. Promise me."

"Of course I will. I grew up in the city. And believe me, I learned my lesson with Harrington."

"Will you be going on trips for the Montague job?"

"Not for a while. Most of the shoots will be in a studio." She shrugged. "He said something about going to New England in September. But I should be in the city for most of the summer."

He couldn't tell her that he would come back and see her. He wouldn't do that to her. Making promises he couldn't keep was a thing of his past.

"If you need anything…" He had to leave it like that.

Something like compassion gleamed in her eyes, and she reached up and kissed him softly on the mouth. "Be safe, Brennan, and thank you for everything."

It felt like a dismissal, like she wasn't hurting nearly as much as he was. And, dammit, wasn't that what he wanted? He didn't want her hurt or sad. He wanted her to live a long, happy life.

Still, he couldn't resist leaving an impression. Pulling her into his arms, he took advantage of the small gasp she released and covered her mouth in a soul-searing, body-melting, devouring kiss. His tongue plunged, retreated, and he ate at her lips, sucked hard, and plunged again. Over and over, until their bodies were plastered against each other, their hands touching, caressing, creating a need that would never be fulfilled.

Finally, he pulled away. They were both breathless, both aching. He stared at her for one more long second, and then he was gone.

Chapter Thirty-Eight

"Arch your shoulder just a bit more.

"That's right, love. Okay, just a little less smile. Give me a dreamy look… There you go. Tilt your head…not that far. Okay… okay that's good. Keep moving like that."

The camera clicked multiple times, and not for the first time Kacie was grateful for her training. Smiling when you wanted to cry wasn't easy, but it was doable. Smiling as if you're the happiest person on earth took work. Insinuating that Montague's new Kacie Dane cosmetic line could change a life, or at least make your life happier, was her job. A tall order at any time, but when your heart was broken, it was almost impossible.

Yet she smiled, laughed, and joked as if life couldn't be more perfect, when everything inside her felt as if it would disintegrate at any moment.

It had only been hours, yet she missed Brennan as if he'd been gone for weeks. Perhaps it was the dread of knowing that when she returned home, he wouldn't be there. She would miss their morning coffee together—she wasn't the most cheerful person in the morning, but Brennan had somehow always made her smile even when she was grumpy. They used to review her agenda while sipping that first cup, and she would always laugh at how he'd gripe about this event or that. She had liked his sense of humor, his realistic way of looking at life, and his kisses…oh, how she would miss his kisses.

Even if he had stayed, he wouldn't have been around much. She knew from talking to Skylar that an LCR operative was on call twenty-four/seven. And an operation could take days, weeks, or even months to complete and close. But at least she'd have known that he would eventually come home to her. Now, he wouldn't come back at all.

"That's a wrap, love. Great job."

Kacie smiled her appreciation for the photographer, who was both a professional and not a jerk. He was a Montague exclusive, and she would be working with him on all the photo shoots. She'd worked with enough unkind and downright cruel photographers to appreciate the ones who not only enjoyed their craft but also made the shoot pleasant for the models.

Even though it had been a short gig, just so the photographer and advertisers could consult on their vision for the campaign, Kacie realized she was beyond exhausted. She'd gotten almost no sleep last night because both she and Brennan had been insatiable. And this morning she'd gotten her heart broken. That was enough to tire out any girl.

A nice cup of hot tea for the blues, a couple of ibuprofen for her pounding head, and a long, hot bath for her tense muscles were all in her immediate future. After that, she would have to wing it. An hour-long crying jag sounded tempting, but since she had another shoot tomorrow, she couldn't indulge.

Settling back into a taxi, Kacie closed her eyes and wondered what Brennan was doing at this very moment. Was he on another case already? He had told her about his training, and Noah wouldn't have hired him if he wasn't an expert in his field, but she couldn't help but worry.

"We're here, miss."

The taxi driver's voice jerked her awake. She hadn't fallen asleep in a taxi in years. The idea that she might actually be able to sleep tonight perked her up. She paid the driver and stepped out onto the street.

"Kacie, where's Brennan Sinclair? Did you two break up already?"

Carlton Lorrance stood in front of her. The mean gleam in his eyes made her think of a rabid wolf looking viciously at his next meal and not giving a damn who he had to tear apart to fill his belly.

He had disappeared from the scene for the past couple of weeks, and Kacie hadn't spared a moment thinking about him. Too bad he hadn't stayed gone.

Not wanting to waste a single moment of breath speaking to the jerk, Kacie turned her head and ran toward her building. The flash of a camera bulb told her he'd brought a photographer, so any lies he told would be accompanied by photographs.

Refusing to even look their way, Kacie dashed into her building. The second she entered, Vincent, the security man on duty tonight, stepped in front of Lorrance and barked, "Get out before I phone the police."

"I've got rights."

"Not in this building you don't. Now get."

Flashing a grateful smile and wink to Vincent, Kacie made rapid strides to the elevator. She needed to remember to give him an extra tip for his help.

Finally making it to her front door, Kacie went inside. Quickly dealing with the security panel on the wall, she then leaned back against the closed door, and breathed her first easy breath of the day.

It hit her once more how very lonely the apartment felt. After living in each other's pockets for so long, not having Brennan beside her felt as though she had a limb missing.

Refusing to fall into that deep abyss of self-pity and loneliness that called out to her, Kacie set about doing what she'd promised herself. She first went to the kitchen and poured water into a kettle for her tea. While she waited for the water to boil, she went to the half bath off the hallway and downed a couple of painkillers.

The shrill cry of the tea kettle brought her back to the kitchen. With quick efficiency, she made a large mug of tea and then headed upstairs to her bedroom. Feeling quite proud of herself—after all, she'd already accomplished two of her three agenda items—she opened her bedroom door and flicked on the light.

The tea dropped from her hand, and Kacie barely registered the sting of hot liquid as it splattered over her legs and feet.

Breath rasped from her lungs, and her entire world expanded and then shrank into a dark hole of horror. Her walls were once again covered in photographs of William Harrington raping her. Who…what…?

A noise sounded behind her. Whipping around, almost stumbling, she faced her nightmare, her horror…her very own boogeyman.

William Harrington III had risen from the grave.

"Hello, my jewel. At last we're together again."

An electrifying pain clenched her muscles in a hideous mass of agony. With a small cry, Kacie tumbled into a dark, evil whirlpool of horror.

The Gulfstream G650 leveled out at 35,000 feet. The instant the pilot announced it was safe to move around, Brennan heard the other LCR operatives unbuckle their seat belts, talking and laughing.

He hadn't lifted his head since he'd sat down. Lying before him was the entire file on Kacie's case, from beginning to end, including all the background information on every person they'd investigated. Though Brennan knew the facts backward and forward, something kept niggling at his brain. Something wasn't right, but for the life of him, he couldn't pin it down.

"You going to join us, Sinclair?" McCall called out.

Lifting his head, he saw that everyone had gathered around the small conference table in the middle of the jet. Hoping whatever was bothering him would come to him soon, Brennan went to join his new co-workers.

He dropped into an empty seat and half-grinned at a comeback Sabrina Fox gave her partner, Aidan Thorne. He'd met the two only an hour or so ago and could already tell they were the type of partners who not only respected one another, but liked each other as well.

Tall, with long auburn hair, sparkling green eyes, and a surprisingly wicked sense of humor, Sabrina Fox made him think of the Raquel Welch poster from the old movie *One Million Years B.C.* She was both beautiful and powerful looking.

Her partner, Aidan, with his golden-blond looks and toothpaste-ad smile, had the kind of model handsomeness that would be more at home in Hollywood or on a magazine cover. Earlier, Sabrina had referred to him as LCR's Adonis. The vulgar comeback Thorne had given her had only made her laugh louder.

The dynamics of the two LCR partnerships he'd seen so far were interesting and seemed polar opposites. Whereas Fox and Thorne ribbed and snarked at each other like they were siblings, or best friends, Riley Ingram and Justin Kelly barely spoke to one another. Yet, other than a couple of disagreements, they had seemingly worked well together in New York.

As soon as everyone was seated, McCall said, "Let's have a final look—"

A cellphone close to Sabrina buzzed, and McCall tossed her an amused glance. "Fox, tell your husband that if he wanted to be in on LCR meetings, he should have accepted my job offer."

She stood and grinned. "Sorry, boss, Declan is just a little more anxious these days than usual."

"Understandable. I talked to him a couple of times last week, but if he has new intel, feel free to put the call on speaker."

"Will do." She walked a few steps away and said, "Hi, darling. Anything wrong?"

While they waited for Sabrina, Brennan noted a marked difference in the atmosphere. Thorne was looking at Sabrina with an angry and frustrated expression, while Justin and Riley actually looked at one another as they talked in low voices.

Apparently seeing his confusion, McCall said, "To give you some background, Sabrina's husband, Declan Steele, leads a government agency few people are aware exists. A few months back, Sabrina was abducted and tortured because of her relationship with him. We rescued her and managed to uncover the name of the man responsible. Declan killed the man, but the one who hired him…the bastard behind it all, remains elusive.

"Last week we learned that a bounty has been placed on her and Declan's heads. Quite substantial. Declan is understandably… concerned for his wife.

"As Sabrina is one of our own, we've agreed to share any info we obtain with Declan's people and vice versa. We'll do so until this man can be caught or eliminated."

Aidan stood and began to pace within the small area as if he couldn't contain his rage. "And the thing is, this asshole has been around for years, and not one damn person seems to even know what he looks like. He's responsible for the deaths of hundreds, if not more. And now he's got a bounty on my partner."

McCall nodded. "We're not usually so willing to share intel with other agencies, no matter how friendly they are. And Declan's agency doesn't like to share either. However, not only do we have a mutual need to keep Sabrina safe, this man was responsible for both Sabrina's and Declan's abductions. He had them tortured. Taking him down will not only save more lives, but will bring a lot of people peace."

Before Brennan could ask questions, Sabrina returned to the group. "Sorry, he has no new intel, just wanted to check in with me." She grimaced. "Oh, he did have one piece of news. Apparently, the bounty on my head has been raised to $3 million, instead of the $2.5 million it was before."

"And I would imagine Declan's went up as well," McCall said.

"Five million for him. He's not the least bit flattered that his is higher." Though she kept her words light, Brennan saw the worry in her eyes.

"The bastard has never had two highly trained agencies working together to bring him down either," McCall said. "Working together, we'll get him."

"I know." Her eyes encompassed everyone. "Sorry for the interruption."

"No worries." McCall's eyes zeroed in on Brennan. "Everyone has a copy of Kacie's file. After an op, before putting it to bed, we review it and discuss what went right, what didn't."

Sounded damn fine to him. Maybe they could shed light on what he missed. "I just went through everything, from the beginning, when the threats began, until Molly's death." Brennan hesitated. How could he describe a gut feeling with no facts to back it up?

"And?" McCall prompted.

"There's something I'm missing. Something's off, but I can't place the problem."

"Then let's figure it out." McCall opened his own folder, and there was immediate silence as everyone reviewed what Brennan had been reading through.

After several long minutes, Sabrina looked up from her folder. "Tell us what you see, Brennan. All of this looks consistent with what I heard from Justin and Riley. What's got you concerned?"

Good question. Maybe if he talked it out himself, he could find the inconsistency.

"The first incident—the one in the park. We thought Tara was responsible because of the convenience. She's the one who encouraged Kacie to go out, even suggested she go to the park. We now know that Molly orchestrated everything to make Tara look guilty."

Brennan paused, and when everyone nodded their agreement, he went on, "But how did Molly know that Kacie would be in the park? She couldn't have camped outside the apartment twenty-four/seven, with a team of Rollerbladers all set to follow and scare the hell out of Kacie. And as guilty as Billy Barton looks, I believed him when he said he had no idea Kacie was involved."

"You think she had another accomplice, besides Billy and the guy she hired who killed Kacie's doctor?" Aidan said.

"What other explanation could there be?"

"Keep in mind," Justin reminded them, "Molly wasn't lacking for money. I agree she might've had more help, but it could've been some other Joe Schmoe, like Billy, who she paid to keep an eye on the apartment. And Kacie was gone from the apartment for over two hours. Plenty of time for him to call some buddies and tell them where to find her, and what to do to scare her."

"Both valid points," McCall said. "What else, Sinclair?"

"Molly admitted to Kacie that she cloned her computer, but LCR's tech people never found a laptop that belonged to Molly, and her office computer showed no evidence of cloning."

"And if it wasn't cloned," Riley said, "then she actually got into the apartment to send the emails and download the video. But Molly admitted to stealing Kacie's key from her purse and making a copy of it, as well as getting her security code from her password book."

"So if she had easy access to Kacie's apartment, and therefore her computer, why tell us she cloned the computer when she didn't? Or didn't have to. It doesn't make sense. What if she told us that to throw us off?"

"Throw us off what?" Justin asked.

Hell if he knew. Brennan was aware he wasn't making a lot of sense. But that's what was bothering him—too much didn't make sense, didn't add up. Whether he had McCall's approval or not, he already knew he would be heading back to NYC. He never should have left her alone.

"That could explain Molly's last words," Riley said.

"What did she say?" Aidan asked.

"That it wasn't over, that she had only begun. We took that to mean that when Molly's real identity was discovered after her death, Kacie's secrets would be revealed."

"But what if it didn't?" Justin said. "That would mean Kacie's still in danger."

And then it clicked, what had been hounding him that he hadn't been able to connect. "The email Kacie received at the beginning."

"The one supposedly from Harrington?" Sabrina said.

"Yes. Kacie commented that she'd looked through the emails before she decided to leave them until later. Then when she returned from her foundation's event, she read through the emails, and that's when she saw it."

"Yeah...and?" Aidan said.

"So if she looked through the emails before and didn't see it, then that would mean someone would've had to come inside her apartment and place the email there."

Everyone nodded.

"But Molly was with Kacie the entire night. They all went to the event in a limo and came home in it, too. Even if Molly left and then went back, the event was all the way across town. There's no way she would've had time to do that, especially not knowing when Kacie would want to leave. Someone else would've had to put the email on that stack."

Brennan muttered the words none of them wanted to accept, "Kacie's still in danger."

Without commenting further, McCall picked up the phone beside his seat and pressed a button. "Jack, change of plans. We need to get back to New York ASAP."

Doing what he'd been dying to do since he'd left her a few hours ago, Brennan pressed Kacie's speed-dial number on his cellphone. The phone rang, Brennan held his breath. No answer. As her voice mail came on, requesting the caller leave a message, Brennan went to the heart of the matter. "Kacie, you're still in danger. Get to the police immediately. And call me as soon as you get this message."

Brennan ended the call, wanting to say more…wanting to say anything that would stop what he already feared had happened. He had left her alone, vulnerable. And though there was no evidence that anything had happened to her, Brennan knew to his soul that it was already too late.

CHAPTER THIRTY-NINE

She woke up crying. At first she had no idea why she was so upset, so terrified. Darkness surrounded her, but that wasn't a big deal, not anymore. Since Brennan had come into her life, she had been able to sleep with the lights completely off.

Brennan.

He was no longer in her life. He had left. Was that why she was so sad? But no, it was something else. Something else had happened...something evil. She grasped for answers, but her brain refused to cooperate.

She closed her eyes on a sigh. She would worry about it tomorrow.

No! Her mind told her to wake up, something was very wrong. A fierce whisper told her to get up and fight. Fight what? Who?

Masculine laughter echoed in the darkness, and she froze with an unnamed terror. Who was that? Where was she?

She moved...or tried. Something had hold of her arms, wouldn't let go. She squirmed and wiggled, her heart pounding so hard it drowned out her hearing. Beneath the thunder of her heart, she heard gasping, sobbing breaths. Panic, set free, took control. She was caught, trapped. Who had done this?

Beneath the terror, she felt a moment of deepest despair.

Not again… Please, God, not again.

Lights blazed, and Kacie got her first glimpse of her new horror. Only it wasn't as scary as she'd feared. She was in the living room of a cabin. The décor was rustic, minimalistic. It was an open-spaced area where she could see both the kitchen and dining room from where she sat on the sofa.

She looked down. She was sitting on a sofa? Then why… Now she knew why she couldn't move. Her hands were cuffed together and then tethered to chains attached to the floor beside the sofa. Bound, chained. New panic threatened to explode her chest.

Think, Kacie.

How had she gotten here? She twisted left and right again, her eyes searching. No one was in the room with her. Who had done this? What had happened?

She closed her eyes. The last thing she remembered, she had come home from her shoot. She'd wanted tea and a bath, and then… Gasping gulps expanded her lungs then seized as she began to hyperventilate.

Harrington.

He wasn't dead. He was here. He had taken her.

"Now, now, you're getting all upset, and that's not what I want at all."

Kacie twisted around, trying to see where the voice was coming from. The voice sounded familiar. *Not* Harrington's. But who?

Footsteps came closer, and Kacie pushed away the fear so she could focus. She had sworn she would never be caught in such a predicament again. And though she felt pretty damn hopeless right now, she refused to give up. She had been through too much, had overcome hell, to allow this to happen to her again. She would kill this time. She didn't care who or what, she would kill before she allowed anyone to touch her without her permission.

At last, he came within view. Confusion whirled in her mind. Good-natured family man with two grandsons he adored and a wife who baked him apple pie on Sundays.

"Vincent?"

He smiled, and she wanted to cry, because it was the smile he always gave her. When he was talking about his grandkids, about how much he loved his wife, his kids. Why had this seemingly devoted husband, father, and grandfather kidnapped her?

"I can see your confusion, so let me set the record straight."

He sat across from her and proceeded to become a different person. Hair peppered with gray came off, revealing a slightly balding but much younger head. Bushy eyebrows were plucked off, revealing they had been glued to his other brows. He also removed the slightly yellowing teeth she was used to, revealing a gleaming, white smile. He was easily twenty years younger than the old man she'd known as Vincent.

"Who are you?"

His smile was kind and sweet—that hadn't changed, just the reason for it. "You know me, Kacie. And this is the real me." He spread his hands as if to apologize. "I had to wear this disguise so no one would know about us."

"Know what about us?"

"About how you feel about me. You know how this city is. Magazines and newspapers would have had a field day if they saw us together, the beautiful supermodel and the security guard. But now, we're here together, just like we were meant to be. No one ever has to know about us. We can be together, our privacy intact."

This was beyond bizarre. But he didn't look like he was going to hurt her yet. At least not yet. Maybe she could keep him talking and then try to talk him into letting her go. She refused to believe that wasn't possible.

"You're the one who put up those photos of me... with Harrington?"

"Such a sacrilege, Kacie. How could you let that man do that to you? He was at least forty years older than you."

Telling him she didn't *let* Harrington do anything to her would have been a waste of time and breath. It was more than apparent that Vincent was not playing with a full deck.

"You and Molly planned this together."

"Molly? Oh, you mean Sally? Yes, although you should know that I protected you quite a bit. She wanted to do really bad things to you, and I wouldn't let her."

"How did you two know each other?"

"I met her when she was just a kid. Did some yard work for the family. We kind of hit it off. Friend-like, nothing romantic, in case you're worried. She got in touch with me about her pet project. And, well..." He shrugged. "The rest you know."

"But why would you agree to something like this? You don't look—"

She was going to say *evil* but stopped herself. Antagonizing him wouldn't help her right now. She needed information first.

"I didn't at first. Seemed like a silly little girl's plan, but the money was enticing. I got the job at the building, and then I got to know you. I knew the moment we met we had something special. So I told Sally it was a go. She did most of the work. I just helped her out when she needed me to."

"Like those Rollerblading kids in the park?"

"Yes, I paid them, with Sally's money. But they promised they wouldn't hurt you. They didn't, did they?"

"No...just scared me."

He grinned. "Good. A little scare every now and then never hurt anybody."

"You know that Sally's…gone?"

"Oh yes, she told me it would probably happen. She paid me in advance, just in case."

"She knew she would die?"

"Yes. She told me all about your affair with her daddy and how it ruined her and her family. She really didn't want to live. I even offered to take care of that for her, but she wouldn't let me. Her only goal was to make you pay."

He grimaced as if embarrassed. "I'll admit, when she told me about you, I agreed with her at first…that you should pay. But then, after I met you and you were so kind and loving toward me, I knew I couldn't hurt you like she wanted.

"We agreed on a different plan. She would repay you, then she would die. And then, after that, you would be mine."

She swallowed past the fear. *Keep him talking, Kacie. Let him think this is all okay. Get him to trust you…and then get the hell out of here.*

"When you were at my apartment…before you…brought me here, you pretended to be Harrington. You talked and dressed like him."

"Yes, that was my last promise to Sally. I practiced for days so I could do his voice." His smile was full of pride. "I guess it's safe to say I fooled you."

"Yes, you did. You're very good."

"Thank you."

He acted as if he were going to get up, and she wanted to delay whatever his plans were for her as long as possible.

"So the photos in my bedroom the other times, did you do those, too?"

"Yes, everything that was done in your apartment was done by me. Molly never even went there, except that one time."

"Which time?"

Even though he had been acting almost normal, Kacie had never been fooled that he was sane. The look in his eyes when she asked that question confirmed not only insanity but also evil.

"Remember when you had a wisdom tooth pulled, and the dentist gave you something that knocked you out?"

She couldn't speak, could barely breathe. She nodded instead and waited to hear just how vulnerable she'd really been.

"Sally and I came in and watched you. You were completely knocked out." An unholy light entered his eyes. "Did you never wonder why you woke up naked?"

Nausea roiled in her stomach, and without any option whatsoever, Kacie turned her head and vomited on the floor. Her mind screamed, *no, no, no,* but her heart screamed for Brennan, who would eventually come for her, once people realized she was missing, but he would be too late.

It was all Brennan could do not to stick his head out the window and shout at the other drivers to move out of the way. He had to get to her, even though a part of him said it was already too late.

Once the decision to return had been made, McCall had been almost scarily efficient. Not only were two SUVs waiting on the tarmac when they arrived, but McCall had called in favors at the police department and asked that her apartment be checked immediately.

A report came back within half an hour that all seemed well. Kacie Dane was not in residence, but her security system was on, and there was no evidence of a break-in or anything else. Brennan tried to tell himself all was well. His gut said different.

When LCR pinged her phone and located it somewhere in her apartment, his suspicions were confirmed. He had lived with this woman long enough to know her routine. She might be unpredictable in many ways, but not in this. Never would she leave her phone behind when she went out.

He weaved in and out of traffic, for once glad for his familiarity with the city. McCall sat beside him, Justin and Riley in the back. Sabrina and Aidan trailed behind in the second SUV.

"I shouldn't have left her," Brennan muttered.

"You did what anyone would have done. It was over, Sinclair. We all thought it was over."

He glanced over at the LCR leader. The man was almost impossible to read, but the tense line of his jaw and set of his mouth told the story. He was as worried as Brennan.

Thirty-two minutes later, in what was probably record time but had seemed interminable to Brennan, they pulled in front of Kacie's apartment building. Brennan jumped out of the SUV and stormed into the building.

A man Brennan didn't recognize was at the security desk. He jerked his head up when they burst through the door. Knowing one of the other operatives would question the guard, Brennan raced to the elevator, McCall right beside him.

Seconds later, they were on the sixteenth floor and running to Kacie's apartment. He didn't bother knocking. He still had his key and immediately unlocked the door. An eerie silence greeted him.

"Weapon, Sinclair," McCall said calmly.

Shit, he knew that, knew what he was supposed to do, how he was supposed to act, but this was Kacie. Nevertheless, Brennan drew his gun, and with a nod, he entered with McCall coming in right behind him.

While McCall handled punching in the code on the security panel, Brennan said, "I'll take the upstairs," and ran up the stairway. He went to Kacie's bedroom first. The door was partially opened, and he pushed it farther. At first glance, nothing was out of place. Kacie wasn't a neat freak, but neither did she leave clothes lying around. Everything was in proper order. The bed was made. He checked the adjoining bathroom, as well as the walk-in closet, and again saw nothing wrong.

Taking his cellphone out, he punched in Kacie's number again, heard a ring. Standing in the middle of the room, he slowly turned, trying to locate the ringing phone. The closet. Brennan returned to the closet and stuck his head inside. Kacie had about a dozen purses lined up on a shelf. The phone must be in one of them.

He hit redial on his phone, waited for the ring, and then zeroed in on a small black purse on the second shelf. Grabbing it, he looked inside, and the rapid thud of his heart skidded to a halt.

Striding out of the closet, he met McCall's eyes as the man came into the room. "Everything looks fine downstairs. You got anything?"

"Yeah." Going to the bed, Brennan upended the purse. Kacie's phone, wallet, and keys tumbled onto the spread.

A multitude of emotions swept through him at once, but the overwhelming one was absolute, mind-numbing terror.

Looking over at McCall, Brennan finally said the words his gut had known all along. "She's been taken."

As tenderly as any loving caretaker, Vincent unlocked the ring that attached the cuffs at her wrists to the chain connected to the floor. What would he do now? Punish her? Rape her? Kill her?

Scooping her into his arms, he carried her into a bedroom. Kacie had stopped breathing the moment he touched her. Now, her body, stiff and terrified, lay in his arms. She had promised to fight, and she would, but her hands and ankles were still cuffed. If she tried to hit him to get away now, she wouldn't be able to run, only hobble. He would catch her, and then who knew what would happen?

As much as she hated it, her best bet was to act semi-compliant. No way could she act as if she were onboard with being kidnapped and held hostage. Vincent might be insane, but she didn't believe he was stupid. He'd never buy her immediate acquiescence. She would play it his way until she could take him down and get away.

"There, there," Vincent said. "I know throwing up upset you, and I'm sorry. You're probably suffering from first-night jitters." He grinned down at her. "First dates are always the scariest."

Settling her onto the bed, he took her cuffed wrists and attached them to a chain hanging from a brass rail on the headboard.

"Vincent…really. You don't need to chain me up. We can talk this through, together. We can figure something out that'll work for both of us."

"Now, Kacie. You know we're not that far into our relationship. Trust must be established, then we'll go from there."

Even knowing what his answer would be, knowing it went against her plan to fool him and made her seem weak, Kacie couldn't prevent the plea that tumbled from her mouth. "Please, Vincent. Don't do this. Please let me go."

He sat beside her and smoothed strands of hair off her forehead. "Why on earth would I let you go when I've worked so very hard for us to be together?"

She forced herself not to flinch at his touch. So far, other than knocking her out with a Taser and kidnapping her, he had been non-violent and eerily kind.

"Now, you're probably not hungry, since your tummy is upset, but I could make you some tea and toast. You spilled yours earlier."

She vaguely remembered the splatter of hot liquid. When she didn't show up for work tomorrow, they would call. Eventually, someone, perhaps the police, would go to her apartment. Would there be any evidence of her abduction? The tea would dry quickly. Had he taken the photographs down?

"What's got you looking so concerned?"

The question was so incredibly asinine, it was all she could do not to laugh in his face. "I was just thinking about the tea I spilled in my bedroom."

"Don't you worry about that. While you were sleeping like a lamb, I cleaned that up and even washed the cup. Took down those nasty photos, too." Triumph curved his mouth. "When they search your apartment, they won't find a thing out of place."

He went silent, staring down at her as if waiting. Having no real clue what he wanted, Kacie went with her instincts. "Thank you. I appreciate you cleaning up the mess."

"You're welcome. Don't you know I'd do anything for you?" He bent closer, and Kacie couldn't help herself, she shrank as deeply into the bed as she could.

Disappointment twisted his face for a moment, and then he sighed. "You're still shy, which is completely understandable." His finger touched her nose in a gesture of teasing affection. "We'll go slow, I promise. We've got our whole lives ahead of us."

Standing, he said, "I need to clean up the puke before it sets and smells up the entire house. Rest for a bit, and when I'm finished, we'll take that bath I know you're dying to have."

The minute he walked out and closed the door behind him, Kacie tugged on her cuffs, bruising and tearing her skin painfully. There was no give, no escape.

He'd left the light on, so she took a moment to familiarize herself with the layout of the bedroom. A large window to her left was plenty big enough to crawl through, but iron bars covered the glass on the outside.

The bedroom was just as minimalistic as the other part of the house. A dresser on the other side of the room held nothing on its surface. The nightstand beside the bed had an unopened bottle of water. That was it, the entire contents of the room.

Her head bounced back against the pillow as she fought the defeat that permeated her being, threatening to crumble her insides to dust.

No...hell no. She would not give up. She would not allow this to happen twice in her lifetime. She was strong...a fighter. And today...right at this moment, she was no longer Kacie Dane, beautiful model with a perfect and charmed life. She was once again Kendra Carson, rape survivor. She had fought a monster once before and won.

She would win again.

CHAPTER FORTY

Half an hour later, the bedroom door opened. Vincent appeared with that same smile she'd once thought so sweet. "Everything's in order again. I'll draw your bath water so you can take a nice, long soak."

He paused and waited. Kacie already knew what he wanted and figuring this was her best shot for surviving, she gave him the words he wanted to hear. "Thank you, Vincent."

His smile one of delight, he said, "My pleasure, Kacie."

Instead of going to the door she assumed led to the bathroom, he headed toward the bed instead. "But first, let's get you ready." He withdrew large, silver scissors from his back pocket.

She couldn't help herself. She shrank back, letting go of a whimper.

He shook his head as though disappointed. "Kacie, Kacie, Kacie. What do I have to do to show you I'm not going to hurt you?"

Giving him the obvious answer was probably not in her best interest, so she didn't say anything at all.

As though it was just another routine matter for him, Vincent cut open her blouse, pulled up the small elastic band between her breasts, and snipped her bra. Her skirt and panties received the same efficient treatment.

Her heart thundered in her chest and her breath came out in raspy pants. She shook her head. This couldn't be happening… not again. Dammit, not again!

Within a minute, she was nude.

Standing, Vincent didn't bother to hide his lust or satisfaction as his eyes roamed all over her body. "You're more beautiful than I remember."

He took her shredded clothes and tucked the scissors back into his pocket. "I'll draw your bath."

Shivering, she closed her eyes against ridiculously grateful tears. He hadn't raped her, cut her, or killed her…yet. However, until she breathed her last breath, she would fight. She just prayed she would get the opportunity.

A few minutes later, she heard him return and opened her eyes. He had changed into a loose T-shirt and a pair of gym shorts. "Since I won't be able to bathe you without getting wet myself, I thought it best if I put on different clothes." He bent down, but instead of reaching for her, he withdrew something from under the bed.

"Sit up for me, Kacie."

Refusing never crossed her mind. Time enough to fight when she could make it count. She eased up, wincing slightly at the pull of the chain securing her arms.

"Don't worry, baby. We'll get those cuffs off in a sec. Now bend your head for me."

She did what she was told and felt something encircle her neck. Seconds later, her wrists were unlocked from the chain behind her, then Vincent locked them to the collar he'd fastened around her neck.

"Not the most accessible way to bathe you, but until our relationship deepens, it's for the best."

He withdrew the chain from the cuffs at her ankles then scooped her up, cradling her in his arms again.

She felt like a damn praying mantis with her wrists so close to her neck, she could do nothing but let her hands hang, suspended, in front of her.

Carrying her into the bathroom, Vincent carefully lowered her into a large tub. The water was warm, which was a relief to her cold body and tense muscles. The fragrance of flowers permeated the room.

"That's my girl. Now, soak for just a bit while I go get your tea. When I return, we'll get you squeaky clean."

Okay, time to figure out a way out of this before he came back.

"Oops. Almost forgot." Laughing as if it was just an amusing incident, he reached down, grasped another chain attached to a bolt in the floor, and secured it to the cuffs at her ankles.

"Be right back."

Kacie leaned back against the cushioned pillow behind her. All warmth from the bath receded in an instant. He intended to make damn sure she was securely locked at all times. He'd said until their relationship solidified, trust established. How could she make that happen faster?

Within minutes, he returned with a cup of hot tea. "Now, since you can't use your hands, I'll have to feed it to you. Just little sips, though, because I don't want you to burn your sweet tongue."

Smile, dammit, Kacie!

Drawing on every bit of training she'd had, Kacie gave him a smile of thanks and then sipped from the mug he placed against her mouth. He allowed her several sips and then said, "You can finish it in bed. Let's get you cleaned up."

Taking a sponge from the side of the tub, he squirted liquid soap onto it and started washing her. The instant he touched her, she couldn't control the natural reaction to shrink away from him.

Though he gave a slight huff of exasperation, he didn't reprimand her for her fear. Instead, acting as if it was a natural thing, Vincent once again showed his efficiency by washing her entire body. When his hand went between her legs, she closed her eyes and let the tears fall. He gave her several hard swipes with the sponge and then continued down her legs to her feet.

He then stood, pulled the drain from the tub, and unlocked the chain from her ankle cuffs. Grabbing her as if she weighed nothing, he carried her soaking body back into the bedroom and stood her on the wood floor. Taking a towel he'd thrown over his shoulder, he dried her briskly.

"Let's get you some clothes, and then we're going to have a nice long chat."

Once again, she felt gratitude. He was going to allow her clothes. Though she knew it for what it was—he thought she would soften toward him if he gave her these small allowances. And though she would never *soften* toward him, she would take every allowance he gave her until she could get away.

"This will take careful maneuvering. Please don't try anything, or I will be forced to punish you. And I promise you, my punishments are far worse than anything William Harrington ever even considered."

He unlocked her wrists from her neck and then unlocked her cuffs. "Raise your hands over your head." When she complied, he slipped a nightgown over her head and allowed her to insert her arms into the sleeves. The instant the gown slid down her body, the hem landing several inches above her knees, he cuffed her wrists again.

"Okay, let's get you comfy, and then we'll chat."

Since she could do nothing more than move inches at a time, she waited to see if he would pick her up. But no, he just gave her a smile and said, "Get on the bed."

It was just another way for him to demonstrate her helplessness. Refusing to give him the satisfaction of asking for his help, Kacie shuffled to the bed. She didn't care if it took her the rest of the night. She would not ask for his help.

By the time she got to the edge of the bed, she was sweating and as close to breaking down as she'd been since this nightmare had begun. Turning slowly around, she plopped onto the edge of the bed with all the grace of a drunken monkey.

"I like your tenacity, my sweet, but stubbornness, especially at the beginning of our relationship, will not be to your advantage. If you had asked for help, I would have given it to you.

"Since it took you twenty minutes to walk thirty steps, and I'd like to get some sleep, I'll ignore your childishness and help you get into bed."

With humiliating ease, he lifted her and then dropped her onto the bed. He once again secured her wrists to the headboard and then her feet to chains at the bottom of the bed. She was back where she'd started an hour ago, except now her feet were secured, too. Somehow, that made her feel even more helpless than before.

"Now that you're all settled and comfy, let's talk."

"What are you—"

His hand covered her mouth. "I'll talk, you listen. Do you know why I'm being extraordinarily nice to you?"

She seriously could not answer that question, and thankfully, he didn't seem to expect an answer as he continued. "I read everything that William Harrington did to you. The drugs, the starvation, the beatings, the cold baths filled with ice cubes. Because of his ill treatment, you lost all affection for him."

"I never had any affection for him. I didn't even know the man."

"Now, Kacie, let's not start our relationship with lies. Sally told me how you seduced her father at that party. If you hadn't shown the slightest bit of interest in him, he never would have abducted you."

Long past questioning or blaming herself for what Harrington did to her, she didn't bother to respond to his inane accusation.

"But that's not my point," Vincent said. "What I'm trying to do is show you that although you seduced me just like you did William, with your smiles and your gifts, the special interest you showed me, I will treat you much better. In fact, I will do the exact opposite of everything William did.

"You'll eat delicious food that I will prepare myself. You'll get long, hot baths. I won't drug you. I'll treat you like the precious angel you are. And when it's time for us to be intimate, you'll give yourself to me out of love and gratitude. Your pleasure will not be drug-induced. It will be real."

Of course he had seen the video, knew that she had climaxed because of the drugs Harrington used. But the other things, the starving, ice-cold baths… There was only one way he could know about them.

"You read my files. You're the one who broke into Dr. Curtis's office. You killed her."

"I kind of felt bad about that. She came in and caught me. I had no other choice. She never would have just let me leave with your file." He took one of her hands and squeezed it. "You do understand that, don't you, Kacie? I don't like to kill, but I will if necessary. I'll do anything for us to be together."

She nodded. What choice did she have?

"And that's why I really hope your boyfriend, Brennan Sinclair, doesn't come after you. I really liked the guy and always felt he got a bum rap for all the nasty things people said about him."

He took something from the nightstand and then leaned closer. She smelled the sourness of his breath as it coated her face. "But understand this, I will kill anyone who tries to get in the way of our happiness. That means no matter how much I like Brennan, the guy will die if he tries to take you away from me."

Pulling away slightly, he held up a giant knife. "One slice from this mother, and he'll bleed out like a slaughtered hog."

He laid the flat side of the knife against her neck. Her breath caught in her throat, and she pressed her head deep into her pillow. "It also means that if you defy me, I will punish you severely. And if you make any attempt to escape, to leave me, I'll slit you in half."

CHAPTER FORTY-ONE

New York City

"*The disappearance of model Kacie Dane remains a mystery. Four days ago, the young woman, who was recently named the Montague It Girl, disappeared from her apartment on the West Side.*

"*Friends and co-workers say the last time she was seen was at a Montague photo shoot. One witness, online journalist Carlton Lorrance, claims she chatted amiably with him outside her apartment building prior to her disappearance. Mr. Lorrance stated that he and Ms. Dane are on the best of terms and refuted statements made by others that he'd had an antagonistic dispute with Ms. Dane's boyfriend, who is none other than former New York Jets quarterback Brennan Sinclair.*"

The pseudo-reporter leaned forward as if sharing a confidence. "*One does wonder about the odd coincidence of Sinclair's son's disappearance years ago and subsequent death, as well as the mysterious death of his wife. And now this...the disappearance of his girlfriend.*

"*Is the man cursed with bad luck...or could something more sinister be afoot?*

"*Stay tuned for updates as they develop.*"

"Assholes," Justin muttered.

"I'm sorry, Sinclair," McCall said. "You don't deserve any of this."

Brennan was barely paying attention to the television and waved away McCall's concern. He didn't care, did not give one small damn about his reputation. It hadn't meant much to him before this…and it mattered even less now. His only concern, his only focus, was finding Kacie. It was the only thing he could concentrate on, think about. What was she going through? Hell, was she even alive?

They sat in the living room in Kacie's apartment, which had become their center of operations. Every law enforcement agency, including the FBI, was involved in searching for her. However, this location had been established specifically for Last Chance Rescue. Thankfully, no one seemed to dispute their authority. Though agencies, especially government agencies, were notorious for not wanting to work together, the spirit of cooperation he'd witnessed restored his faith in not only his fellow man but all those agencies as well. Everyone, everywhere, wanted Kacie Dane back home.

Julian Montague himself had put up a three million dollar reward for information leading to her safe return. The amount might seem extravagant to some, but not to Brennan. He, like so many others, knew how very special Kacie Dane was.

The city, the entire state, was being scoured, but so far, there'd been no sign of Kacie or her abductor.

Skylar and Gabe Maddox had arrived only hours after learning about Kacie's disappearance. And though Skylar had looked as worried as any of them, she'd hugged Brennan and assured him that Kacie was a survivor and would either escape or stay alive until LCR could find her.

He'd nodded and agreed with her, but all the time he kept asking himself just how much more could she survive. Just how many hells was this young, unbelievably brave woman supposed to endure?

The good news, if there was any at all, was that they knew who had taken her. Vincent Deavors hadn't shown up for his scheduled shift. Questions were asked, his apartment was ransacked, and a treasure trove of information had spewed forth. His entire apartment was filled with photos of Kacie, not only of Harrington raping her, but also current photos, too.

The wife, kids, and grandkids had been a hoax. The security company had bought Vincent's lies...and, dammit, so had Brennan.

The fact that Vincent didn't seem to care that he would be found out wasn't the least bit reassuring. He didn't expect to be caught.

"We interrupt this program with a special news bulletin. Carlton Lorrance, the journalist who might well have been the last person to see Kacie Dane before her disappearance, has announced he will be making a public statement today at three p.m. regarding new developments that he has uncovered.

"Be sure to join us at three. Now, back to our regularly scheduled program."

"Son of a bitch," Brennan growled. "He's planning to make a name for himself any way he can."

"You think he has anything?" Justin asked.

"No. But we need to make damn sure, just in case. One thing's for sure, he's done dragging people's names through the mud." Pulling his cellphone out, Brennan punched in a number he still knew by heart, even though he hadn't used it a years.

"Roy, it's Brennan." Before the man could speak, Brennan got to the point. "I know it's been forever, sorry I haven't called, but I need a favor."

As he described what he'd already put in place, and what he wanted done, both Justin's and McCall's eyes gleamed with humor.

His former manager, Roy Gilson, still had a large amount of influence in the city. Brennan had seen him use it with the precision of a skilled surgeon, slicing and dicing careers until they were shredded and blew away like ashes. Before the day had ended, Lorrance's career would be demolished as if it never existed.

Brennan already knew enough to bury the man. Knew what he feared, what kept him awake him at night, what secrets he'd buried deep. He hadn't intended to use it, had wanted the info just in case. Now, he would use every ounce of shit and slime he knew about the jerk to bury him for good.

He would tolerate a lot of things, put up with shit that might infuriate most people, but he'd be damned if that asshole used Kacie's abduction to further his career.

The ringing cellphone brought silence to the room. It had been years since Brennan prayed. He'd prayed for his son to be alive, and his prayers had gone unanswered. He'd prayed for his mother's recovery, and she had died anyway. Without a doubt, he knew God existed. What Brennan didn't have faith in was that his prayers made a damn bit of difference. Whatever was going to happen would happen. No matter what he asked for.

However, the second that phone rang, everything within Brennan was praying, pleading. *Please, please, please, let this be information that will help us find Kacie, alive.*

McCall answered and then clicked on speaker so everyone could hear. "What have you got, Angela?"

"Vincent's family owns a vacation cabin."

"Yes, close to Watertown," McCall said. "We already knew that. The police already checked it out. It was empty."

"No, not that one. He had a foster sister, at least for a short while. She said she hadn't heard from him in years, but he called her out of the blue a few months back. He didn't give her any details about himself but asked her a lot of questions. She remembers mentioning that she had a vacation home in Vermont, close to the New York state border, that she'd been trying to sell with no luck. She said the place is empty."

Brennan met McCall's dark eyes, questioning. Hell, it was better than anything else they had right now.

"Okay, Angela," McCall said, "thanks. Send me the coordinates. But keep looking, just in case."

"Will do, Noah. Everyone stay safe."

McCall stood beside Brennan. "Kelly, you and Ingram get your gear and come with Sinclair and me. Thorne and Fox, find this lowlife, Carlton Lorrance, and grill his ass until he tells you something or admits he was lying and has nothing."

Brennan pulled out the bag he'd stored beneath Kacie's dining room table. It had been packed and ready to go for days. Even though he told himself it was useless, he once again found himself praying that he would need the contents of the bag, because they were going to save Kacie.

As he headed out the door, the television news blasted once more. *"As we reported earlier, online journalist Carlton Lorrance had called a press conference to reveal what he said was pertinent information related to the disappearance of model Kacie Dane. However, we've just learned that Mr. Lorrance has been arrested on charges of money laundering and influence peddling, and therefore, his press conference has been canceled. More news as this story develops."*

Eyes heavy with exhaustion, Kacie blinked to clear her vision. Vincent had put her to bed hours ago, but it was still dark outside. What had woken her? A noise, a voice? Was Vincent talking with someone, or was that the television?

This would be the fourth...or the fifth day of her captivity. She had lost count. Every day was the same. She woke and was allowed to go the bathroom. Most of the time, he made her walk, and she knew he did it only for his amusement and to reinforce her helplessness. By the time she got to the toilet, her need would be so bad, she'd almost collapse with relief.

After she finished in the bathroom, he would carry her into the bedroom and dress her for the day. Dresses, no underwear, no shoes. Then he would carry her into the kitchen, seat her at the counter, and prepare breakfast. All the while, he would talk to her as if they were just a regular couple. Politics, sports, where they might go on vacation, places he had visited. He rarely asked her questions, which was good, since if she opened her mouth at all, she figured it would be to scream or curse. But she did listen, hoping at some point he would share something of import.

After breakfast, she was allowed to go to the sofa and watch movies or read. Lunch would be a light meal, usually a salad. Dinner was more substantial. Her appetite wasn't great, but when she had refused to eat the first dinner he'd prepared for her, he'd shoved her face into her food and told her she had no choice. She had obeyed simply because he was right. Until things changed, she had no choice but to do what he said.

Bedtime was the most frightening. She wasn't quite sure why, since he could rape her anytime he liked. But bedtime was when he bathed her, and his eyes would roam over her in an oily, sick way that made her want to vomit.

That had been the routine since she'd been here, and he'd given no indication things would change any time soon. She wasn't allowed to watch regular television, and she assumed it was because the news of her disappearance must be everywhere.

Brennan would be looking for her, as would Noah, Gabe, and several other LCR operatives. She knew they would do everything possible to rescue her. Again.

Skylar must be frantic with worry. She doubted that her mother would be too concerned, but it must be driving her crazy not to be able to admit that Kacie Dane was her daughter. Sonia did so love to play the martyr.

Kacie didn't intend to wait around for rescue. Vincent had already threatened Brennan's life. No way in hell did she intend to give him the chance. This time she would rescue herself, or die trying. Now if only he would give her an opportunity.

Yesterday, for the first time, Vincent had disappeared outside for a substantial amount of time. When he'd walked out the door, leaving her tethered to the chain beside the couch, he'd grinned at her and said, "Don't go anywhere. Will be back in a bit."

Kacie had waited five minutes. When he didn't return, she'd gotten to work. Though it had taken her a while, she'd managed to make it to a long sideboard that was shoved up against a wall in the living room. She'd been eyeing it for days, wondering if she'd be able to find anything inside that she could use. It was the only furniture of significance that she could reach. When she'd opened the cupboards, she'd found a treasure trove of items.

Now she just needed the opportunity to use them.

The door opened, and Vincent came into the bedroom. She had stopped tensing up when he entered, no longer expecting an immediate attack, but she was still wary.

"What time is it?" she asked.

"After midnight."

So he'd put her in bed only a few hours ago. What was he doing in here? He never woke her at this time of the night, never bothered her after her bath. Why...

Breath caught in her throat. She knew why. He was tired of waiting.

He came closer and then sat on the bed. Pushing the sheet aside, he rubbed his fingers lightly on her bare leg. Kacie couldn't move, couldn't breathe. She had thought she would have more time, thought she would be given a chance to move around freely before he did anything more. Hadn't he promised he would give her time?

"Vincent, please, I don't feel as if we know each other well enough yet."

His fingers stayed on her skin but stopped moving. "We've known each other almost two years, Kacie. Some people marry and divorce in that timeframe."

"But you promised."

"I've spent the last few days telling you about myself, my hopes and my dreams. You know me better than anybody."

"But what about my hopes and dreams?"

"Oh, sweet Kacie, I know all about those hopes and dreams. Unfortunately, they aren't consistent with the future I have planned for us. So you'll just have to adjust."

"What do you mean?"

"Simply that you can't continue to model, be in the public's eye like you have been. You're exclusively mine from now on." His hand went back to rubbing her leg. "No one gets to enjoy this body but me."

Kacie worked to settle the terror rising inside her. Okay, this wasn't a surprise. She had known where this was headed from the beginning and had given careful thought to what she would do when the time came. Even if he succeeded in raping her, she would never be the victim she had once been. Never be broken again. Those days were over. But she didn't intend that to happen.

She would get free of him. However, she would have to endure certain things to gain his trust. Could she get him to take off the cuffs at her ankles?

Kacie closed her eyes, willed herself courage that she knew she had within her, and said, "Maybe we could try kissing for a bit?"

Having his mouth touch hers might well backfire, as she wasn't sure she wouldn't throw up. However, if she just outright offered herself to him, he'd see right through her. Acting shy and hesitant went with the persona he'd built up in his mind about her.

"I would like that," he whispered.

She prayed he kept the lights off, because if he saw her eyes, the revulsion on her face, there was no way in hell she would get him to believe she wanted this.

Leaning over her, he pressed a kiss to her cheek, then her mouth. Her lips trembled under his, and she couldn't breathe. *Don't panic!*

"You taste good, sweet girl."

"Th-thank you."

"Open up, and let me in."

She opened her mouth and had to swallow back bile. The strangled sound she made hopefully sounded like a gasp. She didn't know. Blood was rushing in her ears, drowning out everything but the panic.

He pushed his tongue deep into her mouth, and tears swam in her eyes. Brennan was the last man she had kissed and the only man she wanted.

At last moving his mouth from hers, he licked down her chin, to her neck. One of his hands was wrapped in her hair, the other moving slowly down her stomach, toward the juncture of her thighs.

Shuddering, she managed what she hoped was a convincingly sexy laugh. "Don't I get to touch you, too?"

He stiffened for a moment, and she figured she'd gone too far. Then he surprised her by saying, "You really want to touch me?"

"I think to enjoy lovemaking, we should be partners, don't you?"

Without questioning her further, he reached up and unlocked the chain attached to her cuffs. "Let's see how tonight goes, and then I'll consider uncuffing your wrists tomorrow."

No way in hell would there be a tomorrow night. Even if she had to die, there would be no repeat performance.

As if she was thrilled to have the freedom to touch him, she caressed his hair and squirmed slightly as if she were getting excited.

His hand covered her mound, and it took every bit of her willpower not to scream at him. Fortunately, he realized that to be able to penetrate her, he would have to unlock her ankles. It would be the first time her legs had been free since he'd brought her here, and her heartbeat went wild with anticipation.

"Let's get those legs free, so I can get in between them and show you what a real man can do."

And I'll show you what a real woman can do.

The instant the lock clicked and her ankles were at last separated, Kacie bent her knees and, with a quick jerk, slammed them into Vincent's face. She felt the give of bone and cartilage, knew she'd broken his nose. She didn't wait around to see if he was unconscious. Springing from the bed, she wasted no time in running from the room. She stopped briefly for the small arsenal of supplies she'd hidden, and then she opened the front door. The furious shouting behind her told her she had only seconds before it would be too late.

With death breathing down her neck, Kacie ran into the night.

CHAPTER FORTY-TWO

Dawn broke over the trees, giving just enough light to reveal the small cabin nestled beneath tall pines and giant oaks. A light blazed in a small front window, giving Brennan hope that they'd at last found Vincent's hiding place.

They'd parked the SUVs several yards down the road and off to the side, hidden behind bushes. McCall stood beside Brennan. Justin, Riley, and Gabe Maddox were just a few feet behind them.

McCall hadn't wanted Maddox to come, claiming Gabe's affection for Kacie might cause problems. With a raised brow, Maddox had glanced over at Brennan. "More problems than taking along the man who's in love with her?"

All eyes had been on Brennan as the other LCR operatives waited for him to refute that claim. He didn't bother. What was the point of denying something he knew to be true?

After a long, quiet pause, McCall had nodded and said, "Good point." And that had been that.

When they'd been in the air, Angela had sent them schematics of the house and a detailed map. Other than the occasional campground and US Forest Services outpost, miles of dense forest covered the area.

The cabin was small, with only a large great room-kitchen combination and just one bedroom. There were three porches—front, back, and a small side porch, meaning three exits to cover.

"Ingram and Kelly," McCall said, "take the back. Maddox, you take the side. Sinclair and I will take the front." After a pause, "Go," McCall said softly.

Softly, stealthily, the five of them moved as one. A few yards from the cabin, Brennan felt rather than saw Riley and Justin veer right to go around the house. Maddox went the other direction to the side porch.

McCall nodded at Brennan, giving him the okay to go first. Gun at the ready, silent and quick, Brennan ran to the front, took the five steps in two, and eased onto the porch. McCall was a couple of feet behind, to his right.

Though it was daylight, the trees obscured the light. The flashlight attachment on his Glock revealed two disturbing things. The front door was open, and a dark-looking substance trailed from the front door and down the steps. Even without bending to check, Brennan knew it was blood.

Pushing the door open farther, he stepped inside, going in high. McCall came in low behind him. The room, Spartan in both décor and furniture, was empty. A noise to his right had him turning. Maddox stood in the kitchen and gave a shake of his head. Seconds later, Riley and Justin appeared from the back door and gave the same news. Nothing.

Worry clawing at his insides, Brennan followed the trail of blood to the bedroom. Stopping at the door, he swept his flashlight over the empty room. Swift steps took him across the floor, and he quickly checked the bathroom. The small room consisted of a sink, a toilet in the corner, and a large tub. His gut clenched as he noted the chain attached to the floor beside the tub. His mind refused to envision their purpose.

Turning back to the bedroom, he called out, "Clear."

McCall stood at the doorway and flipped on the light switch.

His jaw clenched, rage and sorrow swirled like bitter acid through his veins. The chain in the bathroom took on greater significance as he took in the chain that hung from the headboard.

McCall turned to Riley, who stood at the doorway behind him. "Ingram, go outside and make a thorough search of the perimeter."

When Riley's eyes spotted the chain hanging from the bed, her face went a sickly white and a small moan left her mouth.

"Now, Ingram," McCall barked.

Riley turned away, and Brennan heard her run through the cabin and out the door.

Giving McCall an odd look, Justin came inside the bedroom and let out a low curse. "Son of a bitch."

Maddox and McCall stood at the bed. There was no need for Brennan to get any closer. He could see the horror from here. The entire bed was splattered with fresh blood.

McCall leaned in closer and then gave Brennan a grim nod. "Yeah, there's a lot of it, but not enough to cause death. Whoever it belongs to is injured, not dead. And it's still wet, so we may have missed them only by a few minutes."

Damn sucky timing, but he'd take what he could get. She was alive, that was what mattered.

"There's a car in a shed out back," Justin said. "Unless he's got other transportation, they're on foot."

Hope rose higher. "She hurt him somehow and got away," Brennan said. "He's gone after her."

McCall took one more look around the room. "I agree. Let's go."

Feeling a small percentage better, Brennan stalked out the door of the cabin. He stopped at the bottom of the front porch steps. Which direction would she have headed? Since the sun had just risen, it would've been dark when she took off. Had she managed to grab a flashlight, or was she running blind? Did she have any kind of weapons?

He was aware that McCall was on his cellphone behind him, talking to local authorities. It would be an hour or more before additional help could arrive. No way could they wait.

A minute later, the LCR leader joined everyone in the middle of the yard. "An official search party is being formed. They'll have dogs, helicopters, equipment. If we don't find her, there will be plenty of people here in a couple of hours.

"Let's split up. With five of us covering the area, there are damn good odds one of us will find Kacie. Stay in radio contact. You see the remotest sign of either of them, call it in."

With a nod and good wishes, they separated. Brennan plunged into the dense, thick foliage with only one thing on his mind. Kacie was running for her life, and no matter what he had to do, he would save her.

Breath rasped from her lungs as Kacie leaned back against a giant tree and gave herself a few seconds to rest. She'd been running for at least a couple of hours, maybe more. Though she still had no idea where she was or where she was headed, she had eluded the maniac, and she was calling that a win.

Her tender feet were a mess—bruised, scratched and bleeding. Since there was nothing to be done for them until she got some help, she chose to ignore the throbbing pain.

Her small bag of supplies had been of little use yet. However, if Vincent caught her, she knew she'd be glad to have them.

When she'd opened the sideboard yesterday, she'd had no idea she would find a hoarders paradise. Apparently, whoever owned the cabin had used the sideboard as storage for everything from fishing gear to old dinnerware and everything in between. If someone else saw her pillage, maybe they wouldn't be too impressed, but thanks to Brennan, she saw a weapon in more than half the items she'd found in the sideboard. He had taught her that…and so much more.

So she had gathered her small treasure of unlikely weapons, found a small pouch-like bag to store them in, and then hid it out of sight but within easy access until the time was right.

Though it was probably well past dawn, the thick foliage from the giant trees made it seem like almost nighttime. The small flashlight she'd found was no real help, but it was just as well. She couldn't risk Vincent seeing the light.

He was out there somewhere, no doubt about that. Unless he was an expert tracker, he probably wouldn't be able to follow her tracks. So unless he saw which direction she had taken, he might be in a completely different part of the woods.

She could take no chances, though. She needed to get going. Her goal was to find either a road or another house. Either one could lead her to safety.

Her breathing now at a manageable level, she pushed off from the tree and took a step. Then went still. For the last hour, the only noises had been chirping birds and squirrels scampering through the ground cover. A noise to her left sounded like neither of these creatures. Breathing halted, she tilted her head to listen intently. Yes, there it was again. Definitely larger and moving fairly rapidly.

Finally locating which direction the sound came from, Kacie turned, and then every limb froze. Less than thirty yards away stood Vincent, and in his hands was a shotgun. He was standing where she could see his profile. Blood stained his face, and even from here, she could tell his nose was off-kilter. Even as terrified as she was, she knew a moment of triumph. She'd definitely broken the lunatic's nose.

Now she just needed to figure out what to do. If she made any movement whatsoever, he might see the motion out of his peripheral vision. The shirt he'd put on her after the last bath was his. Though it reached almost to her knees, it was white and would be easy to see. If she didn't move, he could turn any second, and she would be a sitting duck.

Run and risk a bullet in her back? Or face a pissed-off crazy man with a weapon that could easily cut her in half? Either way, she might be dead. But if he didn't shoot her right away, he would take her back to the cabin, and she had no trouble imagining what he would do to her then.

She took a breath, let it out slowly. Running away would at least give her a chance to survive. Being a captive again? She'd rather be dead.

Inhaling a silent breath, sending up a quick prayer for strength, Kacie made her choice and ran.

The blast of a shotgun cut through the quiet of the forest. Brennan took off, running toward the sound. He didn't care about making noise. Attracting attention might well get Vincent's focus off Kacie. He'd gladly stand in front of a shotgun and take a bullet if it meant saving her life.

McCall's voice sounded in his ear. "Anyone able to tell which direction that came from?"

"Yeah, boss," Justin answered. "Hard to tell with a shotgun in this kind of terrain, but sounded like it was northeast of me. I'm headed in that direction."

"Roger, that," Maddox said. "It was south of me."

"Sounded west of me," McCall said, "I'm headed that way."

Breaking protocol, Justin said urgently, "Riley?"

Sounding winded, Riley answered, "Yes. Heard it, too. North of me, I think." She swallowed and added, "Sorry, just had the pleasure of almost running into a mama black bear and her cub."

"Shit," McCall said softly. "Are you clear of them?"

"Yes. They're gone."

"Okay," McCall said. "Let's find Kacie."

Brennan sped through the undergrowth, soaring over tree limbs, jumping over stumps. He told himself one shot could mean a lot of things. Vincent had thought he saw Kacie but missed. He'd fired a shot in warning. Hell, maybe he'd stumbled, the gun had dislodged, and he'd blown his own fucking head off.

Only, Brennan knew they wouldn't be that lucky.

He should be close now. Brennan slowed and adjusted his plan. Sneaking up on the man would make it easier to take him down. Never had he been more grateful to have had three Navy SEALs put him through the most grueling, brutal training imaginable. One of the many valuable lessons he'd learned from them was walking through the woods without making a sound.

The sound of rough, raspy breathing hit his hearing. Sounded almost like a man sobbing in grief. Brennan stopped, strained to listen. Yes, to his right. He took a few steps forward. Several large bushes obscured his sight. He pushed the limbs aside. His breath hitched and caught in his throat, the sight that met his eyes the stuff of nightmares.

Vincent was looking down at his feet where a half-clothed Kacie lay facedown on the ground, unmoving.

Crap, she hurt. Even the slightest breath made the pain in her chest almost more than she could bear. He had shot at her and missed. If he had hit her, she wouldn't be breathing at all. She told herself pain was good…it meant life. Didn't stop her from hurting, though.

When the gun had blasted, she'd jerked in surprise, lost her footing, and rolled down a hill. With her hands still cuffed in front of her, she'd had almost no way to protect herself or stop the momentum. She had just continued to roll and had finally landed several yards from where she'd been. Unfortunately, there'd been no way in hell she could get up and move quickly enough for her to avoid him. She knew without a doubt he wouldn't miss again.

Amazingly enough, even tumbling down the hill, without any control over her body, she had kept hold of her small pouch of weapons. When she'd finally come to a stop, she was facedown with the bag beneath her. Could she move her hands and open it without him seeing? He was now standing beside her…she could hear his harsh, sobbing breaths right above her.

Maybe if he thought she was dead, he would just leave. No, he would reach down and double-check to make sure she was dead. And when he realized that not only was she still alive, but also that he hadn't shot her, what would he do?

She had to get to the small bag of weapons beneath her. She already knew which item she would use. It was her only hope of surviving. She refused to consider that it was barely a weapon by anyone's standards. It was all that she had, so she would make do.

Now, if only something would distract him.

She heard the snap of Vincent's shotgun and then his oddly cheerful voice saying, "Well, lookee who's here. Hey there, buddy."

And like an answered prayer from heaven, Brennan's deep voice growled, "You son of a bitch. Put your weapon down. Now."

Brennan told himself he was no stranger to pain. Losing his son and his parents had been hideous agonies that had left scars on his soul that could never be healed. Seeing Kacie's body lying so still and lifeless felt as if the bullet had entered his own chest and left a gaping, seeping hole of anguish. He told himself to push the pain aside, he would deal with it later. His fault if she was dead…God, his fault again.

His mind barely acknowledged that he now had a shotgun pointed directly at his chest. He quite simply did not give a damn. Whether Vincent got off a shot or not, this bastard would die today. "Put your weapon down, Deavors."

"Now Brennan, I know how this looks, but she made me kill her. I wasn't even really aiming at her, and she got in the way. But I told her what I would do if she left me. I warned her."

"You sick fuck. Put the gun down, or I swear I will blow a hole through your worthless heart."

Vincent sneered. "Which bullet do you think is going to hit its target first? That little Glock or my man-sized shotgun?"

"If you think that matters to me, think again. I don't give a damn if I die, but you'll be going with me, I swear to that."

Cursing erupted in his ear, sounding like Justin. It was quickly followed by McCall's calm voice, "Keep him talking, Sinclair. I'm only a minute or two away from you." To the others, McCall said, "Listen up, whoever gets there first, take him down. Kill him if you have to, but take the bastard down."

Brennan agreed with part of McCall's statement. This monster would go down, but Brennan would be the one to do it, and he intended that the man would never rise again.

A small, infinitesimal movement close to Vincent's feet caught Brennan's eyes. Had Kacie moved?

To get Vincent's attention away from her, Brennan raised his gun higher and shouted, "Put the gun down, or I'll shoot!"

The decision was taken out of his hands. An agonizing look came over Vincent's face, and he shrieked like a banshee. Stumbling, he turned the shotgun back toward Kacie.

Without hesitation, Brennan took the shot, and a neat little hole appeared in Vincent's temple. As the man fell backward, Kacie scrambled to her feet and ran toward Brennan. No blood. Thank you, God, she really was okay.

Grabbing her hand, he pulled her behind him and then walked over to where Vincent lay on his back, his mouth gaping open, light already faded from his eyes. Blood seeped from the hole in his forehead where Brennan's bullet had entered. Even more blood pooled at the back of his head where he'd struck a boulder on his way down and cracked his skull.

Brennan kicked the shotgun away and bent down, checking his pulse. Definitely dead.

Turning, he pulled Kacie into his arms and held her to him. They were both shaking like hell, grasping and holding onto to each other tightly. Their hearts a matching rhythm of thunder.

"I thought I'd lost you," Brennan breathed against her hair. "God, I thought I'd lost you."

Her face burrowed against his chest, she whispered hoarsely, "I thought you had, too."

He pulled away to look down at her. Her face was covered in streaks of dirt, she had some angry looking scratches on her cheek and forehead, and he knew he had never seen anyone more beautiful in his entire life. Kacie, precious and whole, was alive and in his arms.

He pulled her closer again, and when she flinched, he said, "Tell me where you're hurt."

"I think I've got bruises on about ninety percent of my body."

"Let's get you out of here."

Running footsteps crashed toward them, and Brennan glanced up to see McCall and Maddox come from over a rise. Seconds later, Riley came from the right, followed closely by Justin.

"Everybody all right?" McCall asked.

"Everybody but Vincent," Brennan said, then looked down at Kacie. "What did you do to him?"

"I stabbed him in the ankle with manicure scissors."

"Like I've said before, you're my hero, Kacie Dane."

She tried for a smile but didn't quite make it. Tears pooled in her eyes as she whispered, "Take me home, please."

Scooping her into his arms, he answered with the absolute truth, "I'll gladly give you whatever you want, my love."

CHAPTER FORTY-THREE

She remembered little on the trip back to the cabin. Noah had miraculously produced a small key and unlocked her cuffs. When she was free, he had patted her hand gently, cautiously, and told her he was glad to see her. Gabe had given her a brilliant smile and told her that Skylar would be crying tears of joy as soon as he called her. Justin had given her a smile and said welcome back. And Riley... Riley had given her a quick nod of greeting and then stepped back, her eyes sad, almost haunted.

She knew they had to be several miles from the cabin, but not once did Brennan slow. She'd told him she could walk, and he'd just given her a strained, silent look. He was on the edge. She could feel the tension in his body. So instead, she just burrowed into his arms and remained quiet, peaceful at last.

At some point, each of the men had offered to carry her. He'd answered each time, "No," and kept going.

She had no concept of time but knew it had to have been a few hours before they finally reached the cabin. She took one look at the place of her nightmare and shook her head. "I can't go back in there."

"No one's going to make you, sweetheart," Brennan said.

Relieved, she glanced around at the mass of activity. Like bees around a hive, people were swarming everywhere. Noises overwhelmed her. Whirling helicopter blades, bloodhounds barking, dozens of voices, some shouting. Unable to deal with it all, she kept her face buried against Brennan's neck. Here, she felt safe, secure. Here was where she wanted to stay. The rest of the world could fall away.

"Kacie, I'm going to lay you down so the EMTs can check you out."

For a moment, she clung to Brennan, not wanting to let him go. Then, taking a breath, she pulled away and said, "Okay."

He placed her on a gurney. She held tight to his hand a moment, and he squeezed it gently. "I'm not going anywhere. I'm right beside you."

Reassured, she released his hand and let the EMTs examine her. Even though strange hands touched her, she locked her eyes on Brennan, who stood as close he could. He was her anchor. As long as he stayed by her side, she would be fine.

At last, one of the EMTs patted her hand and said, "She's a little shocky and dehydrated. Multiple bruises, a few shallow cuts and scrapes. Worse on her feet than anywhere else. I've cleaned and bandaged them. Once we get her to the hospital, they'll be able to—"

"No. I'm not going to a hospital."

"Kacie." Brennan stood over her. "Sweetheart, they need to treat you."

"I'm fine. I don't need—" And then she saw the stark pain in his eyes. He thought she'd been raped. And why wouldn't he think that? She was wearing a man's shirt and nothing else, plus she'd been in the clutches of a mad man for several days.

She motioned him to come closer. When he leaned over her, she said softly, "He didn't rape me, Brennan."

His eyes went wide with both surprise and relief and then filled with tears. "God, Kacie. I—"

She raised a trembling hand and wiped his tears away. "He planned to, but he didn't. That's when I got away. I'm fine, I promise."

Blowing out a harsh breath, Brennan kissed the palm of her hand and straightened. "She doesn't need a hospital," he said to the closest EMT. "I'll make sure she's seen by her doctor as soon as we get her back to the city."

"But, sir—"

When the EMT's voice shut off abruptly, she assumed he was on the receiving end of one of Brennan's stern *don't argue with me* looks.

Trusting Brennan to handle things, she closed her eyes, content to drift.

"Kacie?"

She opened her eyes to see Noah standing over her.

"How are you holding up?"

"A little tired, but overall, I'm doing just fine."

The smile in his eyes told her he agreed. "The police need to talk to you but have agreed to wait until tomorrow."

She nodded, relieved. Tomorrow she could do it. Tomorrow she'd be back to being the strong, spirited Kacie Dane, ready to take on the world. But for right now, she doubted she could battle a flea, much less go into detail for a total stranger about her ordeal.

She heard Brennan's voice as he spoke in a low tone to the one of the EMTs, who then adjusted the gurney she was on, allowing her to sit up.

"Here, sweetheart," Brennan said and handed her a cup of hot, liberally sweetened coffee.

"Thanks." Kacie sipped it, relishing the warmth and the surge of energy from both the caffeine and sugar.

Brennan gently brushed a strand of hair from her forehead. "Ready to go home?"

"Yes, please."

In a surprisingly short amount of time, Brennan was scooping her back into his arms and settling into the back of a big black SUV. Even though she kept her eyes closed, her face still buried against Brennan's neck, she was aware of what was happening around her. She knew Noah was driving, and Gabe was in the front passenger side. Riley and Justin followed behind in another SUV.

Apparently fearing they'd disturb her, Noah and Gabe spoke to each other in quiet tones. Brennan stayed oddly silent.

Tension seeped from her bones as she finally accepted that she was fine. She had survived, and she was going home in the arms of the man she loved.

Judging by the location of the sun, it was probably late afternoon...bright enough to see Brennan's face. His mouth was set to grim, and his beautiful eyes looked haunted. This week had been horrendous for her and for him, too.

"It's not your fault, Brennan. There's no way anyone could have known Vincent was working with Molly."

Instead of agreeing with her, or arguing, he just tightened his arms around her and said soothingly, "Just rest, sweetheart. We're about half an hour from the airport. An LCR plane is waiting for us, and then we'll be home soon."

Kacie frowned. Okay, maybe it was time to stop acting like a fragile flower who needed to be cosseted and show her man the support and comfort he obviously needed.

Loosening her grip on his shoulders, she sat up in his arms. "What's wrong? You need something?"

"Yes, I need you to stop blaming yourself."

Aware that she'd gotten both Noah's and Gabe's attention, she turned her head to include them in her announcement. "Now hear this. No one could have predicted those two were working together."

"It's our job to see things like this coming, Kacie. We totally missed it. I'm sorry," Noah said. "You paid the price for our screw-up."

"Oh, for heaven's sake, Noah. He fooled everyone."

Gabe turned so he could see her. "Looks like the spit has returned to your eyes."

She grinned at one of his West Virginia sayings. "I'm going to take that as a compliment and move on."

Noah glanced at her from the rearview mirror. "You feel up to talking about what happened?"

Surprisingly, she did. The strength she gained from being in Brennan's arms made her feel as though she could talk about anything, even the scarier parts of her week.

As succinctly as she could manage, she told them what happened, starting from when she discovered the photographs in her bedroom and Vincent's creepy impersonation of Harrington all the way to when she finally managed to persuade him to free her arms and legs so they could *make love*, and she'd kneed him in the nose and escaped.

She described how he'd gone out yesterday for a few hours and how she'd hopped to the sideboard and gathered weapons for her escape. When Noah had asked her how she'd thought to put those things together, she said, "Brennan. If it hadn't been for him, I might not even have considered doing that."

She looked up at the man who, whether he wanted to admit it or not, had saved her life once again. "Remember your first day protecting me? You bought all those seemingly innocuous things and told me anything can be used as a weapon. You were right."

"Damn ingenious," Gabe said. "So, how'd Molly hook up with the bastard?"

"He'd done some yard work for her family a few years back. When she started looking for an accomplice, he apparently came to mind."

"Like attracts like," Noah said. "She was disturbed, and maybe she recognized the same thing in him."

"He told me she intended to die all along, that her end game was to die and"—she swallowed and couldn't prevent a shiver—"then he could have me to do what he wanted."

Brennan's arms tightened around her as he pressed a kiss to the top of her head. Then, as if to reassure himself she was really there with him, he softly caressed her face. She smiled up at him to reassure him that she was not only there with him, but was perfectly fine. The hollow look in his eyes said he wasn't convinced.

How could Kacie act so strong, so indomitable, when he felt as though he was breaking apart inside? She kept giving him smiles of reassurance, wanting to make sure he knew she didn't blame him. How could he not blame himself? It was his job to protect her, and he'd done a damn lousy job.

She talked about her ordeal as calmly as if it'd happened to someone else. The shock hadn't worn off yet, but at some point, it would. She would remember what the perverted creep had done to her, said to her, how and where he'd touched her. The thought of his slimy hands on her body made Brennan wish he'd been able to beat the shit of Vincent before he'd killed him. The psycho had gotten off way too easy.

"So how did you guys find me?"

"Angela," Noah said.

"But of course," Kacie said, and then she laughed.

She laughed. How the hell did she get so strong? The musical sound seeped inside Brennan, healing something he hadn't even been aware was broken. Kacie had overcome trauma after trauma. That unconquerable spirit was as much a part of her as the purity of her smile. It was in her DNA, in her bones. She had backbone to spare, and she made him feel strong just by existing.

Truth swept through him, settled into knowledge. They had things to talk about. He had amends to make. And then he needed to do something he swore he never would. But for Kacie? God, he would do anything for her. Cut open old wounds, bleed himself dry. She was worth it.

CHAPTER FORTY-FOUR

Kacie eased down onto her sofa, pleased that her body didn't protest nearly as much as it had a few days ago. Even though the EMTs had assured her she was just bruised, she had thought for sure she had broken at least a rib or two. But after she returned home, a doctor had visited and had agreed that, while she was bruised almost everywhere, nothing was broken.

Her body wasn't her biggest worry. Her mind wouldn't stop whirling. With fears and nightmares, yes. In an odd way, that felt incredibly normal. At least she knew how to deal with them. After years of nightmares, these weren't anything new. At least she wasn't starting from scratch.

No, her worries focused on another area. One she wasn't sure she could face, though she wasn't sure she had a choice. Her mind wasn't going to let this go.

"What are you doing out of bed?"

She turned to smile at Skylar, who was standing on the stairs with a motherly expression that seemed totally incongruent with her incredible elegance.

"You look beautiful. Has Gabe seen you in that gown?"

Her cheeks flushed a becoming pink. "He's already tried to take it off of me…twice. The man will do anything to keep from going to my father's birthday party."

She came all the way down the stairs, her long gown swaying around her ankles. "And don't think I didn't notice that you changed the subject. Why aren't you in bed? Your body needs rest to heal."

"It can heal on the sofa just as well as in bed. Besides, I think better down here." She didn't add that her bedroom had too many memories, both good and bad. At least down here, all of her memories were of happier times.

"Are you sure you're okay with us going? There are going to be hundreds of people attending the party. I doubt my dad will even notice I'm not there."

"Jeremiah James's only daughter not showing up for his birthday bash? It'd lead tomorrow morning's news.

"Besides, I won't be alone for long. Brennan will be back in a couple of hours. He's got some sort of meeting going on." Her mind clouded at the thought. He hadn't told her where he was going, what he was doing, just that he was going out to meet someone. Apparently, it was none of her business.

"What's wrong?" Skylar sat beside her, wrapped her arm around her, and whispered, "You know you can tell me anything, don't you?"

A lump developed in her throat. They may not be related by blood, but no one could have a better sister or friend than Skylar had been to her.

Laying her head on Skylar's shoulder, Kacie gave her the reason for part of her worries. "I don't think he's going to stay."

Brennan had slept by her side each night, held her gently in his arms, whispered reassurances to her when nightmares attacked, but not once had he made any promises.

"Have you asked him to stay?"

"I did when he left before. It broke my heart when he said no. I just don't think I can handle it again."

"Men are incredibly stubborn creatures, and LCR operatives seem to have an extra dose of pigheadedness."

"I wouldn't have him any other way, just like you wouldn't have Gabe any other way."

"No, but that doesn't stop me from wanting to knock some sense into him occasionally."

"I think Brennan loves me. I just don't know what else I can do to make him love me enough to stay."

"When you were missing, we were frantic, but there was a lot of downtime where we could do nothing but wait for intel from Angela. I talked to him a bit, got to know him."

She trusted Skylar's judgment as much as she trusted anyone's. "And?"

"I can see why you love him. He was sick with worry, not that he'd say so. You know those LCR types. Tough on the outside but with gooey centers."

Kacie giggled. "Are we talking about LCR guys or candy bars?"

Skylar laughed. "Both." Then she sobered. "It sickens me the way he was vilified about his son. Anyone who spends more than five minutes with him can see the man he is inside."

"Brennan didn't care enough about public opinion to set the record straight. And I'm not sure anyone cared to dig deeper. The things they made up were so much more titillating than the truth."

"That might be the reason he feels he can't stay with you. He loves you enough to leave."

"What do you mean?"

"Kacie...sweetie. The press has bludgeoned the man for years. They made him into this wicked, greedy, soulless man who sacrificed his child's life for his career. Now he's fallen in love with the famous Kacie Dane, the face of innocence, wholesomeness. The woman parents want their daughters to be like. A role model for all the vulnerable young people who are searching for their identity."

Kacie raised her head, stared in horror at Skylar. "You think he believes he's tainting me by being around me?"

"I think he worries that the press will see you differently and your career will suffer."

"My career isn't my life. If he wanted me to walk away from it tomorrow, I would."

"Do you know how wonderful it is to see what a strong, courageous woman you've become? I am so proud of you, Kacie Dane."

"That's only because I had the best role model in the world."

Skylar gave a small, elegant sniff. "Stop it, or I'll have to redo my eye makeup." She pressed a quick kiss to Kacie's forehead. "Talk to him, tell him what's in your heart, on your mind. Make him talk to you. Remember those stubborn types also have sharing issues, too."

Kacie set her chin to firm. Skylar was right. She would talk with him, and if he was choosing not to be with her because he thought it might hurt her career? Well, then she would hit him over the head with her love. Nothing in her life mattered more.

"So I heard you had a confrontation with my mom."

Temper flaring in her eyes, Skylar shot a furious look up the stairway. "I told him not to say anything to you."

"It was right that he did. I needed to know. Besides, I have no illusions about my mom. I haven't in a long time."

"I know, I just didn't want you to add one more thing to the list of reasons why she's not worthy to be called your mother."

"What happened? Gabe didn't give details. Just said it was a heated exchange."

"An exchange that lasted all of three minutes. I called her after you disappeared, thinking she had a right to know, that she would want to be informed."

"Let me guess, she had a manicure or facial appointment and couldn't be bothered."

Skylar huffed a soft, frustrated breath. "We never got that far. In a nutshell, she said that whatever was happening was only what you deserved and she didn't want any details."

The hurt didn't come. It would have years ago. Even months ago, her mother's absolute disdain for her might have crushed her. But experience had developed wisdom. Sonia didn't have the capacity to love anyone but herself. It was her failing, not Kacie's.

"And I assume you told her what you thought of her?"

"I simply told her that you didn't deserve to have a shallow, cold-hearted bitch for a mother and that if she tried to get any more money from you, I would make sure she was brought up on charges of extortion."

Kacie grinned. "You really have that kind of influence?"

Skylar laughed, sounding much more like a teenager than a wife and a mom. "No, but I talk a good game. She knows I still have influence here."

"Thank you for defending me."

"I just told the truth. She's not worth another moment of your time."

"I know." She glanced down at her hands, surprised to see she'd been twisting them nervously.

Skylar's hand covered hers. "There's something else bothering you. What's wrong? Is it Vincent?"

"No, even though I still have nightmares, he didn't have near the impact on me that he and Molly wanted him to have. I just..." She shrugged. "There's something that's been on my mind the last couple of weeks. I needed to work out details, logistics, need to get it right. I've talked to Noah about it, wanted to make sure he had no problems with it, that nothing would blow back on LCR."

Skylar frowned. "Sounds really mysterious. What is it? Can I help?"

Stumbling a little, Kacie explained her ideas and the reasons behind them. Skylar was the one person who understood her better than anyone else. She would recognize not only the chance Kacie was taking but also the scrutiny she was inviting.

When she finished, tears filled Skylar eyes. "Oh, to hell with my makeup." She hugged Kacie tight. "I am so incredibly proud of you and support your decision a thousand percent."

Kacie took a bracing breath. Okay, two of the people she respected most in the world wholly supported her decision. That not only set her mind at ease, it also confirmed she was doing the right thing. When Brennan came home, she would tell him, too.

Then, she just had to find the courage of her conviction to carry out her plan.

If anyone had told him that at some point in this lifetime he'd willingly be sitting across from a reporter again, Brennan figured he would've punched them in the nose and walked away. After his experience, the press had become his number one enemy. It had always amazed him that a person could be considered an icon one day and a pariah the next, but it had happened numerous times. He had just never figured he'd be one of them.

He was doing this for one reason only. He just hoped to hell it didn't backfire. Hurting Kacie was the very last thing in the world he wanted.

Sheldon Mooney glanced around the room as if looking for hidden cameras or perhaps a trick. Brennan had chosen this venue with care. He hadn't gone extravagant like the Plaza or humble like a budget hotel. Instead, he'd chosen a small conference room in a midprice hotel. The décor was understated, not especially elegant, but not chintzy either.

Brennan had also chosen the reporter carefully. The man was a respected freelance journalist and had no affiliation or known preference of news outlets. He would sell this story to the highest bidder. And without a bit of ego, Brennan knew the man would be paid handsomely for the story.

"I have specific requests," Brennan said.

Mooney shrugged. "It's your show. I'm just along for the ride." He threw a glance over his shoulder. "My photographer is outside. You said no video, but—"

"I'll agree to one photo. That's it."

"Fair enough."

"First, I'd like to make a statement. Then you're welcome to ask me anything. However, if you ask me a question that I don't believe is pertinent, I won't answer."

The reporter nodded, but doubt clouded his eyes. He was most likely wondering if he would get the entire truth or if the interview was Brennan's feeble attempt at whitewashing a tarnished reputation with only carefully selected information. It wasn't, but Brennan would give him no assurances. The man would know soon enough that this was no setup.

Mooney placed a small voice recorder on the table. "Ready when you are."

With a nod, Brennan began. "There are several reasons I never spoke publicly about my son's death and my wife's suicide. For one, it was simply too painful. Public scrutiny never bothered me before, simply because I enjoyed the limelight, the fame. I was a shallow, vain man with talent I didn't appreciate and a family I didn't deserve.

"After my injury, reality hit me. I was stupid enough to think my only responsibility was recovering so I could play again. I told myself that my wife and my son depended on me, and recovering should be my only focus so I could earn the money to take care of them.

"By example, my father taught me to be a hard worker. He worked two jobs to support his family, and I believed that that was what it took to be a good husband and father. But my dad did it because he put my mom and me first, not himself. I didn't realize until too late that a good parent or spouse puts their loved ones' needs before their own. You have to love them more than you love yourself. Not doing that was my greatest mistake.

"While I was working my ass off to recover..." Brennan shook his head. "No, even before my injury, my career came before my family. I was a bad husband and an even worse father.

"My wife never meant for our son to die. She wanted a divorce—very rightly, I might add—but because she couldn't talk to me or trust me, she chose an avenue that had devastating consequences. At the beginning, I blamed her for everything. And though it was poor judgment on her part, I was the catalyst. My lack of maturity and utter selfishness drove her to do what she did."

Brennan tried to swallow, but the gigantic lump in his throat prevented the action. His voice, thick with emotion, rasped out, "And our beautiful son paid the price."

Feeling as though he'd run a marathon at warp speed, Brennan worked hard not to collapse in his chair. Not that he minded showing his vulnerability. Hell, he'd just bled himself dry; pride was the last thing on his mind. However, he knew Mooney would have follow-up questions, and he needed to be able to answer coherently.

"That was a…surprisingly candid statement, Brennan. Few people, especially men, would have the courage to confess their sins, much less take full responsibility for their weaknesses. Is there a specific reason you're doing this now?"

He had known that would be asked but had hoped it would come later. Still, his answer would not change. Damned if he would tell a reporter that he was hopelessly in love with Kacie Dane before he told her himself.

"That's a question I won't answer. Do you have more?"

A small smile played around Mooney's mouth, as if he had guessed what Brennan's answer would be. However, all he said was, "Oh yes, I most certainly do."

The questions went on for almost an hour. Why had he walked out in the middle of an important game? Did he not appreciate the thousands of fans who believed in him? Why should anyone believe what he said now after all these years of silence? If he could say one thing to those people who still doubted him, what would it be?

Other than that first one, Brennan gave open, honest, and sincere answers to all of Mooney's questions.

He knew this interview wouldn't be a cure-all. He'd pissed off too many people, burned too many bridges. A hero had fallen, and some people would never forget their disappointment or forgive Brennan's disgrace. However, this had been his best hope. He loved Kacie with every ounce of his being. He also knew she loved him. And because of her love and incredible selflessness, he knew if it came down to it, she would willingly sacrifice her career to be with him. He didn't want her to do that. Spilling his guts and laying open his soul on the altar of public opinion was a small price to pay to be with the woman he loved.

CHAPTER FORTY-FIVE

When the doorbell rang, Kacie knew a small moment of concern. It couldn't be Brennan—he had a key.

Skylar and Gabe were staying at Mr. James's estate tonight. Noah and his LCR team, with the exception of Brennan and Gabe, had already left the city. Any other person visiting would need to be approved by her before being allowed up. So who was at the door?

She brushed off the paranoia. Not only had building security been overhauled, but she knew that Brennan, Noah, and Gabe had personally met with the building owner. From now on, security would be a helluva lot tighter.

Still, she was no fool to just answer the door without checking the peephole. Seeing Brennan on the other side of the door gave her a start. He still had a key to her apartment, didn't he?

Opening the door, she was about to ask that very question when a giant bouquet of red roses appeared from behind his back.

"Oh my, what's this?"

"It's occurred to me that I have never wooed you."

Something that felt like optimism made her heart leap. Laughing her delight, she took the flowers and sniffed them appreciatively. "I don't believe I've ever been wooed by anyone before."

"And no one deserves it more." He paused for a second and said, "Can I come in?"

"Oh. Yes, sorry." She backed up, and he walked inside. Closing the door, she breathed in the delicate scent of roses.

"I'm just not used to such a lovely gesture." She might have received numerous gifts of flowers and other things through the years, but none had ever meant more to her.

"Then I'll just have to make sure you have many more."

She lowered the flowers and took in his appearance. His words held a significance she needed to get her head around. Her first thought was he looked tired. Tension lines around his mouth and eyes said he'd had a stressful day. Even his broad shoulders seemed to droop a bit. Her gaze went back to his eyes, and she revised her opinion. Yes, he looked tired, but his eyes told a different story. Had she ever seen such peace in them before?

"That sounded almost like a promise."

A small smile curved his mouth. "Almost? Then I'll have to do much better. It was definitely a promise."

No longer able to wait, she steeled her spine and braced herself, hoping she hadn't misinterpreted his meaning. "You're staying?"

"If you'll have me."

With a squeal of joy, she threw herself into his arms. As they closed around her, she peppered his face and neck with kisses. He was doing the same, kissing her everywhere he could reach.

She pulled slightly away from him and met his eyes. They shared a moment more intimate and revealing than any words, touch, or sexual act could convey. In that look, she told him what was in her heart. Her love, devotion, trust, and total commitment were his.

Brennan's eyes revealed the same, and then he took it a step further. "I love you, Kacie Dane. I am in awe of your courage and your incredibly tender heart. The way you live your life. The way you love the people in your life is an inspiration. I want to spend the rest of my life with you, showing you exactly what you mean to me."

No one had ever said more beautiful words. None could ever mean more to her. And she had to give him her own.

"And I love you, Brennan Sinclair. I love your kindness and your nobility. Your strength makes me stronger. Your gentleness makes me feel treasured. Not a day will go by that I don't thank God for bringing you into my life."

She didn't expect to see tears from this big, strong man who had more courage than anyone she'd ever known. But they were there, and she pressed her face against his, mingling their tears.

Then he kissed her. His mouth moved tenderly, softly against hers as they sealed their devotion and commitment. As inevitably as the tide rises, so did their need. Kisses turned ravenous, demanding. Words had confirmed their commitment. Now their bodies would, too.

Clothes dropped to the floor. Brennan took the flowers she still held in her hand and placed them on a table.

"I probably should put them in water."

His smile sexy, his eyes hot, he shook his head slowly. "They'll be fine for a few minutes."

She grinned. "So this is only going to last a few minutes?"

Bending her slightly backward in his arms, muffling his laughter against her skin, Brennan kissed a soft, fragrant spot between her neck and shoulders. "I'll try to hold out a little longer, but…" His hands cupped her silky, firm ass. "My need is quite fierce."

"As is mine," she whispered.

Words stopped, replaced by gasping moans from Kacie and low groans from Brennan. She tasted like every sweet, precious dream he'd ever had…and had given up on. This beautiful, vulnerable, incredibly strong woman had changed his life.

He slid on the condom he'd snagged from his pocket. Then, lifting her in his arms, he growled, "Wrap your legs around my waist and hold on tight."

The instant she complied, Brennan thrust deep into her and almost lost complete control. So wet…so hot…so damn tight. Taking a few steps to his right, he carried her to the large leather chair in the living room and dropped down into it. When her knees hit the cushion, he went even deeper, and they both groaned.

Easing her slightly away from him, he checked her face for signs of fear or shadows. It had only been a few days since her abduction, and though she insisted she was fine, damned if he would be the cause of the darkness returning. Instead of doubts or fears, all he saw was heat, need, and happiness.

Reassured, Brennan cupped her breasts in his hands, suckled one and then the other. With a moaning sigh, Kacie arched her back, giving him greater access. Never had he seen anyone lovelier or more sensual.

When he could no longer wait, could hold out no longer, he grasped her hips and pulled her up until just the tip of his cock was inside her, then he dropped her. Her eyes widened on a gasp, and she spasmed around him. Unable to hold back any longer, Brennan held her down on him and exploded inside her.

They were both gasping for air as they recovered. Then, without warning, Brennan barked with laughter.

"What?" Kacie asked.

"Did that even last a minute?"

She laughed softly. "We'll try for two next time."

Unable to stop caressing her, kissing her, he pulled her tightly against his chest. Never had he felt such contentment, such completion. He didn't want to move from this spot. Holding Kacie, staying inside her sweet, giving body, was his idea of heaven on earth.

A stomach growled.

"Was that yours or mine?" she asked.

"I think it was both. Apparently, they're talking to each other."

She leaned back in his arms and grinned at him. "Can you understand what they're saying?"

"I think mine said it would love Chinese."

"Oh really? How did mine respond?"

"It was kind of a mumble, but I think it said something like, 'Kung pao chicken sounds damn good to me.'"

She gasped. "My stomach curses?"

"Yeah, but only when it's really hungry."

"Then I guess we'd better feed it."

Talking nonsense with Kacie was more fun than any day he'd ever spent on a football field winning games. More than aware that he was grinning like an idiot, Brennan kissed her quickly again. "I'll order the takeout."

"While you do that, I'll put my flowers in water. Then…I guess we need to talk."

"Something wrong?"

"No, I just want to talk to you about something."

He pressed a quick kiss to her nose. "Guess I need to tell you something, too."

She met his eyes, revealing a flash of vulnerability. "But we're okay…here? This is for real?"

"This is for real." Cupping her head in his hands, he leaned his forehead against hers. "This, my love, is forever.

EPILOGUE

It was standing room only in the small auditorium. Kacie had chosen this elegant venue for a reason. There was nothing clandestine or cheap about the news she would impart. And she'd nervously and jokingly said that if things went sour, they could just have a cozy dinner party.

Beautiful beyond belief, she stood at the podium on the small stage. Never had he seen such poise, grace…or more courage. Never had he been more proud of anyone in his entire life.

He had wanted to be up there with her, to hold her hand, lend his support…something. But she'd just given him that sweet smile he adored and said that she needed to do this on her own. Still, as she waited for the crowd to quiet down, her eyes met his. In that one look, he tried to convey everything that was in his heart. All the love, all the devotion, all the support he could. No matter how this went down, he knew he had never known anyone braver.

The last few days had been a whirlwind of activity. The article on his interview first appeared in the *Times*, and then was picked up by every news outlet from New York City to Bangladesh. He doubted the news spread so wide because it was his story, believing it had more to do with the shock value. Not too many former celebrities were willing to cut themselves open and bleed themselves dry in the media.

The article had been met with a surprising—at least to him—compassion. Having lost faith in most people, especially himself, he hadn't expected a lot of sympathy or understanding. Especially when he didn't deserve it. But Kacie had thought differently, predicting that when his story was finally told, public opinion would rule in his favor. He was okay with good press, but that hadn't been why he'd opened up. And his plan seemed to have worked. So far, nothing negative had been printed or reported about Kacie because of her engagement to him. That was all that counted.

And now she was about to reveal her own secrets, her own pain. Brennan swallowed hard as emotion surged up his throat. This beautiful, caring woman, who would soon be his wife and someday the mother of his children, was about to bare her soul.

Everyone of consequence in Kacie's life had been told what she would reveal. Every single one of them had voiced their total support. Julian Montague had added to his previous support, offering to donate a portion of every Kacie Dane sale to the Kacie Dane Foundation.

Kacie's voice came loud and clear through the speakers, catching everyone's attention and successfully quieting the crowd. "Thank you for coming on such short notice. I have a brief statement and then will take some questions."

He watched as she visibly took a breath and then began. "Kacie Dane is not my real name. Almost four years ago, I legally changed it and created a new background and new life for myself.

"My real name is Kendra Carson. A little over five years ago…"

As Kacie continued with her revelation, she watched the sea of people around her. Most looked shocked. A few appeared on the verge of tears. She wasn't doing this to gain sympathy and most certainly not more fame. This was all about the need to claim herself, be proud of who she was and what she had become, and show that healing was possible. She'd given her time and her money and put her famous name behind helping other abuse victims. However, she'd hidden herself. But now, thanks to the love and support of so many, she realized that had been a mistake. She had been a victim, and not because of anything she'd done wrong. Hiding had not been the solution.

Her gaze zeroed in on the man in the front row, the one who had not only made her see herself in a different light but had given her the courage to see this through. Before she met Brennan, she hadn't realized she'd been living only half a life, hiding in the shadows, and never allowing the real person behind the famous façade to show. And because of him, because of his faith and love in her, she could reveal herself.

Brennan's courage in giving his own interview to the press had gone well beyond anything she could ever have expected of him. But it hadn't surprised her. From day one of their first meeting, Brennan had shown her what true courage looked like.

Now, every secret, every flaw would be revealed. Brennan's confession had been met with a kindness and compassion that thrilled her. And no matter how today's reveal went, she could never regret her decision. Her journey had been a long, often painful one, fraught with mountain peaks and the lowest of valleys. But she had survived. And whether she was Kendra Carson or Kacie Dane, she was happy and at peace with the person she had become.

She was too realistic to believe it would be all smooth sailing from here on out. Life wasn't like that. But with Brennan Sinclair, her love and real-life hero, at her side, she knew without a doubt that together they could weather any storm.

**Thank you for reading Chance Encounter,
An LCR Elite Novel.**

If you like this book - or any of my other releases - please consider rating the book at the online retailer of your choice. Your ratings and reviews help other readers find new favorites, and of course, there is no better or appreciated support for an author than word of mouth recommendations from happy readers. Thanks again for reading my books!

Other Books by Christy Reece

LCR Elite Series
Running On Empty, An LCR Elite Novel

Last Chance Rescue Series
Rescue Me, A Last Chance Rescue Novel
Return To Me, A Last Chance Rescue Novel
Run To Me, A Last Chance Rescue Novel
No Chance, A Last Chance Rescue Novel
Second Chance, A Last Chance Rescue Novel
Last Chance, A Last Chance Rescue Novel
Sweet Justice, A Last Chance Rescue Novel
Sweet Revenge, A Last Chance Rescue Novel
Sweet Reward, A Last Chance Rescue Novel
Chances Are, A Last Chance Rescue Novel

Grey Justice Series
Nothing To Lose, A Grey Justice Novel

Wildefire Series
Writing as Ella Grace
Midnight Secrets, A Wildefire Novel
Midnight Lies, A Wildefire Novel
Midnight Shadows, A Wildefire Novel

Acknowledgments

**Special thanks to the following people
for helping make this book possible:**

My husband, for his love, support, numerous moments of comic relief, and respecting my chocolate stash.

My mom, who patiently listened as I ranted and raved about stubborn characters and plot points that unravel.

My Aunt Billie and Uncle Marlin for once again opening their home on the river to me.

Joyce Lamb, for her copyediting, fabulous advice, and not giving me an exact number of ellipsis she deleted for me. Thank…you!

Marie Force's eBook Formatting Fairies, who always answers my endless questions with endless patience.

Tricia Schmitt (Pickyme) for her awesomely beautiful cover art.

Reece's Readers, my incredibly supportive and fun loving street team. Thank you for all that you do!

Anne Woodall, my first reader, who always goes above and beyond, and then goes the extra mile, too. You're awesome!

Kara, Hope, Crystal, Alison, Kris, and Jackie, my beta readers, for reading so quickly, all the catches you guys made, and your great advice.

Linda, my proofreader, who did an amazing job and in an unbelievably tight timeframe.

And a very special thank you to all my readers. Without you, this book and all the others, past and future, would not be possible. You make my dreams come true!

Christy Reece is the award winning and New York Times Bestselling author of dark and sexy romantic suspense. She lives in Alabama with her husband, three precocious canines, an incredibly curious cat, two very shy turtles, and a super cute flying squirrel named Elliott.

Christy also writes steamy, southern suspense under the pen name Ella Grace.

She loves hearing from readers. You can contact her at Christy@christyreece.com

Praise for Christy Reece novels:

"The type of book you will pick up and NEVER want to put down again." *Coffee Time Romance and More*

"Romantic suspense has a major new star!" *Romantic Times Magazine*

"Sizzling romance and fraught suspense fill the pages as the novel races toward its intensely riveting conclusion." *Publishers Weekly, Starred Review*

"Flat-out scary, and I loved every minute of it!" *The Romance Reader's Connection*

"A brilliantly plotted book. Her main characters are vulnerable yet strong, and even the villains are written with skillful and delicate brush strokes haunting your mind long after the book is done." *Fresh Fiction*

"A passionate and vivacious thrill-ride! ... I feel like I've been on an epic journey after finishing it.... Exquisite." *Joyfully Reviewed*

Turn the page for an excerpt from

Running On Empty,
An LCR Elite Novel

Running On Empty,
An LCR Elite Novel

Prologue

Paris, France

Sabrina Fox stood at the window of her apartment and looked down at the bustling street below. Since she lived on the thirty-sixth floor, recognizing anyone from this distance should be almost impossible. But she would know him…she would recognize him from any distance. From the moment she had met Declan Steele, she had *known* him.

Not that it had been love at first sight. A smile tugged at her mouth as she thought about those early days. She had hated Declan with a passion unrivaled since the fury she had known as a kid. He had infuriated her, challenged her…made her see things in ways she had never considered before. She had wanted to succeed in everything he taught her, but at the same time had resisted him with every fiber of her being. Even then she had realized her hatred for him was different. He had been her trainer and harder on her than anyone else in the class, but even in their darkest moments with each other, she'd felt as if an invisible force had been drawing her to him.

Still, there were many days she'd left her training sessions plotting his excruciatingly painful death. Dangerous, since he had been teaching her how to kill.

Having been born into the very definition of a dysfunctional family, she had endured a childhood of sheer hell. She had been rescued from that hell by Albert Marks, who had offered her a job, bringing her into the dangerous world of covert ops. The job had saved her life.

The Agency, EDJE (Eagle Defense Justice Enforcers), was known to only a few, including the president and his closet advisers. When assassinating terrorists and dictators, the fewer people who knew about such things, the better.

When Albert had told her about the Agency, she'd laughed in his face, sure that it was just another gimmick or trick. In her world, adults did one of three things—lied to you, abused you, or drugged you. They didn't offer you an escape.

Albert's patience, sincerity, and sheer determination had convinced her. She would always be grateful to him, not only for saving her life but also for introducing her to Declan.

Because of Albert and the Agency, she had learned to believe in herself, to realize there was more to Sabrina Fox than being a victim to beat, demean, or rape. She had worth.

And Declan? He had taught her many things, but the most important was that she deserved to be loved.

Leaving EDJE hadn't been an easy decision to make. She still believed that what she had done for them was right and just. She admired what the Agency stood for. But it had taken its toll. With each new assignment, she had felt as if she lost a little part of her soul. She would have hung on, doing the job even as it destroyed her, but Declan had seen the damage, too. He had been the one to introduce her to Jordan Montgomery, who had left the Agency years ago to become an operative for Last Chance Rescue.

Even though she'd known about LCR, Sabrina had never encountered any of their operatives. Jordan had met with her, told her a little about the organization and then arranged a meeting with Noah McCall, LCR's leader. From that first meeting, she had been hooked. Rescuing victims as opposed to killing? Doing good without taking lives? The chance to work for LCR had felt like a gift from heaven. So she'd joined the Last Chance Rescue team and never regretted it for a second.

The emerald and diamond band on her left hand captured the sunlight, creating a colorful prism on the window. It felt strange to be wearing it. Unless she was on an undercover assignment, she rarely wore jewelry. No one at LCR, other than her boss, knew she was married. She kept her personal life private for many reasons, but one of the biggest was her concern for Declan. As one of EDJE's top agents, his life was in constant danger—she refused to add to it by revealing her connection to him.

Just over a year ago, she and Declan had exchanged vows in the sanctuary of a small church. Other than the minister and his wife, there had been no witnesses. Then, for five glorious days and even more glorious nights, Declan had been hers and no one else's. No calls, texts, or email warnings of dire events and impending doom.

Breath caught in her throat. There he was, getting out of a cab. As if he knew she would be watching, he looked up. She couldn't see his face from here, but his image was etched in her memory. Square chin, stubborn and implacable, but the hint of a dimple in the center gave it a slight softening. His cheekbones, as if carved from stone, were the kind a camera would love to capture. Unfortunately, with his job, photos of any kind weren't possible. He had a high, intelligent forehead and a slash of thick black brows that he often arched when he was expressing himself passionately about something. And beneath those expressive brows were startling, deep-blue eyes that could glint like a sapphire flame when he was angry or sparkle like jewels when he was amused. His nose was a noble blade that she had once teased him would look perfect on a Roman coin. And his mouth…oh, Declan's mouth would make angels weep. Full, sensuous, delectable. Firm and hard when he was in a mood, but soft and delicious when he was kissing her.

If that wasn't enough, all of that masculine beauty was surrounded by ink black hair so thick that it took a strong wind to even ruffle a strand. And his body—six feet, five inches of masculine perfection. Broad shoulders, muscular arms, a sprinkling of hair on his well-defined chest led down to granite-hard abs. Long, powerfully built legs that could run for hours without tiring. To make it doubly unfair, he possessed a keen, intelligent mind, a quick wit, and a good heart. When God had been passing out special favors, Declan had been standing at the front of the line.

She turned at the sound of the door opening, and there he stood, looking even more wonderful than she remembered. He barely took one step inside before she was across the room. The door closed behind him, his luggage dropped with a thud, and then she was in his arms.

"I've missed you." She spoke against his neck and inhaled, loving the fragrance of her man. He smelled of the aftershave she'd given him the last time they were together and clean male musk. Pulling slightly away from him, she gazed up into those deep-blue eyes and her insides melted.

"I missed you, too, Little Fox."

Little fox. She smiled at the nickname he had given her when he'd first started training her. At first it had infuriated her. She'd come from a family who called her derogatory names more often then they'd used her given name. She had been sure it was an insult. And her? Little? Okay, she was smaller than Declan, but at five feet, eleven inches in her bare feet, she was far from little. She was sure he had meant to demean her. But then, after she had come to know him better, she had heard the affection behind the name.

Her fingers traced a slight crease beside his mouth, one she swore hadn't been there the last time they were together. "You're well? No new bumps, bruises, abrasions?"

"Nothing to speak of. And you?"

"Not a scratch."

The relief in his eyes was a reflection of her own feelings. This was the life they'd chosen but that didn't lessen the worry.

"And now that you're in my arms, I'm perfect."

"I couldn't agree more," she said softly.

Lowering his head, his smiling mouth covered hers and time disappeared. His taste deliciously familiar, heady, sexy, rocketed her from simmering need straight to full arousal. Declan's big hands, callused and urgent, roamed over her body. She was so immersed in him, lost in her desire, it took a moment or two to register cool air washing over her.

Pulling away slightly, she laughed breathlessly against his lips. "What's so funny?"

"You're the only man I know who can strip a woman without any effort."

He looked down at her black skirt and aqua blue cashmere sweater lying on the floor. A lacy black bra and bikini panties lay several feet away as if flung by impatient hands.

His grin was wicked. "Be warned, this is how I intend to have you all weekend."

"You'll get no complaints from me, but how about you?" She took a step back. "Think you can undress yourself as quickly as you did me?"

In seconds, he showed her how he could be even faster. Ripping his shirt open, they both ignored the buttons that fell to the floor. He toed his shoes off and pulled his pants, underwear and socks down in one determined move. And he stood before her, gloriously aroused, gloriously hers.

He pulled her back into his arms and growled, "Ready, wife?"

"Always," she answered softly. Melting into his embrace, she allowed him to possess her body, just as he possessed her heart. Everything she had, everything she was, belonged to him. Her husband, her lover, her life.

Hours later, Declan stood beside their bed and gazed down at his sleeping wife—the woman who had become the beat of his heart. She was everything he'd ever dreamed of having in a mate and was the biggest reason he fought against the shit he faced daily. How she had become so vital for his survival still surprised him.

Having lost his entire family years ago, he had never planned on loving or having deep feelings for anyone again. And now here he was today, incredibly, undeniably, and fiercely in love. Every ounce of tender emotion he possessed was tied up with this beautiful, intelligent, courageous woman.

Everything else in his life was duty, but Sabrina was his purpose, his reason to exist.

Holding back a heavy sigh, he strode over to the reading chair across the room and dropped into it with an uncharacteristic lack of grace.

All the plans he'd had were now shot to hell. Would she hate him when she learned the truth or would she understand? She had been in the game a long time, too. She knew better than anyone that you did the job no matter how objectionable. If you let emotions get in the way, people died.

The ache in his chest might be shame. It had been a long time since he'd felt this way, so he wasn't sure he would recognize the emotion. Didn't matter. He had a job to do and would do it to the best of his ability.

When the assignment was over, he would tell her everything. Didn't mean she wouldn't be hurt or royally pissed. When they married, he had recited vows—ones he had written himself. At that time, he had meant every single one. In those vows, he had promised to never willingly hurt her. What a stupid, idiotic thing to have said. In one way or another, he'd been hurting people all of his life. Why would he think Sabrina was any different?

He had known from the beginning that their marriage wouldn't be like others. His job as a top commander of EDJE didn't allow for normal. Maybe if he were still just an agent, still in the field, it could have been semi-normal. But when his pay grade had been upped, the danger had increased, and semi-normal had gone to hell.

Regretting his decisions would do no good. He believed in what he did, what EDJE stood for. Protecting his adopted country, one that he loved as much as he loved his homeland of Scotland, meant sacrifice. He just damn well hated certain parts of it.

"For a man who recently gave his wife ten orgasms, you're looking awfully serious."

Throwing aside his dire thoughts for the moment, he glanced over at her. "You're keeping count?"

"Hell yeah. If I don't, how will I know when you're slipping?"

"So is ten better or worse than the last time?"

"Better." She beamed at him. "Thank you very much!"

He chuckled and shook his head. Only Sabrina could pull him from the darkness. "I ordered a meal for us…that little Italian place down the street you like so much. Should be here in about twenty minutes."

Her movements graceful as a dancer, she rose from the bed. "Just enough time for me to shower." Her naked body seductive, enticing, she held out her hand. "Join me?"

Declan followed her into the bathroom. All the worrying in the world wouldn't stop the inevitable, but for a few hours more he could hold back the sense of impending doom that shadowed his every step. Reality would come soon enough.

Placing her fork onto her empty plate, Sabrina leaned back in her chair with a satisfied sigh. Nothing like incredible, mind-blowing sex to increase her appetite. "That was wonderful."

"More wine?"

"No, thanks. Good choice, though. It was fabulous with the risotto."

"I was surprised the restaurant had a bottle. It's sometimes hard to get."

What she knew about wine or the finer things of life, she had learned from Declan and her Agency training. Odd that knowing such things as the correct wine or proper fork were important, but when infiltrating certain organizations to get close to the leader, that knowledge could be paramount. Men and women who perpetrated some of the most heinous acts on mankind often cloaked their evil ways behind wealth and privilege. Blending in had been vital to her success.

Working for LCR was a refreshing change in many ways, but more than once she'd had cause to be grateful for her earlier training. Though she now rescued kidnap victims instead of assassinating evil leaders, she occasionally went deep cover. Her skills had come in handy.

She eyed the beautiful man across from her. Though Declan could hide any emotion or thought behind a cool, implacable facade, she had known him for twelve years, loved him almost that long. Making a career of being someone else enabled him to hide behind a mask, but she knew every nuance and expression… something was bothering him.

Their time together was so limited that neither of them liked to bring the outside world in, but she knew that was about to happen. And if it was bothering him, then she definitely wanted to know.

"You want to talk about it now or do you want to wait till later?"

She appreciated that he didn't bother to pretend he didn't know what she was talking about.

He swallowed as if what he was about to say was difficult and gave an odd, twisted smile. "I've been giving a lot of thought to our marriage. What I want out of life."

She wanted to tease him and say she was glad he'd been thinking about her. The darkness in his eyes prevented that. "You want out?"

He jerked slightly. "No…hell no."

Relief flooded through her. "Well, then…what? If you don't tell me quickly, I'm going to imagine all sorts of terrible things."

"I want more than this…clandestine, too dangerous life. I want a family, a house with a yard, I want pets…maybe a kid or two."

Frozen in dismay, she could only stare. Never had he indicated that he wanted something like that. The nature of their careers made those things almost impossible to carry off. "I…uh…"

He grinned. "Damn, I love seeing you speechless."

"But, Declan, the Agency is your life. You've been with them for years."

An intense light entered his eyes. "The Agency is not my life, Sabrina. You are. Never forget that." Then, as if pulling himself back from the force of those words, his body relaxed and his expression cleared. "I'm proud of what I've accomplished. But I want to be with you more than a few days out of the year. I was fooling myself thinking I could have both. I don't want both. I only want you."

Happiness burst within her. To have him out of danger. To not worry while watching news of bombs exploding and people dying in war-torn countries if he was there in the midst of it all, trying to stop the chaos. To not worry about that middle-of-the-night phone call telling her he'd been killed or injured. Yes, yes, yes!

"So you're leaving the Agency? I mean, really, seriously leaving it?"

"Yes. I talked to Albert about it already. He was surprised, to say the least, but he understands. I have just a couple of minor issues I need to rectify. Nothing major. Won't take more than a month or so to finalize everything, and then I'm all yours."

"So…you want to, uh, like…get a regular job? Nine to five, the whole deal?"

"I've got some money saved up, so I don't have to make a decision right away."

She bit her lip. While she was thrilled that Declan would be out of the dark, gritty, and dangerous world of covert ops, she wasn't sure how he felt about LCR. She loved her job, and though it was dangerous, often just as much as his was, she didn't want to leave it.

A thought flashed across her mind like a meteor. "I have an idea. How would you feel about working with me? I'm sure that No—"

His fingers covered her mouth. "Let me get this out of the way, and then we'll see. Okay?"

Even though she was a little disappointed at the lack of enthusiasm for her suggestion, she told herself it was understandable. Here he was finally giving up a dangerous job, and she was asking him to jump right back into the fire.

"So the things you're finalizing. Is it an op or—"

He leaned forward and grabbed her hand, squeezing it gently. "Don't ask, darling, and I won't have to say no."

Even though she understood, it still hurt. It wasn't because he didn't trust her—she knew without a doubt he did. His reticence to share was always about one thing—protecting her. And that scared her most of all.

"I love you." She didn't know why, but she felt the need to say it once more.

His face softened. "I know. Believe me, sometimes it's the only thing that keeps me alive."

"Don't say that."

"For now, it's the job."

She nodded. They'd had this discussion before. Either of them could be killed on any mission. They'd agreed to make the most out of their lives, their marriage. Soak in as much as they could. But that conversation hadn't seemed as grim as it did now.

"You've got that look on your face that I don't like. I can't tell you what I'm finishing up, but I will say that it's much less dangerous than usual. Very routine. Mostly paperwork and assignment shifts. Absolutely nothing covert."

Why did she suddenly feel as though they were talking about two different things? She shook away her disquiet. His news had just thrown her off-kilter, that's all.

Realizing their discussion had changed the atmosphere of their time together and wanting to get back to enjoying themselves, she asked one last question, "When do you need to leave?"

"Tomorrow."

"Tomorrow? But we—" She held her tongue. This was the job, too. Missions rarely came at convenient times. If he could've delayed it, he would have.

She drew in a silent breath. Okay. All right. Complaining about it would do no good and only spoil their last few hours together. No way was she going to let that happen. And once he was finished, he'd be back with her permanently.

"Then let's not waste time we don't have."

His smile of appreciation washed away the taut atmosphere. Still seated, he pulled her into his arms, onto his lap. "*Tha gaol agam ort.*"

She smiled her delight. Other than some sexy time when he was seducing her or turning her on in bed, Declan's Scottish heritage rarely showed itself anymore. Occasionally, she'd catch a hint of brogue, but for the most part he sounded as American as she did. However, he knew she loved it when he spoke Gaelic to her. His words, *Tha gaol agam ort* meant *I love you*.

Surprising her even further, he did something incredibly odd, something he had never done before. He drew her closer, cupped his hand around her ear and said in an almost soundless whisper, "You're my everything, Little Fox. Never ever forget that."

Last Chance Rescue Headquarters
Paris

"For right now, I'm offering the job only to those with special ops or covert experience."

Sabrina sat before Noah McCall, her boss and the leader of Last Chance Rescue. Even though she'd been with LCR for four years, she had not yet learned how to read him. A few months back, he had hinted that there were going to be some changes for LCR. She had never anticipated this. Not only was Noah moving the main headquarters to the States, he was creating another branch, LCR Elite.

She loved being an LCR operative, but this sounded even more exciting. And with her background and training, a natural fit for her. Rescuing victims from the most dangerous places in the world. Totally unsanctioned and off the grid. Every mission a high-stakes risk. Her blood pumped with excitement.

"So. You interested?"

His black eyes coolly assessing, Noah asked the question with no emotion, not a hint of coercion. Not that the LCR leader would ever try to persuade an operative to take on an assignment. That was not his style. However, the question he'd asked her wasn't as easy to answer as it might have once been. With the changes Declan wanted to make in his life, how would this new job mesh with it? If only he would come back so they could discuss this together.

"I actually don't know yet."

Black eyes flickered with compassion. "Still no word from your husband?"

She shook her head. "He said he'd be gone for no more than a month…it's been almost two."

"He ever been gone this long before?"

"Yes, but for some reason, this feels different." She wasn't much for psychic premonitions, but she did trust her gut. Something wasn't quite right.

Aware that Noah was waiting for her answer, she said, "How soon do you need to know?"

"You've got some time. I've commissioned the building of a training camp outside Tucson, Arizona. Three former Navy SEALs are designing it. Once it's done, they'll be chomping at the bit to put us through their own version of Hell Week."

Adrenaline surged within her. She loved challenging her physical and mental skills, pushing herself to do more. Hopefully, Declan would be back before she had to give Noah her final answer.

"I saw Aidan leaving when I arrived. I'm assuming you offered him a spot, too?"

"Yeah. With his Special Forces background, Thorne is a natural fit. If you join, you can continue as partners. You work too well together to mess with that."

That was another reason she'd hate to turn down this offer. She'd be losing Aidan Thorne as a partner. They'd been watching each other's backs for a long time. She'd miss the man she considered a friend.

"Just a warning. He's already expecting that you'll be on the team. And since he doesn't know you're married, he might be a little confused if you turn it down without explaining."

She inwardly winced. She had been putting off that conversation for too long. Her brutal childhood had trained her to keep her mouth shut about private matters. And her Agency training had only reinforced her reticence to share personal information. Breaking a thirty-one-year-old habit was damned hard, but she owed her partner the truth.

"It's time I told him."

"Any reason why you haven't? I know it's not because you don't trust him."

"No, trust isn't an issue." She shrugged, unable to explain what probably was a defect in her personality. Getting the hell beaten out of you for telling personal details created an adult who had trouble opening up to others. She'd fought with all her might to overcome her past but still carried scars, both physical and mental. Declan had been the only person she'd ever been able to be completely open with, allowing him to see the real Sabrina.

"Aidan's like a brother to me." She'd never had a real brother, but her stepbrother had been a monster, so that was probably not the best description of their relationship. "Outside of you and Declan, there's no one I trust more."

"Good to know. I—"

The ring tone on her phone played Rod Stewart's *Purple Heather. Declan!* Heart leaping to her throat, she jumped to her feet and barely took the time to throw Noah a look of apology before she dashed out the door. The amused glint in his eyes told her he understood completely.

The instant she was out of Noah's office, she read the short text: *Meet me in Florence tomorrow at 3:00. Salvatore's Café. Have a surprise for you. DS*

Her feet flew to the elevator, thinking about all the things she needed to do to get to Florence by three tomorrow. Didn't matter what she had to do. She would not miss this opportunity.

Florence, Italy

Sabrina rushed out of the airport. Flying commercial and getting somewhere at a specific time rarely meshed anymore. Why hadn't Declan given her more notice? She was going to be at least fifteen minutes late, if not more.

Waving madly at a taxi, she caught the attention of the driver. Barely waiting for it to stop before she opened the door, she threw herself into the backseat.

Giving the driver the location and street address, she sat back into the seat and tried to make herself relax. Silly. She didn't know why she was so anxious about being late. It wasn't as if he'd leave without seeing her. In fact, she was a little surprised he hadn't already called to check on her. She'd called his cell phone to let him know she was running late and gotten his voice mail.

She tried not to be disappointed that it was just going to be a quick visit. If he were through with his assignment, he would have come to Paris. She'd already given Noah notice that once Declan was finished for good, she would be taking several days off. Her boss was a happily married man and understood.

The taxi driver slammed on his brakes as a gridlock of traffic loomed ahead. Cursing softly, Sabrina spoke in rapid Italian, "I'll just walk from here." She dropped several euro into his outstretched hand and jumped out of the car.

She stood in the middle of the stopped traffic to get her bearings. Up ahead was a traffic jam of massive proportions. Horns were blaring, people were getting out of their vehicles and shouting. Any other time she might have enjoyed the entertainment of drivers spouting colorful and inventive curses. Today, she was too focused on her target—getting to Declan.

She spotted a street sign and realized she was within three blocks of the café. Even though she'd worn heels and a dress, she didn't let that stop her. Weaving in and out of stopped cars, she got to the sidewalk and then started hoofing it toward her destination.

She stopped at a street corner and caught a glimpse of the café in the distance. Squinting against the afternoon sun, she focused on a man standing beneath the canopy in the doorway. That was Declan, or was it? He was the right height and coloring. She waved and was glad to see he waved back.

Traffic had picked up again, and she was going to have to either wait until the light turned red to cross the street or take her life into her own hands. She assessed her chances of making it across the busy street without getting hit—not good. Shrugging slightly, she waited. She'd rather arrive alive.

The instant the light turned red and pedestrian traffic was allowed, Sabrina crossed the street at a run. Declan was still there. Odd, but he looked as though he'd put on some weight. She grinned at the thought of teasing him about secretly hiding away and stuffing himself.

She took another step and barely registered the jolt and massive noise before her feet flew out from under her, and she was propelled backward. As she landed with a hard slam onto her back, her breath left her body. She lay for several long seconds as her mind scrambled to comprehend what had happened. Pain radiated throughout her body. What in the world…?

Breath finally returned, and gritting her teeth, Sabrina sat up. Horror washed over her. The restaurant was gone. Flattened. Demolished. The remains were heaps of ravaged brick and burning wood. The building had exploded.

Declan? Declan!

Darkness threatened, and she fought against its comforting pull. She went to her knees, and then stood, wavering. Her head swam, and blackness skirted the outer edges of her vision. An odd numbness swept up her right arm. Absently, as if she was looking down at a stranger, she noticed a large piece of wood sticking out of her shoulder. Blood dripped down her arm to the ground.

Sabrina tried to hold on to reality, to the fierce need to get to Declan. He couldn't be dead. He was trained for things like this. He would have heard the beginnings of the blast and flung himself away from the building. Yes, he might be injured, but he wasn't dead. She refused to even consider the possibility.

She took a step, felt a vague, distant pain on the bottom of her feet. Odd, but she was barefoot. Her shoes were gone. Ignoring the smoldering wood that scorched her skin and the broken glass that shredded her feet, she weaved and hobbled her way closer to the demolished building.

Declan was fine, she continued to reassure herself. Still, she needed to find him so they could help others. She jerked to a stop. A few feet from where the café had stood lay an arm beneath the rubble. Her heart stalled, her breath halted. It was tanned, large, obviously male, and on the hand was a wedding ring identical to Declan's.

Shaking her head, mumbling, "No, no, no," she pushed the debris out of the way and pulled on the hand. It came loose. She stood among the ruins of the destroyed building, holding an arm. No body was attached. Her mind screamed in denial, black mist swirled around her, and she fell forward into a blessed, mind-numbing darkness.